THE DEAD

THE DEAD

Ingrid Black

ISIS
LARGE PRINT
Oxford

First published in Great Britain 2003
by
Headline Book Publishing,
a division of Hodder Headline

Published in Large Print 2004 by ISIS Publishing Ltd,
7 Centremead, Osney Mead, Oxford OX2 0ES
by arrangement with
Headline Book Publishing,
a division of Hodder Headline

British Library Cataloguing in Publication Data
Black, Ingrid
    The dead. – Large print ed.
    1. Serial murderers – Ireland – Dublin – Fiction
    2. Detective and mystery stories
    3. Large type books
    I. Title
    823.9'2 [F]

ISBN 0–7531–7239–9 (hb)
ISBN 0–7531–7240–2 (pb)

Printed and bound by Antony Rowe, Chippenham

FIRST DAY

CHAPTER
ONE

The forecasts had been right. Rain was general all over Dublin. It was falling on every part of the dark city, from Howth Head to Dalkey Hill, and invisibly into the sea between, falling softly on quay, square and station, on stranded trees and ghostly cathedrals. It was falling too on lonely churchyards, on crooked crosses and headstones, glistening silver on the spears of little gates, falling to its last end on all the living and the dead.

It was the first day of December, and I was sitting at the window of a café somewhere in the dark early morning maze of streets between St Stephen's Green and the river, a cave of light and warmth in all that encroaching winter, eating eggs on rye and drinking black coffee, idly glancing through a two-day-old *Boston Herald* in search of news from back home.

I came here most mornings. Same place, same time, same table, same breakfast. The food wasn't up to much, but it was the one place in town where I could be sure they wouldn't have the radio on, the one place that valued silence as much as I did.

There wasn't much of interest in the paper that morning, which was why I glanced up as the door chimed and saw him coming in, looking round, shaking

3

off the rain violently like a dog, as if offended by the very business of being wet.

I quickly turned my gaze back to the coffee, a moment before his eyes would have found mine. I knew he was looking for me, because Nick Elliott wasn't the sort of person who could feign an accidental meeting even if he wanted to — he didn't have the subtlety or intelligence to carry it off — but I ignored him in the hope that he'd take a hint and leave me alone.

Elliott, though, didn't even realise he was being ignored, and headed straight to my table.

"Saxon," he said, faking a smile, and ruffling his hair in what someone with a cruel sense of humour must have once told him was a charming way. "Some weather, huh?"

I didn't bother to return the greeting.

Nick Elliott was a freelance with one of Dublin's largest papers, the *Post*. He did crime mostly, some interviews, profiles, the occasional why-oh-why column when his editor couldn't find anyone with anything more interesting or incisive to say to fill half a page — though for my money you could've picked a name at random out of the phone book and they would have had something more interesting and incisive to say than Elliott.

I'd never liked him, and he knew it, probably because I'd failed on every occasion we'd ever met to get to the end of the conversation without pointedly reminding him of the fact. I just felt that he was the kind of person who might benefit one day from being repeatedly told

4

that he was unlikeable. It hadn't had the desired effect so far, but I lived in hope.

"Can I join you?"

Even his introductions were predictable.

"No," I said.

Elliott laughed. Some people always take rudeness for ironic humour. They don't realise that sometimes it's just plain, honest-to-goodness rudeness. He eased himself into the chair opposite, and laid a thin brown A4 envelope gently between us on the table.

I didn't give him the satisfaction of looking at it. If he wanted something out of me, he could just come right out and ask.

"Can I get you something?" he asked instead.

"I've been coming here five years for breakfast, Elliott, I can order for myself. I speak English too, you know."

"Then I'll get something. What did you have?" He fingered the menu, pretending to consider, and I closed the paper, giving up any hope now of silence. "The *Boston Herald*," he observed. "You must be pining for home, Special Agent. Ever read the Irish papers?"

"The day they put something interesting in them, I'll start reading them."

"You don't like Dublin."

"Ten out of ten for observation, Sherlock."

"Then why live here?"

"Remember when the Germans ask Bogart why he came to Casablanca and he says he came for the waters? There are no waters, they say, we're in the middle of the desert."

"And Bogart says: I was misinformed." Elliott looked smug.

"Well," I said, "I was misinformed about Dublin."

"That's still no answer."

"It's the only one you're ever going to get."

I signalled over the waitress, who had been making "who's that?" gestures at me behind Elliott's back. "Same again for the man from the *Post*," I said for her benefit, "though you'll understand, Margaret, that when I use the word 'man' I only mean it linguistically. And two coffees, black. There, breakfast as you asked. Now, what do you want, Elliott?"

"I want your help."

"Let me guess. You're getting married, and you want me for a maid of honour."

"Not that sort of help, Saxon. Don't be smart. You know what I mean."

"A story?"

"That's the general idea."

"It must be a big story if you've come to me, and it must be a big story if your paper's interested enough to consider giving the readers a break from all the usual small-town intrigues."

"It is. Big, I mean."

That's not what I've heard, I was tempted to say.

Instead, I said: "Come on then, out with it."

"I want you to take a look at something for me."

Without thinking, I glanced at the envelope.

Damn. I'd looked. Strike one to Elliott.

He smiled, realising that I'd dropped the uninterested demeanour.

"Something came to the office," he said.

"For you?"

"That's right, for me. It happens. It came a couple of days ago with the morning's mail. No one knows about it so far but me, the editor, a few people higher up. Somebody wants it published, but we want to check it out first."

"And you want me to do the checking?"

He nodded.

"Some sort of consultant, that's what you want me to be?"

"That, yeah, and there'll be writing involved. Some background and follow-up pieces. Your impressions, conclusions, the usual sort of thing. We'll pay you, of course."

"You're damn right you'll pay me, if I'm going to be writing for your rag. I won't do it for less than fifty thousand."

"Quit messing, Saxon. You know that's impossible."

"Ten, then."

A pause. "Look, we can discuss all that. The editor'll be reasonable."

So it *was* important. Important enough for them to throw money at me for a few lousy articles and my so-called expertise.

The return of the waitress with Elliott's breakfast masked my surprise, and I waited as he set to, stabbing fussily at the eggs like some ancestral hunting memory had flashed into his mind and he was worried lest they make a break for freedom before he could free his spear.

"OK," I said, trying to wrestle my thoughts away from the spectacle of Elliott eating, "I'm interested. But first I want to know what it has to do with me. I wouldn't've thought I'd be your first choice, not seeing how much you know I don't like you."

"It's from someone you used to know," he said, his mouth still half full. "At least, it's from somebody claiming to be someone you used to know."

It was strange really, it was almost as if I knew what was coming next. Before his lips had even formed the words, I heard them chime in my head, the tolling of a long-stilled bell.

"It's Ed Fagan," he said.

A space opened delicately in my head as Elliott spoke, filled with sudden light. I glanced sideways but the window was still streaked with rain, the street still dark. But there it was anyway, the light, sneaking in past my eyes and scraping out my thoughts.

A moment only, and then it was gone, leaving behind nothing but the beginning of what I felt sure would be an epic headache, the *Ben Hur* or *Spartacus* of all headaches, Elliott's gift to me that morning. I longed to close my eyes, longed for him to be gone.

But there he still was.

"Did you hear what I said?" Elliott was pressing.

"Yeah, yeah, I heard you. Fagan," I said, and took a long draught of coffee, buying time for a normality of sorts to return to my face. I checked out Elliott. He didn't seem to realise there was anything odd. There were benefits to his stupidity.

"You remember him?"

"Of course I remember him," I said. "Fagan's not the sort you forget in a hurry."

Seven years ago, Ed Fagan had been picked up on suspicion of the murder of five prostitutes in Dublin in the previous twelve months. Julie Feeney, aged twenty-four, had been the first to be found, strangled on rough ground next to the Grand Canal only a mile or so from where we were sitting now. A month later, in a churchyard not far from there, came Sylvia Judge, nineteen, a history student at University College Dublin who was working part time for an escort agency. Tara Cox was next, two months after Sylvia. She was strangled too, though cause of death was actually multiple stab wounds inflicted, police thought, as she struggled to escape her attacker.

A six-month gap and then Liana Cassidy and Maddy Holt were killed within the space of two weeks, neither of them older than twenty-five and both found in exactly the same way.

With each of the bodies a scrap of paper was left on which was typed some wild quote from the Bible. *To be carnally minded is death*: that was the one I remembered best. The first note was found in Julie Feeney's purse, then the killer started leaving them inside the women's clothing, touching hair or nipple in some vicious echo of intimacy. The final one was stuffed inside Maddy Holt's mouth: *Purge me with hyssop, and I shall be clean: wash me and I shall be whiter than snow*. From Psalms, apparently. The words were stained with blood.

Fagan was picked up for kerb crawling six days after Maddy died, and licence number checks showed he'd been in the area on at least three of the nights when the women went missing. Police found garden twine in his car too that matched fibres taken from the throats of each of the five victims, and there was further DNA evidence linking him to at least two of the deaths. He was also positively identified by the only known eyewitness.

He protested his innocence, they always do, badgering newspapers and politicians to take up his cause — he had some influential friends — but he was charged on what police felt were the two strongest counts of murder and committed for trial.

He spent the following seven months on remand, only for the prosecution case against him to collapse on the fourth day of trial when it was discovered that a senior detective in the Dublin Metropolitan Police had planted the DNA evidence in an effort to secure a conviction.

I'd been commissioned to write a book about the case — a sympathetic account of Fagan's ordeal and police corruption, was how the publisher put it to me. Only problem was, it soon became obvious to me that Fagan was guilty as charged, planted DNA or not. I was on the verge of proving it too when he disappeared — everyone assumed because I was about to expose him — and he'd never been heard from since. I hadn't written the book, but I thought about him often.

Nick Elliott, meantime, had just written his own book about Fagan, *Deepening Shadows: Inside the*

Mind of an Irish Serial Killer, which the *Post* had carried interminable daily extracts from the week before. It was the usual cuttings job, made up of equal parts sensation and speculation, all tarted up with Elliott's most purple prose — more of an insight into his mediocre mind, if truth be told, than Fagan's.

"Fagan's dead," I said when I finally realised the silence had gone on too long.

"Disappeared isn't the same as dead," said Elliott. "He might just've been out of the country, maybe out of the city somewhere enjoying the fresh air."

"For five years?"

"Some people do."

"Not Fagan. People like Fagan aren't made to be inconspicuous; they get themselves noticed whatever they do, they can't help it. They gotta do what they gotta do. And what they've gotta do is hardly conducive to a quiet, unobserved life."

"You don't know that."

"You wanted my expertise, well there's my first bit, for gratis. Serial killers don't stop unless they're stopped."

"Well, not according to what's in that envelope," said Elliott, slurping his coffee. He'd finished eating now, thankfully. "According to that, Fagan's alive and kicking."

"And does it say why he's suddenly decided to make contact again?"

"He objected to my book, wants to correct a few factual errors. Set the record straight, you might say. He wants us to publish his reply in the *Post*."

I couldn't help but laugh out loud.

"Let me get this right. You're going to have a serial killer writing a column for you? Who you going to get to write the problem page — Jack the Ripper?"

"Keep your voice down, Saxon," said Elliott, glancing nervously to where the waitress was now looking over wonderingly at my laughter. "We don't want this getting out. And don't get on your high horse about it either. It's not like we're going to have him write the fucking editorials. He's just written this one piece, and we feel —"

His use of the word "we" was beginning to bug me. He was obviously getting very chummy now with the people higher up, as he put it. He'd seen his chance to get in with them and was already rehearsing his excuses. I cut him off before he could get going.

"What else does it say?" I said.

"It says he's going to kill again. And not just once either. Look, it's all in there."

The envelope; a nod of the head.

"Does he say who?"

"There's a name, if you can trust that."

"Does he say where, when, how? Does he say why?"

"No. At least, maybe part of the how, and it's in Dublin because, well, you'll see . . ."

"Right. So you get this article from someone claiming to be a serial killer. Why don't you take it to the police?"

"All in good time. We don't even know if it's genuine or not. Don't look at me like that. This is a great story. The police can get their hands on it once we've worked out what to do with it, what it is, whether it even is anything. That's why we came to you. All we're asking is that you take a look at it, tell us whether it's genuine. You know Fagan."

"Knew."

"Knew Fagan, then. You were writing a book on him, just like me. You worked with him for months on it. You might still be writing a book for all I know. You knew him better than anyone. Just tell us if it's him, that's all we ask." He paused, waited, but he was getting nothing that easily from me. I wanted to see the desperation in him when he finally asked.

Here it comes.

"Will you do it, Saxon? Please?"

"I'll look at it. That's all I can promise. I'll look at it. You can call me later, and we'll discuss it."

"We'll make it worth your while, really. The editor's going big with this. There'll be money in it for everyone."

"I thought you hadn't decided whether to print it."

"Well, you know."

Yeah. I knew.

"Just give me the envelope," I said. "I have to go."

He put his hand on it as if about to swear an oath.

"You won't show this to anyone else?"

"Of course I won't show it to anyone."

"You promise?"

"I promise. Jesus, you'll be wanting me to cross my heart and hope to die next."

"It's just that it was my idea to come to you, so if this gets out I'm in serious shit."

"The envelope, Elliott. Give me the envelope."

He handed it over with the reluctance of a man passing back the consent form for an appendix op with Dr Frankenstein.

I drained my coffee, picked up my jacket, left Elliott to pay.

Went back out into the rain.

I felt his eyes watching me as I walked, and had to force myself not to run. Steady now, Saxon, easy does it. Only a few more steps to go. There, a corner turned. Out of sight at last, I closed my eyes like they hurt and laid my face against the wet, cold stone of the wall.

Elliott wouldn't believe me when I said that Ed Fagan was dead — why should he? — but I didn't have that luxury. Only the dead can haunt the quick, and I had been haunted by Fagan from the last moment I saw him. Fagan was as dead as he'd ever be, and I knew it because I'd killed him myself five years ago. He wasn't coming back.

Of convicted murderers, it seems, one can say almost anything, make any preposterous, half-baked claim or allegation and we are expected to take it on the chin. Do we not bleed too?

That is not to say I have not been fascinated by the extracts from the book by your correspondent Nick Elliott, which you have lately serialised; but let me make a few points.

One, Julie Feeney was not sexually assaulted prior to her strangulation, as stated. The apparent sexual assault was a misdiagnosis stemming from the pathologist's misreading of the rather obvious signs of Julie's hazardous occupation, as subsequently admitted by the police. Two, Sylvia Judge was nineteen years old, not twenty, when she died. Three, I did not pick her up on Baggot Street Bridge, but in Lad Lane. Four, there were not thirty-seven stab wounds on the body of Tara Cox, but thirty-six. Nor, five, was she the only one of the victims to be stabbed. There were thirteen post-mortem stab wounds on the body of Maddy Holt, one for each of Christ and the Apostles. Six, I could not have used the Ford to take Liana Cassidy and subsequently Maddy on their last journeys, because I had exchanged it two weeks earlier for a Volvo, for reasons of safety. Seven, the tyre tracks found at the scene of Liana's killing were also never identified as mine. They probably were mine, but the results were inconclusive. It's a minor quibble, perhaps, but it's better to stick to the facts. To continue. Eight, the waistcoat I wore on the first day of my trial at the Central Criminal Court was not scarlet but cherry.

Nine, the scriptural instruction to kill prostitutes which was found underlined in my *King James Bible* comes from Deuteronomy, not Leviticus. And ten, my late wife did not die of cancer. In fact, she took her own life when her suffering from the disease became unbearable.

I could go on adding to the catalogue of amateurish errors, but you get the idea; and whilst it would obviously have been difficult for Mr Elliott to check his facts with me, there are numerous public records which he could have consulted to guard against error. It was unprofessional of him not to do so and I would be grateful if you published these corrections.

Worse still, however, is Nick Elliott's effort to make a case for me as the most likely suspect in the murder of Helen Cranmore, whose body was left in the grounds of the Dublin Metropolitan Police headquarters at Dublin Castle a year before Julie Feeney's death. His theory is that I left her body there in order to taunt the murder squad, which is all very well, except that I did not kill this unfortunate woman, as anyone with the most basic understanding of my method, not to mention so-called criminal psychology, would have recognised immediately.

He then compounds his mistake by absolving me of blame for the abduction of Sally Tyrrell, who disappeared whilst walking home from a Christmas party in Dublin city centre nine years ago and whose body, despite an extensive search, was never found.

I must confess that I did indeed kill Sally, and as a sign of goodwill I am even willing to reveal the location of her remains — so long only as you print this epistle of mine.

Meanwhile, despite my hopes of eking out the remainder of my days in quiet retirement, I realise now that I must be about my Father's business again. For it is written: "I have seen the ungodly in great power and flourishing like a green bay tree." And in that tree's shadow, all that is righteous and precious and holy is corrupted and defiled. So the tree must fall.

Five deaths I shall offer up, one for each of those which came before. And I give you seven days in which to find me; one day for each of the seven months I spent in prison. After that, I shall disappear once more, finally this time, my work done.

The seven days will begin with Mary on the feast day of St Agericus. I have been watching her now for some time. She will suffice. Pray for her soul.

CHAPTER
TWO

I jumped when the phone rang, and checked the number before picking it up.

"Fitzgerald," I said. "You read it?"

Detective Chief Superintendent Grace Fitzgerald was senior investigating officer of the murder squad division of the Dublin Metropolitan Police, and one of the first people I'd really befriended on coming to Dublin. One of the only ones, come to that. She'd contacted me over the book I was writing on Ed Fagan and one thing led to another. Now she stayed over sometimes, and when she didn't I missed her.

I'd faxed her Elliott's letter as soon as I'd read the two neat, closely-typed pages that it comprised, hurrying back to my apartment on the seventh floor of a converted Victorian warehouse off St Stephen's Green, desperate to be somewhere familiar. Now I was pacing up and down on the terrace outside my window, smoking a Cuban cigar, one of my few indulgences, and watching the half-hearted bustle of passers-by below impatiently shrugging off the rain.

I'd promised Elliott I wouldn't show it to anyone, but a promise to Elliott wasn't like a promise that needed to be kept. It was more like . . . well, a convenient lie. I didn't feel bad about it. He'd have done the same thing to me, and with less reason.

"So," she said, "where'd you get it?"

Straight to the point as always. That's my girl.

"From Nick Elliott himself."

A snort. I knew how she felt.

"Apparently it arrived at the office a couple of days ago," I said. "Elliott cornered me this morning over breakfast, wants me to authenticate it so that they can run it in the paper. Also, I don't know, I guess they want me to write some charming me-and-my-favourite-serial-killer pieces about Fagan, to give it the ring of authority. Elliott mentioned something about that."

"They're definitely going to publish it then?"

"That's the impression I got. They're still talking in ifs and maybes, but that's all for show. It's going in."

"Jesus," said Fitzgerald, which just about summed it up. "They'll print anything so long as they can pretend it's in the public interest. I think they even fool themselves sometimes. You think it's genuine?"

"You mean do I think it's Fagan? It couldn't be."

"You sound pretty sure."

"I am sure," I said steadily. "Fagan's dead."

"Missing's what it says on his file."

"Dead. Look, whatever. I know this isn't him. I know Fagan, I spent enough time with him to know what he was like. Don't get me wrong, there's plenty here that *could* be from Fagan. That buttoned-up, pedantic *let me make a few points* tone. But it doesn't fit."

"Fagan wrote something for the *Post* once before, didn't he, proclaiming his innocence?" Fitzgerald said.

"That was when the attention was at its height," I recalled. "It was the usual thing — denouncing the media campaign against him, the police for harassing him, accusing them both of putting the courts up to lock him away on a fake charge. Of course he got the *Post* to publish it, you know what suckers they are for that liberal knock-the-police crap. But it's not Fagan. This is an admittance of guilt, for one thing, and Fagan wasn't the confessing type. Wasn't the explaining type either. There was certainly none of this corny *I have seen the ungodly in great power* routine. And look at that reference to *convicted* murderers. Fagan was never convicted of so much as littering. Why would he get a detail like that wrong?"

"OK, I'll buy that. So who did write it?"

"Could be anyone. There's not exactly a shortage of cranks out there who might've got turned on enough by Elliott's book to want to muscle in on the action, just for the thrill. It sure reads like the sort of letter that was written one-handed. Happens all the time. Fagan had a son too. Jack," I added. "I wouldn't put it past him. Fagan brought him up alone after the mother died. Started out as a straight-A student too, but somewhere along the line he went wrong. He dropped out of college, drifted from job to job, basically fell apart; spent some time in prison on car theft charges. He went on TV not long after Fagan went missing. Didn't go so far as to say that his father deserved a medal, but made it pretty clear that the women got what was coming to them."

"Nice guy."

"*To be carnally minded is death*," I reminded her. "Word of the Lord. Who are we to argue? Maybe that's a double meaning there in the part about *my Father's business*."

"What happened to him?"

"The son? He took his mother's maiden name. Mullen. Hung around Dublin for a while spending Fagan's money. Fagan had sold up and left everything to Jack a few weeks before he disappeared, almost like he knew he wasn't going to be around much longer. When the money ran out, he left for England. It might be worth checking out where he is now. Buckley too."

"Buckley?"

"Conor Buckley, you remember. Fagan's defence lawyer. Sharp suit, sharp mind, sharp tongue, not so sharp in the legal ethics department."

"Christ, yes. How could I have forgotten him?"

"Hell, it could be Elliott himself for all I know," I said, throwing down what was left of the cigar and stamping out the glowing tip on the wet stone. "Some sick PR stunt. He wouldn't recognise a professional principle if it was behind bars at the zoo with a sign ten feet high telling him what it was, and this is certainly going to do wonders for sales of his book, wherever it came from. He sure was jumpy when we met this morning too, but then he's always jumpy round me."

Fitzgerald laughed. "You have that effect on some people."

"Not enough to scare them off for good, unfortunately. But Elliott? I don't know. I'd say Elliott loves himself too much to hold his own book up to public ridicule. That stuff about Helen Cranmore is bang on the money; blaming Fagan for her death was ridiculous, and if Elliott really knew that, why would he include it in his book only a few weeks ago?"

"Maybe he's being clever."

"This is Nick Elliott we're talking about, remember?"

Before she could say anything more, a voice entered the background on her end of the line, muffled, complaining. "Five minutes," Fitzgerald said to it. "Yes, Dalton, you already said. You'll just have to wait." Seamus Dalton then, the least house-trained detective in the DMP murder squad's history. "Sorry about that, Saxon," she said to me once he'd gone. "I can't talk long. There was a shooting this morning on the Northside, I think Dalton wants to head over there soon as he can to rough up some suspects. We were supposed to be at the scene half an hour ago."

"Rushed off your feet?"

"Rushed enough not to want some crank letter coming through the fax machine, that's for sure."

I said nothing.

"You do agree this is just a hoax, don't you?" she said.

"I never said it was a hoax."

"But I thought —"

"I said it wasn't Fagan. That doesn't mean I don't have a real bad feeling that whoever wrote this is going to *do* what he says he'll do."

"You think he's going to kill five women? Come on."

"OK, so you're not convinced. But you know how it is, Grace, you get a feel for this sort of thing. I just . . .

I don't know. It's not Fagan, but it's someone who wants us to *think* he's Fagan, and that means he'll take on Fagan's mission, Fagan's handiwork. Can't you at least get the original from Elliott, have it analysed for fingerprints, DNA, whatever? It must have come in an envelope. You could maybe get something that way. Also, start tracking down people who used to know Fagan, friends, colleagues, anyone like that, and see what they're up to."

She sighed. "Want me to solve the Lindbergh baby mystery whilst I'm at it?"

"I'm being pushy again," I said.

"Not pushy, just unrealistic. I'll not get authorisation to do anything, not today, and definitely not if the Assistant Commissioner thinks I've got nothing but some nut's word to go on — and before you say anything, I meant the letter, not you. There's no way I can siphon off resources to follow this up."

"So we just wait until some woman gets killed?"

"I'll tell you what," she said. "I'll pass the word around, see if anyone has any idea what this is all about. Will that do? And you know something?" she added. "I can probably spare Boland for an hour or two. I'll get him to make some enquiries."

"Boland?"

"Detective Sergeant Niall Boland. He's just joined us from Serious Crime. He's following me round, getting the hang of things, settling in. I'll have him go down to records and dig out the file on Sally Tyrrell. Then maybe send him over to the *Post* to try and get his hands on the original, see where it was posted at least. You think Elliott will let us have it without a warrant?"

"Not a chance. You didn't see the excitement on his face this morning. He thinks this is his big break. He's probably got plans for a second edition of his book, co-written by the subject. He's not going to let this one go," I said, "even if you do put the fear of God into him."

"Let's put it into him anyway, just for the heck of it." She was about to sign off when an idea suddenly came to her. "By the way, Saxon, when *is* the feast day of St Agericus?"

"I looked that up," I said. "It's today."

Afterwards, I stood and stared at my reflection in the glass for what felt like an age.

"Thumbelina with attitude" my mother used to call me when I was a kid. Now the rain had made my short hair spikier and darker than usual — it needed cutting; my corduroy jacket hung off my shoulders like I'd shrunk somehow without noticing; and my face had thinned out till I'd swear I could see the shadow of my bones. I didn't look after myself enough at the best of times; Fitzgerald kept telling me, so it must be true. But now it was like I was disappearing, almost like I'd known what was coming and my body had huddled in on itself to escape.

I had to pull myself together. Whatever Fitzgerald said, this Thumbelina was going to need all the attitude she could muster in the coming days.

24

CHAPTER
THREE

For the rest of the day it rained on and off and I stayed indoors, in hiding was how it felt, trying to get some take on the questions that sang crazily through me.

No matter how many times I read it, the letter refused to make sense.

Why would someone suddenly want to blame Fagan for the disappearance of Sally Tyrrell? It was absurd. And even if he *had* been responsible, how could the author of the letter know it, given that Fagan wasn't in a position to be telling anyone his secrets any more? Could he have confessed at one time to whoever wrote this letter? Could he have had an accomplice?

I shook my head to stop myself. Fagan had nothing to do with Sally's disappearance, I felt sure of that. I'd looked into her case when I was writing my book and quickly discounted any connection. Fagan always left his dead to be found; why would he have changed his MO that one time? Sally wasn't a prostitute either, but a former secretary with the police. No. The most likely explanation was that it was the author of this letter who'd abducted and murdered her. But then why was he trying to add the killing on to Fagan's tally rather than claiming the credit for himself?

In the end, I did what I'd been avoiding doing ever since speaking to Nick Elliott at the café. I went to the safe in my office at the back of the apartment, dug out the satchel in which I kept my files on Ed Fagan and carried it over to the table for the first time in five years.

Here was the unfinished manuscript of my book, together with my research notes: old newspaper clippings, tapes and transcripts of interviews with Fagan, his son, colleagues, neighbours, police, as well as friends and family of the five victims. There were crime scene reports too that Fitzgerald had let me see, evidence inventories, witness statements, all of which I'd copied and filed away together with photographs of the various scenes that I'd taken myself.

There was even a shot of Fagan somewhere, another of him with his freaky son. I didn't want to look at those just yet. I didn't feel ready. I certainly didn't feel ready for putting a tape on and hearing his voice. He was real enough to me right now. Too real.

I hadn't looked at the notes in years, not since I'd put the book, metaphorically speaking, out with the trash. They remained out of sight, if never quite out of mind. I don't even know why I kept them. Fagan wasn't a subject I relished thinking about, and I didn't need notes to remember.

It was forgetting that was the difficulty.

Somehow there they still were, a presence always at my back as I wrote; but since it was increasingly rare these days for me to write anything, that wasn't such a bind.

I'd been delighted when I got the contract for the book about Fagan. I'd only been in Dublin three months, and Fagan was something of a cause célèbre. Others, hungry as Nick Elliott, would have leapt at the chance to write about him, and they might have been better at it too. I, though, had a measure of fame behind me by that point, and at such times you stumble into opportunities as easily as a drunk into lampposts.

That fame came from my first book. I'd been lucky. I'd started out studying archaeology of all things at Boston University, though my boredom with prehistoric Aegean civilisation and the micro-morphology of terrestrial sediments quickly started to outpace even my boredom with myself, which was some achievement on its part. Eventually I'd risen to the goading of an old boyfriend and, to both our surprises, found myself accepted on a training programme by the FBI in New York. In one fell swoop, I ditched boyfriend, Boston and boredom. It was what I'd always wanted, though I'd been reluctant to admit it even to myself. I was always fearful of failure.

Three years' training, four in the field as a special agent in New York state, and I was part of the team, a small part, that uncovered the serial killer Paul Nado, aka the White Monk.

Archaeology hadn't been so far removed, I quickly realised. What was I doing now but deciphering the hieroglyphics of psychopathology? But what I realised even quicker was that I didn't have what the FBI took — and what the FBI took from its agents was everything. I was drained by the White Monk investigation; wasted; I couldn't function.

All I needed, maybe, was some leave; but with my usual talent for self-destructive gestures, I resigned from the Bureau and retreated back to New England to write a book about the hunt for Nado. Before I knew what was happening, I'd sold book, film rights and — according to my former colleagues — soul, and my life had changed for ever. For the better? I'd never know.

Since then they'd been deciding which Hollywood actress should have the pleasure of playing me. I was a great part; from what I'd seen of an early screenplay, I was now responsible for catching Nado single-handed, if not for the entire security of the United States, which would have astonished my old colleagues if any of them were still talking to me. I was past caring, and if I had cared, the cheques that kept arriving would soon have soothed my misgivings.

I'd written three books quickly after that. A follow-up to the White Monk story, in which I scraped the barrel of my experiences as a special agent to fill another three hundred pages; a study of offender profiling, much in vogue at the time; and a cuttings job on a notorious hired killer out of Boston with Irish roots, which was what first brought me to Dublin. That, and a desire to escape to some place where few knew Paul Nado's name or mine.

And that was when I was offered the chance to write about Fagan.

He was only recently out of jail then, and he'd been a regular interviewee in newspapers and on television, decrying his treatment at the hands of the police and the courts, enjoying his new-found fame immensely. He knew exactly how to handle it.

He was a lecturer in theology at University College, where Sylvia Judge had studied (she'd even stayed briefly in a house which he rented out during college term-time); he'd published numerous articles in the academic quarterlies; he was a popular speaker at conferences in North America and Europe; he'd sat on some of the Church's policy-making committees. Ultimate irony, he'd even written a book on Christianity's ancient problem with women, and had come forward to the police to offer possible insights into the thinking of the perpetrator of the prostitute killings. Nudging in on the investigation, happens all the time. Afterwards he tried to claim that's why they'd picked on poor little him to frame.

Fagan's wounded innocence story wasn't really my thing, but he, apparently, had hand-picked me for the job and I had nothing else to do. I agreed.

He obviously expected me to be flattered by his endorsement of me. In fact, I took an instant dislike to him. He was arrogant and overbearing, with a crude, cruel sense of humour which would've shocked many who thought they knew him best. The more I delved, the more my doubts grew — which was when Grace Fitzgerald materialised. She called me unexpectedly one day asking for a meeting. She'd heard about the book, and wanted to put me on the right track.

She was a mere superintendent then, but knew the detective in charge of the case well. Kevin Donnelly was old, was how she saw it, tired, nearing retirement; he'd overcompensated in his urge to get Fagan convicted, but his instincts were sound. The DMP were simply too concerned with getting out of an embarrassing spotlight to admit it; under pressure from the so-called civil liberties crowd, they just wanted to bury the whole mess, be done with it. I knew at once that she was right. Too much fitted. Together we set about trying to nail Fagan properly.

Of course, he couldn't stand trial on the same charge a second time, but he'd only been charged with the murder of two of the five victims, due to a lack of direct evidence in the other three cases. He could still be reeled in if only we could find the right bait. So I went on working during the day with Fagan on the book he hoped would prove it was the police who were to blame for his troubles, and at nights with Fitzgerald weaving the web in which Fagan could be finally enmeshed. And step by step, we felt ourselves closing in.

Till I made my way one night to a place in the mountains, just where the city gave way to the wild, where I'd arranged to meet Fagan — there was some witness in a remote pub out there who would prove he couldn't have murdered Maddy Holt, he told me, and I could think of no good excuse to get out of going without rousing his suspicion — only to find him waiting for me in the dark by the side of the road, masked, taunting, knife and green garden twine in hand.

My secret, as they say, was out. I guess I wasn't as good an actor as I thought.

Fagan's disappearance, as she saw it, hurt Fitzgerald, and it hurt me that I couldn't ease that hurt for her, not without danger, and I was satiated with danger by then.

I may have shot Fagan in self-defence that night in the mountains, but even self-defence would not be much of a plea in a city where carrying a firearm was still a criminal offence. Here the law decreed that only criminals should be allowed to carry guns, whilst the cops and victims went unarmed. It was a dumbass rule, but I didn't relish arguing it in front of a jury in a country which still looked down on Americans as trigger-happy desperadoes who always shoot first and ask questions later, or better still just shoot and screw the questions. I wasn't supposed to have a gun at all, but it isn't hard to pick up a weapon in a city if you know where to look.

Half-heartedly now, I got the picture of Fagan out of the satchel, and stared at that thin, smirking, superior face again, remembering that night, remembering the gasp from him as I spun away from his hand, pulled the gun from inside my coat and fired, remembering the exhilaration, the satisfaction, yes the pleasure, as he realised I was not for the taking like all the others.

A single shot and Fagan slumped. A shot that shattered the silence, scattering birds through the branches in the trees; and then I was looking down at a man with half his face blown away. In that moment, Fagan entered my consciousness in a way he had never done when alive, and I knew that I would never be rid of him, not really. I may have dragged him into the trees and buried him so deep that it was nearly light by the time I'd finished digging his grave, but I would never be free of him.

Now I sat in my apartment, as the day darkened and died, staring again at the photograph of Fagan, and going over in my head one more time, always one more time, Elliott's letter, trying to piece it all together, and I realised for the first time exactly what never being rid of him meant. Since he'd disappeared, Fagan had been a private nightmare of mine, and that was bad enough. Now somehow he'd slipped out of my head when I wasn't paying attention and gone walkabout by himself. Wherever I went, I'd be stepping over his bones. Or worse yet, the bones of some woman who was living her life this minute thinking she was safe.

It was late afternoon before I forced myself to leave the apartment again and go looking for bagels. I couldn't exist on cigars for long. Couldn't exist on bagels for long either, but it was all I felt I could manage. The city looked just the same. I'd half expected it to have changed, just because I had. We're all solipsists at heart. It was good to see it even so.

By the time I got back there were two messages waiting. Always the way.

The first one was from Fitzgerald. She'd run a check on Mullen, and guess what? Fagan's son had been back in town about three months, basically bumming around after his job as a hospital porter went belly up in England thanks to his drinking.

"Why don't you follow it up?" she said.

I would. Job loss was a classic stressor that could tip a potential offender over the border into violence, and Mullen certainly had the ancestry for it.

The other message was from Elliott.

He'd called to let me know that I was a two-faced, conniving bitch, I was going to get what was coming to me, I'd pay for betraying him, nobody treated him like that. Oh, and I was ugly too. Now *that* hurt. On and on it went. He'd run out of tape if he wasn't careful.

Detective Sergeant Niall Boland, newly transferred from Serious Crime, had paid Elliott a visit after all. From such small pleasures is the wreckage of a day salvaged.

CHAPTER
FOUR

The call came shortly before midnight. It would've roused me from sleep, if sleep had been possible. As it was, I was watching the baseball on cable and picked up the phone as soon as it started ringing.

"We found her," said Fitzgerald. "Do you want to come down?"

"No," I said, "but I'm going to."

Five minutes later, I was on my way.

There were still plenty of people in town, despite it being so late and despite the cold. Someone was singing on the other side of St Stephen's Green, some old Irish ballad, and there was the sound of music behind glass and a smell of cheap food in the air. Somewhere else, a siren shrieked. It was headed in the opposite direction to me, but somehow it all seemed connected. Drinkers shambled out of pubs, laughing, shouting, and it seemed obscene that they should be so happy. It wasn't their fault, but I hated them at that moment for their innocence.

Soon I'd left them behind, crossing over Baggot Street for the back lanes, making my way down towards the canal through empty streets, past black windows.

A few hookers lingered by the railings at the Peppercanister Church, watching me suspiciously; the odd car crawled by; but apart from that there was no one about.

I wasn't worried; I knew these streets well enough, just like I knew the place that Fitzgerald had directed me to over the phone. It was where Ed Fagan had left his first victim, Julie Feeney, almost down at the point where the canal reached the docks. I should've guessed the author of Nick Elliott's letter would pull a stunt like that. Another mistake from me.

By the time I was within a couple of hundred yards of the site, I could see the already stark winter trees lit with blue flashes from the patrol cars, as if lightning was trapped among the branches, struggling to get free. Turning the corner, I saw them all parked up ahead, Fitzgerald's car among them, circled conspiratorially like wagons round a camp fire.

She, whoever she was, had obviously not been found long. The uniformed officers were still securing the scene, and I could see familiar faces from the murder squad's scene-of-crime unit standing round waiting, drinking coffee, talking quietly: Dalton, Ray Lawlor, Sean Healy.

Tom Kiernan, the unit photographer, who, incongruously enough, had done the author shot for my last book, had also only just begun taking his first overlapping pictures of the scene, stopping after each shot to scribble a note of what he'd just photographed.

Everything by the book. The way it had to be.

A young policeman tried to bar my way when I got there till Fitzgerald, who'd been talking on her mobile a few yards apart from the rest of the murder squad, saw me and came over. She was wrapped up tight against the cold, grim-faced, her black hair yanked back severely from her brow, her breath a frost, skin so pale that her own breath made it fade temporarily from view. She looked like she hadn't slept for a week, but it was still good to see her.

It always was.

"It's all right, Sergeant," she said. "This woman's here at my request." If he thought it unusual, he didn't say anything. He was hardly going to contradict a chief superintendent.

"Where'd you park the Jeep?" she said when we'd stepped out of hearing.

"I walked."

"You should be more careful." It was automatic by now, this show of concern. She never liked my habit of night walking.

"Don't worry about me. You look like you're ready to drop," I said simply.

"Maybe it'd be better for everyone if I did."

"What the hell do you mean by that?"

"You know what I mean," she said. "I shouldn't have been so quick to dismiss the letter as a hoax. It was unforgivable. Just because I had a lot on my plate."

"You weren't to know," I said.

"*You* knew," said Fitzgerald. "You get a feeling for this sort of thing, you said. Well, where's my feeling for it?" She was avoiding looking at me now, and I had no answer. "And the worst of it is, if this was true then the rest of it must be true as well. This is just the start."

"You'll find him," I said.

"You think so?"

"I wouldn't be here if I didn't."

She managed the trace of a smile at that. "Come on then," she said. "To work."

She turned and led me back to the tape, close as she could — obviously, I wouldn't be allowed in. Beyond there were a few trees, and a path heading down to tuck under a low bridge. It was one of the last bridges before the narrow canal broadened out into the dock on its last stop before the sea. Prostitutes often took their clients there, if the clients weren't too fussy — and they wouldn't be in this part of town if they were.

Looking through, eyes adjusting to the shadows, I could make out a lonely shape sprawled in the dark — a foot, twisted, a stiletto heel, perhaps an arm outstretched, ghost-white flesh — before the screen went up to keep her out of sight. Out of sight of the spectators who were beginning to gather on the other side of the road, and out of sight especially of the cameramen and reporters who surely wouldn't be too far behind.

"She was found about half an hour ago by a man out walking his dog," Fitzgerald began. "It's always a man out walking his dog, have you noticed that? If there weren't dogs to be walked, I sometimes wonder if we'd ever find any bodies."

"Strange time to walk a dog."

"Tell me about it. I'm going to ask him about that myself later, once he's given a statement. It's probably nothing. Some people get a kick out of hanging round places like this."

"Was she strangled?"

"It looks like it. Some sort of ligature. You can see the mark it's left round her neck. But she's still face down so who knows what we'll find when we turn her? Looks like she's been dragged down some way towards the water too, like maybe he wanted to throw her in but couldn't manage it. Wonder why he didn't just wait till they were down there before strangling her? Why strangle her here where he'd still be in sight of the road? Risky."

"Maybe the fact that he was still visible from the road was part of the thrill for him," I suggested. "Maybe he got too excited and couldn't wait. Maybe he got frightened she might stop him somehow, that she might get away? Who knows? Any sign of a note?"

"Not yet."

"She's a prostitute, though?"

Fitzgerald nodded. "No ID on her yet, but I'd say so. She has about ten condoms in her bag, about seventy in cash, a little hash. Obviously no robbery motive. Doesn't seem as if she's been raped either. We'll know more when Lynch gets here." She meant Ambrose Lynch, the city pathologist. "*If* he ever gets here. Where is the old walrus?"

A sudden burst of light made her look up, blinking.

As if on cue, a car was making its way down the road towards us, diving into the dark from the city at its back. Lynch's black Mercedes, headlights on full. Everyone's head turned as he slowed to a halt and shifted his considerable frame out of the door.

Lynch had been city pathologist here in Dublin for almost twenty years, and he looked as if each one had only made him more weary, more melancholy. He drank too much, which didn't help, but then pathologists always drank too much. It came with the job, it was part of the act, like the gruesome humour and eccentric air of abstraction; world over, they were all the same. I think they must make them in a factory somewhere. Lynch's own trademark was misanthropy. "I am free of all prejudice, I hate everyone equally" was how he'd put it to me the first time we met, and since I recognised it as one of WC Field's better one-liners he'd decided to give this sucker at least an even break.

Right now his unkempt hair spoke of a man who'd been dragged reluctantly out of bed, though the dress suit, bow tie and expensive shoes told another story.

He nodded at me in greeting as he came to the tape. He'd obviously been drinking. Even at a distance, I could smell whiskey, faintly. It was a wonder he was never pulled over and breathalysed when he was driving to crime scenes, or maybe not such a wonder. He was the only pathologist they had, after all; they couldn't be throwing him away.

"Forgotten your coat, Ambrose?" I said.

"Left it in the car. Didn't want it getting dirty. It's cashmere, you know. My tailor would never forgive me," Lynch replied. "What about you, Saxon? Doing well?"

"I've been better. How's Jean?"

Ambrose pulled a pained expression. "My dear wife has left me, Saxon. Three weeks ago. For some reason, she found this life of mine trying. Can't imagine why. There I am, midnight hour beckoning, finishing a final brandy before blessed sleep after a night at the opera when the phone rings. Message from Fitzgerald. Come down at once, urgent urgent urgent. So down I come. My wife, however, finds life more agreeable at present in London with her redoubtable spinster sister, Miss Alicia King, enthusiastic patron of the Anti-Ambrose Society."

"I'm sorry," I said, and I meant it. I always liked Lynch. He rarely complained.

"Can't be helped, can't be helped," he said. "What *would* help is a deputy pathologist to ease the workload, but I've been asking for the last five years without success. Still, it seems a trifle irrelevant to be making a fuss about a little thing like that, considering why we're here."

"I guess so."

Fitzgerald had stepped aside for a moment to whisper to Dalton. They'd found something, I could tell from Fitzgerald's face. Now they came over and she shook Lynch's hand.

Dalton ignored me as usual, chewing gum.

"What is it?" I said.

She held up a small transparent plastic bag, sealed at the top. Inside, a note. Typewritten, same face as Elliott's letter. *All wickedness is but little to the wickedness of a woman.*

"Shit," I said. "What's wrong with people?"

"Healy just found it in her bag."

"I thought her bag was searched?"

"Only quickly, looking for ID," Fitzgerald said. "This was inside a tear in the lining, folded up tight." That was like Julie Feeney too. Our boy was playing out Fagan to the letter. "Seems we have a name too. One of the uniformed officers reckons it might be one Mary Lynch. That fits. It should be easy enough to verify. Most of the girls round here have a record."

"Relative of yours, Ambrose?" said Dalton.

"Most amusing," said Lynch with a tolerant smile. "I fancy we moved in rather different social circles. More likely one of your old girlfriends, I should have imagined."

"Touché."

"Look, boys, if you don't mind," said Fitzgerald, "we're just about to start a sweep of the scene, see if anything else's been left, so if you want to get started, Lynch, I'll take you over."

Lynch nodded, and ducked heavily under the tape as Fitzgerald held it up. "So much for the shoes," he said. "Ah well, all in a night's work." He raised a hand at me in farewell.

"I'll have to get back too," Fitzgerald said to me. "Catch you later?"

I understood, offered a smile, then she was gone. Dalton took out his gum and threw it to the ground at my feet, and followed. He hadn't looked at me once.

I retreated to the other side of the road, every step emphasising my distance. People had gathered now to watch what was happening, distracted on the way home from bars or roused from sleep in nearby apartments. Police work always draws a crowd, like car smashes and lovers' tiffs. Whispers mingled with the low crackle of police radios, a murmur of excited rumour. Some watched me, wondering what connection I had with the scene, though none dared to ask.

I leaned against the wall, lit a cigar, creating my own silence, looking at the lights of the city at the edges of the darkness, watching the blue flash in the trees, as Fitzgerald's unit started their slow circles one way and then the other round the body of the forsaken Mary Lynch.

I knew the routine. For now it was about sketching, measuring; looking for blood spatters, and taking samples — hair and soil, fibres and leaves; and making notes, there were always endless notes. Above all, now was the time for collecting what physical evidence they could find in the vicinity of the body, though there wouldn't be much of that tonight, I guessed.

This was as bad as it got for any scene-of-crime officer: out in the open, winter weather, the rain just starting again and heavier with each moment that passed, though they couldn't rush. There certainly wouldn't be much chance of finding fingerprints. Mary Lynch's killer wouldn't have hung around long enough to leave any; and anyhow they didn't show up on wood, stone, rocks, leaves, or indeed on most types of cloth, and here that was all there was.

Worse, there were so many footprints — hooker and client, hooker and client, in joyless procession — that finding an intact one to lift would be almost impossible.

It was strange that I felt so excluded. I had been at scenes like this before, many times, watching over the broken and the dead. It was always the same scene, the same calm going-about things that only ever seemed to be a cover for some inner scream.

A place where there had been such pain and terror was always afterwards so quiet, and yet it would never be entirely free of its past. Bad things lingered, and it turned those places bad in turn, so that other bad things happened in time. One evil act could instigate a chain that, if not snapped, would unravel for ever. I had always wondered if that was what ghosts were: the accumulated bad memories of places where things that could not be forgotten, should not *be* forgotten, had happened. I shook my head, irritated by my own thoughts, and thought about Fagan. About Fagan's ghost. About Julie Feeney. About Mary Lynch.

It was a few moments before I realised there was somebody standing next to me. I turned my head, and there was Nick Elliott, watching, smiling. I wondered how long he'd been there.

"If you're here to start a fight, Elliott," I warned, "don't bother. I'm not in the mood."

"I'm not going to say a word. What's done is done. It's my own fault for showing you the piece. I should have known you'd play the Good Samaritan and pass it on."

"I wasn't playing. What else could I have done? It might've saved somebody's life."

"Didn't, though, did it?" Elliott replied smugly, and he came to stand by me, lighting a cigarette from the remains of the last one, pulling his coat hard around him.

"Perhaps things would've been different if you'd handed the letter over soon as you got it, instead of hanging on to it for a few days," I said, though what difference *would* it have made? No one had believed it anyway, except me and Elliott. "I suppose this means now you're going to run with your friend's little written contribution to the academic debate on crime?"

"We shall see what we shall see."

"That means yes."

"If you want to know, buy tomorrow's paper," he said. "What about you, anyway? Your friend Fitzgerald give you anything juicy?" He always said "friend" with that faint leer.

"If she did, I wouldn't tell you," I said. "You'd just have it on the front page next day, spiced up and attributed to one of your legendary sources."

"Well, I have as much as I need for tomorrow's edition anyway. I spoke to one of the detectives about ten minutes ago. He tells me it was a prostitute, and the name seems to match. I've been having a word with some of the local ladies of the night too."

"They offering you a discount in return for a mention on page one?"

"I like that, that's funny," Elliott said, and he actually laughed, as if it was.

He was on a high, I could tell. Buzzing. He wasn't really thinking about the murdered woman, he was just thinking about his letter from Fagan, or the person he thought was Fagan, and what an impact it would have when it was published. His name was up in lights in his head. Or maybe he was just refusing to be distracted from his work. As soon as the letter arrived, it was obvious some woman would die. We had all written someone off, we just didn't know who it was that we were writing off. Perhaps Elliott was just being realistic.

He had a job to do, and that letter, this death, gave him a chance of making something better out of it. Indeed, the killer had struck so quickly following my handing the letter over to the police that it had probably saved Elliott's skin. Any longer and someone would've talked, news leaked out, bang would've gone his exclusive. This way it didn't matter any more.

That was why Elliott was so ready to forgive my handing the letter over to the murder squad — because it hadn't ultimately stopped him getting the story. He wasn't going to waste any more energy on being angry with me when fame beckoned.

"Look, here comes your great source," I said just to irritate him, seeing Ray Lawlor emerge from the shadows by the path, step under the crime scene tape and make his way back towards his car. I was pleased to see Elliott flinch.

"Lawlor's not my source," he said.

I shrugged dismissively. Everybody in the DMP knew Lawlor had been taking money from crime reporters for passing on information for years, and not just from Elliott. I'd seen the two of them out drinking at various bars round town myself; it wasn't hard to plot the connection between their nights out and Elliott's sudden insights into an investigation.

"You surprise me," I said. "I always thought you couldn't possibly be as stupid as you looked. Hell, was I wrong."

"I told you —"

"Yeah, whatever. Better hurry now before you miss him."

I shut my eyes to shut him out, and when I opened them again he was gone. I hung around a little while longer after that, but it was obvious I wasn't going to be able to talk with Fitzgerald again, and there wasn't much point staying otherwise. Around three I finally set off for home, taking the same streets, emptier than before yet somehow more sentient, more aware. Inside my apartment was almost colder than out, and the central heating wouldn't switch on automatically for another hour or so. I was weary, worn out. All I wanted was to sleep.

I was about to climb into bed fully dressed when my clothes reminded me of the scene down by the bridge. I took them off, and tossed them into the basket. Then I climbed into bed, and was asleep immediately. Fagan was waiting for me in the darkness, dead, resurrected Fagan, and the face of Mary Lynch, whoever she was. I wasn't too surprised to see it was my own.

SECOND DAY

CHAPTER
FIVE

I was one drink ahead of Fitzgerald by the time she finally arrived at the bar where we'd arranged to meet for an early lunch.

The eyes that sought me out in the gloom were black-ringed and exhausted. She'd obviously not gotten much sleep last night, if any. I'd not gotten much myself; I'd been up again before six, checking out the news, not liking what I heard.

"You're not drinking?" I said after she'd ordered an orange juice from the waiter.

"Better not," she replied. "Long day ahead."

We ordered sandwiches, and whilst we waited for them to come she took a copy of that morning's *Post* out from her coat and tossed it on to the table in front of me.

"Have you read this yet?"

"I resisted buying a copy," I said, "in case the proximity of the words Nick Elliott and exclusive turned my stomach."

I glanced down at the front page: *Night Hunter Back*.

Fagan had been the Night Hunter since the second killing. Once he'd been arrested, some newspapers tried to make play of his academic background and call him Doctor Death, but it had never caught on. Doctor Deaths were two a dime, after all.

"They always have to have a nickname, don't they?" I said. "Angel of Death, Alligator Man, Candy Man, Red Spider, Ripper."

"White Monk," said Fitzgerald.

"That wasn't my choice," I said. "They only called him that because he always killed his victims close to a church or a monastery. You know how the legends start: some high school kids decided it was the ghost of an old monk, the freesheets ran with it and a nickname was born. After we caught him, that was what Nado seemed proudest of. Said he was going to use it for the title of his autobiography. *White Monk Blues*, can you believe that?"

That was the problem with the sort of coverage the *Post* was providing. For some, killing was their way of making a mark, of asserting who they were, even of finding out who they were; but once they started, then the reactions of others reinforced their behaviour. They weren't just some pathetic sack who cut up women for kicks any more; they were the Angel of Death, the Red Spider, the White Monk, the Night Hunter, and then it was that which they acted out, always wanting to become more like that image. It was a vicious circle, and the victims were caught right in the middle.

"Take a look at the rest of the paper," said Fitzgerald. "You might as well depress yourself some more while you're at it."

The first nine pages were devoted to last night's murder. Picture after picture on the first few: grainy long-distance shots of incident tape stretched between trees and crime scene techs in white overalls; one of Fitzgerald talking into a mobile phone; another of the covered body being lifted into the mortuary van. The paper had obviously printed late.

I checked the name: Simon Mee. A staff snapper with the *Post*. I hadn't seen him around the night before. He must have turned up after I left.

There was background too by Nick Elliott, incontinent reams of it, together with photographs and stories of Fagan's five victims, and an analysis, if it could be called that, by one Maeve Curran, an undistinguished clinical psychologist whose pieces I'd occasionally come across and who always seemed to me to be more screwed up than most of her clients.

"*The perpetrator of last night's awful murder is filled with rage against women*," I read out, shaking my head. "*He will kill again*. Does she get paid for this or does she do it for a joke?"

And there, on pages six and seven, the letter.

Pressure from the Dublin Metropolitan Police had stopped them saying that the letter definitely *was* written by Ed Fagan, but they as near as damn said it. In fact there was a photograph of Fagan alongside the article, which made the link inevitable, and an anonymous quote from a police source — hello, Lawlor — that police had "no doubt" Fagan was the killer.

It was all there. The perfect blueprint of the classic serial killer. Even if he'd been frightened off by what had happened last night, there was no way our perpetrator could give up after this sort of accolade. It was an open invitation to live up to his billing, to be the sort of monster they wanted him to be. And it was an invitation that I didn't doubt he'd take up.

"It's worse than I expected," I said. "They'll be giving him his own TV show next."

Fitzgerald nodded. "And this was just the first death. Our guy promised more. They're almost wetting themselves, waiting for the next instalment. Unless we can stop him. Only benefit is, he promised to give details of where Sally Tyrrell was if the *Post* published. Well, they sure lived up to their end of the bargain, and then some. Now we'll see if he lives up to his."

The sandwiches came, and as we ate she told me that detectives from the murder squad had started door-to-doors in the area first thing, interviewed a few people who knew Mary Lynch, searched her house. It didn't seem yet as if they'd come up with anything that would help. Other prostitutes in the area weren't exactly queueing up to be cooperative either.

"No funny customers to tell of, no strange clients?"

"Only all of them," Fitzgerald said. "They'll take more breaking down yet. It's my fault. I put Seamus Dalton on it. You know what a gift he has for dealing diplomatically with people." She pulled a face. "Dalton. Christ, what was I thinking?"

I wasn't surprised that they'd hit a wall in the streets round the scene. Where Mary Lynch worked and died wasn't the sort of area whose residents relished talking to the police. In fact, it wasn't the sort of area where

52

residents noticed much of anything. They got used to turning a blind eye, a deaf ear. It was all either short-term rentals who came to be nearer where they could buy drugs round the clock, or else high-rent high rises where they only cared that their cars were safe.

"I could have a word," I suggested. "I know some of the girls round there. They might talk to me."

"That's what I told Draker."

Assistant Commissioner Brian Draker was her immediate superior at the murder squad. Rumour was that he had never actually worked a case in his entire career, but that hadn't stopped him leapfrogging over those who had, like Fitzgerald, to the top job when it became vacant. He was one of nine assistant commissioners who ran the various police departments in the city.

"What did he say?"

"He didn't like it, told me that I should concentrate on working the scene instead of wasting my time bringing in outsiders. Like he ever worked a scene in his life. But he was just giving me the assistant commissioner act, showing me who's boss. He recognises you know more than anyone else about Fagan."

"I thought we agreed this wasn't Fagan?"

"You know that. Maybe I know that. But they don't know it. Fagan's the obvious follow-up to them. That's where they want to concentrate resources. It makes it neat and tidy for them. They can't see past the letter, the stuff from the Bible, the MO."

"They're all bullshit. You know that."

She shrugged. "Path of least resistance, that's Draker's favourite route. If the papers want it to be Fagan, then Fagan's what it'll be for him. At least till he's shown otherwise."

"I could show him otherwise."

"Then show him. Show him why it can't be Fagan. That's your way in."

"I'm not sure I want in," I admitted.

Fitzgerald looked out of the window, pushed her sandwich away half eaten.

"It's your choice, Saxon. No pressure."

"Meaning?"

"Meaning there's a place for you if you want it. As a consultant on the case. We're putting together a major crime team; I had a word, said you could help. I don't have as much influence as I'd like. The label might say Chief Superintendent, but Draker's still jerking my strings. But he did listen to me on this. He knows your background well enough. He's willing to take input from you, as long as it's unpaid, let you sit in on meetings, interviews, read the case notes, review the evidence. But if you don't want to, fine. Just don't beat yourself up about it."

I caught her eye. "You're one to talk about beating myself up after what you said about Dalton."

She smiled. "Two of a kind, that's you and me."

I held her eye and smiled too.

"I'll do it."

She touched my hand lightly in thanks. "I knew you wouldn't be able to resist," she said. "That's why I told Draker you'd be offering your services."

54

"You already told him I'd agreed?"

"I told him you *would* agree, there's a difference. And it's as well you did. I don't mind admitting I have no idea where to start with this. You can help me out. You always have ideas."

"I have ideas all right. Ideas are about the only thing I do have. It's a way of making anyone listen to them that I don't have."

"Precisely. And that's what I can give you. Just get me started."

I felt impatient all of a sudden, like the bar had gotten too small and I wanted to be out walking.

"Then start with Fagan," I said.

"But you said —"

"I know what I said. But like *you* said, all roads lead to Fagan. It can't be Fagan, but that doesn't mean it isn't someone who's connected to Fagan. The Fagan references must mean something. Whoever has done this has picked on him for a reason. Maybe there's a message there. He didn't have to *be* anyone, he could have killed who he liked. But he wanted to become the Night Hunter, wanted us to think that he was the Night Hunter. That must mean something."

"Maybe he just did that in order to conceal his true identity, to send us on the wrong track," Fitzgerald said. "To get a kick from watching us disappear up our own backsides."

"That's possible, but I don't buy it. There are plenty of other ways of screwing with our heads than borrowing the shade of some dead serial killer, and that causes problems in itself. Most killers are trying to

55

assert some semblance of identity, to say 'this is who I am'. They think the world's misunderstood them, done them down, so murder is their way of making their mark, making *themselves*. So why has this one decided to subsume his identity in Ed Fagan's when all experience suggests he should want to assert his own?"

"They're not going to like that back at headquarters," Fitzgerald pointed out. "You tell them most serial killers do what they do to assert their identity and they're going to tell you that's exactly what proves it has to be Fagan."

I conceded the point with a shrug.

"That's why we have to eliminate the Fagan connection as quickly as possible, so they don't get fixated. And the only way to do that is by going back to Fagan. Sounds contradictory, but there you go, that's where I'd start. Why Fagan? And why now? Those are the two questions."

I took a long drink, then pushed it aside. It tasted bitter now and I needed to think clearly, however much I might've longed any other day to sit there and drink myself into forgetfulness.

"When's the autopsy?" I said.

"Late afternoon," said Fitzgerald. "Ambrose is in court till then and we're still doing the follow-ups. The autopsy's not going to tell us anything we don't know. It's more important that we concentrate on the door-to-doors — there has to be a witness somewhere — then see what we can get from forensics at the scene."

"Find anything so far?"

"Nothing that'll be worth anything is my hunch. A few hairs from Mary Lynch's clothing was about the best we got, but again they could've come from anywhere. We might be able to make a match if we can get a suspect in for this, but they're not going to actually lead us *to* anyone, unless he's really stupid and has been caught before." She drained her glass of orange juice. "There was one other thing, now that you mention it. A bottle."

"The canalside's littered with bottles."

"This one was underneath the body. The crime tech boys found it when they came to lift Mary and take her to the mortuary. A Coors Light beer bottle. Looked like it had been placed deliberately, like the body was dragged on top of it for a reason."

"Could be that's why he dragged her down the bank."

"That's what I was thinking," she said. "We bagged it up anyway and took it with us, took some other bottles from the scene for comparison. You never know, we might be able to lift prints off it, get somebody for littering if nothing else, make sure the night wasn't a complete waste of time. Though knowing my luck," she added pointedly, "Conor Buckley would turn up in court to represent the litterbug and tear all our forensic evidence to shreds, and we'd end up paying out damages. Christ, listen to me. Getting morose and I've not even been drinking."

"You need to sleep."

"Sleep be damned. That's what graveyards are for, right? God's way of telling you to get more rest." She checked her watch. "I'm out of time. Tell me quick what you want and I'll get it for you."

"Reports going back from Vice, Serious Crime," I said. "Attacks on prostitutes. Murders. Sexual assaults. Things like last night don't come from nowhere, they always leave a trail, there's always a buildup, a progression. That might be where this nut's trace'll be picked up."

"How long do you want?"

"Say the last five years. Everything since Fagan. You may not have the time or manpower to go through them all. I do."

"I'll get Boland on to it soon as I get back. And I appreciate this, Saxon. I'm only sorry we can't pay you anything. Bringing you in is shock enough for Draker; asking him to write a cheque for you'd probably tip him over the edge."

"I wouldn't want his money, even if he was willing to give it me. For my own peace of mind, I just want to see what you've got, reassure myself all the angles are being covered."

Alone again when Fitzgerald had gone, I realised she'd left the newspaper. On purpose, I guessed. She knew me well enough to know it'd annoy me so much I'd be itching to get going.

But it did more than annoy me. The *Post* was making all fingers point to Ed Fagan, and that was my fault. They wouldn't think Fagan had killed Mary Lynch if they knew where he'd spent the past five years. But was I going to give them Fagan? And if I didn't, wouldn't I be responsible when the next woman died?

58

CHAPTER
SIX

The idea to call Fisher came to me as I was making my way back to my apartment. Why hadn't I thought of it before? Soon as I got in, I rang directory enquiries for his number.

Where was it he lived these days? North London, wasn't it? Highgate or Hampstead, I could never remember which. Whichever's the one with the cemetery. It seemed fitting.

A criminal psychologist for twenty-five years, Dr Lawrence Fisher had spent most of those years in prisons across England, professionally speaking, investigating the roots of pathological psychosexual behaviour, publishing his findings in small learned journals, helping the police behind the scenes with particularly obdurate cases when asked, before a starring role in my book on offender profiling had brought him belatedly to wider attention.

Since then, Fisher had been the subject of a number of TV documentaries, as well as a radio series on the BBC, and he'd written four bestselling accounts of his work mapping the criminal mind. By now, I sometimes half suspected, he was just making up his past cases; he surely must've run out of them after the first couple of books. His latest project was a TV series in which he cooked up profiles of the perpetrators of ten infamous unsolved murders.

He was quite the celebrity, as criminal psychologists go, but still found time to spend two days a week working on an ongoing project to update and refine Scotland Yard's serial offender database. Fisher, in short, was one of the good guys.

When he finally picked up the phone, I could hear the sound of a kettle and children in the background, ordinary family noises. It must be his day off. I tried to remember the names of his children in case I needed to make small talk, then gave up when I realised I couldn't even remember how many he had, never mind their names.

"Long time no hear, Saxon," were his first words.

"You too, Lawrence. I see you're keeping yourself busy."

Phoebe, was that one?

"It keeps me off the streets. What about you? Still stuck in dirty Dublin?"

"Seems like it."

"I thought you'd have been back in the States by now," he said, "begging them to let you back in at the Bureau."

"Not a chance."

Eleanor? Jake?

"Not a chance of you getting back in, or not a chance of you wanting back in?"

"Both."

"I'll buy the first one. So, what is it you're doing now?"

"Right now, what I'm doing is waiting for you to cut the preliminaries so I can get round to what I called about."

"I see you haven't changed. Go on then. Shoot."

"I want you to run something through that fancy new computer system of yours," I said.

"This would be the fancy new experimental computer system of mine which isn't up and running officially yet?" he said. "Is that the one you mean?"

"The very one. This is important. There's been a murder."

"This is news? Join the queue."

I ignored him. "A prostitute, strangled. Freak who did it claims he's Ed Fagan, guy who did the five murders in Dublin a few years back."

"I remember Fagan well enough, Saxon, but you're not listening," Fisher answered. "Do you have any idea of the kind of backlog we're trying to work through here? And I'm not just talking about murders; we've got rape, child molestation, stalking, pornography. Sometimes I get to thinking it's HAL 2000 they imagine I'm setting up here, they're trying to get me to do so much."

"You sound harassed."

"I *am* harassed, which is why I don't need to add to my workload with extra cases from another jurisdiction."

"Case, not cases. Singular."

"Singular always turns to plural. That's the first rule to remember when the police come knocking. What makes you think that you'll get anything from me, anyway?"

There it was, the first chink in the armour. That wasn't the sort of question you'd ask if you were really planning to give someone the brush-off. Never get too interested: that was the real first rule. I took my chance.

"The suspect spent some time over there before coming back here," I explained. "Three years. Moved round a bit, but he was mainly in London. And it gets better. It's Fagan's son."

"You think Fagan's son is following in Daddy's footsteps?" Fisher sounded incredulous.

"Someone's certainly following in Fagan's footsteps, and the son looks as good a place as any to start. Name of Mullen, by the way. Jack Mullen." I could hear him writing it down. "Murder always leaves a trail, you know that. And if Mullen really is our man, then you're best placed to pick it up."

"Before I make a decision," he said, "just answer me one question. Is this the DMP's prime suspect or one of yours?"

"Would it make a difference?"

"Try me and see."

"He's more prime to me than them, but he fits all the patterns they're looking for. There. I admit it. All I want," I said, "is for you to check it out for me. Fitzgerald here can pull up his criminal records from Scotland Yard, but that's no help if he's been keeping his nose clean. There are unusual features in this case.

What I want to know is if you've had anything with points of similarity over there. It's not much. You fax me through the forms, I can fill them out, then you just run them through your system and see if anything matches. It's important."

"You've already used the *it's important* line."

"OK, let me think. What if I try the line about how you can maybe clear up some of your own unsolveds as well?"

"Better," said Fisher appreciatively, "but still no prize. You know, I think this is probably the point at which you're supposed to try the *you owe me one* line."

"Well, it's funny you should say that," I said. "I was saving that up for the next favour I was going to ask."

"There's more?"

It was a testament to his trusting nature that he genuinely sounded astonished.

"I need a profile," I said.

"Now I know you haven't been listening. I have enough to do. I'm working three cases for three different police forces this week alone, there was another on the phone yesterday looking for help, I've got a backlog longer than your list of social inadequacies . . ."

"Yeah, yeah, plus the au pair's got flu."

"The Black Death, actually. *And* I've got to film inserts for my new show."

"I saw that. You know, I think you've put on some weight."

I heard the smile in his voice, but he didn't shift.

"I mean it, Saxon. I have learned to say no. To delegate. Keeps me sane. Why don't you ask Tillman?"

"Tillman?"

Now it was my turn for astonishment. Mort Tillman was the profiler who'd worked the White Monk case when I was still in the FBI. A psychologist out of Notre Dame in Boston, he'd been my personal recommendation for the job. We'd been friends for years, though things had iced over since then. I'd been hard on him in my book on the Paul Nado investigation.

Too hard? He thought so.

In fact he'd thought I was virtually accusing him of having caused further deaths by bungling the evidence analysis. I didn't think I was, but if he'd written things like that about me I guess I might've felt the same way. It was years since I'd seen him.

"Is that supposed to be some sort of joke, Lawrence?" I said. "Why on earth would I ask Mort Tillman?"

"Because he's in Dublin. Didn't you know?"

"Tillman's in Dublin?"

"Saxon, this conversation's going to take all day if you insist on repeating everything I say. Yes. Tillman's in Dublin. Been there a couple of weeks now. He was invited over by Trinity College to give a couple of guest lectures for the Psychology Faculty. So you see, he's in a better position to help you than I am. He's there already, in your boy's shadow. In yours too."

"Be realistic. I couldn't ask Tillman."

"That's your choice, Saxon, but I'm not doing it. Listen to me. Not doing it, got that? I'll run this fruitcake through the system for you, glad to help, but I'm not doing a profile. Look, I'll even have a word with Tillman if you like, butter him up. I'll tell him you've been looking for him, desperate for his help."

"You'd better have plenty of butter," I said. "He'll not help. He'll probably not even speak to me."

"Tillman isn't the sort to hold a grudge, especially not if you give him the chance of being the big hero. Isn't it worth a chance at least?"

I couldn't argue with that.

"OK," I said. "Do it. Call him. Tell him I want to speak to him. But do it quick, all right? The end of the day at the latest. We don't have much time. And the check on Mullen —"

"I'll fax you the forms soon as I can. You just send back the details."

"Thanks. I'll speak to you again. Give my best to Ellen and the kids."

"Laura actually, but it's the thought that counts."

After the line to London went dead, I called Trinity College.

Mort Tillman, I learned, was indeed in town as a guest of the Psychology Faculty. He'd be delivering his first public lecture later that week; meanwhile he was giving private lectures and seminars for the students alone. And when was the next one of those? Four that afternoon.

"Shall I take a message for him?" said the girl at the desk.

"That won't be necessary."
"If you give me your number, I —"
She never finished. I hung up.

CHAPTER
SEVEN

Within an hour of having left my early lunch with Fitzgerald, the buzzer went and a man's voice crackled over the intercom from seven floors below.

"Detective Sergeant Niall Boland?" it said, as if he was making an enquiry rather than an introduction. "Detective Chief Superintendent Fitzgerald told me to bring these notes round?"

There's formal for you.

"Come on up," I said, and released the switch to let him in.

A few minutes later Boland was at the door, labouring under the weight of a large cardboard box filled, I noted, with files and papers. I held the door open for him to carry it in.

The newest addition to Fitzgerald's murder squad team was not quite what I'd expected. He looked less like a city cop than some plodding country sergeant, not that appearances can always be relied upon. God knows what anyone'd conclude from how I looked.

There was certainly something ponderous and meaty about him, though. He had thick fat fingers that looked like someone had blown them up with a bicycle pump, and his shirt strained at a bullish neck. He was like an oak tree that had uprooted itself through sheer will but was still clumsy on its new feet. His hair needed cutting too, and his jaw was dark. Not so much a five o'clock shadow as the sort of day-long shadow that never really went away.

There was a shyness about him as he lingered at the door, looking around at the large apartment, openly appreciative, his eyes drifting to the huge window overlooking the city, and the terrace beyond, like visitors' eyes always did, before remembering why he was here and depositing the box down on the table with a sigh.

"Thanks," I said. "You want coffee?"

"There's another one in the car."

"You'd better get it then."

"Right you are."

He went back down and returned with a second box, sweating now despite the cold. He made his own skin look uncomfortable. The lift must've been broken again. It usually was.

"You could do with more exercise, DS Boland," I teased.

"I don't know about that," he said, "but I wouldn't say no to that coffee you promised."

"See that over there? That's called a kitchen. You'll find what you want in there. Cups in the cupboard."

"Oh, right. I'll do that. You want some, Miss . . ."

"Saxon. Just Saxon. And no, I got some already."

"Right," he said again, and did as he was told.

Out of the corner of my eye, I saw him opening cupboard doors with the aimlessness of a man who had never actually been in a kitchen before and was alarmed by what he was finding.

"Second on the left. No, left. There. Now top shelf."

He lifted down an I Love NY mug and poured coffee from the percolator.

"I didn't see you last night at the canal," I said as he carried it back.

"Off duty," Boland replied.

"I didn't realise there *was* such a thing as off duty in a murder case."

"There is if you're out drinking and you've left your pager back at the station," he said. "It was only when I got home later that I realised everyone was looking for me." He took his first mouthful of coffee and winced. "That's strong," he said. "Not bad, mind, but strong. I'm more of an instant man myself."

"I guessed."

He gestured at the mug.

"Is that where you're from, then — New York?"

"No." I opened the box and started sorting through the papers inside. "That's just a souvenir. I'm from Boston."

"What brought you all the way from Boston to Dublin, if you don't mind my asking?"

"I don't mind you asking. Everyone asks me that question."

Was he waiting for an answer? He could wait.

"I suppose," he tried again, "you must be one of those Irish Americans we're always hearing about."

"Not me. I'm one of those American Americans you never hear about. My grandparents came from this side of the Atlantic, if that's what you mean. One from County This, the other from County That. They all thought of themselves as Irish."

"You don't?"

"I was born in Boston, raised there, went to college there. I pledged allegiance each morning to the flag. American is what I am. All that Irish American, Italian American, Whatever American stuff doesn't really interest me. I guess it must've skipped a generation. Is this all there was?" I said to change the subject, gesturing at the boxes he'd brought round from Dublin Castle.

"It's all I could find at short notice. There may be more. I'll check with records again once I've another free minute. They've been working me pretty hard since I transferred."

"You came from Serious Crime, that right?"

He nodded once more. "About a month ago. Didn't get on with my superior, I was going nowhere, I needed a change, Fitzger — the Chief Super was looking for new blood."

"And now you're lugging boxes up six flights of stairs for some interfering outsider."

"Ours is not to reason why, isn't that what they say? Ours is but to do and die? And I won't always be the department dogsbody. They say it's only till I find my feet in Murder. Besides, you're not just any interfering outsider. From what I hear, you used to be FBI."

"Seven years. Not that long. I've spent longer out of it than in, but yeah, that's what I did. Plus I used to know Ed Fagan, knew him well, that's why I've been roped into looking through this lot." As if they could've stopped me.

"Looking for clues," he said. I couldn't tell if he was being sarcastic.

"Looking for patterns," I said. "There's always patterns, always connections. It's only a question of sorting out what's important from what's not. Let's hope it's here."

I mustn't have sounded very hopeful, because he immediately asked: "Is this not what you wanted? I brought copies of everything that was there."

"It's fine," I said. "Just wondering where to start is all. What about you? What've they got you doing?"

"Me?" said Boland. "I'm tagging along with the Chief Super in half an hour to talk to the man who found the body."

"The dog-walker."

"That's the boy. Stephens, you call him. Matt Stephens."

"I thought he was already interviewed."

"He was taken down last night to make a formal statement. Now it turns out that he hangs out with some group who patrol the streets round there at nights trying to reform prostitutes, bring them back to Jesus, only he didn't mention that in his statement. A uniform came through with the information a couple of hours ago. He recognised the name, put two and two together. The Chief Super wants to follow it up straightaway."

"Sounds promising."

"Detective Dalton reckons they just like hanging round red-light districts," Boland said. "He thinks they get off on it."

"He's probably right. They could bring anybody back to Jesus if they wanted. Gamblers, shoplifters, even lawyers if they fancied a real challenge." Boland smiled at that. Cops always appreciated a joke at the expense of the enemy. "But it's hookers every time. Next best thing to picking one up, maybe. Cheaper too."

"They even have an office in one of the streets backing on to the canal," Boland said. "Registered charity, if you can credit it. That's where he's arranged to be interviewed again. I think he was hoping there'd be safety in numbers. What're they called now?"

He struggled for a name.

"The Blessed Order of Mary," I helped him out. "I've heard of them."

As I spoke, a thought flashed into my mind. Blessed Order of Mary . . . Mary Lynch . . . I wondered if that was significant. Another hidden message, like the bottle?

I'd bring it up with Fitzgerald next time we spoke.

"You'd better be on your way," was all I said to Boland. "You don't want to be late."

Once Boland had gone, I sat down with the boxes and started going through them, slowly, methodically, file by file, page by page. Basically I was looking for any evidence there might be of Mary Lynch's killer having struck before. Premeditated, ritualistic murder was rarely the first act. Rather it was the culmination of a process which might have taken years to come into shape, moving inexorably through increasing levels of brutality, audacity, cunning, to its final flowering.

Mary Lynch's killer was unlikely to be any different. He'd be in here somewhere, I was sure of it, refining the fantasy, rehearsing for Mary, waiting his chance.

I started with murders all the same. It seemed the obvious place. Only three prostitutes, I soon learned, had been murdered since Ed Fagan's day (only three? What was I saying? Three was a universe), and two of those could be quickly discounted.

The first, Susan Levy, had died, along with her two-year-old son, in a fire at her high-rise on the Northside of the city. Petrol had been poured through the letterbox and set alight. Police suspected a grudge attack over an unpaid loan. The other, Jo Philpott, was found stabbed to death a couple of years after Fagan's own disappearance, in a laneway off Benburb Street just across the river from the Guinness brewery. This was another red-light district, where only the most desperate prostitutes worked, even more desperate than those who worked the Grand Canal, and Jo was the most desperate of all. She was forty-two and eight months pregnant when she bled to death.

The woman's boyfriend/pimp went missing shortly after the crime, and on discovery, confessed. He'd done it, he said, because she'd been cheating on him. She'd had sex with other men scores of times a day to feed his drug habit, and then he lost it when she slept with one for free. Her blood was found on his clothing which, criminal genius that he was, he'd stuffed in a refuse bin next door; his fingerprints matched those on the knife found at the scene.

He was now in Mountjoy doing a ten-year stretch, having pleaded temporary insanity, diminished responsibility, deprived childhood, you name it, but was expected to be released soon when, no doubt, he'd find some other Jo Philpott to finance his prodigious chemical intake.

It was the third murder which stood out, that of one Monica Lee, whose naked body had been found in the Dublin mountains two years ago, three weeks after going missing.

Finding her was an act of pure chance. She'd been thrown down the side of a deep vale that was used by locals for dumping, and was already in an advanced state of decomposition due to bad weather. There had been gnawing of the body by rats too, which meant identification was only possible by dental records. What was more, the physical environment had been torn up by three weeks of heavy rain and the usual comings and goings from the dump. Tyre tracks were too numerous to distinguish, and those of three weeks back had long since been obliterated.

Ambrose Lynch's autopsy report was appended to the case notes. I skipped through the pages of details to the conclusions at the end. Death had been by massive brain haemorrhaging caused by indeterminate frontal blunt-force injury, possibly with a brick. Fragments of stone had been taken from the wound and sent for analysis, though no conclusive evidence as to its nature had been found. She was probably raped too, Lynch thought — two separate traces of semen were found inside her, no match on records, and there was some internal damage — but the poor state of the remains was so bad that he couldn't say for sure. Cautious as ever, that was Lynch.

And maybe he was right to be cautious. Monica was known to have rough sex with clients without a condom if they paid extra; she made no secret of it. Proving that she was raped would be virtually impossible, even when it did come accompanied by a brick to the forehead.

There were, of course, some obvious differences between this killing and that of Mary Lynch last night and Fagan's own victims.

The body was concealed, for one thing, not left in the open to be found. Monica Lee was naked, not dressed — her clothes were never found. There was the probable rape. Method of death, crucially, was different too, and this killer had used restraints on both the victim's hands and ankles, and a gag. Plus there was no note left with the body, no religious angle.

The only possible hint there was the absence of a crucifix which, the dead woman's friends assured police, Monica Lee had always worn; but that was a long shot. If the crucifix was all that was taken, it might've suggested a significance for the killer, but everything Monica had on her that night was taken, so whatever symbolism there might've been was hidden.

No witnesses saw Monica get into the car that took her away on the night of her death. No witnesses saw her body dumped. No witnesses saw her in between, however long that might be. Fitzgerald's hunch had been that Monica had a prearranged meeting that night with a regular client rather than being picked up at random on the street. Perhaps a client by the name of Gus who she'd mentioned to some of her friends. Other girls working that night certainly recalled her taking a call just before her disappearance, and laughing familiarly.

Efforts to trace the mysterious Gus proved fruitless, however, and the investigation was, reluctantly, wound down. A note and extension number on the cover of the report indicated that the case was now being dealt with by a DS Donal O'Malley, and I made a note to contact him later and see if there was any information he could add.

When it said that an unsolved case like this was being handled by a lone officer, that usually meant the officer in question was responsible for keeping the file updated with any new evidence which might, but rarely did, come in, and that he was expected to get the file out occasionally and blow off the cobwebs, see if anything had been missed previously; also to call the various witnesses and relatives to give the impression that something was being done. But to all intents it meant the investigation was closed and police didn't expect to make further progress. Still, there was something about this one that made me want to know more.

The deaths of five other prostitutes in the same time period took me less time to get through. They didn't seem relevant to any investigation into Mary Lynch's murder.

One had fallen from the bridge, knocked her head and drowned in the canal. Autopsy showed excess alcohol and the presence of four different stimulant narcotics, including LSD and Ecstasy. Two had overdosed in the same crack house off the South Circular Road, not far from where Mary had lived, four months apart, but each was considered a clear case of accidental death. Another had suffocated on a plastic supermarket bag filled with glue. It would've been put down as accidental too had she not left a suicide note. The last to die had been knocked down and killed not far from the city centre at the corner of Fitzwilliam Street and Merrion Square.

Eight women, eight dead women, just names now, eight women reduced to ghosts in the pages of a few meagre case reports. And only remembered now because Mary Lynch had gone into the darkness to join them.

It was only when I laid Monica Lee's photograph on the table, wanting on a sudden impulse to check if she looked anything like the picture I'd seen of Mary Lynch in the *Post*, whether that might be a connection, that I realised it was getting dark already. Out the window, lights were coming on over the city. The sky was streaked with black clouds. More rain.

I checked the time. Four thirty. Fisher hadn't called back, and Mort Tillman certainly hadn't been in touch. I wondered if Fisher had managed to speak to Tillman yet, and if he had, why he hadn't called to tell me. I rang Fisher's number in London again but there was no answer. What time was Tillman's seminar? Four o'clock, wasn't it? I could be down there before it was over if I hurried. And once that thought was planted in my head, there was no uprooting it.

What I had left of good sense told me I should wait till I heard from Fisher — but I told what I had left of good sense to go to hell.

CHAPTER
EIGHT

Trinity College rose above the traffic that flowed round its base like an ancient sacred rock out of some fast-flowing dirty river, seemingly untouched by the surrounding noise and chaos. It had been here for over four hundred years and it wasn't looking bad for its age.

Certainly better than I did for mine most days.

I walked through tall gates into the cobbled courtyard within. On the far side, a queue of tourists still waited, late as it was, to get into the library to see the Book of Kells, an eighth-century illuminated manuscript in Latin, stolen from Scotland, some said, by Irish monks and which the Irish showed few signs of handing back. And why should they? It was obviously doing good business, though I'd never been to see it myself. I was waiting for the paperback to come out.

It didn't take long to find the Psychology building, nor, once inside, to climb the stairs and find the room I was looking for; but once there, my nerve almost failed me.

The door had one of those glass panels in it patterned with squares, like the sort of paper on which children do their math homework, and through it I could see Mort Tillman sitting by the window, head framed by darkening sky, legs crossed, hands folded, listening intently as one of the students, an anxious, fidgety young man in John Lennon glasses, made some point.

Mort looked just as I remembered, with that same air of distracted, shabby grandeur, that same seemingly permanent frown, above all that same inexplicable fondness for over-large grey corduroys and bright waistcoats, the latter his one concession to style. It was as though he'd once seen a 1940s print showing a caricature of the standard eccentric college professor and the image had become imprinted in his head, unerasable except by invasive surgery.

His hair was still too long for a man of his age as well, though closer to grey now than the silver he always used to be so proud of, and the goatee looked rather worn.

He was the middle son of a grand New England family of attorneys who'd expected better of him and made sure he never forgot it. Grandfather in the Senate; summer house on Martha's Vineyard; winter ski lodge in Vermont — why wouldn't they have expected better? Tillman had courage in his own way to defy them. It was just a pity that he couldn't have defied them that bit more by not sharing their own assessment of his shortcomings.

A glance up from Tillman showed that he'd seen me as I pushed open the door and entered as unobtrusively as I could manage, but if he was surprised by my appearance he wasn't showing it. Did that mean Fisher had managed to contact him? Or had he been expecting me to come round ever since he arrived in Dublin?

A couple of other people near the back of the room looked up too, but most of the other twenty or so students who'd turned up for Tillman's seminar were too engrossed in the dialogue that was going on between him and the fidgety young student to take any notice of me.

Theirs was an argument I'd heard many times before. If something was acidic, the relevant test would always show it to be acidic; it couldn't be mistaken for, or pretend to be, anything else. But if an actual or potential offender knew the parameters of a profiler's tests, he could subtly change his own behaviour to buck the test, escaping detection to carry on killing.

"You can even download VICAP forms from the Internet now," the student insisted, referring to the FBI's Violent Crime and Apprehension Program analysis reports. "I've done it myself. You know what the police are looking for. And once you know, you can beat it."

"In theory, maybe," Tillman said when he got the chance. "I've never claimed that profiling is faultless, I've never even used the word science. Offender profiling is a technique, that's all, an application of psychological principles to the realm of criminology. It's still up to the police to determine how to use the application of those principles in the solving of a crime."

"But how can they apply the principles at all if the principles can't be relied on?"

"It's more complex than that, Tim," Tillman replied. "An offender may know the principles involved, but he still won't alter his behaviour in the most part because what he's doing has its own compulsion. He is working out, usually, an elaborate ritualistic fantasy of his own, perfecting it each time to make it right. Not only is it not possible for him to change his behaviour, he also wouldn't want to because that wouldn't satisfy the urge."

"But he *could*, if he chose to."

"Sure he could, if he wanted to make an abstract academic point about profiling," Tillman agreed. "But most murderers aren't interested in playing those sorts of fussy intellectual games. They're obeying a more primitive instinct. You can't get away from sex."

"Tim manages it most weekends," another student piped up.

Everyone laughed, though Tim didn't even seem to have heard the mocking. He was listening too intently as Tillman continued.

"Even if our hypothetical murderer wanted to buck the profile," Tillman said, "every contact leaves a trace. Every physical contact leaves a trace — that's the principle of forensics. But every contact leaves a psychological trace too. We may only be at the start of finding out how to interpret that trace, but we need to keep at it. Even if it's only knowing if the killer was in a hurry, if there was excess violence, whether he's organised or disorganised. It all adds up to building a rounder picture of the offender. We can't hide the way we are in our actions. We can change aspects, but how we behave still has an inner logic of its own that can be mapped."

Tim shrugged, unconvinced.

"Don't just take my word for it. Ask Saxon here."

He nodded at me, and twenty heads turned in my direction. I shifted uncomfortably in my seat.

"Saxon," Tillman said, "is an FBI agent."

"Former FBI agent," I corrected.

"Clarice Starling or Dana Scully?" asked someone with a laugh. The same class wit who'd wound up Tim.

"Nowhere near as effective as either, sadly," I said. "That's why I left."

"And why she now writes books. She was working on a book about our friend Ed Fagan when he went missing. The one the local newspapers tell us is up to his old tricks again."

There were a few nods from people who obviously recognised who I was. A look of embarrassment on a few other faces too, as those who'd bothered to read up about their guest lecturer realised his uneasy relationship with me.

"Are you helping to catch him?" one girl asked.

"As I said, I don't work in law enforcement any more."

"You're not here to ask Dr Tillman's help then?" she said; but before I could think of a noncommittal answer, a bell sounded outside in the courtyard for five o'clock, and Tillman rose to his feet with what seemed very much like relief.

"Time's up," he said, and he started gathering his papers together into a briefcase as the students filed reluctantly out.

He waited till the last one had gone before speaking.

"I have a meeting," he said then.

"This won't take long," I said. "I'll walk you there."

He considered it, then nodded, though with little enthusiasm.

"Interesting bunch of students you have," I said as he showed me out and we set off down the corridor, Tillman greeting people occasionally as they passed. He seemed to have become pretty well known in his first couple of weeks in Dublin.

"Bright kids," he agreed. "This is a new ballgame for them. The college has only invited me here for a few months to see what interest there is in classes on criminal psychology. So far, it's going well. They're learning quickly."

"Like Tim."

"Tim's got a first-rate mind," he said. He didn't elaborate.

"I was surprised to hear you were in town at all," I tried again. "Small world. You should've called me."

"Why?"

"We could've had dinner. A drink."

"For old times' sake?"

"Something like that."

"You've had better ideas," he said.

"You're still mad with me about my book."

"I'm not mad," said Tillman. "I got over it. It just changed our relationship, that's all. I don't think it's going to be root beer and potato chips for us from now on, you know?" His sarcasm made root beer and potato chips sound like an offensive suggestion. "But that's no reason why we can't keep things professional. Like now. You wanted to see me. Why?"

"I need a profile of the man who killed Mary Lynch," I said.

No answer.

"Did you hear me? I said I need a profile."

"I hear you," said Tillman. "Loud and clear." He stopped walking abruptly, and looked at me. There were tufts of grey flowering in his eyebrows too these days, I saw. "What is it? Am I a charity case now? No, don't bother answering that. Like I told Lawrence Fisher when he called earlier with the same message, if you need a profile you should ask a profiler."

"That's what I'm doing."

"Correction, Saxon. You're asking an ex-profiler, just like you're ex-FBI. At least that's what you told my students in there. I stopped doing individual cases three, four years ago."

"You worked an abduction case for the police in Paris last year, I read about it in the newspapers. Some college student had been reporting a stalker for three months, then went missing shortly before her finals. They came to you for help."

"They came to me because I was the only FBI-trained profiler who could speak French, and the French police didn't want the extra expense of an interpreter," Tillman said. "Anyway, if you know so much about it, you should also know that it failed."

"It didn't fail. The profile you drew up was a ninety per cent match for the man now doing time in prison."

"The girl was found trussed up like a caterpillar and suffocated with her own underpants. That's a failure in my book."

"You were hired to do a profile. You did a good profile. It wasn't your job to stop the girl from dying."

He started walking again, down the stairs and out into the courtyard.

"You didn't think so in Paul Nado's case," he said without breaking step.

That threw me.

"I never said you should've caught Nado," I replied. "You were overworked. You were under pressure. You missed things. Strong hints of familiarity between him and the first victim, for one thing, possible staging of the scenes. We all did."

"Clear signs that, if spotted and acted upon, could have prevented other victims dying. As your book made plain."

"I had to be honest when I wrote it."

"You didn't have to write it at all."

I had no answer to that. He was right. The world could have managed quite well without another book on serial killing.

"Look," said Tillman, "can we change the subject? I told you, I don't do profiles any more. I mean it. Get someone else."

"There isn't anyone else."

"There's Lawrence Fisher."

"If you spoke to him, you know he won't do it. I already asked."

"I wasn't the first choice then?"

I ignored the jibe. "Just take a look at what we've got and see if anything comes to mind, that's all I ask."

"Take a look at what *we've* got? What happened to the *I don't work in law enforcement any more* act?"

"It died with Mary Lynch on the canal," I said, "with a cord round its neck and the blood vessels bursting in its eyes."

Cheap shot, but it worked. Tillman paused and looked into the distance. The picture was in his head, where I wanted it.

"You know, years ago I had the choice between psychology and medieval French literature," he said at last. "If I'd taken the latter, I'd probably be a professor now, thinking beautiful French thoughts, taking long vacations in Rouen, Chartres, Montmartre, calling it work. But I got it into my head that psychology would make me more attractive to women. Look where I am now. Head full of serial killers."

"At least it's some use," I said. "More useful than another book on medieval French."

"You reckon? At least I could sleep nights if I'd stuck to French poetry." He stopped and rubbed his eyes. "Look, I don't know why I'm saying this, but if you're so convinced it's not Ed Fagan who killed your Mary Lynch, and you wouldn't be after a profile from me if you weren't, then I'll take a look. Send round what you've got, and I'll see if anything comes to mind."

"I'll do that. And why don't you come along to the crime team meeting tomorrow morning? I could pick you up beforehand and after it we could run out to the scene."

He nodded.

"And Mort?"

"Yeah?"

"I won't forget this."

"Don't worry. I'll make sure you don't. Now if you'll excuse me, I have to go make some calls."

"I thought you had a meeting?"

"I do," he said. "I just didn't say what day."

I smiled, then swore softly as a call came through on my mobile. I checked the number first as usual. It was Fitzgerald.

"Wait there," I said, "I'll only be a moment."

I backed away a few steps and pressed to answer.

"Grace?"

Tillman must have seen something in my eyes when I returned a few minutes later, for he said: "Bad news?"

"Mary Lynch's killer made contact again about an hour ago," I said. "He sent a text message to the golden oldies request line of some local radio station, giving them the location of Sally Tyrrell's body."

"He's doing what he said he'd do," Tillman said. "That's good. Something else to go on at least. He still wants to play the game. It'd be more worrying for you if he'd retreated, gone back in on himself."

"Nine times out of ten, I'd agree. Only problem is," I said, "Fitzgerald just told me it isn't Sally's body that they found."

CHAPTER
NINE

"Is it true?" said Elliott. "That they've found another body?"

I turned and there he was, lurking at my shoulder. I should have him arrested for stalking. I'd only come into the store round the corner from my apartment on the way home from Trinity in order to pick up something for dinner. I was supposed to be cooking for Fitzgerald tonight, though I didn't know if she'd remembered — the arrangements had been made before either of us had even heard Mary Lynch's name — or what time she'd be there if she had.

"What do you do?" I said, turning back and reaching up for pepper. "Do you follow me?"

"I saw you come in, that's all," he said. "I was passing. It's a small town. Look, why don't you just tell me what I want to know and then I'll be out of your hair? Is it true?"

I tried to remember what it was he'd said to me last night down by the Grand Canal. Yeah, that was it. "We shall see what we shall see," I reminded him.

"Screw you, Saxon," Elliott said.

In his dreams.

"There's no point lying to me," he went on once he realised I wasn't paying him any attention, "because I already know the police found another one. I don't get it. We printed his letter like he asked; why didn't he come to us with this instead of some trashy radio station?"

"You know how it is, Elliott, love fades. Even between a serial killer and his pet reporter. Maybe he's been seeing other crime reporters behind your back. Maybe he wants a trial separation, an open relationship even. You get to write about other sickos, he gets some other reporter to jerk him off."

"You think that's what I'm doing?"

"What'd you think, that he hates all this attention?"

"I'm only doing my job," said Elliott sulkily.

"I think you'll find that the usual excuse is you were only obeying orders," I corrected him. "Copyright Nuremberg, circa 1945."

"So I'm a Nazi now?"

"No, Elliott, you're a Pulitzer Prize-winning lyric poet and an all-round humanitarian. Satisfied now?"

I tried walking on, but he just wouldn't quit.

"I only want you to tell me one thing," he said, catching me up. "One thing, all right. I have a deadline coming up, I need something for tomorrow's edition. Just tell me if it's Sally."

"I can't."

"Not even that?"

"Your boyfriend said he'd reveal where Sally Tyrrell was if you published his deranged ramblings," I said. "You published them. So what do you think?"

He stared back, trying to read me, like it was a trick question; which of course it was.

"I think it's Sally Tyrrell," he said at last.

"You think you can trust him?"

"I think so, yes."

I'd heard it all now.

"Well then," I said, "you've got your answer."

I wished I felt guiltier about deceiving Elliott once again, it was getting too easy; but he was out of my mind the minute he left the store.

My mind was still a couple of miles away, in the churchyard of St John the Divine in Ballsbridge, where the as yet unidentified body of the latest woman had been found.

I hadn't been up there to see her for myself. I'd get the reports later; right now, I'd only be in the way. And I certainly didn't need to go there to fix a picture of the place in my head.

The churchyard at St John's was where Sylvia Judge, Fagan's second victim, the student, had been murdered. We were back to the same pattern again, and once again I'd missed it. Missed it because it seemed too obvious after Mary Lynch, but that only proved how clever our busy, communicative little killer was turning out to be. He knew that going back to the scene of Fagan's second killing was too obvious as well. That was exactly why he calculated he'd probably get away with it. The obvious was always the last thing on anyone's mind at a time like this. Even if there were watches put on Fagan's other scenes now, it was already too late.

Fitzgerald had called me as soon as she got there and talked me through what she found.

The dead woman had been laid down in a corner of the cramped churchyard, close by a moss-covered wall. She had been dead some time, Ambrose Lynch estimated; killed somewhere else, dumped here; but he was talking weeks, not years. If it *had* been Sally Tyrrell, she should have been little more than bones by now. What was more, the clothes which the victim was wearing when she died suggested an older age range, as did the apparent loss of elasticity to the skin.

Lynch, though, wouldn't immediately hazard a guess as to when exactly she died, or how, and for once his legendary reticence could be forgiven, for this woman's head was completely missing — "Cut off cleanly," Fitzgerald told me flatly over the phone — and likewise her hands, and . . . Fitzgerald paused whilst she made sure . . . yes, her feet as well.

"Looks like a single stroke for each of them," she confirmed.

She sounded bewildered and I didn't blame her.

Removing the head was one thing. Perhaps the killer simply wanted to delay a possible visual identification of the victim. Taking away the hands similarly could be explained if the dead woman had a criminal record and could be tracked through fingerprints.

Or perhaps it was that the killer feared there might be traces of his DNA under the fingernails, where the victim had scratched his face — or was it *her* face that was damaged? He might have bitten her cheek, say. An offender's teeth are as unique as his prints. Whatever it was, there were plenty of reasons why he might have chosen to dismember the corpse.

But why cut off the feet as well? That didn't make any sense. That only made it seem like there was some deeper symbolic significance to the act, but what? Fagan had certainly never done anything remotely like it. Nor was there any clue in the neat typewritten message which was found, just like with Sylvia Judge, tucked inside the dead woman's bra.

Go, see now this cursed woman and bury her.

The Bible was indeed a charming book.

I got back to find that Lawrence Fisher had faxed through the promised form while I was out seeing Tillman. The sheets, all thirty of them, lay curled separately on the floor where they'd fallen and I had to gather them up and arrange them in order before I could begin.

Basically it was an amended version of the VICAP form that Tillman's student had mentioned earlier. There were scores of questions about the victim — what build was she, what ethnic grouping, did she have any physical abnormalities, missing teeth, did she wear glasses, what colour was her hair, did she have tattoos or scars and if so where, what kind of clothes was she wearing when she died, what was her last known location?

Questions too about the killer's MO. Did he use restraints and if so were they in excess of what was needed simply to restrain? Was the face or body covered after death? Was any clothing missing? Torn? Did the body show signs of being re-dressed post-mortem? Did the attack take place in a vehicle, in an open field, in a wood, near a school? Was the body concealed?

On and on the questions went, each one a separate line of enquiry, each one a separate road unwinding out possibly to eternity. I had filled out similar forms many times in the past, too many times, but this time I felt myself drowning in detail. I knew so little about what had happened to Mary Lynch; I'd have to wait for Fitzgerald to fill me in on all these points.

And what about this latest body? That meant another form — and still there'd be more to come. Not months later, or weeks, but only days and hours away.

Frustrated, I laid the form aside and went to wash my hands.

Then I washed them again.

I felt stained.

I put on a pot roast to cook slowly, and wondered as I did so what Mary Lynch would've been doing this time last evening. Eating dinner, watching TV?

I wanted to imagine her wired into some normality like that, but I only wanted it for me; it was no good to her any more. And anyway, I knew in truth that what she'd probably been doing was scoring heroin off her dealer, or screwing some fat loser to pay for it.

And what had I been doing? Waiting for Fitzgerald to call. Waiting for Mary to die.

I shook my head to clear my thoughts. Thinking of Mary Lynch was no use to anyone right this minute. Work was, and it was time to get back to it. I took a

Coke from the fridge, and sat down to recommence my ascent up the north face of the incident reports.

The next few hours made for miserable reading. Prostitutes were always reluctant to report trouble to the police, didn't matter what city you were in, so if this was only the tip of the iceberg then it was a wonder the city hadn't ground against it and sunk years ago.

Week after week, going back through the records, there was the same forgotten story. Prostitutes were robbed, raped, beaten, harassed, followed, on the streets, in rented flats, in massage parlours. One had been stabbed by a dirty needle, and sent for an Aids test. The report gave no reason to believe that officers had even followed up to find out if the test was positive or not.

The case files for most of these incidents were so thin that sometimes I had to open them just to convince myself there was anything inside. Usually there was an incident report from the (inevitably) lowly officer sent to the scene, with an accompanying victim statement, the odd picture if the photographer was available, and that was that, wham bam thank you ma'am.

The most recent such report came from only two weeks ago, and concerned the rape of a prostitute by a punter she'd picked up in Lad Lane, not far from where Mary's body had been found. The victim said she wouldn't even have bothered reporting what had happened, but she was so badly beaten that a friend had taken her to Casualty, where nurses called the police.

It was the name, Jackie Hill, that alerted me as much as anything. I knew Jackie. Hadn't seen her for months now, but I knew her. I'd met her first when I was researching my book on Fagan. She'd been a prostitute back even then, and had been friendly with a couple of his victims, which was how she'd come to my attention. Every time we'd met since, she'd promised me she'd quit, soon, next year, once she'd got herself sorted out. I'd heard them all.

Would this finally persuade her to get out? Probably not, knowing Jackie. Why would it, if what Fagan did to her friends hadn't?

What really disturbed me as I read the account of her attack was that she hadn't been robbed. Rape of a prostitute was usually followed by the taking of whatever money she'd earned; most attackers seemed to derive pleasure from that final humiliation. Jackie's attacker had taken nothing. He'd also told her he knew where she lived and would kill her if she talked to police.

She'd been hysterical, unsurprisingly, when the police interviewed her, convinced that she would die if she talked, but eventually they'd managed to take a statement from her, some DNA samples to send for forensic analysis. She hadn't been able to provide a description. Because it was dark, she said, but knowing Jackie it probably had more to do with the fact that her brain was fractured from her last fix. Then they'd dumped her on to Victim Support, who were supposed to be arranging a follow-up visit, though I couldn't help doubting they'd ever get around to it. Jackie Hill wasn't the type to insist on her rights.

I made a note to find out who was dealing with her case. Rape was outside the Fagan pattern our killer had adopted for himself, but then so was dismemberment and that hadn't stopped him; and even if he was acting out the role of the great Night Hunter, that didn't mean he wasn't up for some freelance sexual assault when out of his adopted persona.

He'd said he knew where Jackie Hill lived. The author of the *Post* letter had said he'd been watching Mary Lynch too. It wasn't much, but I wasn't willing to let any possible connection, however implausible, go begging. I had to start somewhere.

I rubbed my eyes roughly, trying to hurt myself back into alertness, then looked again at the boxes of files which Boland had brought round earlier that day. I couldn't be much more than halfway through, and on and on it went, this bizarre catalogue of human malevolence, the endlessly lapping waves of a poisoned tide. Where did it end?

A picture of Fitzgerald entered my mind out of nowhere. A hot volcanic pool outside Reykjavik, Grace splashing her feet and drinking vodka, refusing to get in because she couldn't swim. We'd been on holiday, it was after midnight and the Northern Lights were showing off among the dull jealous stars; they seemed to get tangled in her hair when she turned her head.

Now someone had switched off the Northern Lights and Grace was most likely at her desk down at headquarters, making the same lists as me, seeing no end.

It would all be followed up in time. We'd convince ourselves we were doing something, scurrying after each lead, but roads had led to nowhere before. What if they led us nowhere again? What if our precious lists only led to more lists, files to more files? What then?

CHAPTER
TEN

Fitzgerald buzzed around nine, and as always I felt immediately guilty that I hadn't given her a key. I always meant to, but something, just as inevitably, always stopped me. A key would have meant something, and I didn't know if I was ready for what it would mean.

Fitzgerald never asked, and she certainly didn't ask tonight. She just came in wearily from climbing the stairs and shrugged off her coat.

"Something smells good."

"Shall I put it out?"

"Not just yet. Pour me some of that first." She took the glass of wine out of my hand and tasted it. "Not bad. What is it?"

"Don't quote me on this, but I think it might be wine."

"That's not what I meant."

"Yeah well, you know me. I only picked it up because I liked the label. It's Italian, I think. Distilled on the slopes of the Appalachian Mountains by Corleone and Sons Winemakers. It was sitting there on the shelf, making me an offer I couldn't refuse."

"Spirits are distilled, wine's fermented," Fitzgerald said, taking another sip. "And the Appalachian mountains are in America, not Italy. Remember *Appalachian Spring?*"

"Can't say I do. Was John Wayne in it?"

"It's a symphony by Aaron Copland. Don't Americans know anything about culture, even their own? You must have been thinking of the Apennines," she added, peering distractedly at the label. "Besides, this is French."

"Wherever." I paused. "Bad day?"

"Is there any other kind?" she said. "I'll tell you about it over dinner. I'm going for a shower first. Is that OK?" There it was again. The asking for permission. She wouldn't ask for permission if she had a key. For a moment I wondered if the asking for permission was a rebuke, but I didn't want to ask in case it was.

"You know where everything is," I said instead, and she smiled and took the wine into the bathroom.

A moment later I heard the shower, a hard rattle like gravel thrown against a window.

I sat by my own window and looked out over the city. The rain was back out there too, but it was a soft rain, the sort of rain that blurred the streetlights rather than obliterated them. Traffic moaned quietly below. Sitting here sometimes made me think of Boston, and the differences, and then I'd get homesick, recalling how long it had been . . .

"What are you thinking?" said Fitzgerald.

My eyes snapped open. I must have nodded off momentarily. I hadn't even heard her come up and put her arms about my neck.

"Nothing," I said. "Or dinner. Take your pick."

She was wearing my sweater, I saw; she wore it so often now it smelt of her rather than me. I didn't mind. It suited her better. Most of my things did.

"Come on," I said, "let's eat."

I may not know much about wine, but I can sure cook a Class A pot roast. Even Fitzgerald, who had long since got used to snatching whatever food she could get hold of at short notice and now rarely noticed what she ate, had to admit that it was good.

For decency's sake, I waited until she'd almost finished before I asked about the latest body. The plan was to wait until she'd finished entirely, but waiting was never my strong suit.

"I wondered how long it'd be before you got round to that," she said.

"Any indication yet how she died?"

"She was only taken away about an hour ago," Fitzgerald said. "The crime tech boys got so little from the scene of Mary's death overnight, I think they just wanted to make sure they didn't disturb anything in the churchyard as well. Lynch said he'd do the autopsy tomorrow morning. I'm going round there after the crime team meeting to sit in on that one as well."

"Anyone see her being dumped?"

I conjured up a picture of the churchyard in my head. It was overlooked by a convent on one side, a terrace of houses on the other; a narrow lane branched off from the main road and round to an entrance at the side. Someone must have seen something, surely?

"Teenagers drinking there last night claim they heard a car pulling up about one a.m.," Fitzgerald said. "But it was dark, they didn't actually see anyone coming in."

"That would only've been a couple of hours after Mary was killed."

"He probably had the body in the boot of his car when he picked Mary up. Drove to the canal, killed *her*, then on to the churchyard, where he dumped the body of this one."

"Risky," I said. "That's two chances of being seen."

"*If* that's when the body was left in the churchyard. It's only the evidence of the kids that puts it at one a.m. She might've been left there earlier. The car might be unconnected."

"If she *was* left there at one, that puts the dog-walker in the clear," I pointed out. "He was conveniently giving a statement to the police down by the canal around that time."

"Stephens," said Fitzgerald contemptuously. "Don't talk to me about Matt Stephens."

"I assume from your tone of voice that you got to speak to him today."

"How did you know about that?"

"Boland told me."

"Boland, right. Well, I did — if you can call it talking. Pleading and whining'd be nearer the mark. Creep. He's the sort who, if you ask him the time, starts squealing 'I didn't do it, I'm innocent.' He admitted knowing Mary by sight, but he denies ever having

102

talked to her, and he insists he didn't know it was her when he reported finding the body. He says he didn't admit to being in the Blessed Order of Mary at first because he didn't want to drag them into it. Didn't want them knowing he was doing a little freelance loitering in the red-light zone, if you ask me, but for now we're going to have to take his word for it. Unless we get something on him."

"His knowing her might be significant," I said. "Eighty-five per cent of victims know their attacker."

"Fifteen per cent don't," Fitzgerald pointed out, and I couldn't argue with that.

"What about Jack Mullen then? Fagan's son? Did you get a chance to check him out?"

"That's the other bad news," said Fitzgerald. "Mullen has an alibi. About twenty of them, to be exact. He was drinking last night in a bar near his place up by the North Circular Road. He told Healy he didn't leave there till after two in the morning."

"Is he telling the truth?"

"It'll be straightforward enough to check out."

"I had a real feeling about him too," I said, and I felt sick all of a sudden. Mullen had been perfect. Mullen had made sense. If Mullen had an alibi, then we were right back to the beginning — but I wasn't accepting that quietly.

"You haven't asked me about the autopsy on Mary Lynch." Fitzgerald interrupted my gloomy thoughts, reaching over to the wine bottle and refilling her half-empty glass.

"I didn't know if you'd want to talk about it yet," I confessed. "I remember what it's like. It's never easy."

"You wouldn't say that if you saw Ambrose at work," Fitzgerald said. "He doesn't bat an eyelid."

"There are worse than Lynch. I knew a medical examiner in Vermont once used to lay out his sandwiches on the mortuary slab so that he didn't have to stop for lunch."

"That's sick."

"Sick's right, but then we all must be a bit sick, working this field, true? So come on," I said, "tell me. Any surprises?"

"On cause of death? No surprises. In fact, it was all pretty straightforward. Congestion of the face, cyanosis, petechial haemorrhaging in the skin and eyes, particularly prominent in the lips and behind the ears, slight bleeding from the ears. Numerous petechiae on the internal organs too, apparently, though I didn't hang around for a closer look. Didn't need to by then."

"A textbook strangulation."

"That's what Lynch said. If you ask me, he was secretly impressed. Said he was going to keep the photographs to show in his lectures."

"Get anything on the ligature?"

"Lynch lifted some fibres from inside the wound."

I guessed before she said it. Green. Fagan had used green garden twine too. There was even some in his car boot when he was arrested. Conor Buckley, incredibly, had tried to have it discounted as evidence on the grounds that Fagan was a keen gardener, which was the first his garden had ever heard about it.

104

"Whatever it was, it was certainly pulled tight," Fitzgerald said flatly. "There was serious damage to the thyroid cartilage, and the hyoid bone was broken."

That was significant. A broken hyoid bone in the throat was associated more with manual strangulation. That it was broken in Mary Lynch was a sign of just how much force had been used by her killer, much more force than was necessary simply to render her dead. In Fagan's five victims, the hyoid had been broken in only two.

"What about knots?"

She shook her head. "The ligature was crossed over at the back, but there was no knot."

That was like Fagan too. The killer was obviously keen to ape every part of his MO.

"Any other injuries?" I said.

"Some bruising on the neck where she tried to pull the rope away," Fitzgerald said. "Scratching. We took scrapings from under the nails. It'll all trace back to her is my guess." She paused. "What a civilised conversation for the supper table. Do you want more wine?" I shook my head. "That's not like you. I think *I'll* have another."

And that wasn't like Fitzgerald. I was losing count.

"Any other tampering with the body?" I said as she started to pour herself yet another glass and, finding the bottle empty, reached over for the corkscrew to open a second.

"No evidence of rape or sexual assault, if that's what you mean. We'll have to wait on the lab results to know for sure, of course, but Lynch seemed fairly confident they'd be clear."

"What about Forensics?"

"They'll get the results to me soon as they can. I'm quoting now. They're short-staffed. They can't perform miracles. When is the Commissioner going to approve their new facilities?"

Fitzgerald ticked off the complaints on her fingers, then sighed, avoided my eye.

"I'm getting too old for this," she said.

"It takes time," I said. "You'll get there."

"Like I did with Fagan, you mean?"

Now it was me avoiding her eye. I didn't trust myself. "That wasn't your fault," I replied evenly. "You know that. And you also know it has nothing to do with what's happening now."

"Doesn't it?" she said. "That's not what they think at headquarters. Draker, Dalton, the Commissioner."

"The Commissioner? What's he said?"

"Phoned this afternoon. Wanted to know how I was getting on, that was how he put it, but it was Fagan's name he kept coming back to. Even Lynch told me he thought that whoever killed Mary had killed before. Too neat and tidy for a beginner, he said."

"It's not Lynch's job to make those kinds of judgements," I said sharply. "It doesn't exactly take a PhD and twenty years' training to strangle a seven-stone junkie and get it right."

"He was just offering his opinion," said Fitzgerald. "Same as you. All they see is the same MO, same victimology, same locations, same sick little trademarks, plus a published confession in the morning's newspaper. Strangling's not exactly a common method of serial murder, Saxon, yet we're asking them to believe they've got the second one in a decade."

I was glad to see it was still *we* who were asking them to believe it, at any rate. I didn't know what I'd do if she started believing it was Fagan as well.

"All I'm saying," she continued, "is that it's not easy standing there and telling them that they have to ignore the one obvious suspect they've got, the only suspect, and start back at the beginning again looking for someone else."

"There are *differences*," I said. "Look at the state of the body you found this afternoon. Hands missing, head missing. Does that sound like Fagan? And Dublin isn't New York; Fagan couldn't simply wander round here without being seen by someone he used to know. It doesn't add up, and they know it. We just have to find whatever it takes to make them admit it."

She didn't answer, so I took the opportunity to stand up and carry the plates through to the kitchen. Neither of us had much of an appetite any more for what was left of the pot roast.

Her voice, quiet now, followed me across the room.

"There was one other thing. One *difference*, as you put it."

I laid down the plates and turned round.

"Go on."

She didn't look at me, just swirled the wine round inside her glass, staring at it.

"There was a symbol of some sort, written on the sole of Mary Lynch's left foot. They found it when they took off her stilettos to send them for analysis along with her clothes. Thought it was a tattoo at first. It had been written on her skin with a fountain pen."

"Are you going to tell me what it was?"

"It's hard to explain. Wait there," she said, like I had anywhere else to go. "I made a copy."

She put down the glass, got up and walked, a little unsteadily, to where she'd left her coat tossed over the chair. It took her some time to root through her pockets, but at last she found what she was looking for. It was a scrap of crumpled paper. She handed it to me to unfold, though it still didn't make much sense when I did.

The symbol was like a letter x that was starting to curl, but made with thicker, darker pen strokes. I tried to imagine what it looked like on the dry, dead parchment of Mary Lynch's skin, then wished that I hadn't.

"You going to tell me what this is?" I said.

"That," she said, "is aleph." She spelt it out. "First letter of the Hebrew alphabet."

"You're joking."

"I am only repeating what the wise Ambrose Lynch himself told me this afternoon. Comes before beth and gimel." She didn't bother spelling those out. "Literal translation from the Hebrew: ox."

"Well, if this doesn't persuade Draker and the Commissioner that this isn't the work of Fagan, nothing will," I said. "Fagan may have left around a few quotes from the Bible, but nothing like this. No symbols, certainly no writing on the skin of his victims. Wonder how the *Post* will explain that away if they're still intent on insisting that it's him?"

"Let's hope they don't find out," said Fitzgerald, draining her glass again. "Not for a few days, anyway. That way there'll be more time for us to work out what the hell's going on."

"Maybe I can help there," I said.

"Don't tell me. You've been taking a night class in Hebrew scriptology." It was reassuring to see that alcohol hadn't affected her sarcastic sense of humour.

"I called Lawrence Fisher today. The profiler, you remember?"

"I remember Fisher. You wrote about him in your book. The third one, the one that didn't sell. He's working on a new serial offender database for Scotland Yard, isn't he?"

"Among other things. I asked him to run the details of Mary Lynch's killing through the system to see what comes out. I thought seeing as Mullen was in London up until a few months ago . . ." I didn't need to join the dots. "That looks pretty futile now, of course, but you never know what'll turn up. He faxed me through the form this afternoon, but I wanted to check some of the details with you first and take a look at the initial crime scene and autopsy reports."

"They're all in my bag. Help yourself."

"I asked whether he'd consider drawing up a preliminary profile too."

"I'm not sure about that," said Fitzgerald carefully. "Draker's not exactly the world's greatest fan of profiling. Far as he's concerned, it'd be like bringing in a witch doctor or a psychic to help with the investigation. Even when I suggested making enquiries to see if there was some significance in the quotes the killer had left so far, and whether there was anything in his choice of the feast day of St Agericus for the start of his seven-day sequence, he nearly went through me. Gave me his working-the-scene lecture. I couldn't release the funds without his authorisation."

"Money's not the problem," I said. "The problem is that Fisher turned me down and passed me on to Mort Tillman instead. Yeah, that Mort Tillman. Turns out he's going to be in Dublin for a while, giving some guest lectures over at Trinity College."

Fitzgerald whistled softly.

"Do you think he'll talk to you?"

"He already has," I told her, "and he's agreed to help. And there's no need to look so surprised either. He can't hold a grudge for ever. Anyway, I told him to come along to the crime team meeting tomorrow morning and said I'd bring him to the scene afterwards — if that's OK with you. Maybe it's what we need right now to throw some light on this hieroglyphics bull."

"I hope you're right, because I have a feeling we're going to be needing all the help we can get." She reached for her glass again, only this time she knocked it over and red wine spilled across the tablecloth. "Shit," she said. "Sorry."

110

"I'll do that," I said, but she wasn't making any attempt to clean it up anyway.

She had her elbow on the table, her chin in the scoop of her palm, and the other hand was pinching her nose. "I think somebody must have kicked me in the head when I wasn't looking," she said. "Have you got any aspirin?"

"You can have aspirin in the morning when the wine's worn off," I said. "Why don't you just go to bed? I'll clear up."

By the time I got back with a cloth, she'd gone. I found her lying on top of the bed, too tired to even pull back the quilt and climb in. I fetched her coat and laid it over her, then went to find a blanket to lay on top of that. The night was going to be cold. She would need it.

CHAPTER
ELEVEN

Help yourself, Fitzgerald had said, so help myself I did.
I lifted the reports I needed out of her bag and made
two photocopies, one for my own files and another for
Mort Tillman. Then I boxed up his set and called for a
courier to take them round to his guest rooms at
Trinity. It wasn't even midnight yet, he'd still be up
probably; and if he wasn't still up, he should be.

Once that was done, I sat down and finished filling
out the blanks in Fisher's form using the same
information, then fed the pages back into the fax so it'd
all be there for him in the morning.

What now?

Too restless to sleep, I took the Jeep from the
underground car park and started to drive, nowhere in
mind. There was hardly any traffic at this hour, and in
no time at all I'd made my way to the seafront, where
the road followed the railway line along the curve of
the bay, and was driving with the city on one side and
the black water glittering on the other.

Somewhere out there, Howth Head rose out of the
blackness, the lighthouse blinking at its foot, and there
was a ship winding its way in across the Irish Sea to
sweep cumbersomely into harbour, where another

lighthouse blinked back. Here was where the city came to pause for breath, and I felt for the first time since yesterday morning that I was pausing for breath too.

On Dalkey Hill, I got out and smoked a cigar, and tried to tune my thoughts again to the unhurried beat of the lighthouses below as they called to one another silently across the water. It was so cold that the self-pity was frozen out of me. But I resisted a second cigar, climbed into the Jeep again instead, turned the heater up high, and made my way back to the city.

Soon I was making a circuit of the streets and lanes around where Mary Lynch's body had been found, where the prostitutes always lingered, along the canal, past the Peppercanister Church, spinning round Fitzwilliam Square, looking for a familiar face.

It was months since I'd seen Jackie, and I felt guilty after reading what I'd read about her that night. I knew she'd still be out here, though. This was her beat, her domain, same as Mary.

A momentary panic gripped me when I thought she wasn't there, a vision of what might have happened to her, but I forced it back down. I'd no right to console myself with this show of sudden concern; she was out here every night.

OK then, but I still needed to talk to her, for Mary Lynch's sake if not for hers; or if not for Mary Lynch's sake, for she was long past concern, then for the next Mary Lynch and the next one after that. There were always Mary Lynches.

Finally, by chance, I found her sheltering in the pale light of an insurance broker's architect-designed

113

doorway, dressed for the cold as usual in microskirt and fishnet stockings and leather jacket, the standard international uniform of the streetwalker.

She'd told me once that she was sixteen and only weeks on the street when Fagan killed his first victim, so she couldn't be more than twenty-four now, but she could have passed for forty on her worst nights, and this was definitely one of those. Her skin looked stretched and parched, her eyes wide and heavy-lidded under thick black make-up, her hair lifeless as straw.

I pulled alongside her and wound down the window. "Jackie," I said. "Long time."

"What can I say?" Jackie said thickly when she realised who it was. "I've been busy. People to see, things to do, cookies to bake, you know how it is."

She was putting on an American accent, she always did when we met. She thought it was funny and I always smiled, like I would at a child. But there was no disguising her rough accent, or the rasp in her voice that told me she was as far from conquering the habits that kept her out here as she had been last time we met.

"You got any fags?" she asked.

"I don't smoke, remember?" I said. "Don't smoke cigarettes, that is. But get in. I'll go get you some."

"I'd better not, it's not been a good night."

"Jackie, get in. I'll make it worth your while." Friendships in this part of town were always sweetened with money, that was part of the deal, but I could still see her wavering, right up to the moment when she came over and climbed in.

"Heated seats!" she said once she'd slammed shut the door. "Jesus, I wish you were a man, I'd do you for free just to get out of the cold. Heated seats, shit. This is some motor."

"Same one as last time, Jackie."

"Last time was summer. Everything was different in the summer." She shivered as warmth slowly took hold, and I could see the shadow of the bruises still festering under her make-up. I could see why the nurses in Casualty had called the police.

"You been out there long?" I said as I pulled away.

"An hour, a bit more," she said.

I found a look of sympathy coming to my face, then stopped it. I wasn't going to sympathise with her for not finding any strangers to abuse her. No strangers meant no money, then maybe she'd sort herself out. I'd tried often enough to help in the past.

"It's last night," she said. "You must have heard what happened. It always keeps the punters away for a while. Some of the girls haven't even bothered coming out. They think the cops'll be all over the place, scaring the cars off. It wasn't too bad earlier on, but now it's just dead —" She stopped short at the word, alarmed by it. "Do you think there'll be . . . more?"

"Killings?" I said. "There's always more."

"If it's Ed Fagan there will be. That's who they reckon did it, don't they?"

I said nothing to that, kept my eyes on the road.

A moment later I pulled into the forecourt of a garage, and hopped out for cigarettes, picked her up a sandwich while I was at it. I handed them to her along with fifty in notes.

She made a half-hearted attempt to give it back. "Hey, Saxon, you don't have to . . ."

"Take it," I said. "It makes me feel better."

She'd already taken out the first cigarette and lit it from the car lighter. Now she looked at the sandwich, almost shyly, as if wondering what that was about, why I'd bought it, unsure what to do with it, almost amused. She turned it over a few times in her fingers and then put it up on the dashboard. I kept the car ticking over but made no attempt to drive away.

"I heard about what happened to you," I said in the end. "I'm sorry."

"Yeah?"

"I only saw the incident report tonight. I'd no idea."

"Goes with the territory," she said, willing herself hard. "Least I kept the money. They catch who did it yet?"

"Not yet."

"Are they even trying?"

I remembered the crime scene report, how thin it was, and avoided the question with another one. "Victim Support been in touch yet?"

She saw what I was doing and ignored me.

"Look," I said, "I just want you to know you can call me any time. You have my number."

She nodded, but I don't think she was really listening any more. The appeal of the heated seats was wearing off. She didn't want to talk about what had happened.

"I just need to clarify a few things," I tried to explain.

116

I thought she was going to ignore me again, she took so long to answer, but she simply asked: "What good will it do?"

"I don't know. Maybe I can help the police find who did it. The Chief Superintendent's asked me to help out with the enquiry into Mary Lynch's death. Maybe there's a connection."

It took her a moment to realise what I was saying.

"You think the freak who killed Mary was the one who raped me?"

"What do the police call it? A line of enquiry. That's all it is I'm following. Had you ever seen the man who attacked you before?"

"Not sure." Begrudging, but at least it was an answer. "I might have."

"What did he look like?"

"I — I was wrecked, wasn't I, all right? I didn't even know what fucking day it was." She raised her voice to cover her embarrassment at having to admit she'd been taking drugs, though it wasn't as if she could hide it. "He just walked up to me, didn't he? It was dark, he had one of those hooded tops, I didn't really get a good look at him. We just went down by the canal, down where Mary was . . . where Mary died . . . and then he went nuts and attacked me."

"Near there, you mean, or the exact place?"

"Same place, I think, from what I saw in the paper."

I tried to keep my voice level. It hadn't said in the report exactly where she'd been attacked. It probably hadn't seemed important at the time.

"Did he suggest going there or you?"

"Him," she said firmly. "I hate it down there. There's rats there, I've seen them, I don't like going under the bridge. But he offered me another twenty if I'd do it. Twenty's twenty."

"And did he say anything to you during the attack?"

She shook her head.

"After?"

She gave a snort.

"He said I should go and sin no more."

"Those were his words?"

"Yeah. Bastard. Like it was me who was in the wrong."

Go thou and sin no more. I was no theologian, but even I recognised that.

"Just a couple more things, Jackie, and then I'll leave you alone. The report said the man who attacked you told you he knew where you lived, is that right? Try to remember. Did he *tell* you where you lived, or just say that he knew? To frighten you, you know?"

"I think . . . yeah, I think he told me where it was. Said he knew I shared a house with Penny. That's my cousin. She moved in with me a couple of months ago. She was the one made me go to Casualty. He said he'd seen me with her, said he knew we lived down the Coombe."

"The Coombe, that was all? No address?"

"He might've done. I can't remember. I'd been taking these pills, on top of everything else, to help me sleep. The doctor said they might make me confused. I don't . . ." She trailed off again, before gathering

118

herself. "What else? You said there was a couple of other things."

"So I did. I want you to look at a picture, see if you recognise the face."

"I keep telling you, I can't remember."

"I just want you to take a look at it, see if anything looks familiar."

"Is it the one who did it?"

"It's no one."

"If it's no one, what do you want me to look at it for?"

"Will you look?"

I reached into my pocket before she could think of any more reasons why she shouldn't cooperate, and brought out the photograph of Jack Mullen.

I'd snipped it so his father wasn't in the shot; I didn't want Jackie recognising *him*. The photograph was more than eight years old, but it was all I had.

"Who is it?" said Jackie.

"Just someone I'm checking up on. You recognise him?"

She looked at Mullen's face briefly, then shook her head.

"Take a longer look, if you like," I said.

She took the photograph from my fingers and stared at it for a long time.

"There's *something* about him," she said presently. "The eyes, maybe."

"What about the eyes?"

"Something familiar maybe . . . no. No. Sorry," she added as she handed it back.

I tried not to show my disappointment. I had no right to be disappointed.

"That's OK. You did great."

"Fat lot of good it'll do anyway," she said bitterly. "The police aren't going to find who did this to me any more than they're going to find who did that to Dolly."

"Dolly?"

She looked at me like I was stupid.

"Mary. That's what we called her — Dolly Parton. She said that's what she'd do, you see, if she ever got rich, go get her tits done like Dolly Parton. It was a nickname."

"I didn't realise you knew Mary Lynch."

"Sure I knew her," Jackie said. "All the girls out here knew Mary. I used to let her crash at my place sometimes when she was stuck. She was with me the night before she . . ."

She didn't need to finish.

"Did she seem worried?" I asked.

"Why should she be worried? She didn't know what was going to happen, did she?"

"She didn't give you any hint that she might be in danger? That she might've been followed recently, or threatened, anything like that?"

"She was just the same as usual," she said. Then she smiled, remembering. "We had a good laugh about her fancy man."

"Fancy man?"

"That was her name for him," said Jackie. "It was a joke. He was just a client, he'd picked her up one night a few months ago and he'd been back a couple of times a week ever since, more some weeks. Said his wife was dead and told Mary he wanted to marry her. As if."

"Did she say what his name was?"

"Let me think," she said. "Gus, was that it? Something like that."

Gus, the same name that had come up in the Monica Lee investigation.

I felt numb.

"Did you tell all this to Dalton?"

"Who?"

"Seamus Dalton from the murder squad. He was supposed to have been conducting interviews with the people who knew Mary Lynch."

"Well, he never conducted one with me." And she glanced pointedly over at the clock on the dashboard and sighed loudly. "Look, can I go now?"

What was I, her fifth-grade teacher?

"I'll drop you off," I said.

Jackie kept her nose to the glass like a child as we drove, pressing her palm flat to wipe away her breath every time she needed to peer out and see who was there. She was looking for her boyfriend, now she had the fifty, so the both of them could get stoned. I wished I'd had the courage not to give her any; I'd only done it because it made things easier for me.

"Here," she said. "Pull over."

I pulled to a halt and let Jackie out. There was a man standing in the same doorway where I'd picked her up earlier, obviously waiting, knowing she was bound to be back there if he waited long enough. He started hopping from foot to foot in his baggy designer pants

121

when he saw her climb out of the car; scenting money. What was Jackie afraid of rats for when she picked vermin like him for company? He'd never end up lying dead on the bank of the canal with a cord around his neck. Dead in an alleyway with a needle stuck in his vein maybe, but that was his choice.

I tried to put him out of my mind as I drove away and left him jumping about like a hyperactive kid in my rearview mirror. Finding Gus was more important now. Was it Gus who'd become Elliot's communicative new little friend? Was Gus the so-called Night Hunter?

Night Hunter —

Stop.

I screeched the car to a halt and jumped out. There it was, a fresh poster for next day's edition of the *Post* hanging outside a shop. I'd seen it out of the corner of my eye as I passed.

Night Hunter Writes Again.

Again?

Apologies about Sally Tyrrell. As it is written in Psalms: "He who works deceit shall not dwell within my house; he who tells lies shall not continue in my presence."

Though did the Hebrew midwives not lie to Pharaoh about the birth of Moses? He would have killed Moses otherwise. And did Judith not lie to King Holofernes to save her people? "Smite by the deceit of my lips the servant with the prince and make my speech and deceit to be their wound and stripe, who have purposed cruel things against thy covenant."

Nor, to be blunt, am I prepared to endure lectures on falsehood when I have been the victim of such absurd and lurid speculations as appeared in your newspaper following the demise of Mary Lynch. I refer in particular to the article published under the name of Maeve Curran which accused me of harbouring a "hatred of women". This is nothing but a repetition of the vile libel which Nick Elliott perpetuated against me in his book. Hatred is a highly pejorative term and I repudiate it absolutely, just as I resent being subjected to what are little more than hysterical outbursts of semi-literate bargain-basement popular psychology.

If anything, I do not hate women so much as pity them; and in that, I concur with no less an authority than our Church Father Chrysostum who said of women that "they need greater care precisely because of their ready inclination to sin . . . the whole sex is weak and flighty." Women need protecting from their own natures. Is offering that protection then to hate them?

123

Indeed, one must ask whether it is those who lazily throw accusations of misogyny at me who are in fact guilty of hating women. It is they, after all, who are equating all women with those that I am foresworn to eradicate. In the words of Martin Luther: "The evil spirit sent these whores here and they are dreadful, shabby, stinking, loathsome and syphilitic."

It is certainly ironic that my critics seem unable to grasp this simple distinction when those who might be expected to disagree most fundamentally with my methodology, such as Mary Lynch, say, grasp it immediately. That is the advantage of working with prostitutes. They know the rules. They seem to realise at once that what is happening was bound to happen eventually and that indeed it had to happen; they recognise the justice of it. There is none of that tiresome indignation. I commend their resignation. I commend their instinctive appreciation of the proper order of things, of the urgent need for the wicked to accede to the authority of the virtuous.

Alas, too few have the necessary understanding. That much was obvious from Tara Cox. She just did not seem able to understand that I had nothing against her personally, any more than I would against a rat beneath the floorboards of my house. Prostitutes are the carriers of a deadly plague, and I am the poison, I am the arsenic in the bloodstream of the city; taste me.

Not Tara, though. Oh no. Tara thought she was better than that, a cut above, though it was my cut which sent her below in the end. Now there's poetic justice — but no, I must not boast. I am but an instrument of the Lord and through me He manifests His divine will.

And if only one stinking, loathsome, syphilitic whore should turn from the path of wickedness as a result of my work, shall it not have been worth it? Remember that "joy shall be in heaven over one sinner that repenteth, more than over ninety and nine just persons which need no repentance." Five dead to save a city from its own festering corruption is hardly excessive.

But who next? There's the rub. It is, you may be sure, a matter to which I have given the most careful and devout consideration. To be the means by which a people are cleansed and purged of their impurity is a singular honour and one would not want to throw it carelessly away on the ungrateful or unworthy, especially with so many candidates from which to choose.

So let it be Mary again. Mary the First fulfilled her part in the sacrifice commendably; I have no reason to suspect that her namesake will disappoint. I shall know soon enough.

Pray for her.

THIRD DAY

CHAPTER
TWELVE

Mort Tillman wasn't there when I stopped outside the front of Trinity to pick him up on the way to the crime team meeting next morning; but then I *was* pretty late. I'd dropped round to the offices of the *Post* first to confront Elliott about the new letter, though as it was I hadn't managed to get past security — which was probably just as well for the reporter's good health.

I couldn't believe what Elliott had done. I'd woken Fitzgerald last night soon as I found out that the killer had written to the *Post* again, and she eventually tracked him down and got the whole story out of him. He'd received a call from the killer about eleven, just as they were about to go to press with Elliott's front-page story about the body in the churchyard being Sally Tyrrell — another stroke of luck for him. The voice was muffled and slow, he said, like the caller was using some kind of device over the mouthpiece. It told Elliott to get down to the public garden next to St Patrick's Cathedral, where the next letter would be taped under one of the park benches.

So that was what he did. The killer had him well trained.

Elliott claimed that he'd tried to contact Grace a number of times on her mobile to tell her, but it was switched off. So instead he sent the story to the presses. Like you do.

I waited a while for Tillman, and when he still didn't show I decided just to carry on up the hill from Trinity towards Dublin Castle. I was nervous enough about the crime team meeting without being late as well. I only hoped he'd gone on ahead without me.

By the time I found a parking space, I was ready to kick something with impatience. I settled for slamming the car door instead, before hurrying across the yard to the front door of the police headquarters, glancing up as I did so at the statue of Justice on top of the old tower to the north, her back turned disdainfully away from the city. Till they were mended, I'd once heard, her scales used to tip when it rained. And it always rained. That just about summed up my mood.

I say castle. There was certainly one in there somewhere. Thirteenth century, apparently. But now what was called Dublin Castle was really just part of an untidy complex of old and new buildings tucked away near the summit of Dame Street as it climbed lazily out of the heart of the city. It had been home to the Dublin Metropolitan Police from the force's inception some eighty years ago, and nothing much seemed to have changed in the interim.

I went in at reception, and waited whilst a young female uniformed officer disappeared into the back for the pass that Fitzgerald had promised would be waiting for me. Then she led me up the stairs to the room on the first floor where the meeting was to be held.

I was relieved to find that it hadn't started yet. The room was still filling up with detectives from the murder squad, others from Vice and the crime scene forensic unit, some I'd never seen before. I just slipped in and took a seat near the back. There was no sign of Tillman.

A few glances came my way, but nobody challenged my right to be there. Then again, nobody exactly made an effort to speak to me either. Voices dropped a notch. I felt like the pass pinned to my lapel marked me out as an intruder. Fair enough. That's what I was.

I ignored them, and deliberately picked up a copy of that morning's *Post* which had been left on the chair next to me. I'd already seen it last night, of course, and had no desire to look at it again, but I gratefully hid myself in the pretence of reading it all the same, until a pair of oversized shoes appeared in my line of sight and I looked up.

"DS Boland," I said. "Good to see a friendly face."

"Can I get you coffee?"

"You don't have to get me coffee," I said. "Make me get my own. It'd do me good."

"Only if the coffee doesn't kill you first," Boland said.

"That bad, is it?"

"Worse." Making the chair look as small as a child's, he took a seat next to me. Well, no one else had. "Is it just my imagination," he said, "or did the temperature drop five degrees when you walked in?"

"Serves me right," I said. "At least now I understand how outsiders used to feel when they were brought in on investigations for the Bureau. This feels like payback time."

"They'll get used to you," he said.

"I don't care if they get used to me or not. I just wish they wouldn't make me feel like they're about to drag me down to the cells for interrogation."

"There aren't any cells here," said Boland. "This is all administrative. They'd have to take you to Pearse Street station for that."

"That makes me feel a whole bundle better."

"Only trying to help, Special Agent."

He was the second person to call me that this morning, but the truth was I didn't much feel like a special agent at that moment, not even a former special agent.

I looked round the room. Everyone else seemed to have something to do, some purpose for being here. What was I doing here? What use was I any more?

Over by the coffee machine, Dalton and Lawlor were sharing a joke. Paranoia made me think it was at my expense, then I recalled the old line: just because you're paranoid doesn't mean they're not out to get you. And where those two were concerned, they usually were.

My eye was drawn to a whiteboard on the far wall with a photograph of Mary Lynch — no doubt stolen by Dalton from a frame on her mother's mantelpiece; that was his usual way — fixed to the rim, and others taken by Tom Kiernan, the squad photographer, ranged about.

One showed Mary's face laid flat against the grass by the canal, tongue protruding thickly from between her teeth, eyes open wide more in astonishment than fear or pain. That was often the final look. Another showed a close-up of her neck, the mark left by the ligature standing out on the skin like a snake's winding trail in the sand. Another close-up of that scrap of paper and its vicious words: *All wickedness is but little to the wickedness of a woman.*

So much for the killer's professed annoyance at being accused of hating women.

I wondered idly why Ed Fagan had never used that quote himself; it was the religious misogynist's creed in a nutshell. Made a mental note to check out where exactly it came from.

There were photographs too of the body which had been found in the churchyard of St John the Divine yesterday. It was the first time I'd seen her for myself and I wasn't sure now I wanted to. The shape in the picture bore the same relationship to a real woman as a shank of raw meat hung from a butcher's hook bore to the animal out of whose skin it had been torn.

What had happened to her?

Inside the rough circle formed by the photographs hung a map of the city, two red pins to mark the spots where Mary's body and that of the latest woman had been found.

And what was that? It was hard to make out, but it looked like another pin, white this time, immediately to the left of the red pin for Mary Lynch.

Julie Feeney, I realised at once.

My eyes tracked across the map, following Fagan's path. Where each woman had fallen, another white pin. The churchyard for Sylvia Judge. The Law Library on Constitution Hill for Tara Cox. The Royal Canal and Prospect Cemetery on the Northside of the city for Liana Cassidy and Maddy Holt, Fagan's last two victims in the weeks before he was arrested.

Boland saw me looking, saw me getting angry.

"Draker's orders," he said.

"What kind of asshole is he?" I said, realising at once why I was needed here, how awry Draker could send the investigation if he was unchecked. So much for him lecturing Fitzgerald about working the scene. "He's got no evidence that Mary Lynch's death has anything to do with Fagan! Since when was an article in the gutter press accepted as Exhibit A?"

"Don't get mad at me," Boland said. "He just said we should explore the possibilities."

"Is that how he put it? *Explore the possibilities?*"

"His exact words."

"Prick."

I would've said more, but at that moment the door opened and Fitzgerald came in, looking better than she had any right to look after last night, checking the room to make sure everyone was there, her eyes gliding over me without stopping. I wasn't sure how many people here knew about our relationship, but she was clearly determined not to give them any added reason to bitch. The investigation would be difficult enough as it was.

"Quiet, everyone," she said as she reached the desk next to the whiteboard. "This won't take long. Ambrose

134

Lynch has kindly given us a little of his precious time this morning so we can get the second autopsy done, so we'll have to keep this short." There was a murmur of familiar laughter. They knew Ambrose well. "Dalton, I want you along for that. Boland too."

"I've got an interview at ten," said Dalton. "Mary Lynch's dealer."

"Lawlor can do it," Fitzgerald said. "Think you can manage that, Lawlor, without Seamus along to hold your hand?"

"I'll do my best, Chief."

"You do that. Now," she went on, "two things. First, you all saw this morning's edition of the *Post*. This guy isn't hanging around. I want you all to dig deep and see if there's anything in this latest letter that strikes a chord. There isn't much to go on, but anything that comes to you, anything at all, bring it to me. Turn your minds to the Mary angle. Why two Marys? Is that a coincidence or does he have some kind of fixation on the name? And if so, why? Are we looking at some twisted Virgin Mary angle? Does he have something against *all* women called Mary?"

"That could be you, Boland, what about it?" said Dalton loudly.

I glanced across at Boland for an explanation. He looked embarrassed.

"My ex-wife was called Mary," he said quietly, avoiding my eye.

"Better make sure you have an alibi!" Dalton laughed.

"That's enough," said Fitzgerald. "Think about it, that's all I ask. Just because you can't grasp the meaning of something doesn't mean it doesn't have one. *Everything* has a meaning. Now, second thing. Some of you may have noticed that we have a new face here with us. Those of you who haven't noticed, you're in the wrong job. Saxon, say hello."

I nodded hello coolly. I wasn't going to seem too eager, or make them think I was after their approval. Besides, I was still too furious with Draker to give a damn what they thought.

"Saxon's going to be along for the ride, so try and make her feel welcome. I know you won't, but I'm saying it anyway. I'm sure you know who she is. She's got a lot of experience, so make use of it. And oh, if any of you have a problem with her being here, have it out with her on your own time. We're here to work, understood? This guy gave us seven days in which to find him before he runs to ground again. If we don't pull together, we're doing his dirty work for him."

"That's telling them," whispered Boland, then he lifted his head sharply as Dalton laughed out loud again at some remark by Ray Lawlor. I felt that nag of paranoia return.

"Seamus, do you have something to add?" said Fitzgerald.

"Just clearing my throat, Chief."

"Well, now it's cleared, you can start. Show us all what a good little policeman you are. Let's see what you've got on Mary Lynch."

And so it began. I'd been here many times before, not in this room maybe, but ones like it. It didn't matter what city it was, or who the victim; the routine was always the same: the same air of tension, excitement, especially in a case like this when everyone knew how time mattered, that the clock was counting down to the next death; the same patient putting together of each tiny fragment that detectives brought back with them off the street; the slow amassing of detail in the hope that it would eventually fall into shape and amount to something.

There wasn't much to work with here, though.

According to Dalton, the last known sighting of Mary Lynch was about 10.45p.m. on Baggot Street Bridge on the night of her death. Her body was found about half eleven. Dalton refused to say which of the two was nearer the time of death — too many variables, he said — but she probably wasn't dead much more than half an hour if the last sighting was to be trusted.

"Probably not even that long," Dalton added. "It's not Connolly Station out there, but it's busy enough. There's punters and prostitutes coming and going all the time, and she wasn't exactly well hidden. She'd have been found earlier if she was there to *be* found, is my guess."

"Then that means discovering where she was between ten forty-five and eleven thirty," said Fitzgerald. "Are we making any headway there?"

"Short answer," said Dalton, "is no."

Detectives had spent all the first day trying to track down and isolate witnesses, but so far they hadn't come up with a single person who would admit seeing Mary after 10.45. Taxi drivers gave the same story, and they were usually good for information. People got used to not noticing other people in the city, that was the problem. It became a habit.

CCTV footage from businesses in the area was more hopeful, but it would take weeks to get through. Even now they had a list of over a hundred number plates to follow up. Some drivers who'd been in the area at the time had already identified themselves in response to an appeal for information. Others would take longer to track down and eliminate, or not, from suspicion. Lone walkers identified by the same pictures were proving harder still to trace. A hotline had been set up to gather in information. Fitzgerald was going to make a televised plea for witnesses.

"Any luck with family and friends of the dead woman?"

Dalton made a gesture of dismissal. "Half of them are out of their heads on pills and booze," he said, "and the other half just didn't want to get involved."

"What about Jackie Hill?" I spoke up for the first time.

Dalton glared at me contemptuously.

"Who?"

"Jackie Hill," I repeated. "She's a prostitute, works much the same beat as Mary Lynch. They were friends. She was raped a couple of weeks back by some Bible-quoting nut in exactly the same spot where Mary died. Plus she says Mary had been talking lately about some man by the name of Gus who'd gotten interested in her and kept kerb-crawling back to pick her up."

"Do you know anything about this?" Fitzgerald asked Dalton.

"First I heard," he said carelessly.

"Did you even speak to this Jackie Hill?"

"Her name didn't come up, no."

"Well," said Fitzgerald, "this puts a whole new slant on things. Dalton, you're going to have to skip the autopsy and go back and interview everyone again, find out what they know about this Gus. Maybe someone will have seen Mary with him, seen a car at least. Maybe she confided in someone. Oh, and try not to miss anyone else who knew her this time, yeah?"

Dalton nodded curtly, his eyes telling a story that his tongue wouldn't dare. There went my chance of a Christmas card, anyway.

"Your turn now, Boland." Fitzgerald switched quickly. "What did you get from fingerprints?" And Boland, taken by surprise, briskly ran through what he had.

It was the same dead ends. He'd spoken to staff in the *Post*'s mailroom, who confirmed that the first letter claiming to be from Fagan had come in from a city-centre sorting office, addressed to Nick Elliott, the day before Mary died. Following it back through the system showed that it had been posted at a box not far from Trinity College late the previous afternoon.

The envelope had been taken away and dusted for prints, but no matches came back save for those of the staff themselves, who'd all volunteered prints without complaint. Frankly, I was amazed the editor hadn't tossed off an indignant editorial about police abuse of civil liberties.

As for results of the fingerprint tests on the letter taped beneath the bench last night in the garden next to St Patrick's Cathedral, they weren't in yet; but no one was feeling very hopeful.

And that — give or take some background from Vice on Mary Lynch's sorry record of long-term drug abuse and short-term prison stays, and a report from Healy on whether anyone on the register of sex offenders looked like a contender for prime suspect (they didn't) — was that.

I could feel the unacknowledged despondency in the air as Fitzgerald handed out the tasks for the day and the meeting broke up. It didn't surprise me. It's often said that the first forty-eight hours after the discovery of a body are the most important — and ours were almost up.

"Boland, do me a favour," I said as we got to our feet and the rest of the team filed past us to the door. "Point someone out for me."

"Anyone in particular, or are you not fussy?"

"Someone called DS O'Malley. Donal. Ring any bells?"

"Don?" said Boland. "Pointing him out might be a problem. He's dead."

"What?"

"Yeah. Killed himself about six months ago."

"Great sense of timing he had," I said. "What was wrong with him?"

"How long've you got? Stress. Depression. Panic attacks, last I heard. His wife left him."

"I'm not surprised. He sounds like a basket case."

"She left before he got sick," said Boland. "She was why."

"Ambrose Lynch's wife left him too," I pointed out. "Your marriage broke up. You both still manage to keep things together. You're not having panic attacks."

"Lynch wouldn't allow himself to. He's like Dr Spock out of *Star Trek*. He'd think they were illogical."

"Mister," I said.

"What?"

"Mr Spock out of *Star Trek*. Dr Spock's the baby guy. Everyone makes that mistake."

"Oh, right. What did you want O'Malley for, anyway?"

"Just a case he was handling I wanted to talk about," I said. "Monica Lee, another prostitute, killed about two years ago. Thing is, the report says that she was seeing someone called Gus as well. I wanted to know if he'd ever tracked him down."

"Interesting. I think I remember the case. Was that one of Don's? I'll dig out the file and have a look at it myself, if you like."

"Are we set?" Fitzgerald said, as she arrived to take Boland to the autopsy on the still unidentified body. "It doesn't do to keep Ambrose waiting, you know."

"I'm set, Chief."

"What about you, Saxon? I thought you were meeting up with Tillman."

"So did I, but there's no trace of him."

"Well, you can tag along with us, if you like. Lynch is always pleased to see you."

"I'll give it a miss, if it's all the same."

"Can't say I blame you. I can think of better ways to spend a morning."

CHAPTER
THIRTEEN

On the way downstairs, we met Tillman coming up in the other direction with Ambrose Lynch.

"I found this fellow loitering around outside and thought I'd haul him in for questioning," the city pathologist quipped.

"Dr Tillman, I presume?" said Fitzgerald, stepping forward and shaking his hand. "Saxon's told me all about you. I only hope you realise how much we appreciate any help you can give us, anything at all. We're not exactly buried under the weight of leads here."

"That's not so surprising this early in an investigation," Tillman said, nodding a curt greeting at me as he caught my eye and reaching out a hand to Boland. "As I was saying to Dr Lynch as we came in, you're a long way from finished yet."

"You mean it will take more killings before we get a breakthrough?"

"I'm not here to make anyone feel better." He shrugged. "So yes, that's probably the way it will be. Unless you get lucky. An element of luck lies behind most closed cases in the end."

"So where do you come in?" said Ambrose.

"Sometimes my job is simply to point out the obvious. There's always a danger of investigators making a case more complex than it really is. Most murders happen for very primitive reasons. Rage, lust, the sheer thrill of transgression, the desire to be heard."

"Thwarted creativity," said Ambrose.

"That too. Often the mistake is to become convinced that there's any great mystery involved. Things are generally simple enough once you reduce them to their basic elements. But," and he opened his hands and held them in front of him as if fending off any more enquiries, "if you think I'm going to give you my profile before I've even seen all the evidence . . ."

"Not at all, no," said Fitzgerald. "But you know, quick as you can, that's all we ask. I don't need to remind you that the calendar is against us."

"I appreciate what you're up against. This morning should be helpful. The initial reports that Saxon had couriered round to my rooms last night in Trinity were intriguing, but what I really want is to see the scenes for myself."

"I wish I could come with you," said Ambrose. "I'd like to see how a profiler works. We don't get much opportunity in Dublin. Where murder is concerned, we are still, alas, a quiet, sleepy backwater, very much in the lower divisions of crime."

The ghost of a smile brushed Tillman's face.

"Not so sleepy any more," he pointed out.

"True," said Ambrose. "Things have certainly perked up."

"What are *you* doing here, anyway?" Fitzgerald asked the pathologist.

"Just dropping in the autopsy report on the second victim," he replied cheerily. Then he stopped when he saw the surprise in Fitzgerald's face. "I thought you knew," he said, appalled. "Assistant Commissioner Draker telephoned me yesterday and insisted that he wanted the report on his desk first thing this morning. I explained that you were due in this morning to watch over me as usual, but he said not to worry, that had all been sorted out. I'm sorry, Grace, really I am. If I'd realised you knew nothing about it, I would have called you."

"It's not your fault," Fitzgerald sighed. "This is obviously just Draker's way of putting me in my place, reminding me who's in charge of the department. Is that it there?"

She nodded at the file Ambrose had tucked under his arm.

"Yes," he said. "Here, take it."

"At least I get the results quicker this way," she said as she reached out for it. "That's one consolation." She opened the front cover and quickly turned through the pages inside. "Wait, what's this? Cause of death wasn't strangling?"

"The damage caused to the neck by the cutting off of the head makes it difficult to state definitively that there *wasn't* strangulation, but there were certainly none of the normal signs of strangulation I'd expect to find in the internal organs," said Ambrose. "But there *were*

145

severe abrasions and bruises, not to mention numerous fractures, consistent with a sustained assault."

"With?"

"I found nothing that pointed to a weapon."

"An old-fashioned beating then?"

"Looks like it. The outline of a shoe was imprinted on the skin of the lower back too."

"Is there a time of death here?" Fitzgerald said. "I can't see."

"She was killed thirteen days, twelve hours and" — Ambrose glanced at his watch — "twenty-four minutes ago. Though that is merely a rough estimate, naturally."

"I'll take that sarcasm as a no then, shall I?"

"You know what I think about estimating times of death, Chief Superintendent," said Ambrose. "It's as much guesswork as science. But if you insist on forcing me to indulge in it against all my principles, then a couple of weeks is the best guess I can offer."

"So where has she been since?"

"From the preserved condition of the remains, I'd say in someone's freezer."

"Lovely."

"She was in her *forties*?" said Boland suddenly. He'd been reading the report over Fitzgerald's shoulder and now looked like a schoolboy who'd been caught cheating in a test.

"Again, you have to take all provisos into consideration, but yes," said Ambrose, "mid to late forties. She wouldn't have made the hockey team any more, put it that way, but she was still in fairly good physical condition for her age. You seem surprised."

"When I heard that the body in the churchyard was older than the others, I didn't think it meant *that* old. Not that mid forties is old," he added quickly, "just old for a prostitute."

"What makes you think she was a prostitute?" said Fitzgerald.

"Well . . ." Boland seemed confused for a moment. "Isn't that who Fagan . . . the letter-writer, I mean . . . said he was going to kill?"

"That doesn't mean we have to believe him," she said sharply.

"I'm sorry," said Boland. "I just assumed."

"Don't," said Fitzgerald. "Assume nothing till you know it for a fact. As to that, you'd be surprised how many prostitutes there are over forty. I once arrested one who was sixty."

She snapped shut the file, but didn't hand it back to the pathologist.

"Don't worry about taking this up to the Assistant Commissioner's office," she said to him instead. "As the little red hen once said, I'll do it myself. I think Draker and I have a few . . . how shall I put it? . . . issues to sort out, and it's about time we made a start." She turned to Boland. "As for you, Sergeant, I want you to dig out the missing persons files and get reading. I want a name to put on this woman. She must be in there somewhere. And since you were so interested in the autopsy report, you should also be aware that the dead woman had an old fracture of the left ankle and had never had children. That should help narrow it down."

"I'll get down to records straight away."

"I suppose that leaves me free to tag along with you children then," said Ambrose to me and Tillman. "What an unexpected treat for you both. Shall we make a start?"

We rode in Lynch's car, mainly because he refused to ride in mine. He'd only put his faith in German engineering, he said, but I suspect the real reason was that he'd only put his faith in his own driving. I knew the feeling. I made a bad passenger; and I was tense all the way from Dublin Castle, sitting in the rear, looking at the backs of Ambrose's and Tillman's heads.

The traffic was foul, and we were caught in it all the way through town. Lynch was listening to some opera on the radio and humming, tapping the wheel. He seemed to be possessed of some serenity gene which meant he never got annoyed with the traffic. The wipers swished on a thin rain that barely needed them. I settled back and thought again about Ed Fagan. About Ed Fagan dying. Harbouring my secret in the car made me feel cheap.

The scene of Mary Lynch's death wouldn't be preserved much longer, but there was still an officer on guard when we arrived. He looked bored and stood stamping his feet to keep warm.

He recognised Ambrose Lynch as soon as he'd pulled to a halt and climbed out, and he didn't even ask who Tillman and I were. Ambrose had that natural air of authority that other people deferred to without thinking, without even realising they were doing it.

148

"That's where she was found," he explained now, pointing, as we stepped under the tape. "You can still see an indentation in the ground — there — where she fell."

The rain was growing harder each minute, and I turned up my collar, trying and failing to light a match so that I could smoke, damn, trying and failing again, and finally giving up.

Tillman was even worse dressed for the weather than I was. Hadn't brought a coat at all. I wondered if that was deliberate, if he wanted to feel the cold as Mary Lynch must have felt it on the night she died, for she'd had no coat either, just a thin jacket that didn't even cover the hem of her mini skirt, much less her bare legs. They were raw with cold that night. And colder now.

Or maybe he'd just forgotten his coat. The simplest explanations often make most sense, as Tillman himself had said. I stood and watched as he set to examining the scene.

A crime scene a few days after the body is gone is a strange thing, Momentarily, it seems to be stripped of its macabre mystery. Everything that brought it to attention is gone, everything that marked it out as different is erased, and yet here it still is separated from the world. Often it seems too inconsequential to have made itself noticed. Only much later, when the police have gone, the tape torn down, the scene left again to the elements, does it return to itself, and then something of a dark, tortured spirit attaches to what's left, or rather comes out of hiding again.

Tillman, any profiler, was expected to see beneath the surface inconsequentiality to capture again that moment — only a moment, if the victim was fortunate — which had wrested a place into disequilibrium. He was expected to live that moment again. At least that was the theory. What he actually felt when he walked a scene was his own secret.

Tillman was certainly inscrutable today. Occasionally he paused and closed his eyes, looked back at the road and down at the canal, but that was about as dramatic as it got. The rain was streaking his spectacles, but he didn't even take them off to wipe them.

"What is he doing?" said Ambrose in a low voice as he came to stand beside me.

"Getting a feel for what went on here, that's all."

"I could tell him what went on here," said Ambrose. "I saw it well enough when Mary Lynch was laid out on the table in the mortuary, and I'm not likely to forget it."

"You know what was done to Mary Lynch, but you don't know why, or what it felt like to do it," I answered. "That's what Tillman's trying to do. He needs to know what it was like for the killer that night, what he was thinking, what it all says about him."

"And he can tell that just by walking about a bit and frowning, can he?"

"You're too practical," I said. "You need the certainties of science. You find powder tattooing round a gunshot wound, you know the victim was shot at close range. You need to know if a victim drowned in fresh water or sea water, you just check the dilution of

150

the blood in the heart. You know what those things mean when you find them because that's what they've always meant. There's no formula that tells him what it means to find Hebrew letters written on the heel of a dead prostitute; but he's expected to come up with an explanation all the same."

Ambrose looked unconvinced.

"You remind me of one of his students," I said, cupping my hands to my mouth and blowing into them to try get them warm. "Boy by the name of Tim, thinks profiling is only so much mumbo-jumbo."

"Sounds like an intelligent chap."

"But you're both missing the point. In the end it doesn't matter what you think of it," I said, "because it's just another piece of the jigsaw. Fitzgerald can decide what she wants to do with the piece once Tillman's finished cutting it out. She doesn't have to do anything with it, there's no obligation, it's just another road to explore. But just because you don't take every turn-off on the highway doesn't mean there mayn't be something worth exploring down them."

"Saxon, you're mixing your metaphors."

"They can stand a little mixing," I said.

I looked back again to Tillman and saw him bending down where the body of Mary had lain. Ambrose had been right, you could see an indentation in the grass; there was almost a shadow there, a fairy ring, a cursed mark. Or was I just imagining it?

Ambrose, meanwhile, reached into his inside pocket and drew out a hip flask, then fumbled with his gloves as he unscrewed it, took a swig.

151

"Purely medicinal?" I said.

"Central heating, my dear," said Ambrose. "Central heating. One needs it at my age. You wouldn't deny an old man his pleasures, surely?"

"You're not so old," I said.

"I feel as if I am," he said in reply. "And yes, I know that drinking will only make me feel older still, but there it is . . ." He trailed off.

"Have you heard from Jean?" I said after a pause in which I'd wondered whether to raise the subject or let it drop and in the end decided what the hell.

"There was a message waiting for me when I got back home last night," he said. "Naturally, I was out. Some fight outside a bar, a young man stabbed. Bloody awful mess. I thought about returning the call, but it would only have led to another row. I can't help doing what I do."

"Jean knows that," I said. "She's probably just pissed at you because you weren't there one time too often. It happens."

"Do you get annoyed when Grace isn't there because she's working?" he said.

"That's different," I said. "I've been there. I know what she has to deal with."

"That doesn't make it any easier."

"You're wrong, it does make it easier. At least it does for me," I said. "Jean's what? A schoolteacher? Of course it's going to be harder for her to understand."

"Three weeks is a long time to stay, as your delightful expression has it, pissed with me."

"Ambrose," I said, "she'll come home."

"No, she won't," he said, and he looked me straight in the eye as he said it, and at that moment I knew he was right. Just then he did look old, and I had a vision of him getting older, alone, drinking whiskey out of a hip flask and telling everyone it was for the cold.

He smiled tolerantly as I struggled and finally gave up trying to find the words to say he was wrong. What was the point?

"Well then," I said with sudden bitterness at the world for his loneliness, "if she's not coming back . . . then fuck her."

"Yes," he said. "Fuck her."

And the words sounded so odd coming from his mouth that we both laughed nervously, before glancing round guiltily, remembering where we were and seeing Tillman coming towards us, not even looking up in enquiry as to why we were laughing. He probably hadn't even noticed.

"We were just discussing someone who looks increasingly likely to be my ex-wife," said Ambrose. "I don't suppose you have any advice on that score, do you?"

"Who, me? No, never married. Never fitted in with the job."

He was distracted still, affected by the scene. He was shivering, almost as if he could sense the evil which still lingered. Maybe he could. At his back, cold, pale light shone on the water. There was laughter from afar. The hum of the traffic. He'd shut it all out and now it was returning slowly, like waking from a disturbed sleep and not quite remembering where you were.

"You OK, Mort?" I asked.

"Sure," he said. "Just thinking."

"That's what you're here for," said Ambrose.

"I'm not sure anyone would want to share my thoughts right now," Tillman confessed. "What I was thinking is that maybe it's time I got a different job."

"Join the club, my good man, join the club."

CHAPTER
FOURTEEN

Later, I called the records office from the back seat as
Lynch drove Tillman and me back into town from the
churchyard of St John the Divine, where we'd gone
briefly after the canal — Mort wasn't as interested in
that scene, he told us, because it wasn't where the
victim died.

Boland wasn't there.

"He left about twenty minutes ago," said the girl who
answered the phone. "No, I don't know when he'll be
back. Can I help?"

"Just page him and tell him to call Saxon, all right?
Just Saxon, yeah. He'll know what it's about."

"Maybe he's managed to ID the body," suggested
Tillman.

"Already?"

"Why not?" said Ambrose. "How many missing
forty-somethings can there be in one city?"

"I guess."

"Where can I drop you off, anyway?"

"Anywhere," I said. "In fact, here'll do."

"Here?"

"That's what I said."

"You're the boss."

Ambrose pulled his Mercedes to the kerb, probably enjoying the admiring glances it drew from passers-by as I got out.

"Thanks for the lift, Ambrose," I said. "And I'll catch you later, Mort, yeah?"

I watched the traffic swallow them up again, and then stood for a moment staring at nothing, almost forgetting why I'd asked Lynch to stop here, before suddenly remembering.

The bookshop, that was it. Where was it? I'd seen it as we passed, a glimpse through the window on to a street crowded with bookshops. *Ex Cathedra Editions, specialists in theological and religious books.* Draker didn't have to believe there was anything of significance in the choice of quotations this killer had left at the scene, but he didn't have any hold over my time.

I made my way back up the street to where I'd seen the shop window, and as I walked, my phone rang. I held it tight to my ear and put my hand over my other ear to drown out the traffic.

"Saxon, you wanted me?"

"Is that you, Boland?" I said. "I can hardly hear you. Where are you?"

"Just taking a break. I'm down in Bewleys. You know it?"

"Of course I know it. Which one?"

"Westmoreland Street."

"I'll be there. Give me another ten minutes. There's something I have to do first."

★　★　★

Boland had taken a booth to himself in the dimly lit café and covered the table with thin clip files, each with the word MISSING stamped in red ink on the cover. A half-eaten sandwich lay forlornly on a plate next to a mug of what looked like cocoa covered with a cold skin like a wrinkled eyelid.

"Isn't that stuff for bedtime?" I said as I eased myself into the booth opposite him.

"Saxon, you startled me." Boland's head jerked up like he was surprised to see me, surprised to find himself here at all. "What were you saying?"

"Just commenting on your choice of drink. Wondered if once you'd drunk it you'd be getting a hot-water bottle and a pair of pyjamas out of your bag and settling down for the night."

"Too much coffee makes me edgy," he explained.

"Is that a problem?" I said, glancing round.

Involuntarily, he followed my gaze.

"What are you looking for?"

"A waitress."

"Then you're out of luck," he said. "This is a self-service café, you'll have to queue like everyone else."

"I forgot. Screw that," I said. "I hate queuing. I'll just wait until you want another cocoa and have you get it for me."

"At the meeting this morning you said I should make you get your own coffee. You said it would do you good."

"I changed my mind. Woman's prerogative."

"Well, whatever it was, I hear and obey."

Once Boland had risen to fetch me coffee, I turned to look at the files.

There must've been about thirty in all. Ten or so were stacked neatly at the far end of the table next to the wall; there was another pile of three next to it; most were fanned out on the table still waiting to be read; one was open flat where Boland had been sitting.

I couldn't read it upside down so I lifted it over to my side right way up.

Cathy Neill, aged forty-nine, British tourist reported missing at Hallowe'en whilst on holiday in Dublin. Boland had added a handwritten note: *Turned up safe 3 November.*

"Aren't these supposed to be under lock and key in records?" I said to Boland when he eventually came back.

"What? Oh, the files. Don't worry about those. Who's going to steal a bunch of missing persons files?"

"I'm not grouching," I said. "I just had you down as more of a stickler for regulations."

"To hell with regulations," he said. "I had to get out. Spending too long down there is worse than prison, and it'll never get any better till the Commissioner finally comes up with the funding to computerise the records. Here, lend me a hand, will you?"

I cleared a space for him to put down the tray, then lifted off my coffee and took a first tentative sip, biting my lip at the jab of heat. My first shot of the day, I realised.

"You find anything yet?" I asked, putting it back down to cool.

"I'm getting there," he said. "You know, there were hundreds of files and that was just for the last few years. They're not all missing persons officially, of course. Sometimes just husbands who've gone out on the tear and who'll turn up eventually when they sober up, teenage kids who've run away for a few nights because Daddy won't buy them a new car like Tabitha or Jeremy next door. Goes on all the time. Someone calls in and reports a missing person, the officer on duty opens a file on it, then no one remembers to update the file when the person turns up, so it just sits about in records for years until now when it gets dragged up again."

"Like Cathy Neill?" I said.

"Who?"

"Cathy Neill," I said, nodding at the file lying open before him.

"Oh her." He shrugged. "Classic case. Tourist rents a room for a couple of weeks, one evening she doesn't come back, the hotel gets worried and reports her missing, and it turns out that she's simply gone west on an impulse for a few days; but does anyone in the department bother writing that in the file when she wanders back into town in blissful ignorance that there's been a search for her? Of course not. It's left to muggins here to do it."

"It's like fishing for tuna," I said. "You end up with all the other fish in the net that you didn't want as well."

"Not to mention that someone's day gets ruined, usually mine in my experience, ringing round trying to find out the status of each file so that it can finally be closed."

"A bureaucratic nightmare," I said.

"Well, I'm exaggerating a little," he admitted. "It wasn't too bad. I was able to discount all the men and children, then everyone under forty and over mid-fifties; Lynch was pretty specific about the age range of the victim for once. That left about thirty. Some of them have been missing more than a year, though, and Lynch said this woman died about two weeks ago."

"Someone could've been keeping her somewhere in the interim," I said, then shook my head because I didn't want to think about that. "What do you like the look of so far?"

"So far, those ones," he said, indicating the files piled at the far end of the table next to the wall.

I reached out for the taller pile, but his hand shot out and stopped me. "No, not those," he said. "They're no good. Either they've turned up in the mean time, or the age is all wrong, or the height or build. The other pile's the ones that match."

"Those three? Is that all?"

"At least it narrows down the search, as the Chief put it."

I took another sip of coffee, grateful that I could drink it now without needing reconstructive plastic surgery on my lips. It tasted good and I didn't give a damn if it made me edgy. I liked being edgy. Another mouthful and I flicked open the top file and looked at the photograph inside. A police mug shot.

160

"Tanya Grant," I read. "Ex-prostitute, forty-seven. How long has she been missing?"

"Two months," said Boland.

"Sounds promising."

"It does until you read the rest of it. She disappeared in September with a kilo of cocaine which she was meant to be taking north for her lover. Moral of the story: a man should never cross an ex-prostitute who has a kilo of his best cocaine."

"So she's on the run rather than missing?"

"Looks like it." Boland reached over and turned to the second page, jabbed a finger at a paragraph near the bottom. "According to that, Spanish police have reported two sightings of a woman who matches Tanya's description living the high life in a resort on the south coast."

I shut the file. "And these are the best ones, you say?" I said.

The next file was for a woman who'd vanished whilst on bail for credit card fraud. Age fifty-one, five foot four. No sightings this time, but police didn't seem unduly concerned.

"It's something of a habit with her," said Boland. "I arrested her once myself when I was in Serious Crime and it was nine months before we found her after she skipped bail."

"And judges keep letting her out?"

"That's lawyers for you," he said. "If I had a fiver for every villain I've caught who's been released on bail and done it again, well . . ."

"So that's Kim Whelan out. What about this last one?"

"Now that," he said, "is interesting. Open it and see."

"Mary Crosby," I read. "I see why."

"I don't know if there is any significance in the choice of names so far," said Boland, "but she's inside the age range *and* she's been missing only two weeks."

"Plus she's a prostitute," I noted, reading down the details of her last known movements. "What did Fitzgerald tell you? Hookers come in all shapes and sizes and ages."

"High-class escort girl," corrected Boland sardonically. "Used to work the hotels, servicing out-of-town businessmen who were in Dublin for conferences, lunches, business meetings, not to mention the opportunity to catch an exotic disease from a stranger in a hotel bedroom."

"Forty-one's low on the age range."

"That's my one quibble," said Boland. "Lynch said we were looking at someone nearer fifty, but, you know, even he could be wrong sometimes."

"Ambrose Lynch wrong?" I said, feigning astonishment.

"Clap me in leg irons for even suggesting it. But surely even God makes mistakes?"

"He does indeed," I said. "Have you ever been to Canada?"

I looked at Mary Crosby's photograph again, then back to the notes. She'd gone missing before, I saw: days, weeks, even months at a stretch. Each time her family reported it to the police; each time she turned up again as if nothing was wrong. Had she gone walkabout again, or had her walk this time taken her no further than the churchyard of St John the Divine?

"So," I said, "you have one ex-prostitute probably living it up on the proceeds of cocaine trafficking on the Costa del Crime, another career criminal with an allergic reaction to doing time, and a prostitute . . . sorry, high-class escort girl . . . who goes missing after a romantic night at the Gresham Hotel with a — let me see, it was here somewhere — a travelling biscuit salesman." That certainly made me pause. "Travelling biscuit salesman?"

"It's a dirty job, but someone's got to do it."

"I guess so. Not much of a haul, is there?"

"I still have these to go through." He indicated the fan of files that covered the table. "They might throw up something. You're welcome to join me."

For the next half-hour, we sat reading the remaining files. It was lunchtime and the café was beginning to fill up. There was noise all around us — carefree voices, the scrape of chairs as customers came and went, the rattle of cups — but we sat enveloped in a melancholy silence of our own making, adding only the rustling of thin pages to the music of the day.

Each file, once read, was added to the tall pile if it was useless, to the smaller one if either of us felt it merited further investigation. There weren't too many of those.

It was like we were reading job applications for a post that nobody wanted. Situation vacant: one unidentified

163

corpse, probable victim of an aspiring serial killer, apply within.

It was too horrible to think about, so it was better not to think, only switch to automatic pilot, flick past any photographs of the missing women that might be clipped to the front of the file, and just look at the what, when and where of their disappearance, see what matched.

It's astonishing how many people just vanish from the radar screen of a city, how easy it is for the real to become shadows. People are there one day and gone the next. That's how the world works now; people move around, paying rent by the month, switching between jobs, between lovers, with nothing to tie them down. It was easy to forget that each name and number in the missing files represented some family somewhere who might never get to know what had happened to their sister, father, husband, wife, and who would always assume the worst, assuming the worst being one thing at which the human mind has always excelled.

There they all were, scattered across the table of a café in Dublin — a few more spoonfuls that fate had added to the bottomless well of human misery; and sometimes that was the way the missing wanted it. Sometimes they *wanted* to be missing, even took pleasure in the misery that they left behind them. Sometimes the prospect of the misery to come in their honour was what spurred them into making themselves missing in the first place.

At the end, we were left with one large, teetering pile of files containing the names of women who could, for now at least, be ruled out as possibilities, and another pathetically meagre pile of seven which might, conceivably, contain the name of the woman whose body had been found in the churchyard, victim, so it seemed, of a savage beating.

But where was the spark, the feeling that, yes, this was the one? I hadn't felt it, not even with Mary Crosby, though she was promising in so many ways, and I knew from looking at Boland as he rubbed his eyes frustratedly that he hadn't felt it either. It was like that game you play as children, hiding something and then getting someone to find it by telling them if they are hot or cold, near or not. Everything today had felt cold.

"We should be getting back," he said when he caught me looking at him, and I nodded.

We both reached out at the same time to pick up the tall pile, the coldest pile, and in the confusion of hands it toppled over, files spilling off the table and on to the floor.

"Shit," muttered Boland, and he seemed angry.

"No harm done," I said. "Look, I'll help you pick them up."

But Boland bent down heavily for each file, not waiting for help, not wanting it, until he'd gathered them all together and brought them back to the table to shuffle into neat piles.

I hadn't moved.

I'd noticed a name on the front of one of the files as it fell and I'd picked up only that. Now I sat reading, my hands tingling with sparks.

"You missed this one," I said.

Boland leaned over to see which one I meant.

"Susan Fuller," he said, still breathless from bending down, "I remember that one. Hers was one of the first files I looked at, but she was outside the age range."

"Only just," I said, reading. "She's forty-two. That's nearer than Mary Crosby. It says here that her husband, Tom, reported her missing more than two weeks ago — that fits with what Lynch said. Came home from work one night and she wasn't there. No note, no signs of disturbance. He reported her missing the next day, police sent someone out to take a look. He interviewed the husband, called friends and colleagues, followed up a few leads, but came back with nothing."

"I suppose we could add it to the list if you think it's worth it," he said.

He didn't sound convinced, but I didn't need to match her up point for point with Ambrose Lynch's autopsy report to know that Susan Fuller needed further investigation.

"I know her," I told Boland. "If it's the same one I'm thinking of — and face it, how many Susan Fullers can there be? She was a lecturer at University College when I met her."

"Where Fagan worked?"

Was he getting that spark too?

"Different department, that was all, And it gets better," I said. "Or worse, for her maybe. She was Ed Fagan's lover in the months leading up to his arrest."

"Get away," said Boland. "And now she's missing. That's some coincidence."

"Too much of a coincidence for my liking," I said. "What say you and I pay her husband a call?"

CHAPTER
FIFTEEN

"She's dead, isn't she?" said Susan Fuller's husband as soon as he opened the door to see Boland and me standing there at the top of his steps. We hadn't even had a chance to ring the doorbell.

"I know she's dead," he went on. "Soon as you called, I realised."

"Mr Fuller —" began Boland.

"Look, you'd better come in."

Fuller took a step back and ushered us into the hall. It was only a half-hour since Boland had called and asked if he'd see us. He'd agreed eagerly and now here we were following him into the hall of Susan's Victorian terraced house close to Phoenix Park in the leafy north of the city.

It was just as I recalled from the time I came here to talk to her about her relationship with Ed Fagan: polished antique floorboards, stripped doors, restored this, original that. The walls were bright with colour and life and I could only imagine they were Susan's colours, Susan's life, for her husband was nothing like that. I'd not met him then, she'd made sure he was out before she talked to me, but he was just as I'd expected from her description. Not a button was out of place on his jacket, not a hair in his moustache; his tie was knotted tight.

"What makes you think Susan's dead?" said Boland when Fuller had closed the door behind us and we stood, awkward still, in the hall.

"What would you be doing here if she wasn't? It's that woman they found, isn't it?"

"The woman whose body was found yesterday is still unidentified," said Boland. "Your wife's name simply came back among the list of missing persons, and we're going through the list trying to eliminate names. We have no reason to believe it's Susan. Can we sit down?"

Fuller, pacified for the moment, led us through into the sitting room. It was a huge room, running all the way from the front of the house to the back, where an arched window looked out on trees and glimpses of other houses. Books filled the shelves either side of the fireplace. A fire had been lit, but it gave off no warmth, only a thin trickle of smoke

"I know who you are," he said to me once we were sitting. "You met my wife before. You were writing a book about Ed Fagan."

"You remember," I said.

"It's hard to forget a man who was screwing your wife," he said, then he looked away quickly. Ashamed. "Do you think he came back and killed her?" he said after a pause.

"Fagan? No, I don't."

"Why not?"

"Because Fagan's dead, and there's no evidence that your wife is dead at all."

Boland immediately flashed me a warning look. He hadn't been sure about my coming here in the first place; I had no business interviewing Tom Fuller about his wife's disappearance, as he'd pointedly reminded me back in the café when I first suggested paying Fuller a call. He'd only agreed to my tagging along because knowing who I was might make Susan's husband more forthcoming; but it was still only on the condition that I leave the talking to him. Now this.

I returned Boland an apologetic look. The words had been out of my mouth before I could stop them — hell, that was the story of my life.

Fuller seemed unaware that anything was wrong. "Yes, you said that already," was all he said, derisively, to my reassurance. "That's why you're both here."

"I know how it must look," said Boland.

Fuller didn't answer, just stared into the fire. I took the opportunity to get to my feet and look at the photographs that were lined along the mantelpiece between the bookcases.

"Do you mind?" I said.

I took down one of Susan. It had been taken at the university where she'd taught alongside Fagan eight years ago. She was an attractive woman, still looking good for her age. Too — there was no other word for it — alive for the moribund Tom Fuller. The sun was in her hair.

"Explain how you realised she was missing," I heard Boland ask behind me.

"It was about two weeks ago now," Fuller said. "I'd been working, I'm a company director in town, specialising in office supplies." He seemed to think it was important that we should know that. "Paper clips, photocopier fluid, envelopes; well, you know, all sorts really."

Christ, that was all we needed, an analysis of the office supplies industry.

"We'd been having problems," he said, "but we were supposed to be going out that night, patch things up, make a go of it, but I had to phone to tell her I was working late." Probably a run on staplers, I thought unkindly. "There was a bit of an argument, we both ended up shouting, and she put the phone down. Slammed it down, I should say."

"What was the argument about?" Boland said.

"Nothing. Everything. It was just an argument."

"You don't have to tell us if you don't want. We're not here to check up on your marriage. We're just trying to put together a picture of Susan the day she disappeared."

It was hard to tell if he heard. He was staring at the fire again. I caught Boland's eye and saw the same thought imprinted there as on mine: this was going to be difficult.

"So what then?" Boland tried again. "You came home at what time?"

"About nine o'clock," he said.

He'd heard that then. Maybe that was what he needed. Direct questions, straight to the point. I could see he'd be that sort of a man. Difficult to live with? It'd certainly be hard to be always straight to the point when half the fun of life was straying off it.

"I'd brought a bottle of wine with me," he was saying. "A peace offering, I suppose you could call it. You know the way you can tell when a house is empty even before you've looked round it? Well, that's the way it was. I went through to the kitchen and I just knew. It was like my voice was echoing. She'd taken her handbag and gone."

"There was no message, no note saying when she'd be back?"

"Nothing."

"What did you do?"

"I made myself something to eat, opened the wine, watched the news."

"After that?"

"Washed up, went to bed. Next day I went to work."

"Did you try calling her?"

"I tried. I tried her here and at the college. I wanted to see if she'd talk to me, if she was still mad, but she hadn't gone into work that day, and when I came home she wasn't here again."

"Which was when you called the police to report her missing."

"Leave it twenty-fours hours, isn't that what they tell you?"

He seemed proud of doing it all to the letter.

"Weren't you worried?" I butted in.

Another glare from Boland.

"Of course I was worried!" Fuller answered. "I was desperate with worry. But I didn't think anything bad had happened to her. I mean . . . look, there's no point pretending. She'd left before." He glanced up at me.

172

Looking for sympathy? I kept my face impassive. "It was an old schoolfriend of mine, actually. Roy Green. She went to live with him for a while, but she came back. Like I said, we were trying to work things out. So when I saw she wasn't here, I thought maybe . . ."

He didn't need to finish.

"How long ago was this?" said Boland.

"Last summer."

"And did you ring him once you realised Susan was missing, to see if he knew where she was?"

"I couldn't. I wouldn't . . . trust myself to talk to him. I phoned a few of her friends, but they didn't seem to know any more than I did. As for the college . . ." He grimaced.

"You don't like your wife's college?"

"I certainly didn't like her friends from there," he said. "It's just not my world, that's all. I couldn't share it with her. It — they — made her . . . dissatisfied."

"Is that what she was before she vanished — dissatisfied?"

"No more than usual."

But I got a sense that the usual dissatisfaction was probably more than enough for either of them to bear.

Whilst Boland and Fuller went on talking, I made an excuse to go to the bathroom. I could see Fuller wrestling with how best to phrase a refusal and failing to come up with anything.

"Top of the stairs on the left," he said frostily.

At the top of the stairs on the right was what I was actually looking for. Susan's office. Door ajar. I remembered it from my last visit, when she'd brought me here to get us both out of the way in case Tom came home early. It was only a storage room really, but it had been kitted out with a desk, built-in shelves, a computer, fax; there was a tiny window in the wall high up. I noticed spots of rain on the glass. Another day giving up the pretence it wasn't winter.

The desk was untidy with papers, letters. Had *he* made this mess as he searched through Susan's things after her disappearance, or was this how Susan had left it?

I lowered myself gingerly into her chair and quietly opened a drawer. There were essays from her students waiting to be marked; a couple of books she'd borrowed from the university library, with a rubber band round the middle and a note telling her that another book she'd asked for was unavailable.

Ordinary, everyday clutter. And there — her diary and address book.

I flicked through them hopefully, but it was merely a list of appointments, lectures to attend, scraps of paper torn from newspapers naming books she intended to read, movies to see, concerts and public talks to attend. There was certainly nothing personal, much less confessional, in her diary, though occasionally a date would be underlined faintly in pencil. Days when she was meeting a new lover unbeknown to Fuller? Or maybe not so unbeknown.

I was starting to think that maybe Susan *was* the woman whose body had been found in the churchyard, with no more appointments to make, concerts to attend, books to read. When I closed her diary, it was with something that felt grimly like finality.

I retreated back down the stairs to the hall.

Boland came out of the sitting room with Fuller as I neared the bottom. Susan's husband looked at me suspiciously. Did he know I'd been snooping? How could he?

"We'd better be getting back," Boland said to me. "And thanks for your time, Mr Fuller, we'll be in touch. Just one more thing. In order to rule out Susan from our enquiries, we need some details, anything you can think of, that might help identify her."

"You want a photograph?" said Fuller, confused at first. Then something clicked into place in his head, and there was a moment of alarm in his eyes before he composed himself again. "Oh, I see. I . . . I suppose I could give you the name of her dentist."

"Dental records are no good," said Boland. He didn't elaborate. "I was thinking more if there was anything else distinctive you could tell us about. Birthmarks, tattoos."

"Susan didn't have any tattoos," he said.

"What about fractures? She ever have to go to Casualty in the past?"

Fuller was about to start shaking his head again when a shadow of recognition appeared in his eyes. "Now you mention it," he said, "she did. About ten years ago, she fell off a horse whilst we were on holiday. Had to wear a plaster on her leg for a couple of months."

I felt chilled, remembering what Ambrose had said; but it was something finally, I couldn't deny that. Somewhere on her medical record there'd be an X-ray of her fractured leg. All the police had to do was call it up, then match it against the X-rays Lynch had taken during the autopsy of the body from the churchyard, and they'd have an answer. Fractures are perfect witnesses, after all. They never change.

Fuller scribbled down the name and number of her doctor for us, and then reached out to unlatch the front door. He didn't even bother hiding his relief that we were going.

"Do you mind if we go out the back way instead?" I said.

Boland looked almost as surprised as Fuller.

"The back?"

"If that's OK."

Irritated once more, Fuller pointed down the hallway.

"Through there," he said, and he followed us into the kitchen and lifted down a key from a hook on the wall. He handed it to Boland.

"You'll have to unlock the gate at the end of the garden, then go left to get back to the road," he explained. "Just leave the key in the keyhole when you've done."

A moment later, we were out.

The rain was heavier than spots now, and promised worse.

"What was that all about?" said Boland to me, but we were still too near the house to talk and I took no notice. I'd seen what I wanted down the garden from a window upstairs and now made my way along the path towards it, trailing Boland behind me.

"What do you think of *that*?" I said when we were out of earshot.

He looked where I was indicating.

"It's a garage," he said.

"Well spotted. You know, you should be a detective."

Like everything else in the garden, the garage was in immaculate condition. There were people who lived in rougher conditions than Fuller provided for his car. Or *was* that his car? We smeared a space in the rain and pressed our noses to the window at the side to peer in.

"Convertible," said Boland. "Nice."

"Nice big freezer too," I said, "right behind it."

It took him a moment to realise what I was saying.

"You don't think he . . .?"

I shrugged. "All these high walls and trees, who's to see if he carries his wife's body down to the garage in the night then stores it in the freezer till he can get rid of it?"

"Why would he kill her?" said Boland.

"Because she didn't love him, because she loved someone else, because she was going to leave him. Need I go on?"

"I can't believe that," Boland insisted. "If that's Susan Fuller in the morgue and he killed her, then that means he must've killed Mary Lynch too. Where's the evidence?"

"Who needs evidence? I'm just batting round ideas here," I said. "Line the suspects up then knock them down one by one, that's my technique. Last man standing takes the rap."

"Call me a naive, sentimental old fool," said Boland, "but to me he just seemed like a man who was sad because his wife wasn't around any more. I can relate to that."

"But do you have a copy of Nick Elliott's book on Ed Fagan stashed away under the chair in your sitting room?" I said.

"What?"

"That's right, I saw it when I passed his chair. A little corner peeking out. *Deepening Shadows: Inside the Mind of an Irish Serial Killer.* Fuller was obviously reading it before we arrived, then tried to hide it away. His guilty little secret."

"Reading Elliott's book isn't a crime."

"Then why hide it?" I said.

Boland didn't have an answer to that.

Suddenly, I sensed that we were being watched and looked back.

There was Tom Fuller, doting husband, king of the office supplies, at the window. He didn't look away when he realised I'd seen him, only went on watching, unsmiling, still.

I stared back at him, wondering if it was him or the rain that was making my skin shiver.

CHAPTER
SIXTEEN

The rain was coming down hard again by the time we made it, long way round, back to the car. It was getting dark too. Another day dying, as if the light couldn't be bothered trying to hold on any more.

"Can I drop you somewhere?" said Boland once we'd climbed in.

"The National Library," I said. "I've arranged to meet someone there. Professor Salvatore. You know him?"

"Should I?"

"He used to know Fagan," I explained, "though that's not why I'm meeting him. He's a theologian. The owner of a religious bookstore down on Nassau Street gave me his name, said he might be able to help me track down the quotes our boy's been leaving."

"*All wickedness is but little to the wickedness of a woman.*"

"Amongst others. Salvatore's going to be there all day, researching his latest book; he agreed to take time out for me."

"What time's your appointment?"

"Four."

"Then I'd best hurry."

The quickest way from Fuller's house near Phoenix Park to the National Library, I thought, was down towards the railway station by the river and then along the quays into town; but Boland made a 180-degree turn and headed off in the opposite direction.

"The traffic will be murder down by the station," he explained, not appearing to appreciate the oddity of the word he'd chosen. "This way'll be quicker. Trust me."

I settled back, not really caring, hardly even noticing after a while which turnings we took, though the roads seemed to bristle bad-temperedly with traffic whatever way we went.

"Do you mind if I turn on the radio?" he said once we were under way.

"Damn right I do," I replied.

He didn't protest, and I closed my eyes and put my head back against the rest, listening to the quiet, hypnotic swish of the wipers. Doubts instantly began to prick me once more in the dark, and I found myself wondering as always what I was doing here.

Everyone had something to do except me; I didn't even know what my role was meant to be. Expert consultant, my ass. I didn't even have enough pulling power to get on to a crime scene without prior permission, yet I was supposed to be some help here? Come on. It was nothing but vanity on my part, an inability to let go. I'd have been better off back in my apartment just waiting for Fitzgerald to come and tell me how things were progressing. Are you sitting comfortably, Saxon? Then I'll begin. Even Boland was more use than I was.

I wasn't sure I rated Boland as an investigator. He wasn't slow, but he was a plodder. He'd come to the murder squad from Serious Crime, but why he'd come was harder to figure. It didn't seem like he had that energy about him that all effective murder detectives need, that passion. He investigated murder like it was a speeding offence.

The difference, though, was that Boland would earn his place on the team eventually, whereas I would do my job this once and then be out of here. But out of here to where?

That had always been my problem: I never felt settled, never felt that, finally, I knew where I wanted to be. Some people instinctively know where that is. Like Fitzgerald. She had a place here, a purpose; she fitted. I was just loitering.

The thought came to me, though, as we drove, the car heater making me sleepy: would she go with me if I asked her? If I told her I had to get away, on to the next place, wherever that was, would she come? Could she leave this life she had behind? It wouldn't be fair to ask her. I wouldn't ask her. But say I did, would she come? At that moment I desperately wanted to know.

"Hello, hello, hello."

I opened my eyes at Boland's stage policeman's exclamation, as reluctantly as if I'd been sleeping. Light irritated my brain at once and I resented it.

It took me a moment to get my bearings and recognise the narrow street where Boland was slowing down. There was a church not far from here, I half recalled, infamous because the corpses in the crypt never rotted. Something ancient and dry in the air had preserved them against decay, and visitors used to descend the steep steps to shake their hands.

Now the blue flash of a patrol car splashed the walls of the narrow street.

A crowd had gathered.

Raised voices.

A hundred yards from where we were parked, a market opened out to fill all available space. To our left, hemmed in by tall grey buildings, the stalls were out, the day's trade at its height. Traders, shoppers, idlers should've been milling about, but it was as if some malfunction had unexpectedly pushed the city's pause button and all movement had ground to a halt.

Boland was already out of the car by the time I'd taken in my surroundings, and he was even further ahead before I reached down to release my seatbelt and follow him. I'd almost caught him up when I remembered the car was unlocked and had to double back and reach in to take the keys out of the ignition. This wasn't the sort of area to leave a car unlocked.

But where was Boland now? I was left following the blue flash through the frozen crowds with a strange feeling, like I was wading underwater.

"Let me through," I said. "Police."

A lie, but it did the trick. They parted to let me pass.

An air of unreality enveloped me as I waded. All around were signs of normality. Christmas trees rested against the market stalls, fairy lights hung from metal bars and awnings, there were stupid ornaments for the season and wrapping paper laid out for sale; stallholders wore Santa hats with twinkling lights, and somewhere a radio blared out "Sleigh Ride".

At the back of the market there was a line of what looked like stable doors, secured with padlocks. Stallholders, I guessed, hoarded stuff here out of sight of taxmen and thieves.

One door was open. I saw Boland's shape imprinted on the darkness that flooded out from it, two more uniformed officers close by. He was peering inside.

At what?

"You can't come in here," one of the uniforms began.

"Boland," I snapped.

Boland turned his head and saw me.

"It's OK," he said, "she's with me."

It was an unsatisfactory answer, but it took the quarrel out of the officer who'd challenged me. He had that wide-eyed, pale look that you only get in someone who's just seen the body of a murdered person, for I'd no doubt now that that was what it was we'd come here to see.

I wondered if it was his first. Some officers go through an entire career without seeing a single body, without being tainted with those images; but once they have, the stain never leaves their mind. It makes its mark, brands them. Some never recover. I'd known cops who handed in their notice when they found the first one, because they couldn't handle the memory of it and didn't want to add other memories to it. Others were unaffected, serene.

Boland was one of those, I realised at once; and in many ways so was I. I stepped up to the door and recognised in his eyes the same distant, abstracted look of one who could step outside himself, do what needed to be done. The horror would come later.

I took a deep breath and looked into the dark. Saw her.

"Mary," I said.

She was lying on her back, arms thrown wide, laid out in a corner in the dark, eyes closed, green twine wound around her neck, the front of her dress stained with dried blood. I couldn't see a wound or a weapon, but the blood told its own story.

"Who found her?" I said.

"One of the market traders," replied the uniformed officer. I checked his name badge: DS Simon Turner. "We've taken him for a cup of tea," he continued. "He's pretty shaken up about it. He opened the door here about twenty minutes ago and found her lying there. He called the station in Chancery Street and we were sent out to check up."

"She must've been here all day," I said. "All these people milling about the market, you couldn't carry a body through here."

"Carry a body?" said Boland. "How do you know she wasn't killed here?"

I sighed, irritated all of a sudden that he hadn't seen it himself and not caring at that moment if he knew I was irritated.

"The blood, Boland, look," I said. "Look how much of it there is on her. Her clothes are covered with it, but there's none on the floor or walls."

He nodded, plainly feeling foolish.

"She wasn't strangled then?" he said.

"That's a post-mortem strangling," I said. "See how tightly the ligature's been pulled, yet there's no bulging of the eyes, no protrusion of the tongue. She died of stab wounds all right."

I stepped forward.

"Careful," Boland said, all policeman again.

"I won't touch anything," I said, "I just want to see. Here, you, pass me your torch."

DS Turner handed over the torch without complaint and I shone it down on to the woman's hands. "Defensive wounds, see, where she tried to ward off the blows."

"Like Tara Cox," said Boland with a belated insight.

"Exactly like Tara Cox," I said, for I could see now the open wound in the woman's throat, a single cut.

Everything was the same, except that Tara had been covered with a blanket.

I flashed the light round the dingy interior.

And there it was. The market trader must have lifted the blanket off when he came to open up, not knowing what was underneath. It lay in a heap a few yards from the body.

I was about to point it out to Boland when a movement in the crowd caught my eye.

"Great, here comes trouble."

Scything through the crowd came Seamus Dalton. Civilians fell before him like freshly cut wheat. Make way for the lawman.

"I hope you didn't touch anything," were his first words to me.

"The day I need lessons in crime scene preservation from you, Dalton, is the day I go home and blow my brains out," I said.

"Don't let me stop you."

He glanced briefly into the dark where Mary lay. Almost dismissive.

"She's been stabbed," I said.

"Stabbed, is it?" He actually laughed. "So you're a pathologist as well now? How does the FBI manage without you? No wonder the US has the highest murder rate in the world now that you're not there to take care of law enforcement single-handed."

"You know something, Dalton?" I said quietly. "You're so far up your own ass even your boots are starting to disappear. So let's get one thing straight, OK? I am not one fraction of one per cent interested in spending the next few days tiptoeing round your delicate little male ego so that it doesn't get bruised. I've got more important things to do. So should you."

"Well, excuse me for talking out of line," sneered Dalton. "There was me thinking I was the police officer round here and you were just the Chief's favourite bedwarmer. My mistake. We'll all just go home now, shall we, and let you get on with closing the case?"

"Saxon," said Boland before I could say anything back.

A warning.

I turned my head and saw Lawlor, Healy and the other members of the murder squad moving through the marketplace. No sign of Fitzgerald yet. The blue tape was going up once more. I wasn't going to have it out with Dalton in front of them.

There was something of the wolf pack about their arrival as they fanned out, taking control, re-establishing the hierarchy. First thing they did was summon up jobs for Turner and the other officer from Chancery Street, anything to clear them out of the way.

Then Lawlor stepped forward and whispered in Dalton's ear.

"If it's all right with Chief Fitzgerald's representative on earth," Dalton said as a parting shot to me, "I'll be off now to talk to the man who found the body. You have a good day now."

"He certainly has a way of making you feel like you're only cluttering up the place," said Boland once Dalton had left. "God help us if he ever gets to be chief. I think I'd apply for another transfer."

"Back to Serious Crime?"

"Serious Crime, Traffic, dog unit, you name it."

"He's hard work," I agreed.

"He's great if you're one of the gang," said Boland. "The after-hours-drinking type. It's the ones who go home to their wives once their shifts are through that he can't stand."

"No women allowed," I said.

"Not if he can help it. And especially not if they're chief superintendents."

"Talk of the devil."

A snatch of "She Moves Through the Fair" came into my head as I watched Fitzgerald weaving through the crowd towards us, head bent as always to her mobile phone. Why is it that the mind always throws up such incongruous memories and images at the most inconvenient moments? Our minds conspire against us, that's why, laughing at all our attempts to tame them.

Boland held the crime scene tape up for Fitzgerald as she ducked underneath. She groaned as she stood upright again, pulling her shoulders tight to dislodge the pain in her back.

"He's not leaving much time, is he?" she said to me.

"She must've been dead already before the article hit the news-stands," I said. "She wasn't killed here. That means she must've been brought here in the night, before the market opened."

"It opens at six," said Fitzgerald, "but they start putting out the stalls about five. And Benburb Street's just round the corner" — she meant the red-light district this side of the river — "so there'd have been people in and out of here pretty constantly till, say, three o'clock. That doesn't exactly leave much time in between for our friend to dispose of a body."

"Long enough," I said.

"True. What about a note?"

"I didn't see. I didn't want to touch anything. But if he's still following the Fagan pattern, and it looks as though he is, then it'll be inside her bra; that's where it was on Tara Cox."

188

"Well, we'll find out soon enough," she said, and took a deep breath, she was steeling herself for a dive into icy water. "I'd better go in. What are you going to do?"

"Damn," I said, suddenly remembering. "I have to meet someone."

I checked my watch.

"And I'm late."

"I'll drop you off," said Boland.

"No, Boland, you stay here," said Fitzgerald. "I want to get an ID trace on this woman as fast as we can. We don't have much time. Sorry, Saxon, you'll have to make your own way."

"No problem," I said. "Here, Boland, catch."

"My keys."

"Good job one of us remembered."

I'd almost left the marketplace before I noticed the green dome of the Four Courts rising through the rain above the square. The Four Courts . . . Chancery Street.

Fagan had murdered Tara Cox in the grounds of the Law Library on Constitution Hill. Whoever killed this woman couldn't go back there, not after Mary Lynch and the body in the churchyard had alerted police to his desire to match out the same pattern. He knew they'd be watching, waiting. But that didn't mean the pattern had to be abandoned completely.

Law Library . . . Four Courts . . . Chancery Street. This was Dublin's legal district. Connections didn't come much more tenuous, but it *was* a connection.

So then, where had Fagan's next victim died? Liana Cassidy had been killed in Prospect Cemetery, next to the railway line. That was no help. How many cemeteries were there, after all, how many miles of track? The police couldn't watch over them all.

And then I stopped myself, realising what I was doing. A woman lay dead and my thoughts had already turned to the next one. It was as though I'd written off the chances of catching whoever was doing this before it happened again. And the worst of it was, maybe I had.

CHAPTER
SEVENTEEN

"Professor Salvatore?" I said as I came through the revolving doors of the National Library and a tall, graceful figure rose to greet me from one of the benches that lined the wall. "Sorry I'm late."

"No need to apologise," he said. The bookstore owner had told me Salvatore was Italian, but there was only the faintest trace of an accent in his voice. "And I insist you call me Max."

"Max it is."

I recognised him at once from the photograph printed on the back cover of one of the volumes I'd been shown earlier in Ex Cathedra Books, the only difference being that the mugshot hadn't done him justice. He was an attractive man, with cheekbones you could go skiing on, and he was well-dressed too, with that careless elegance Europeans seem to manage so effortlessly.

"Traffic a nightmare?" he said.

"Something like that," I replied, sidestepping the question. Then I wondered why I felt the need to make up excuses for being late when the events of that afternoon were reason enough. "Actually," I started again, "the truth is that the police found another body."

"That's awful. I'm sorry."

"She was only found about an hour ago, no, not even an hour. I was passing by chance otherwise I'd have been here on time. I'm grateful you waited."

"If this is a bad time . . ."

"No. Or yes, it is a bad time, but perhaps you can stop it getting worse, like I explained on the phone this morning. This man is leaving messages, religious messages, each time he kills. The police have managed so far to keep the details out of the media, but what they really want, what I really want, is to know if they contain other possible meanings beyond the obvious."

"And that's where I come in?" he said.

"You're a theologian," I said. "Former priest, trained in Rome. See, I've been told all about you — not least that you're one of the most important scholars right now in the field of Old Testament eschatology. Whatever the hell that is."

"The study of different concepts of heaven and hell," he laughed.

I noticed he didn't object to my assessment of his importance.

"There you go," I said. "Who better to explain what we're dealing with here? Plus, from what I hear, you used to be familiar with Ed Fagan."

"I didn't know Ed Fagan that well," Salvatore said. "We attended a few of the same conferences, contributed to some of the same symposiums and journals. He reviewed me once. Badly. Never give an academic a bad review, they'll never forget it. We don't make enough from our writings to put up with bad

192

reviews. I wouldn't have minded so much if he knew what he was talking about, but eschatology was not Fagan's field. He was more of a religious historian and a linguist than an Old Testament theologian."

"Fagan was interested in language?"

"Well, he hadn't published much by the time of his arrest," said Salvatore. "It was more of a developing interest. But it was something he told me once he wanted to delve into more."

"Hebrew?"

"Not really. Principally Aramaic, Greek, the languages of the New Testament period. I doubt if he could even read Hebrew. That would be more my line of enquiry."

"Which is why I called you," I said. "I'm pretty sure the quotations must come from the Old Testament. You're the Old Testament expert. It makes sense to put the two of you together."

"I'll do my best," Salvatore answered, "though let us hope that you do not succeed only in exposing my true ignorance. I have spent my whole career trying to keep it hidden."

"Max, my lips are sealed."

"Then let's go up."

Salvatore waved a hand to the stairs at the back of the high-domed hall and we climbed up. At the top of the stairs we turned right and pushed the heavy doors into the Reading Room.

I'd almost forgotten how huge it was in here and how the silence filled it like water in a deep pool. It had that incredible stillness all libraries possess, a quiet broken only by coughs and whispers, pages turning, the squeak of doors and chairs. I'd come here often to read in my early months in Dublin, or more usually just to sit and think. I'd spent all day here sometimes reading, and come out to find that it was dark already. I'd never considered those days wasted. Now I hardly came here at all. Another sign of how my relationship with the city was fraying.

Today it was all but empty and no one spared us so much as a glance as we wove our way among the desks to the back where he'd been working, books and papers scattered across his desk, and where he now pulled up an extra chair for me beside his own.

"You have the quotations with you?" he said.

I took out a piece of paper and slid it across the table towards him.

"This is a copy of the note the killer left on a body we found yesterday," I said.

"*Go, see now this cursed woman and bury her,*" he read out. "Well, at least I shan't embarrass myself with this one."

"You know it?"

"I am the most important scholar in the field of Old Testament eschatology, remember?"

"*One* of the most important is what I said."

"Only one of? Funny, I didn't catch that part." He reached over for a book — a King James Bible, I saw it was — and started to flick purposefully through the pages. "You know," he said whilst he looked, "you could probably have found all this information out for

194

yourself with half an hour on the Internet. You'd be surprised what strange things are out there."

"Technology and I don't get along."

"You and me both," he said with feeling. "I refuse to even have a computer in my office. I still use a typewriter. Ah, here it is. The Second Book of Kings, Chapter 9, Verses 33 and 34."

I read the part he indicated.

So they threw her down: and some of her blood was sprinkled on the wall, and on the horses: and he trode her under foot. And when he was come in, he did eat and drink, and said, Go, see now this cursed woman, and bury her: for she is a king's daughter.

"Who is this woman?" I said.

"She is Jezebel," said Salvatore. "Wife of Ahab, King of Israel. She was denounced by the prophet Elijah for encouraging idolatry, and killed on the orders of a certain Jehu. But you don't need to be a theologian to appreciate the popular connotations of the name Jezebel, no?"

"A shameless or immoral woman," I said. "A whore."

"Precisely."

I glanced back to the story of the murder of Jezebel, trying to work out if the words were intended as a sign that the woman in the churchyard was indeed a prostitute — in which case, how could it be Susan Fuller? — or whether her killer was simply trying to say that all women were prostitutes, all women unclean, all women Jezebel.

As I did so, my eyes saw the words that followed; and the breath caught in my throat.

And they went to bury her: but they found no more of her than the skull, and the feet, and the palms of her hands.

This was getting bizarre.

Why would the killer leave a note referring to the murder of a woman of whom only the skull, hands and feet were found, on the body of a woman with the skull, hands and feet missing? Was it a sick joke? Or was there some hidden meaning in there which only he could decipher?

I looked up and realised that Salvatore was watching me curiously. My face must have betrayed something: incomprehension, excitement, disgust. Cool it, Saxon, I told myself.

The press hadn't been told about the missing body parts, and I wasn't about to betray that secret now. I didn't suspect for one minute that Salvatore would tell anyone else if I confessed the reason for my startled reaction, but I was taking no chances.

"Are you ready to look at the second quote?" I said instead, and he, thankfully, was courteous enough to pretend for my sake that everything was normal.

All wickedness is but little to the wickedness of a woman.

"Now then," he said when I passed him a copy of the message found in the lining of Mary Lynch's bag. "It's not from the Old Testament, I'm fairly sure of that."

"It's not?"

"But it sounds familiar all the same. Let me think, let me think." He was half talking to himself, his eyes closed as if in prayer. "Stay here a moment, there's something I must look at."

I watched Salvatore retrace his steps and start a whispered conversation with the woman behind the counter; watched her go into the back and emerge some minutes later with another thick, leather-bound book; watched him carry it back to our desk, turning pages as he walked.

"You find what you were looking for?" I said.

He certainly had.

Where was my mobile? I must have left it in Boland's car. I cursed as I squeezed into the phone booth downstairs in the library, searched for change, and jabbed out the number.

"Can you talk?"

"I have five minutes," said Fitzgerald.

I told her where I was and who I was with.

"Has he been any help?"

"Maybe," I said. "He tracked down the Mary Lynch quote. Turns out it comes from something called the Book of Sirach in the Apocrypha."

"Come again?"

"That's what I said. Seems that when the Bible was first officially put together, there were all these holy books that got left out because they weren't considered genuine. They were called the Apocrypha and that's where we get the word apocryphal, meaning made up. The story about Judith in the last letter the *Post* printed came from the Apocrypha too. That part about lying being justified in order to smite the enemy was why the Book of Judith was excluded from the official Bible. Lying didn't fit the image of God they wanted to portray — although now I think of it, that part about the Hebrew midwives lying about Moses made it in, didn't it?"

The pause was slight, but it was there.

"Is there a point to this history lesson?" she said.

"It's a message, don't you see? What the killer's saying is that *he's* not genuine either, he's apocryphal, he's not Fagan. All Fagan's quotes came from the Bible proper. Why would he change now?" The silence was longer this time. "Are you still there?"

"I'm here," said Fitzgerald. "Just thinking how I'm going to put this to Draker. He's going to love it. Do I have eyewitnesses, blood matches, a confession? No. But don't worry, sir, I have a two-thousand-year-old book that proves conclusively the killer couldn't be Ed Fagan."

Now it was my turn to go silent.

"Look, Saxon, I'm sorry," she said. "I don't mean to take it out on you. I was just pretty pointedly reminded this morning by Draker, when I confronted him about the autopsy, of how many other people there are who want my job and how much better they'd do it."

"Draker can't fire you," I said.

"He can promote me," said Fitzgerald, "and that's worse. Before I know it, I'll be one step higher up the pay scale, and handcuffed to a desk all day long, going stir crazy."

"He wouldn't do that. You're too valuable to waste away at some desk."

198

"I'm glad you're so confident. Unfortunately, you're not Assistant Commissioner of the murder squad." She yawned quietly. Lack of sleep catching up on her, especially after last night's wine. "Anyway, enough of my troubles. Shall we get back to this . . . what was it again?"

"Apocrypha," I said, "but that can wait. Tell me what you've been doing instead."

"At the scene? Well, we found the knife."

"Naturally. Fagan left one behind when he killed Tara Cox. He wiped it clean of prints first, of course."

"This one wasn't wiped," said Fitzgerald. "There was still blood on it. And fingerprints managed to lift a partial."

"You must be pleased."

"First break we've had, practically. It was Healy found it."

But was the print a mistake by the killer or another part of the game?

"You have a name yet?" I asked.

"That's another thing. She's Mary Dalton. Twenty years old. Prostitute."

"Dalton?"

"I already thought of it. First Lynch, now Dalton."

"There we were speculating what significance there was in the names of the women being Mary and we never even gave a thought to their other names. Is this part of his game as well, do you suppose, picking women with the same surnames as people on the investigation?"

"It sure ain't a coincidence."

"That means he must know who you all are."

"It's not exactly classified information," Fitzgerald pointed out. "He'd only have to read the morning papers, and we know he likes doing that."

"I guess. What does Dalton make of having his name adopted by a psycho?"

"Who knows what Dalton thinks of anything? He's too busy right now rounding up half the market traders of Dublin so that he can practise his hard cop routine on them."

"Sounds like he's getting nowhere."

"He has a few sightings of strange characters hanging round, but the times don't fit. As you said, the body must've been put there before the market opened, and the sightings were all later."

"Maybe he came back to hang around the scene," I suggested. "It wouldn't be the first time. Killers often get a kick out of being there when the body's discovered. Or say he expected it to be discovered earlier, when the market traders arrived to open up — then nothing happens. He might've got nervous and turned up to check out what went wrong."

"That was Tillman's idea too," she said.

"Tillman's down there?"

"He was, up until a few minutes ago. I called to let him know what had happened. I didn't get much of a chance to talk to him, though. He said we could go into all that later tonight. He's invited us both over to his rooms at Trinity for ten o'clock."

I snorted.

"I don't recall Tillman being the type to throw cocktail parties."

"Who said anything about cocktails? This is work. He has his profile ready for us. At least he will have, he assures me, by ten."

"That was quick work."

"He knows how little time we've got left," she said. "Don't knock it."

I looked out of the side window and saw a small line of people waiting impatiently to use the phone. How long had I been talking to Fitzgerald? Too long for their liking.

"One more thing and I'll let you go," I said. "What was the quote this time?"

"Have you a pen handy?"

"Shoot."

Professor Salvatore still had his head bent over the leatherbound book when I returned.

I handed him the slip of paper.

Stumble not at the beauty of a woman and desire her not for pleasure.

"Sirach again, same section," he replied promptly. "I was reading it whilst you were gone. It is fascinating material. You've given me a whole new line of research. Look."

He slipped the book across to me and pointed. There on the page it was. And much more where that came from. *I had rather dwell with a lion and a dragon than to keep house with a wicked woman . . . the wickedness of a woman changeth her face and darkeneth her countenance like sackcloth . . . of a woman came the beginning of the sin and through her we all die . . . give the water no passage, nor a wicked woman liberty to gad abroad . . .*

Convenient excuses, every single one, for a score of murders. And why would he stop at five with such a seemingly limitless supply of inspiration?

"This Sirach had a bit of a problem with women, didn't he?"

"Show me an Old Testament-age holy man who didn't," Salvatore said. He hesitated a moment before continuing. "Listen, I was thinking. Are you hungry? I'm hungry. I thought perhaps . . ."

I should have seen this coming.

"Professor Salvatore —"

"Max."

"Max. Look. I appreciate your offer, really, but I can't go out for dinner with you. It wouldn't be right. It's just . . . trust me, that's all, it's not such a great idea."

"You have a husband, I should have guessed. My mistake," he said. "Still, you can't blame a man for trying, no? I never could resist a pretty woman."

"No," I said. "Me neither."

CHAPTER
EIGHTEEN

Fitzgerald hadn't yet arrived when I got to Tillman's rooms at Trinity shortly before ten after another hopeless evening with the case notes brought round by Boland.

Mort let me in without a word. I was out of breath from climbing the stairs and collapsed gratefully into an armchair in the tiny sitting room, glancing round me as I did so.

"Nice place you've got here," I said.

"You think so?"

"No, I was being polite is all."

"Beggars can't be choosers," he said. "It'll do."

Aside from this small room filled with other people's furniture and lined with other people's books, there was only a door to the left which led, presumably, into a bedroom, and another doorway which revealed a narrow, dingily lit kitchen like the galley on a ship. It was, in short, the standard sub-monastic accommodation that colleges set aside for visiting academics or staff from out of town who just wanted somewhere to collapse for the night.

The only thing festive about the place was an artificial Christmas tree about one foot high sitting in a pot on the desk, draped half-heartedly with tinsel and crowned with a paper star. Someone had obviously put it up to welcome their visitor; someone with a warped idea of welcoming, that is. Still, it was more effort than I'd managed in my own apartment.

"I'll go make coffee, yeah?" said Tillman.

God bless coffee. It fills every silence.

Where the hell, I wondered, as the sound of a kettle boiling filled his cell, was Fitzgerald? I needed her to spare me from the awkwardness that was sparking between Tillman and me.

Out there by the canal where Mary Lynch died was one thing; there was enough space for everyone out in the open. In here was different. There was no escape, and neither of us had the small talk to hand to put up a pretence of normality. But that seemed to be the nature of our relationship now. There was no point mourning. Even when I'd called him earlier to pass on what I'd gleaned from Professor Salvatore, he was distant, and he certainly wasn't trying tonight as he came back with the coffee and sat hunched over it like a patient about to face the dentist's chair.

"Chill out, will you, Mort?" I said eventually. "You're making me feel almost as tense as you look."

"I didn't think anything made you tense."

"You'd be surprised. I'm human too." He looked sceptical. "Humanish, then."

He smiled faintly at that, and seemed about to say something when there was the sound of footsteps outside the door and a sharp knocking, and he rose almost reluctantly to answer it.

A moment later, Fitzgerald swept in, trailing apologies, casting her coat aside on the table and lowering herself into the chair where Tillman had been sitting.

"Busy?" I said.

"Busy doesn't begin to describe it," said Fitzgerald. "Is that coffee?"

"I'll go get you some," said Tillman and ducked into the kitchen. "You know," his voice floated back, "if it'd made things easier, I could've come round to Dublin Castle tonight instead."

"It wouldn't," Fitzgerald said, "believe me. Draker would've only started asking more questions. You being there this morning freaked him out enough as it was. Once he realised you were nosing around down in the market this afternoon too, he collared me and wanted to know all about you." She reached up as Tillman emerged from the kitchen again and took the coffee.

"Maybe he has me down as a suspect," Tillman said.

"That's not a bad idea," answered Fitzgerald. "You come to the city, first criminal profiler we've ever had about the place. Next thing, the bodies start piling up. Watch out or we'll be asking you to account for your movements soon."

"That wouldn't take long."

"I doubt Draker has the imagination to think of you as a suspect, anyway," Fitzgerald went on. "It's just that he's from the old school. What you do makes him . . ."

She searched for the right word.

"Uncomfortable?" suggested Tillman.

"More than that. Nervous. Uptight. Edgy. All of this is too out of the ordinary for him. He doesn't want any of the murderers he has to deal with getting ideas above their station. Husband beats his wife to death with a poker because she was humping the postman: that's the right sort of murder as far as Draker's concerned. All this stuff the last few days, he just sees it as a challenge to his authority. Then you come along and it's the last straw."

"These are like the arguments we used to have in the States twenty years ago. It's about time police stopped fighting every new development, stopped thinking of everything as a threat."

"You'll get no argument from me, but you've your work cut out with Draker."

"Thankfully," said Tillman bluntly, "it isn't my job to convince anyone. I'm simply here to offer my observations as asked and then it's back in my box I go. I've a public lecture to deliver in three days' time that I've barely started writing yet. You're on your own."

"Like I told you this morning," said Fitzgerald, "I'm grateful for any help you can give."

Tillman nodded, satisfied. "Then let's get started, shall we?"

He walked to the desk under the window, opened a drawer and lifted out an unexpectedly large pile of pages.

"What's that — your autobiography?" I said.

"Very funny. I just printed off a few extra copies in case they were needed."

206

He peeled off two of the printed profiles and handed them to us, stapled at the corner. The others he put down on the desk. He didn't bother lifting one for himself.

"I just want to start by stressing that these are only my preliminary observations," he said. "You shouldn't think I'm claiming anything definitive for them."

"Yeah, yeah, we know all that, Mort," I said.

"I'm saying it all the same, so there's no misunderstanding later about what I'm claiming. I'm saying it for me, not for you. These are pointers, nothing more. Are we clear?"

He was looking at Fitzgerald as he said it.

"I understand," she told him. "Just give me what you've got."

"Well, that's the problem," he said. "Normally, in a case like this, what I'd be looking for first are the characteristics of each particular crime scene. What I'd be looking for is some indication of what the offender's done and why he's done it. Why he's done things one way rather than another, that is. But we already know why this offender has done what he's done in the way that he's done it — because that's what your old friend Fagan did. He wants to be as much like the old Fagan as he can; he wants to hide behind that other Fagan."

"You're saying it's definitely *not* Fagan then?" said Fitzgerald.

"Whoa," said Tillman, "I already said there were no definites. I'm just pointing up the difficulty of trying to separate the traces of this killer from the traces of Fagan. Even if it is Fagan, he's still operating according to a pre-existing template, so it's hard to disentangle the now from the then — but I'll come to that in a minute. I just want to make things clear so I can't be accused of missing something later."

Was that a dig at me? Christ, it was about time he got over it.

"So what did the scenes tell you?" said Fitzgerald.

"Start with the basics. One, he's very familiar with those areas. He's clearly confident of coming and going without being noticed too much. He can find his way around. He knows the locations of the CCTV cameras. Has to if he wants to get in and out without being seen."

"Proper little Green Beret," I said sarcastically.

"That's probably how he likes to think of it. Each time it's like a surgical strike. And to do that, he's going to have to know these places as well as he knows his own backyard. That means he'll have spent a lot of time in the area, hanging round, driving round."

"Does he live locally?" asked Fitzgerald.

"Hard to tell, since the places where Mary Lynch and Mary" — he checked his notes — "Dalton were found are relatively far apart. But I don't think so. Not live there. He needs prostitutes, he uses prostitutes, they feed some crucial fantasy element in his life, but he wouldn't want to be contaminated by being that close to them all the time. Plus he's careful of his own security, so he's not going to take the risk of being recognised by a neighbour as someone who's using prostitutes. That would diminish his self-esteem, and this is a man for whom self-esteem will be everything.

How he appears to others matters greatly to him. His reputation. His standing in the world. He couldn't bear that to be slighted. But as I say, he needs them, so he may have a job which allows him to come into contact with them and those areas of the city."

"Taxi driver?"

"I don't think we're looking at a taxi driver, but it's tempting. He strikes at night each time, he's obviously more comfortable at night, he feels it's his domain."

"Familiar with the area, maybe works there, looks for excuses to come and go from the area, to be in contact with prostitutes. Add in the religious angle and we could be talking about Matt Stephens. He even comes there to walk his dog. At least that's what he says."

"I don't want to hear the names of suspects," Tillman said.

"Sorry," said Fitzgerald. "Go on."

"You're looking for a highly intelligent individual. Definitely someone on the same intellectual level as Fagan. He's organised, knows all about police procedure, he's confident of evading detection. He's also operating right now on high stress levels, yet the scenes feel calm, ordered, there's no panic there; he never loses control, even when he's potentially exposed to view, as he was when he killed Mary Lynch. Afterwards he's also finding it relatively easy to detach himself from what he's done, to rationalise it. I'd say he'll want to have photographs of the body as a memento, but outwardly he'll not be behaving any differently."

"Age?"

"Mid thirties, forty-ish. Again it's hard to tell because he's copying an already established pattern in Ed Fagan; Fagan's his screen, and that's the age Fagan was when he began killing. But the fact that this guy is able to do that with ease, at least so far, suggests someone older."

"*Socially invisible*," read out Fitzgerald, glancing down at her copy of Tillman's profile. "What do you mean by that?"

"Put it this way. He's not the type to start ranting and raving about prostitutes in the street. Seen from the outside, he'll be no more remarkable than I am. He's able to form relationships, he's probably married or living with a partner, though she knows nothing about what he's doing. He drives a good car, holds down a steady job, owns his own house."

So much for my suspicions about Fagan's son Jack.

"And," said Tillman, "he's killed before. That's something on which I *am* prepared to be definite. This is no beginner. No one is this good first time round."

"You know what Draker will say to that," said Fitzgerald.

"It doesn't mean it's Fagan," I said, annoyed. "We can already assume that whoever wrote those letters to Elliott probably did kill Sally Tyrrell. Why else would he have mentioned her? He probably killed Monica Lee too. Of course he's not a beginner. Right, Tillman?"

"I never believed the story about Fagan coming back," he conceded after a pause. "Serial killers don't retire, for one thing. If it is Fagan, where's he been the past five years?"

210

"Out of the country?" suggested Fitzgerald.

"It's possible," Tillman said, "but it doesn't fit. There's always degeneration, escalation. Every case I've ever worked, all the literature, it all says there should be escalation. The offender starts with a basic fantasy model and then it varies, develops, because the basic model doesn't satisfy him any more. He's been there, done that, brought home the bloodstained T-shirt. You can see that with Fagan. He starts out with a straight strangulation and a Biblical quote left in the torn lining of Julie Feeney's bag. Next time, with Sylvia Judge, the attack is more intense, her clothing is torn, and the scrap of paper with the quote on it is left inside her clothing. Next, Tara Cox is stabbed and the quote is left inside her bra. He's doing more things to the bodies each time, like he has to do worse each time to keep getting the same kick, the same return on his investment."

"But that's what's happening this time too," said Fitzgerald, confused.

"That's the point," said Tillman. "It's too perfect. Too clinical, too unemotional, too businesslike. He's just recreating what Fagan did down to the last detail. He even cut off part of Mary Dalton's hair so that she conformed to the physical archetype preferred by Fagan."

"What?" I said to Fitzgerald. "You never mentioned the hair."

"Didn't I?" she said. "Oh God, sorry. I thought I'd told you earlier on the phone. He cut it off with the knife after she died. There was blood matted in the ends of her hair. Then it looks like he took it with him. It wasn't anywhere in the storehouse where she was found."

"A trophy."

"You could see it like that," Tillman went on, "but the cutting off of the hair can't be that symbolic in itself, otherwise he'd have done it to the others as well."

"Some profilers would see it as a sign that he knew *this* victim," I said.

"Not this profiler," said Tillman. "This profiler thinks it simply fits in with the offender's desire to be seen as Ed Fagan. There have now been three killings, with only minor variations on the Fagan theme, such as the writing on the body of Mary Lynch, the quotations being taken from other sources, but that only confirms to me that he is playing out some game of his own."

"Dismembering the body in the churchyard isn't a minor variation," I pointed out.

"As to that, I tend to agree with your initial idea that the motive for removing the head was to delay identification. Or to stymie the forensics perhaps," he said. "His own DNA would have ended up under her fingernails if she scratched him; he wouldn't have taken that chance."

"That still doesn't explain the feet."

"The head was gone, the hands were gone," Tillman said coolly. "So why *not* remove the feet as well to make it seem as though the quote about Jezebel has a deeper significance?"

"You don't think there's anything to be gleaned from the quotations?"

212

"I'm not ruling it out completely. What I am saying is that these killings are being perpetrated mainly to prove a point, to play out a game. He doesn't actually believe any of that stuff about the wickedness of women and stumbling not at beauty. He feels contempt for them, sure. They're disposable. But Fagan killed prostitutes because they offended his religious sensibilities; this one kills them simply to mimic Fagan in order to outwit the cops, all the experts."

"So he doesn't want to kill women?" said Fitzgerald. "He has a funny way of showing it."

"No," Tillman stressed. "He enjoys the killing, it's a bonus to him, and that will assert itself ever more strongly the more women he kills. He will start to introduce variations and deviations, he won't be able to avoid escalation. But for now the killing isn't the point. If it was, he would've had to make things conform more closely to his own fantasies already. It's the acting out of the game, this contest of wills, of intellects, which is the point. This little innovation of his in choosing the names of people connected to the investigation confirms that much."

I wasn't convinced. "You don't think you're dismissing the significance of the Hebrew writing on Mary Lynch's body too easily?" I said.

"Of course it must mean *something*. I don't think it's part of his fantasy, that's all. I made a few enquiries of my own, just to see what the ox metaphor might mean. The best I could come up with is that the ox ploughing a field disturbs the earth in order to make it ready for new life, just like he said he was doing in his letter, making the world a better place by ridding it of sin. It's a standard mission motive scenario. It doesn't mean anything except as a statement of intent."

"You don't know that. It might be the key to this whole thing."

"OK, you have it your own way; but even if it is the key, then my guess is it's either going to be so simple that you'll overlook it completely, or so esoteric, so personal, that it's something which will only make sense in retrospect. Either way, all you'd be doing is wasting time. That's what he wants you to do, lose yourself in some artificial complexity."

Fitzgerald sighed and reached for her coffee, took a sip and realised it was cold. "So how the hell do we catch him?" she said, pulling a face and pushing the cup away.

"When's Mary Lynch's body being released for burial?"

"It'll be a while yet. There're still tests to be done."

"Pity. I'd have said have people watching the funeral. I'm sure he'd turn up for it, send flowers, maybe visit the grave later when everyone's gone home, leave a gift."

"Does the same go for the places where Fagan's other victims were killed?" I asked.

"No. He won't risk revisiting them now," Tillman insisted. "It suited the game for him to use the same places as Fagan for the first two killings, but he wouldn't carry it on once it had ceased to be his private joke. He knows now you're watching, waiting.

214

The fact that he didn't take Mary Dalton to the Law Library, like Fagan did Tara Cox, proves that. He might still try, though, to insert himself into the investigation like Fagan did. Check that out. See if there's anyone who's been asking too many questions of a member of your team. Watch out for a witness who keeps ringing up with more details that he's claiming suddenly to have remembered. He'll be obsessed by the media coverage that he's getting too. There's a possible angle."

"How?"

"Use the media against him. Plant stories. At the moment, it's all positive coverage as far as he's concerned, it's all good for his ego. But if the paper started reporting that, say, profiles suggested the killer was sexually impotent, or had a low IQ, bad body odour, then it's going to alter his cosy relationship with the media and maybe make him careless. Look how annoyed he was when Maeve Curran in the *Post* tried to psychoanalyse him. It'd be better if it came through Elliott, because he obviously has a relationship of sorts built up there."

"Elliott wouldn't do it," I said. "He wouldn't jeopardise his love-in with the killer. It's too important to him to keep the exchange going. He wouldn't want to scare him off."

"Then use other newspapers, TV, radio. Call a press conference. Say there was a witness even if you don't have one. Say you have a description, a sighting of the offender's car. Anything to make him start to doubt that he's as much in control as he likes to think."

"And then?"
"And then you wait."
We all knew what that meant.

FOURTH DAY

"God I thank thee, that I am not as other men are." But still I am beginning to grow tired of being ignored. I have explained my purpose, is that not enough? Yet all I hear is hypocritical pity for those through whom I have chosen to work the alchemy of spiritual renewal for all.

It is not as though I have made myself a menace to the innocent; "Woman is a misbegotten man and she has a faulty and deceptive nature. One must be on one's guard with every woman, as if she were a poisonous snake and the horned devil" — St Albert, our Church Father. Surely that is simple enough for you to understand?

"But they seeing see not, and hearing they hear not, neither do they understand."

I would, like Our Lord, that this cup had passed from me if possible. But it was not to be. This is my burden, I was charged with the salvation of souls, the expiation of sins, and still they speak of me as if I was some aberration of nature, some monster. And for what? For taking nothing from these filthy diseased vermin that would not be taken by time itself.

"Set thine house in order, for thou shalt die."

Is that such a complicated concept to grasp? Is it?

They should be envied, that I have chosen them, as I have chosen Nikola — there, are you satisfied now that you have a name to run after? They have escaped from two prisons, the prison of flesh and the prison of this sick lustful earth, and you dare feel sorry for them? "I had rather be a doorkeeper in the house of my God than to dwell in the tents of wickedness." God promises us that the dead shall see Him as he is after the manner of His own being. Why then should the dead be pitied? They know as truth what the wise have only guessed at for centuries.

And now they stand outside of time, as my enemies shall soon be out of time themselves. Seven days I gave and three are spent. Verily was it written: "There are nine things I have judged in my heart to be happy, and the tenth I will utter with my tongue: A man that hath joy of his children and he that liveth to see the fall of his enemy." Though that's two things, surely? Naughty Scripture, cheating like that. Honestly, you just can't trust anyone these days.

CHAPTER
NINETEEN

"Right, people," said Assistant Commissioner Draker. "As you can see, we have another communiqué from our friendly neighbourhood serial killer, Mr Fagan. You should all have a copy by now. Anyone who doesn't can pick one up from the front desk after."

Communiqué? What a dumbass word. And jabbering on still about Fagan was even dumber. Presumably if the killer said he was St Francis of Assisi, Draker would believe that too.

He was standing now in front of the map of the city, to which, I noticed, he'd added another of his little pins to represent Mary Dalton. He always liked to take meetings himself when there was progress to report, Fitzgerald once told me, but was this what he called progress?

To be honest, I was in a bad enough mood as it was without having him to contend with as well. Tillman's profile hadn't exactly delivered what I'd been hoping for; I could have given the same preliminary sketch of the killer myself. I'd been looking for more from him. Some flash. And it hadn't been there. I certainly wasn't as willing as he was to ignore the evidence of the Hebrew writing or the dismemberment of the body. It may have just been part of the game, but leads were sparse enough without dismissing the few that we had as irrelevant.

Now this. *God I thank thee, that I am not as other men are.* Was he for real? *Woman is a misbegotten man and* — Enough already. I was growing seriously hacked off with this half-baked mystic mumbo-jumbo. He didn't really believe he was on a divine mission any more than I did.

Fitzgerald had handed me a copy of the letter that morning as I arrived in the crime team room, less than an hour after she'd been having breakfast in my apartment. I'd read the single closely typewritten sheet half a dozen times since then and despair gnawed at me each time. A name, that's all there was. A less common name than before, maybe, but he wasn't making this easy.

The only possible lead I could see was that phrase about *a man that hath joy of his children.* Could it be a hidden message about Jack Mullen carrying on his father's work?

But even that was stretching it.

At least, I tried to console myself, Tillman had come down strongly against the idea of it being Fagan we were looking for, that was something; but it wouldn't be enough to convince Draker, and he'd made that plain in his opening remarks to the meeting.

He reminded me of Nick Elliott. I'd heard *him* being interviewed early that morning on one of the talk radio shows about his special relationship with Ed Fagan.

222

Did I say being interviewed? Addressing the nation was more like it. All of a sudden Elliott wasn't just some second-division crime reporter guzzling for scraps from the same trough as the rest. All of a sudden he was an expert, an authority, and boy did he wallow in it.

I'd switched off, disgusted, not least with myself. It was my fault Elliott and Draker could throw Fagan's name about so easily, and only I could make them stop. What's more, I was going to have to do it soon. If only I wasn't so afraid of what might happen when I did.

My eyes sought out Fitzgerald. There she was at Draker's side whilst he spouted inanities. She was leaning back against the desk, one hand either side of her body, grasping the edge, legs stretched out, feet crossed. She was looking at her shoes the whole time he spoke. Draker turned to her occasionally, for affirmation or support, but her shoes were just too damn fascinating each time. I liked her style. She made contempt look like concentration.

"It came in this morning's mail to Nick Elliott at the *Post*," Draker was explaining right now about the latest letter. I hadn't been listening, I realised, but I hadn't missed much. "Same postmark, same typeface, same paper. The editor had it sent round to us straight away."

At last, they were learning cooperation.

"Are they publishing it, sir?" said Lawlor.

"They've promised to hold it over for one day. That gives us twenty-four hours to track down this Nikola. We've already been in contact with Vice and the various welfare agencies to find anyone with a record of prostitution over the past few years with that name. So far, nothing."

"For all we know, she might be dead already," Dalton piped up matter-of-factly.

He was sketching spirals on the copy of the killer's letter on his knee. The page was covered with them. He didn't even raise his head as he spoke. I knew what was eating him. He was still unhappy because he'd had to go back and redo all his interviews with Mary Lynch's family and friends in an effort to try and track down her mysterious admirer Gus. He hadn't had any luck, but it was the having to do it at all which bothered Dalton more than the failure.

"Probably *is* dead," he added when he could be sure he'd got the attention of the room. "My little namesake yesterday was dead before the *Post* even hit the streets. No reason to think this one'll be any different."

"She *might* be dead," said Fitzgerald firmly, raising her head for the first time since she'd taken her perch and glaring at Dalton. "But we don't assume anyone *is* dead until they are confirmed dead by the city pathologist. He's the only one round here legally qualified to certify who's dead and who isn't. Besides, I spoke to Mort Tillman about half an hour ago . . ."

There was a low groan in the room at the sound of the profiler's name, and Draker smiled indulgently, making his own contemptuous opinion plain. So much for official appreciation of Mort's efforts. I wondered if Draker had even read Tillman's profile yet. Or if he ever would.

"That's enough," said Fitzgerald, raising her voice. "You catch this offender all by your clever selves, then you'll earn the right to turn up your noses at other methods. Till then we take expert advice where we can get it. And what Tillman says is that he won't kill this Nikola, whoever she is, before her name appears in the *Post*. He's seeking applause, validation. He needs to make it seem as if there's some two-way game going on here in which we're all equal players, hunter and hunted, quarry and prey. So he'll wait."

"Like he did with Mary D?" said Dalton.

"We didn't have prior warning about Mary Dalton because the *Post* kept it to themselves. The killer didn't expect that. How could he? You don't have to go along with it, but Tillman's theory is he'll wait this time to make sure everyone knows what he's playing at before striking. Meanwhile, we do our job. That means all of you calling in all your contacts to see if you can get a lead on this Nikola. She's out there somewhere. It might be someone with the nickname Nikola, the middle name Nikola. We know this guy has already murdered two women with surnames connecting them to this investigation, so bear that in mind too. And don't just expect the obvious. He wants to play a game against you, wants to show he's better than you. Don't prove him right."

"Well, whatever the psychologist says," said Draker, seizing his chance to wrestle back control from Fitzgerald, and managing to make psychologist sound like it was something equivalent to snake-charmer, and equally as useful to the investigation, "it's not going to help us trudge through the evidence any quicker. What about that? Have we got anything at all on the latest victim since yesterday?"

There followed the most depressing part of the meeting. So far, the investigation into Mary Dalton's death had been as fruitless as that into Mary Lynch's. Door-to-doors had failed to uncover a single person who had heard or seen anything unusual on the night she died, much less a witness who had observed her with a possible suspect, or even noticed her at all. We were dealing with the same ghost who came and went without leaving a trace.

Mary Dalton herself was almost as invisible. Hers was a familiar story, mapped out now in retrospect in little more than a list of summonses, court appearances, short stints in Mountjoy Prison, all for relatively minor offences linked to her need to feed her drug habit. She'd even worked as a lap dancer for a time at one of the clubs that were springing up around the city, though she'd been sacked when her pretty obvious status as an addict started putting off the punters, bless their high standards. It certainly didn't take long to summarise her career.

And that was it, was it, the sum total of a life? It seemed so. Then finally it was over, as Lynch's latest autopsy showed, with multiple stab wounds to the body followed by a single expert stroke to sever the jugular, leading to massive and fatal blood loss — exactly like Tara Cox.

As for her boyfriend/pimp, if he knew anything about what had happened to Mary, he wasn't telling; and according to Sean Healy, who took the man's statement detailing when and where he last saw Mary alive, he didn't seem too troubled by it.

His alibi wasn't convincing either, but I doubted that he was the killer. Whoever wrote those letters and killed these women was methodical, attentive, intelligent, like Tillman's profile said. Mary Dalton's boyfriend, by contrast, was as unstable as a homemade explosive. He had a conviction dating back seven years for attacking a barmaid with a broken bottle; another time he'd been hauled in for an assault on a previous girlfriend, though she'd been too frightened to press charges. Violence was encoded in his being; he couldn't hide it.

"What about the print on the knife?" someone asked eventually.

"It's being run against the files this morning," said Draker.

"And the cord round her neck, sir?"

"Same sort that was used to strangle Mary Lynch," he said. "Standard garden twine, available all over. That's a dead loss. We'll never trace it back to a particular batch."

Draker didn't bother asking Boland or me how we'd got on at Tom Fuller's house, or what progress had been made in identifying the body in the churchyard. In fact, he barely acknowledged our presence at all. And that suited me just fine. I wasn't here to earn his respect or approval. Added to which, I wasn't quite sure *what* I made of the Susan Fuller angle yet.

Sure, she matched plenty of the criteria. She was the right age, thereabouts; right build; she'd disappeared at roughly the right time. She was healthy too, a non-smoker, had never had any children, and she had a comparable fracture to that on the body of the murdered woman, though without the X-rays from her medical records that was still only anecdotal and Lynch was still having trouble tracking down her doctor. Plus there was no one else on missing persons who matched, at least no one whose disappearance couldn't be better accounted for some other way.

And yet, it didn't feel right somehow. Susan Fuller didn't fit any of the potential victim profiles, and the only scenarios I could weave around Tom Fuller as a suspect were so off the wall that I would've been embarrassed to share them with Draker even if he'd asked.

I'd been through them all in my head late last night as Fitzgerald slept fitfully beside me. I didn't want to get up in case I disturbed her; all I could do was lie there and think.

Just say, was what I thought, that Fuller had killed his wife, either accidentally during a quarrel or premeditatedly. He's an intelligent man. He knows that if he reports her missing and the body is subsequently found, then the police are going to start sniffing round his wife's history and it won't be long before they have a motive. Susan wasn't exactly the forsaking all others type, and Tom had a reputation for jealousy. So, perhaps he decides, why not let someone else take the rap for it? Someone like Fagan; and carefully he starts laying plans for Fagan's comeback; storing Susan's body in the freezer at the bottom of the garden until the time is right to dump her remains, by which time her death should simply be chalked up to her old lover. Make Susan's murder part of a series, after all, and there's less chance of the police looking at each individual killing, not for a while anyway. They'll see the whole, not the parts. But then the more the plan takes shape, the more Tom Fuller realises what a talent and a thirst he has for killing . . .

I'd put these pieces together forensically in the dark inside my head last night. I knew it answered plenty of the questions that the killings were posing. There was only one problem.

I didn't buy a word of it.

Out in the corridor again after the meeting, lighting a cigar for familiarity's sake after that unfriendly place, I turned on my mobile and found a message waiting from Lawrence Fisher.

I called him back at once. Fisher was a busy man. He never just called to pass the time of day. Never just called *me*, that is.

It was hard to figure out where he was when I finally got through, but it sounded hollow, echoing, noisy. There was a murmur of crowds. And was that a tannoy in the background?

"I heard you teamed up with Tillman again," he said when he recognised who it was. He sounded amused.

"I wouldn't exactly call it teaming up," I said. "And how come you're so knowledgeable, anyway? You boys been talking about me behind my back?"

"Would you mind if we did?"

"What is it they say?" I answered. "It's not when people talk about you that you should worry, it's when they stop talking about you."

"You didn't hear what we said."

"Same difference. But you didn't call to tell me that. Not when you could be opening a supermarket somewhere."

"I have never opened a supermarket in my life," said Fisher, pretending to be offended. "They couldn't pay me enough, for one thing. No, I just wanted to let you know that I may have something for you off the computer records." A pause. "Are you still there?"

"I'm here," I said. "Stunned, but here."

"Why stunned? You're not saying you didn't expect me to find anything, are you? Because if you are, why the hell did you get me to put in all the details in the first place?"

"Just fishing," I said. "And a good job I did too if you've come up with something. Are you going to tell me what it is, or do I have to come over there and beat it out of you?"

"I'll tell you," he said quickly. "From anyone else, I'd take that threat as rhetorical. From you, I know you mean it."

"You'd better believe it."

"But I'm still not telling you right away. Not over the phone. I'll tell you when I see you. I'm on my way over now."

"You're coming to Dublin?"

"That's where you are, isn't it?" Fisher replied. "Where else would I be coming over to?"

"No need to be smart," I said. "I was surprised, that's all. At least that explains what all the noise is behind you. You're at the airport. What time's your flight?"

"Five minutes. I'll be there within the hour."

"You don't give people much warning."

"That's what happens when you have your mobile switched off. I've been trying to get you for the last hour. You wouldn't . . ."

"Pick you up? Of course I'll pick you up. Is that what all the secrecy's about then, Fisher — making sure you get a free lift out of me in return for your information?"

Fisher laughed.

"Well, where's the fun of claiming expenses for taxis if you actually take the taxis?"

CHAPTER
TWENTY

I set off straight away. This time of morning, I'd be lucky to make it across town and find a parking space before Fisher's plane landed. It only took an hour to fly from London.

It was ten minutes alone before I got down Dame Street and crossed the river. Roadworks, according to the notices, though I couldn't see any sign of work going on.

I switched on the radio briefly to catch the traffic update, vainly hoping, like thousands of others, that I'd find the one secret road in the city where cars ran as free as wild stallions. Instead I found myself happening upon a discussion of the Night Hunter case. Their phrase, not mine.

Some feminist was blaming the murders on provocative images of women in the media and the low economic value placed on women's work; another guest had concluded that the slippage in sexual morality since the sixties had made the murders inevitable. The killer would have been proud of that analysis. He had seen the ungodly flourishing like a green bay tree too.

It was always the same story. No matter what happened, those with an axe to grind invariably decided it proved they'd been right all along. Fancy that. I held on until a caller asked the radio panellists what they thought of his theory that the murders were the work of an inner circle of top judges and politicians before realising I preferred the sound of angry horns outside.

I made it to the airport with fifteen minutes to spare, reflecting, as I climbed out of my Jeep in the short-stay car park and made my way across to the terminal, on the irony of modern travel: you can be halfway round the world in the same time it takes to get in and out of the city at rush hour. Airports always make me restless like that. The world seems so close at hand.

All I had to do was get on a plane and I could be back home in Boston in time for dinner if I wanted. Filling up on Mexican food at the Border café, drinking in the Gargoyle —

No. Best not get started on that again.

The arrivals board said Fisher's plane was on schedule, so I simply grabbed a coffee from the nearest kiosk, found a seat and waited.

Twenty minutes and three coffees later, Lawrence Fisher was coming down the escalator, clutching a briefcase and glancing round for me. What about that? He *had* put on weight.

His hair was thinning out slightly too, and there was more grey in his beard than I remembered, but he still looked good, still looked attractive enough in that rumpled, abstracted way of his, still carried himself with that air of confidence which only came from years of being indispensable. He smiled when he saw me and quickened his step.

"Saxon, you're here."

He didn't bother with a handshake. I appreciated that. I hate that sort of starchy formality.

"You're observant as ever, Fisher. Good flight?"

"As good as any flight can be considering that you're flying thousands of feet above the ground, vulnerable to being sent plunging earthwards by a stray bird in the engine, terrorist bombs, pilot error, ice on the wings, passengers with air rage . . ."

"Everyone has to go some time."

"I'd rather go with my feet on solid ground," said Fisher. "Better still, with my feet on a mattress and me fast asleep."

"Stop whining. You're here in one piece. You need to pick up any bags before we go?"

"It's all here." He held up the briefcase. "I'm flying back tonight at ten. Just in and out this time, as the bishop said to the actress."

We made our way through the crowds of fortunate people waiting for flights out of the city, and soon were easing into the familiar traffic to start the slow crawl back into town.

There was nothing I could do to quicken up the journey, so I cut to the chase and asked Fisher to fill me in on what he'd found.

"I was hoping we could have breakfast first."

"With this traffic, you'll be lucky to get breakfast before nightfall," I said. "You might as well use the time constructively. I never was one for small talk."

"That's an understatement," said Fisher.

"Then what have you got to lose?"

So Fisher told me that he'd fed the details of the killing of Mary Lynch and the discovery of the body of the woman in the churchyard into Scotland Yard's computer database, as I'd asked him to do, and last night he'd been rewarded with a tentative match.

A prostitute by the name of Ellen Shaw had been working a night shift behind King's Cross station in London in January when she'd been approached on foot by a punter with an Irish accent who offered her £100 — well above her usual rate, King's Cross being about as classy a pitch in the vice hierarchy as the Grand Canal — if she'd come back to his bedsit.

"She agreed?"

"It was late," Fisher explained, "she hadn't had a punter for a while, it was snowing, cold, the money was good. And you know how it is with these women. When they're desperate, they take risks. So she walked round with him towards Camden, not far, to some old house that had been hacked up into bedsits. They climbed the stairs to the second floor, he unlocked the door, she stepped in. Next thing she felt was a cloth over her mouth and nose and she blacked out."

"Chloroform?"

"Something like that. When she came to, she found herself tied by the hands and ankles and gagged; she was naked and lying on a filthy mattress in the middle of the room, and the walls were plastered with religious prints, pictures of the Crucifixion, quotations from the Bible."

"Nice decor."

"Totally freaked her out, as you can imagine," said Fisher. "She didn't even know how long she'd been unconscious — it was still dark outside the window, but was it two hours, twenty-four? — and her head was aching from whatever it was he'd knocked her out with. She was drifting in and out of sleep, shivering with fear, cold. Remember it was winter. Then *he* came in."

"The Irish entry for the world psychopath games?"

"The very one. He had a Bible with him and he started reading out loud from it; some bull about angels and sin and death, whispering to start with, getting louder, getting excited. Then he raped her, and, whilst he was raping her, he started to strangle her as well."

"And they say romance is dead."

I watched the normal world go on outside the windscreen and wondered, not for the first time, how normal it really was.

"Did he use a ligature?" I asked.

"A tie," Fisher explained. "She blacked out pretty quickly, but he simply brought her round and started again, the same routine. It happened a few times, she didn't remember exactly how many, then she felt the cloth over her mouth like before and she was out cold again. Glad to be out too, as she put it. When she woke next time, she was untied, though still naked. She got up, tried the door, it was unlocked, so she ran out down the stairs to the floor below, where she knocked at a door until someone answered and they called the police. One lucky woman."

"Oh, I'm sure she felt *very* lucky," I said sharply.

"Lucky to be alive is what I meant," said Fisher.

236

"I know what you meant," I said. "Sorry, OK? Don't listen to me. I'm just taking out my frustration. Go on. What did the police in London get from their investigation?"

"Not a thing," said Fisher. "Lots of names of possible suspects, but none of them checked out. There was plenty of DNA evidence in the bedsit and on Ellen Shaw too, but again no match. And there were fingerprints. He'd made no effort to be careful about covering his tracks. Police put out a photofit, some calls came in from people who thought they might know him, but in each case the suspect had moved on. Police did find out that he'd done the same thing to two other prostitutes in other parts of the city, and probably more in my opinion; he had a well-established routine. But neither of the two women had bothered reporting the attacks at the time."

"That's not so unusual," I said, thinking of Jackie, thinking of the similarities to what had happened to her down by the canal a couple of weeks before Mary Lynch died, and pulling out abruptly at the same time to overtake a bus which had suddenly stopped without indicating to pick up passengers. "Going to the police only brings more trouble sometimes."

"That's what the two women said."

"Did police find the places where the others were attacked?"

"Both. Like I said, this attacker wasn't taking any precautions; he didn't care if the women led police back to his little den because he didn't intend hanging around afterwards."

"What about Ellen Shaw's clothes?"

"Never found. Nor those of the other women. It seems like he was coming into an area, renting a bedsit, paying cash up front for a month ahead. After a couple of weeks, when he could be sure the cash was gone and couldn't be traced back to him, he'd invite the latest woman back to the bedsit, drug her, tie her up, do his little biblical prophet act on her and then be gone, on to the next bedsit to start all over again. The police have no idea how many times he'd done it before Ellen, but afterwards there were no more. No more reported, I should say."

"You don't think he stopped?"

"This offender wasn't going to stop," said Fisher. "Quite the opposite. He was getting too much out of it, too much pleasure, and the violence was worse with Ellen Shaw than it had been with the others. Classic escalation pattern. It could only get worse."

"Murder?"

"It seemed like the obvious next step. Instead, things went quiet."

"Then I contacted you."

"And out of the blue we have an actual murderer with an Irish connection, a religious fixation, a thing for strangling with a ligature — oh, and he'd cut off bits of their hair too, like this latest woman of yours, Mary Dalton, did I mention that? Plus you carelessly drop Jack Mullen's name into the conversation, and what do I find but that he left London in September, eight months after Ellen Shaw was attacked and three months before Mary Lynch was murdered."

"He was escalating to murder in London but reached it in Dublin?"

"It's a possibility," Fisher replied. "Enough of one that I had to follow it up, at any rate. If I can get a photograph of Mullen from you, and the police in London get a visual ID from Ellen Shaw and the others, then we can probably move to force a DNA sample out of him."

I said nothing.

"What's wrong?" asked Fisher.

"Mullen might be," I said. "Wrong for us, that is. He claims to have an alibi for Mary Lynch."

"Alibi schmalibi," said Fisher. "DNA's what matters. Fingerprints are what matters. If we can get a match on him for the attacks in London, how long is his alibi going to stand up?"

"You're right," I conceded. "I told you there was something wrong with me today. Your being here might be just what I need to slap me out of it. But you know, you didn't have to fly in personally to get a photograph of Mullen. I'd have couriered one over for you."

"And missed my chance of seeing your happy smiling face again? How could I? To be honest, you should be thanking me. If it hadn't been for me, you would have been landed with Inspector Taylor, undisputed winner of Scotland Yard's most charmless detective competition. He's been handling the Ellen Shaw case from the beginning and it was all I could do when I told him there was a possible suspect not to get on the first plane over here to see what you had."

"Seeing what we have wouldn't have taken long," I said.

"One of those cases, is it?"

"It's always one of those cases."

"Then here's hoping I might be able to make it that bit easier," he said. He glanced briskly out of the side window. "Haven't we just missed the turn-off?"

Where was my head at? I'd been concentrating so much on what Fisher was telling me, I'd completely missed the turning into Dublin Castle. Come to think of it, I couldn't even remember crossing the river. Impatient with myself, I found a gap, turned and went back.

Something was going on, I could sense it the moment I pushed at the swing doors and shepherded Fisher into reception. A barely contained air of — what? Excitement, that was it.

"Lawlor!"

A figure was dashing by. Shouting was the only way to drag it back. Lawlor turned reluctantly, even more reluctantly when he saw it was me.

"What's happening?"

"Haven't you heard?" said Lawlor. "We got a fingerprint match from the knife that killed Mary Dalton."

"Who is it?"

"It's Fagan, of course," he said. "Looks like you were wrong all along, eh? Still, that's what comes of being out of the game too long. You get rusty."

"But Fagan's dead," I said, realising as I said it how stupid it must sound.

"Well, we'll just have to write out an arrest warrant for a zombie, won't we?" laughed Lawlor, and then he was gone, smirking back over his shoulder.

Fisher whistled.

"This is like that old Chinese curse. May you live in interesting times, isn't that how it goes? Saxon? Saxon, where are you going? *Saxon!*"

CHAPTER
TWENTY-ONE

I walked. I left my Jeep and walked. I had no sense of where I was going, I just needed to get away. Rain was falling, and the Christmas lights looked pale and washed out. It was gloomier than usual for a late morning, even in Dublin, and my mood only made it seem gloomier still.

An awareness of each place that I passed brushed against my mind as I walked, but only brushed. A dour church on the corner of Fenian Street; a gasometer not far past Misery Hill (I smiled grimly at the street signs. God obviously did have a sense of humour). Then what was this? Of course, the water, and now I was looking across towards the North Wall Quay without any memory of the streets between. I doubled back to cross the river at the bridge.

I considered walking east to where the city expired into warehouses and shipping ports and the stench of oil, but there was something bleak out there that, even in my present mood, I didn't want to indulge. I might be weary of people at times, perhaps most of the time, but at that moment I wanted them round me all the same. I couldn't face the ghost-town emptiness of the docks. I needed to know the city was still there. Enough had changed in recent days.

Once over the water, I went west instead, through the back streets to Connolly Station, then north to Portland Row and Mountjoy Square, just like I'd done relentlessly when I first came to the city. Walking was the only way to understand how a city worked, how its parts knitted together. Today, though, the litany of familiar names and sights, the rituals of rain and shadow, offered no comfort. Today they only made me edgier still.

The world was disintegrating about me, and I was caught in the collapse. My skin tingled with the proximity of possible danger. I could almost sense Ed Fagan walking beside me, falling into step. I'd never be rid of him.

Time and again, I forced my brain to drag itself back to basics. Deliberately, forensically, I conjured up the image of Fagan dying, of Fagan dead. I had buried Fagan, there was no getting away from that; this wasn't some movie, he wasn't going to claw his way out of the soil after my back was turned, to make the paying audience jump in the final reel.

Fagan was dead.

I needed to fix that thought.

Fagan.

Was.

Dead.

That was the trick with any investigation. If you kept repeating simple facts, a pattern would emerge. It was bound to. It might not give you the name you were looking for, or a face, but it would make an offender-shaped hole at the centre of things into which someone, somewhere could eventually be inserted.

That wasn't happening now, and it wasn't happening because it couldn't. The offender-shaped hole at the centre of this investigation was hiding a ghost, and ghosts don't stalk and murder the living. But no matter how often I reminded myself of that fact, my brain would not compute it and kept tormenting me instead with images of Fagan around me in the city.

Every face I passed seemed to resemble his, every voice echoed his; every laugh made me turn my head in alarm. I wondered if this was how people went mad, if this was how it started, when reality and fantasy made war inside your skull and ended up cancelling one another out.

And the further I walked — round the City Basin and down to the Wellington Monument; back across the river eventually to Clancy Barracks and Kilmainham — the more unstable my thoughts became. Fractured. Splintering. I almost found myself growing angry with Fagan. He didn't even have the decency to stay dead. A man should know when he's beaten.

I must have been walking two hours before the motion finally got through to me, before that rhythm, that systematic step after aching step, managed to instill some order again into my thoughts.

Slowly, possibilities returned, and I was able to sift through them, discarding what didn't feel right, hoarding what remained, like a miser counting her gold to see how it added up.

First possibility: the fingerprints were forged.

That was once considered impossible, even by fingerprint experts, which only proves how little faith you should have in experts. Experts always say something's impossible until someone else does the hard work for them and figures out how it's done.

But who would have the know-how in Dublin to forge Fagan's prints? This wasn't New York, for Christ's sake.

OK then. So not forged. Second possibility: the knife must have once belonged to Fagan himself and been used by the killer to murder Mary Dalton simply to throw police off the scent.

Didn't matter that Fagan was five years dead. Fingerprints were practically eternal; they've been lifted from Egyptian papyrus thousands of years old. And a knife belonging to Fagan wouldn't be so hard to come by either. Fagan's house had been sold off a couple of years after he went missing, and there'd been an auction of his entire belongings round about the same time. Someone might have bought the knife then.

I'd once read too that there was quite a trade on the Internet these days in mementoes of murder. Murderabilia it was called. Locks of Charles Manson's hair; paving stones from the path where OJ's wife was butchered; you name it. Sales were so brisk that as soon as police had finished examining the house in England where Fred and Rose West tortured and killed nine women, it was taken apart, stone by stone, and ground to dust to stop relics ending up on the market.

Would it be possible after all this time to track down who had bought Fagan's belongings? Perhaps — but it'd take months, and there was no knowing how many times the stuff had been sold on since. The knife might have had a hundred owners since it last rested in Fagan's hand.

Third possibility: the knife was the very same one Fagan had used on Tara Cox, and it had been lifted by the killer from the evidence store down in the vaults at Dublin Castle.

An inside job.

Was that possible? Of course. But risky. Whoever had left the knife at the market alongside Mary Dalton's body would have to be confident no one would be suspicious enough to order further tests. And there was another flaw. Only someone on the inside could get their hands on the knife, but anyone on the inside would know there was enough suspicion around that the truth could eventually emerge. Or did the killer agree that it was time for the Fagan charade to end?

I shook my head irritably.

I could go on walking the rest of the day, circumnavigate the whole damn city, wear my shoe leather out on every street, and the answer still wouldn't come to me.

What mattered right now wasn't figuring out the game. What mattered was putting a stop to it, or at least to this stage of the game. I'd known this morning that it was time. All I needed was the courage. Easier said than done.

I was south of the river now, headed back into town. Best place for what I had planned. This was where I felt most at ease, and being at ease was what it took to be invisible.

Check the time.

Two o'clock.

Fisher was flying back at ten. Time enough to take things slowly.

Might as well make a day of it then, I thought; and I went into the nearest bar, one I'd never seen the inside of before, took a place at the counter and ordered a drink.

It was one of those hopeless, dingy, smoked-out places where men with nothing better to do congregated joylessly to drink, out of sight of women and world. They hadn't exactly fallen silent as I came in, like regulars at the saloon in an old western when the stranger rides into town, but I could feel their eyes on me. Half curious, half resentful, as the barman brought me my beer.

I felt no hostility towards them, these ayatollahs hiding out in their cave as the territory which they once considered theirs alone shrank to the size of a room. It was their city too. They had a right to do whatever it was made it bearable for them. I just didn't have the energy to waste mourning with them.

Instead I lit a cigar and set about finding out what the bottom of my glass looked like. Something about me — something maybe about the practised, leisurely way I set to the joint task of drinking and ignoring them; maybe just something about the way I looked — must have reassured the ayatollahs that I was no threat, for I quickly sensed their attention wearing thin.

I ordered another drink, and looked round for a phone.

"Saxon, how's it going?" said Fitzgerald when I got through.

"I've been better."

She sounded excited, out of breath. I recognised that giddy restlessness that comes when you think you're closing in. I hated what I had to do to her.

"We're missing you here," she said.

"I doubt that," I said. "I'm not the most popular girl in town, you know what I'm saying? And I'll be even less popular if I come down there and start trying to spoil the party."

"Why would you want to spoil it?"

"Because the print is bullshit," I said. "It has to be. I've been thinking it out. Someone on the inside must've planted it, it's the only possibility that makes sense. Either that or the killer managed to get hold of something Fagan once owned."

Silence.

"Are you listening to me?" I pressed.

"I'm listening," she said, "but what do you expect me to do? Ignore the evidence?"

"Think about it," I said. "Wouldn't you expect there to be more than just one print? One partial print? If Fagan was there when Mary Dalton died? Plenty of

248

prints from the killer I understand, none I understand better. But why only one? He never left any before."

"What I expected to find doesn't matter," Fitzgerald said firmly, though I could hear the trace of doubt in her voice. "What matters is what the evidence says. You can come up with all the theories you want, but in the end . . . you know, maybe you just have to face the possibility that it is Fagan. You ever think that maybe, just once, you could be wrong? It has to happen sometime."

"It's not Fagan," I said. "I'm not wrong about that. I might not know what the story is with the print, but I know Fagan isn't out there playing with us. Someone else is. Maybe someone closer to home than you like to think."

"What does that mean?" she said.

"Don't you think it's too convenient, finding Fagan's prints just now? It makes everyone's job a hell of a lot easier if they get to pretend to themselves that the murderer is who the whole city wanted it to be from the start. You can see how badly Draker wants it to be Fagan."

"You're not saying Draker planted the knife?" said Fitzgerald. "It was found before he even reached the scene. Besides, Draker's a pain in the butt, but he'd not do that."

"I didn't say I thought it was Draker," I said. "OK, maybe I did. But there are others. Dalton, Lawlor . . ."

Fitzgerald sighed loudly.

"Why don't you come in and we can talk about this?"

"I don't feel up to it," I said. "Not today. You're going to have to cover for me. I need to think. Just do something for me?"

"Out with it."

"Look, Grace, I'm not saying the knife isn't important. Just check it against the inventory taken from Fagan's crime scenes; also against the lists of what was in the house."

"What house?"

"Fagan's house."

The pause was fractional, but it was there.

"I'll do it," she said, "but don't get your hopes up. I know how much you wanted Fagan to be dead. I wanted him dead too, but maybe we both have to face the fact that he got away, and just make sure he doesn't get away this time. I'm not saying it's not hard."

You have no idea how hard, I said to myself. To her, all I said was: "I'll be fine. I just need today to think."

"I'll tell everyone you're not feeling well."

"If anyone asks. Like I say, I'm not exactly Ms Popularity down there." She didn't contradict me. "Here, I have to go," I said. "I'm meeting up with Fisher later to see what he's dug up, and there's a few things I need to sort out before then. Catch you later?"

My drink was waiting when I got back to the counter, but I needed to move on. I paid up and made my way out into the street. Keep moving back towards the centre, that was the plan.

First stop, another bar. A little higher up the evolutionary chain this time. And that's how the day panned out. Drinking, walking, smoking, moving closer to the centre each time.

I ate a sandwich in one. Couldn't say what was in it. I was just going through the motions. And as I drank, I reflected on the irony of what I was doing. Tillman's profile said the killer was using alcohol to stabilise himself too, to prepare himself for each killing, to put him in control, and here I was doing the same thing.

Idly, I wondered what else we had in common, but I wasn't going down that road. It was the differences between people that mattered, not the superficial similarities, and the difference between this killer and me was as wide as that between the dark and the day.

As I left the third (or was it the fourth?) bar, I noticed it was growing grey. Above my head fairy lights danced down the narrow curve of Wicklow Street, swaying and rattling in a cold breeze. This was how a day faded to nothing, if you weren't careful. Drinking, then dark.

But I knew what I was doing; I knew what I had to do. The time was close now. I took my place again, unobtrusively, in a booth at a bar I'd chosen specially for the job.

It was a place I knew well, I drank here all the time, which was why I guessed no one would take any notice of me. It was strangers who got remembered. They stuck out.

I put on my gloves and drank coffee, eavesdropping on the conversation of the woman in the next booth.

Megan had sneaked away early from the office. She was meeting Mark later. She didn't know if it was going to work out with Mark, but what the hell, you were only young once. Did Brenda want another one? Brenda wasn't sure. "Go on, be a devil," said Megan, and Brenda was in a devilish mood. Megan rose to squeeze out from the table, still talking as she went.

Women talk too much. I'm allowed to say that, being one. And sometimes it's as well they do. The eye, after all, sees less when the tongue is in fifth gear.

I glanced back briefly at her trying to catch the attention of the barman as I stepped out of the warmth once more into the street. I wished Megan well. I didn't give much to her chances with Mark, in all honesty, but what the hell, right?

How long would it be before she noticed her mobile phone was gone?

Long enough for me.

I stifled a giggle. Didn't want to draw attention to myself. I'd had too much to drink, obviously; but I do worry myself at times, the ease with which I can turn to crime when I have to.

Still, every girl needs a career to fall back on. And what was the alternative? I couldn't risk buying a phone that could be traced back to me. Couldn't go into a store and risk turning up on CCTV. I only hoped Megan was insured against theft; and if not, well, she'd just have to make her own involuntary contribution to the murder squad's latest investigation.

I found a quiet place halfway between Wicklow Street and my apartment, and turned on the phone. Just another shopper making a call. Hi, honey, home soon. It was awkward with gloves, but fingerprints had got me into enough trouble that day.

Elliott's boyfriend liked text messages. Let's see how he liked this one.

It was time for Fagan to come home.

CHAPTER
TWENTY-TWO

I half expected to find the police waiting to arrest me when I got back to my apartment. Stupid thought — if they were that good, they would have tracked down Fagan's doppelgänger already and I wouldn't have had to do this — but I was used to stupid thoughts by now. All that waited for me was a message from Fisher telling me where I could catch him later, if I wanted, if I was free.

I took off my clothes and stepped into the shower, turned the water as hot as I could bear, then stood still, eyes tight, as the bad aura of the day washed off me and into the drain.

My nerves shrieked at first, then got used to it. There's a neat metaphor for life. What you think you can't bear, you always can, and then some.

Finished, I wrapped a towel around myself and lay on the bed, shut my eyes. Slept; I must have done, for the day felt different when I opened them again, and I was almost cold.

I realised I hadn't eaten since breakfast, apart from that unconvincing excuse for a sandwich which had appeared at one of the day's bars, and only half of that.

What had breakfast been, anyway? Black coffee and dry toast. Hardly the Ritz.

I found myself missing the smell of baking bread that lingered in the streets when I went walking round dawn; missing too the afternoon walk down Clarendon Street to the shop that sold fresh pasta; then there was the Greek place on the river where I sometimes met Fitzgerald after she'd finished with work and I'd finished pretending I had any to do, and where we were so familiar that they hardly now needed to take our order. The spectacle of the dead, and the dead to come, had taken the pleasure out of all those little everyday rituals around which I'd built my life of late, and now I longed for them with a renewed ache, like I was homesick for my old life.

In the end, I pulled on the first clothes that came to hand and padded through on bare feet to the kitchen, cracked and whisked some eggs and made myself an omelette, then sat in front of the TV with the plate on my lap, flicking channels aimlessly.

The phone rang sharply like an alarm after a while, and I switched the mute button to silence the *I Love Lucy* rerun which I now realised I'd been watching without noticing I was watching it, and waited for the answering machine to kick in.

"Saxon, are you there?"

Fitzgerald.

"Look, give me a call, all right? Soon as you get in. It's important. You'll have to get me on my mobile number, I won't be in the office. I'll explain later when we speak. Bye."

Click.

I found myself missing Fitzgerald. It was that *bye* which did it. It felt like for ever since we'd had any time to ourselves, since we were just ourselves, nothing between us.

No, it was longer than for ever. It was another life.

O'Dwyer's, not far from Baggot Street. Another bar. Fisher was sitting at the counter with a pint of Guinness to hand, looking at a copy of that morning's *Post*. He'd obviously only just arrived himself, even though I was fifteen minutes late. His hair was wet; he was out of breath; skin slightly flushed; coat still on. Put him near the fire and he'd have steamed.

"The newspapers certainly love a good murder," he noted wryly as I slipped sideways on to a bar stool next to him.

"That's entertainment," I said. "It's what happens when you make celebrities of serial killers. It becomes self-fulfilling."

"They kill in order to get the media coverage. Is that what you think is happening here?"

"I don't have the first clue what's happening here," I said, "and right now I don't give a shit. No, I don't mean that. Obviously I give a shit. I just wish . . ."

"What?"

"That I was somewhere else," I said. "Someone else."

"You're stressed out, nothing odd about that," said Fisher. "Stands to reason. After all this is over, you should take a holiday. Fly back to the States."

256

When all this is over, I thought bitterly, I'm more likely to be in jail, but I avoided the thought by reaching into my pocket for change as the barman brought me a pint, the twin to Fisher's own, without being asked.

"Don't worry about that," said Fisher. "You can put it on my tab, Joe."

"You've been in Dublin all of a day and you've already established a tab?" I said. "I'm impressed." I raised my Guinness and took a sip. "I'd say Joe's impressed too."

"Joe's a barman. Barmen are impressed by nothing," said Fisher. "They've seen it all before. Anyway, this isn't exactly my first time in Dublin, you know. I spent some time here filming my last series. I've been here for the odd weekend too with Ellen."

"Laura."

"Just testing to see if you remembered."

"No time for sightseeing this trip," I observed, taking another slow sip at my drink, determined to make it last. I'd had enough today already; a hangover was the last thing I needed.

"You can say that again," said Fisher. "I spent most of the day trying to track down anyone who knows about Mullen, but the whole place is buzzing with this print they've found of Fagan's. It wasn't possible to get much information out of anyone."

"They'll get over it soon enough," I said. "Soon as they work out the print's a plant."

"Yes, I could tell you weren't exactly overjoyed about that earlier."

I felt a twinge of guilt.

"Sorry," I said. "About running out on you like that this morning. It's just . . . well, seven days, that's all we had. And the killer knows it. He's the one who made it seven days. Planting the print was a smart move. Planting the print made it one less day. Tipped the scales even more in his favour than they were already. And I don't hear you disagreeing."

"I don't like the print either," he agreed. "It's too easy. Too convenient. I'm not so sure you'll only lose one day over it, though. From what I saw today, it'll take a miracle to persuade them it isn't Fagan now."

"Miracles happen," I said.

Careful. Dangerous territory. But Fisher gave no sign of having noticed.

"In the end, I gave up," he was saying. "I got my photograph, read Mullen's file, then went round to see Mort Tillman instead. He's got his first public lecture the day after tomorrow; he told me he'd like to bounce a few ideas off me."

"Did he show you the profile while he was at it?"

"To be honest, it was hard to get him to talk about anything else. Having got me there, I'm not sure he mentioned his lecture at all. This case is really eating at him."

"Tillman was always like that when he worked a case," I said, rummaging through my pockets for matches to light a cigar. "He never could switch off."

"Maybe you shouldn't have asked him."

"You were the one who suggested I ask him," I pointed out.

"I know." It was Fisher's turn to look guilty now. "I was buried under a heap of work, I didn't know what else to say. After what happened, I just wonder if it's all too much for him."

"The White Monk case? That was ten years ago, for Christ's sake."

"No," said Fisher, "I mean after what happened in Notre Dame." He must have seen the bemused look that came into my face. "You didn't hear? Jesus, me and my big mouth."

"You may as well tell me now."

"Tillman got suspended from his job last summer. That was why he came over here. Dublin isn't exactly the centre of the academic criminal psychology world, you know. Didn't you wonder what he was doing here instead of back in the States? This is all he was offered."

"I never thought," I said, feeling bad again. "What happened?"

"Some allegation of sexual harassment is what I heard."

"Sexual harassment? Tillman? That's ridiculous."

Fisher held up his hands in submission. "I'm only telling you what happened, I'm not saying I agree. Here," he added, catching sight of his own empty glass, "do you want another?"

"I'm good, and you can wait. Tell me about Tillman."

"There was a student in his class, some first-year scatterbrain killing time on Daddy's money, you know the type. Tillman gave her an F. Next thing you know, she's claiming Tillman's picking on her because she refused to sleep with him."

"And the college believed that Tillman would throw away years of his career over some little tootsie who can't even pass first-year psychology?"

"It didn't matter what they believed," said Fisher. "What mattered was they were wetting themselves at the potential bad publicity. Her father was one of their biggest benefactors."

"So they dump him?"

"Self-preservation," said Fisher. "Name of the game."

"Then the game stinks. Tillman's no sexual harasser."

"Well, the row may have cleared up in time on its own," Fisher said, "but Tillman didn't want to eat dirt for the sake of his job. He walked out. He said it was the right thing to do."

"Damn right it was."

As Fisher ordered another drink, I remembered what Tillman had said the day I went round to Trinity to ask him to work on the profile. *Am I a charity case now?* He'd obviously thought I was asking out of pity, throwing him some scraps to make him feel like he was still in the loop.

"Poor Tillman," I said. "He deserves better."

Fisher was silent as Joe returned with the Guinness. He merely reached out to take it in mid air, holding it by the rim as his lips met the foam at its head and came away white, like an Arctic explorer's.

"What did you think of his profile, anyway?" I asked him.

Fisher was noncommittal. "Most of what he's given you is simply the application of standard profiling procedures. I'd have come to pretty much the same conclusions myself. The rest . . ." He shrugged vaguely.

"No shrugs, Fisher," I warned. "I'm not in the mood."

"There *was* something," he said at last. "Something Tillman might have missed."

He reached down the side of the stool, lifted up his briefcase, then sat it on his lap whilst he clicked open the lock. He reached in and took out a copy of Tillman's profile from among his own papers. Notes were scribbled in the margin, I saw. Seemed like this case was eating at us all.

"You got one too?" I said. "What's Tillman doing — handing them out on street corners?"

"He didn't give it to me, I lifted one when his back was turned," said Fisher. "Thought it'd make more interesting reading on the plane home than your last book. Can't do any harm."

"It can if it gets into Nick Elliott's hands," I said.

Fisher wasn't listening. He was flicking through the pages, looking.

"Here it is," he said presently. "See here, where Tillman says the places chosen by the killer will be symbolically important to him, because they were where Fagan killed his victims?"

"I remember. I'd thought of that myself. He said the killer would've spent time there, soaking up the pleasant ambience, reliving it in his mind, long before he got around to killing anyone. So what do you think Tillman missed?"

"*Might* have missed was what I said," Fisher said. "Might have missed the possibility that this killer would also try to mark the final three Fagan scenes in the way he marked the first two."

"We considered that," I said, "but it'd be too risky for him to leave any more bodies there. He might be seen. For all he knows, they could be under twenty-four-hour surveillance. At the least, he'd be assuming we'd expect him to return."

"I wasn't talking about bodies. Of course he won't leave any more victims at those places, but he might leave something else: jewellery, books, flowers, photos. It'd be his way of superimposing himself on Fagan's territory."

I shook my head firmly. "I still think the chances of his being seen are too high right now for him to risk it," I said. "The other sites aren't under round-the-clock surveillance, as it happens, but patrols have been increased and they've all been told to keep an eye out."

"Maybe there's no risk at all," Fisher said quietly.

"You mind explaining how the killer could leave books and flowers at the scenes of Fagan's other murders without any risk of being seen?"

"By leaving them there before he killed Mary Lynch and before he dumped the body of the second woman in the churchyard," Fisher said, and I realised at once that he was right.

"He wanted to mark each scene," I said, "but knew that he couldn't go back there once the police realised he was retracing Fagan's footsteps exactly. So he had to mark them, claim them, in advance, before the pattern was guessed at." Saying it out loud now made it seem so obvious. It *was* obvious. "And you say you suggested this angle to Tillman?"

"I mentioned it in passing," said Fisher, "but he wasn't convinced. That's why I thought I'd bring it up with you. You can easily have the scenes searched tomorrow when it's light."

"Screw tomorrow," I said. "Let's do it now. You've got a couple of hours to kill before your flight takes off for London, and I hate waiting."

"There isn't enough time —" he began, but I cut off his escape route.

"Just the place where Tara Cox was killed then," I pressed. "It won't take long."

He was wavering now.

"Come on, Fisher, where's your sense of adventure?"

He sighed heavily, like Caesar about to wash his hands.

"OK, OK, I'll come," he said, "but if I get arrested, I'm telling them it was your idea."

"Suits me fine," I said. "You never get the credit if you're not willing to take the blame sometimes as well."

"I'll try to remember that comforting little motto when they're reading me my rights."

CHAPTER
TWENTY-THREE

"The car's at my apartment," I said as we came out of the swing doors of the hotel into the cold air and Fisher stopped to put on his coat. "It won't take long to walk back for it."

"You can't drive," said Fisher. "You've been drinking."

"One drink isn't drinking!"

"One drink is too much drinking. And don't bother telling me that was your first of the day," said Fisher. "I'm a psychologist, remember? I can tell when you're lying."

"I'll be fine."

"Read my lips. No. Way."

I was just wondering what to do now, annoyed because Fisher was right, when a movement in the car park caught my eye.

A figure was standing there among the shadows.

"Boland?" I said, squinting to pick him out of the gloom. "Is that you? What are you doing here?"

He edged out awkwardly from behind a car, the light from the street falling on his face.

"I was looking for your car," he said.

"My car?"

"The Chief sent me to track you down," he said. "She's been trying to call you."

"Yeah? I must have my mobile switched off."

"Well, the Chief suggested you might be here so I said I'd drop in on my way home. I was looking to see if your car was here."

"You should've come into the bar," I said. "Here, you might as well say hello. This is Lawrence Fisher. You've probably seen him on TV. Just pretend you have even if you haven't. We wouldn't want to do irreparable damage to his fragile ego now, would we?"

"As a matter of fact, I *have* seen you on TV, Doctor," said Boland, reaching out a hand to shake Fisher's. "Pleased to meet you."

"You too. And it's just Lawrence," said Fisher.

"What did Fitzgerald want with me, anyway?" I said.

"We think we've found Ed Fagan's body," Boland said.

"What?"

That came from Fisher. I was glad he was so surprised; it saved me from having to pretend that I was too.

"What happened?" I asked instead.

"The killer sent another text message. On a stolen cell phone this time. Directed police to a body, just like before. We managed to trace the number. It belongs to a woman called Megan O'Brien. She'd been in town earlier on and hadn't even noticed the phone had been stolen till officers went round to her flat to make sure she was OK. They thought maybe . . . well, you know."

"That the killer had taken her?" said Fisher.

"Exactly. She didn't know where it had been stolen. The officers who interviewed her got the impression she'd been on a bit of a pub crawl. Her new boyfriend stood her up, apparently."

Mark. What a loser.

"Where was the body?" I said.

"In the mountains somewhere," said Boland. "I wasn't out there myself, but the forensic team's up there now, trying to get an ID. The clothing matches the description of the clothing worn by Fagan when he was last seen five years ago, but he's pretty decomposed."

I remembered the clothes: white shirt, black trousers, green corduroy jacket, cowboy boots. He never did have any style.

"Was he strangled too?" said Fisher.

"No, he was killed by a single gunshot wound," Boland said.

"That's an innovation."

"Well, well," I said. "That puts paid to the fingerprint theory."

"If it *is* Fagan," said Boland. "DNA results will take for ever to come back. But it sure looks like it." He seemed depressed. Maybe he'd really thought they were getting somewhere at last. Then this. I searched for a way to make him feel better, but sensed that now probably wasn't the best time to remind him that certainty was better than futile hope. "I don't get it. The knife . . ."

"The killer's playing a game," I said.

266

"But why make us think it's Fagan and go to all the trouble of using a knife on Mary Dalton that makes us even more convinced, only to suddenly own up?"

"I don't know," I said feebly.

"Anyway," he said before I could think what else to say, "that's why I was sent to find you. The Chief reckoned you should know what was happening."

"So this killer murdered Fagan as well?" said Fisher to me. "There's a neat twist to the profile. I can't quite believe it. It certainly makes the killer's relationship to the earlier sites all the more symbolic. It's as if they're truly his now."

Boland looked blank.

"Fisher and I were just discussing a theory of his concering the scenes where Fagan carried out his murders," I explained. "In fact, we were just about to take a run out to where Tara Cox died and have a quick look round before I drop him off at the airport for his flight home."

"You were going to drive?" said Boland. "You've been drinking."

"This is getting to be like a meeting of the Teetotallers' Association," I said. "Is it so obvious?"

"Obvious enough that I can't let you drive," said Boland. "I might not be much help catching serial killers, but I am still a policeman. I couldn't let you get behind the wheel."

"You'd arrest me?"

"I hadn't thought that far ahead," he said with a grin, "but yes, I suppose I'd have to."

I sighed, conceding defeat.

"A taxi it is then."

"No need for that," said Boland. "I'll drive you. My car's round the corner. It'll make a change to be of some help."

"You don't have to get home?" said Fisher.

"I think I can bear to skip the delights of a cold house, a cheap takeaway and an empty bed for one night," said Boland. "If I'm not careful, I'll be turning into Elliott."

"Elliott?"

"His wife left him too, only a few weeks ago. I met him in a bar the other night, drowning his sorrows. He suggested we should form the Abandoned Husbands Club."

"I didn't even know he *was* married."

"Four months ago, apparently."

"And it's over already?" I said. Though when I considered what Elliott was like, it was probably more of a wonder that she'd stuck with him so long.

"Making relationships work can be tough," said Boland.

"Oh, Sergeant, you're making my heart ache," I said. "Better show us to this car of yours before I start crying."

A couple of minutes later we were pulling out from the kerb to join the snake of traffic round St Stephen's Green. Rush hour was over by now, but there were still plenty of cars and shoppers thronging the narrow streets. Tonight was the night for late shopping, I remembered.

268

There they all were outside the window as we passed, as ethereal to me as ghosts. Seeing them was like watching some medieval masque whose outlandish masks and gestures had lost all meaning. A dumb show in every respect. Was that unfair? I didn't care. I was only glad when we crossed the river into darkness and left them behind.

Rivers form a boundary in all cities. North is north and south is south and never the twain shall meet. What is also true is how the people on one side of a river rarely feel that the city that exists on the other side is as completely theirs.

Finding a place that is completely theirs matters to killers too, maybe more than anything. Finding a place symbolically, in the sense of discovering who and what they are; but also physically, finding a literal place where they can be what they are in secret. They need a place where they feel comfortable, so there are no distractions, so nothing comes between them and the act. That's why they pick places to kill which they already know intimately, as intimately as Tillman told us Mary Lynch's killer would have known the area round the canal.

Fagan had switched. He started south of the river, then for the third killing went north instead; no one ever figured why.

My guess was that he simply started to feel the pressure round the canal — Fitzgerald had told me that the police presence was stepped up massively after Sylvia Judge died, much to the detriment of the local trade in female flesh, and Fagan couldn't have failed to notice it as he cruised the streets in preparation for his next killing. So he turned his attention to a place where the hookers were easier to hook. Three women died north of the river, but it was the canal where he felt most like himself, and it was there that he was finally arrested. He'd come home.

Was this, I found myself wondering as we drove, the same route Fagan had taken the night he killed Tara Cox? He'd been working late that night, had stopped off with colleagues for a drink in town, then he'd driven to the dark lane that ran alongside the barracks to pick up Tara.

She'd only been working there a couple of months, and the other hookers who worked the barracks pitch agreed that she was different. The job hadn't defeated her yet. She still believed she was only passing through. They all started like that. But maybe that made her naive as well, so that when Fagan said he wanted to go to the park up by the Law Library for sex, no alarm rang.

And then, somewhere along here, he must have pulled into the side off Constitution Hill, as we now did, and climbed out of the car. We peered through the railings at the huge building set aloofly well back from the road.

"Is that it?" said Fisher.

"That's it," I said. "Dante put lawyers in the eighth circle of hell. Dublin puts them here."

"At least hell would be warmer," Fisher replied with a shiver, tugging his collar tightly round his throat.

"The pay isn't as good, though," said Boland

A few lights glimmered in upper windows of the library, but it was the huge darkness between there and the road that really imprinted itself on the mind. I want to go in there, Fagan must have told Tara Cox. And in she went. Into the darkness. Very symbolic.

"Do you have a torch?" I said.

"In the boot," Boland said, and Fisher and I waited without saying a word until he came back with it.

"Over here. There's a broken railing, we can climb through there."

It took us a while to find it. I squatted down to squeeze through into the grounds.

I conjured up again the image of Tara as we crossed the grass in silence, the light from Boland's torch picking the way. Seventeen she was when she died.

That was three years before I'd even set foot in Dublin for the first time, yet I still remembered the horror I felt when I saw the crime scene photographs. Tara had died of multiple stab wounds; thirty-six of them, as the writer of the first letter pointed out forensically. She'd taken every precaution to be safe on the streets, save for the only realistic precaution, which was to stop selling herself to strangers. A black belt in judo, she'd even managed to wrestle free from Fagan when he attacked her; but she hadn't got far. Thwarted once, he didn't take the risk of being denied again. The knife was his final answer to her resistance.

"Here," I said quietly, realising as I did so that I was probably the only one of us who'd been here before, though it was daylight when I'd come. I hadn't wanted to face it in the dark.

"This exact tree?" said Fisher.

"This tree."

"You're sure."

"I'm sure."

Fagan had left her curled beside the tree, as though sleeping. He'd even draped a sack over her like a blanket, covering her head. The only psychologist the police had contacted at the time speculated, predictably, that the killer may have covered the body out of shame, but I didn't buy that. Animals aren't capable of shame. Fagan only covered the body so that it wouldn't be found too quickly, so that anyone who saw the shape lying there in the shadows would take it for a down-and-out sleeping off another bottle of cheap vodka in the park.

This spot was where he'd wanted her to die, where he'd chosen, though analysis of the footprints and blood at the scene afterwards showed that the fatal wounds had actually been inflicted about a hundred yards away before Tara was dragged back, barely alive, but alive, to bleed to death by the tree.

He'd been angrier than usual that night. Even from the photographs, I'd realised that. You'll die where I say you'll die, he was telling her by dragging her back. You're mine.

"Fitzgerald found her, you know," I said, "though she wasn't Chief Superintendent then, of course. Police got an anonymous call eventually that a body had turned up in the grounds of the Law Library. No details. Just that there was a body."

"Was it Fagan who made the call?" asked Fisher.

"They never established that, but it could've been," I said. "He never called to direct police to any of the other victims, but this one was different, so maybe his reaction was different, maybe he was particularly proud of this one, wanted to show her off. Fitzgerald didn't know that when she came here, though. It could've been the victim of an overdose for all she was expecting. The uniforms were supposed to be on their way, but in the end she got here first. It was about two in the morning and she just saw Tara lying there. And she knew."

"That it was Fagan?" said Boland.

"Fagan always left an aura."

I stepped forward, pointing a finger to mark out the coordinates of the scene.

"She was lying this way," I explained, "head pointed towards the library. Fitzgerald saw her feet first, poking out from beneath the blanket. Fagan had taken her shoes with him; they were never found. The ground around her was black. Fitzgerald said it was glimmering wet with blood. The blood had spread out like wine spilled from a bottle. Lynch's autopsy report said Fagan had severed an artery in Tara's neck and the blood had spurted over a distance of nine feet."

I looked down at the grass and thought about that blood. Blood lasted, that was one of the things you first realised when you were an investigator. Indoors and out. Didn't matter how often you tried to wash it away or how often it rained, it never really went away. It just went into hiding. It was still there, like a skeleton under the skin. The rain could come a thousand times and more and wash Tara's blood into the soil, hammering it down deeper and deeper into the earth to mingle with the stones; but she was still here, scattered through the ground. Each fragment of her DNA, each perfect blueprint of herself, still lingering here to be trampled on. The final insult.

Fagan would've liked that.

For the next ten minutes or so, we searched the area round the tree in silence, stopping now and then if we found something and calling the others over for a second and third opinion.

Sum total by the end of it: a few discarded condoms (were the grounds of the library still being used by prostitutes?), a couple of crumpled pages from a porn magazine, some coins and candy wrappers. It would be easy to read significance into a condom, a porn magazine and a few coins — but it was only litter, I couldn't persuade myself otherwise; it had no meaning.

Well, what had I expected — the killer's address on a scrap of paper with a huge arrow carved into the tree pointing towards it to make things easier? A cryptic crossword with one across spelling out the name of the killer? I needed to get a grip.

"Come on," I said at last, "we're wasting our time."

And I could tell by the way they didn't say a word to object that Fisher and Boland had come to the same resigned conclusion. It was time to call it a night.

Then I saw it.

"Boland, give me the torch!"

Boland handed me his torch and I flashed the light on to the trunk of the tree.

Fisher whistled.

There, carved into the bole of the tree. Not an arrow pointing, but another letter. Another Hebrew letter? How the hell would I know? But it looked like it.

Aleph it was the first time . . . now what?

"You were right," I said to Fisher. "I don't know how you knew, but you were right."

"I wish I'd been wrong," he said quietly.

"Because of Tillman? It's not your fault he missed an angle."

"He's still my friend," said Fisher.

I nodded as if I understood, but in truth I had too much else to think about at that moment to spare any space in my head for Tillman's potential hurt feelings.

The letter on the tree: what did it mean this time? I stepped forward and raised my hand to touch the carving, like it was Braille and I was blind and could read it.

"No," said Boland firmly.

"What's the matter?"

"We're going to have to seal the scene."

"No hurry," I said. "The techs'll find nothing here that we haven't found already."

"Even so," he said. "I don't want to get the blame for contaminating evidence. Great start to my career in the murder squad that'd be. Draker would have a field day with me."

"What are you going to do?"

"I'm going to call through to headquarters, tell them what we found," Boland said. "They'll have search teams out to the last two Fagan scenes within the hour."

"You don't mean —" I stopped, annoyed. "Fisher?"

"Leave me out of it," Fisher said.

"But I thought we were going to search the scenes ourselves?"

"Just where Tara Cox died, you said," Fisher reminded me. "Besides, Boland's right. We should leave well alone now. You've proved your point, and I have a flight to catch."

They wouldn't even look at me. It was pointless arguing.

I knew I should have come by myself.

CHAPTER
TWENTY-FOUR

I didn't relish the idea of hanging around waiting for the crime scene technical bureau to arrive and take over, not least because that might mean talking to Fitzgerald. I wasn't ready for that yet.

Instead I called a cab and ran out with Fisher to the airport. We hardly spoke at all during the journey, both distracted by our own thoughts, and when I offered to come with him into the departure lounge, maybe grab a coffee, he politely put me off.

He stood at the entrance to the terminal, watching as I drove off.

What now?

Then it came to me. I'd call Ambrose Lynch. There was something that had been bothering me since I talked to Salvatore at the library, something he might be able to help clear up.

But there was no answer from his mobile when I tried to call. He'd probably switched it off. He hated carrying one, and only did so because the police insisted he always be in touch in case he was needed at a crime scene. "What's the rush?" he often complained. "The body isn't going to get up and make a dash for it if I'm a few minutes late." Switching the phone off now and then was his quiet protest against bureaucracy and the modern world.

In no mood to wait till morning, I simply gave the pathologist's address to the cab driver, leaned back into the seat, shut my eyes, and let the city flow by unnoticed . . .

Lynch lived in the city's embassy belt, an exclusive neighbourhood where security cameras flowered on virtually every tree and spiked iron gates warned off the curious. At this time of evening, it was an almost straight run across town to get there.

His was a huge detached Victorian villa with a gravel drive, a steep flight of granite steps to the front door, a coachhouse round the back, and enough bedrooms inside to house a football team, though he and his wife had never had any children to fill them. Why they hadn't I didn't know; and to be honest, it wasn't the sort of thing I could imagine asking Lynch about.

I got the cab to pull up outside the front gate and climbed out. The rain had stopped a long time since. Lynch's Mercedes wasn't in the drive but he might have parked it round the back.

"How much?" I asked the driver, then waited till his taillights had disappeared into the darkness before stepping through the open gates and crunching up the gravel to the front door.

I rang the bell.

No answer.

Tried the bell once more. The same no answer.

Lifted the letterbox to peer inside, but there was nothing to see except another door. No light that I could detect. Was he in bed already? Quietly I made my way round the side.

I'd been to this house for dinner with Lynch and his wife a couple of times; there'd even been a cocktail party once at which the Commissioner himself had been present, and some minister in the department of justice whose name now escaped me.

I was the only woman there who wasn't wearing a cocktail dress, and that included Grace. But I'd made a real effort and put on some expensive leather trousers that she'd bought me for my birthday. Grace had looked fabulous in her little black number, but then she always did, whatever she wore; and I thought I looked fabulous too. No one else seemed to agree.

I was like the token eccentric, having to keep everything polite with Grace so the minister wasn't scandalised, endlessly explaining what an American former FBI agent without a cocktail dress was doing in Dublin. But Lynch had been charm itself. He didn't give two hoots what I was wearing — that was how he put it to me, didn't give two hoots, and I found the owlish expression so charming and odd that I took a note of it and meant to introduce it into conversation next time I had the chance, though the opportunity had never arisen. My language was usually more forceful.

I remembered the house as it was that other night, light spilling on to the back lawn through the terrace windows, warm summer air scented with the fragrance of plants (Lynch's wife Jean was a keen gardener), a bright moon in the sky. Lynch had rigged the trees with lights — which is to say, he'd got somebody else to do it; I couldn't see Ambrose up a ladder hanging lights for a party — and the whole garden glittered like something out of a child's picture book. The food had come from an award-winning restaurant down by the river; there was champagne; a string quartet played the Kreutzer Sonata. I know that's what it was because the minister told me; well, chamber music's not my thing. And maybe he was only bluffing to impress me.

In return, I offered him one of my best Cuban cigars — I was obviously feeling generous — and enlightened him as to why exactly he should introduce the death penalty to Ireland, starting with the people who parked illegally outside my apartment.

Now the house looked dreary, forlorn, the garden filled with shadows as I trudged across the grass to the coachhouse and smeared a space on the dusty window to peer inside.

No sign of Lynch's car there either. He obviously wasn't home yet, and it wasn't hard to imagine where he was: some familiar pub, probably, to put off the moment when he had to come home to this blackness. Strange how the absence of one person could have such an effect on a house. Since Jean had gone, the life seemed to have seeped out of the place.

I was just debating whether to drop a note through the letterbox telling Ambrose to call me when a flash of light illuminated the trees and headlights appeared at the far end of the drive. For a moment I was dazzled, till my eyes cleared and I saw him clambering heavily as usual out of his car.

"Lynch," I said.

He was so startled that he dropped the bags he was carrying on to the gravel.

"It's only me. Saxon."

"For mercy's sake," said Ambrose, "you nearly killed me." He sounded breathless, edgy. "Where are you?"

"Over here," I said and I stepped out where he could see me.

"I thought . . ." He trailed off, embarrassed. His hair was wet, as if with rain. He ran his hands through it nervously.

I smiled. "You thought I was the legendary Night Hunter?"

"I don't know what I thought," said Lynch. "Thought my time was up, that's for sure. Jumping at shadows at my age. I should be ashamed of myself."

"I shouldn't have been lurking."

He bent down to pick up his bags. A briefcase first, filled with papers he'd brought home to work on; the other one —

"I'll help you with that," I said.

"I'm fine," he said hurriedly; and I realised there was a bottle inside the second bag, whiskey no doubt, picked up from an off-licence on the way home. "It's you we've all been worried about. Grace was searching high and low for you to tell you what was happening."

"About Fagan? I know about that. Boland told me."

"Did he tell you about the *Evening News* as well?"

"The *Evening News*?"

"Obviously not. They got hold of a copy of the latest letter from the killer. They published it in their final edition late this afternoon."

Why hadn't Boland told me? Did he just assume I knew already? I *should* have known, that was true enough. And I would have known if I hadn't gone AWOL.

"There goes our head start on the killer," I said despondently.

"It's even worse than that, I'm afraid," he said. "They published everything, and when I say everything I do mean *everything*. Their crime reporter got hold of the details of the quotes the killer has been leaving, and the writing on Mary Lynch's body, and the missing parts of the woman in the churchyard. Need I go on?"

"How?"

"It seems that someone telephoned them this afternoon claiming to be an officer with the Dublin Metropolitan Police. He said he wanted to blow the whistle on the investigation in order to expose the corruption and inefficiency of the force."

"And they fell for it? They're worse than the *Post*."

"It gets better. This self-proclaimed shining credit to the force gave his name as Gus Bishop."

Gus. The same name as Mary Lynch's creepy sugar daddy.

"I don't suppose you have a copy of it, do you?" I said.

"Of that rag? My dear, I am grievously insulted. Though you'd better come in all the same," he added.

"No point standing about in the cold even if I have been insulted, is there?"

He took out his key and let me in the door at the side of the house, then led the way down a short passageway into the kitchen. The house smelt like it hadn't been lived in for years. Not dirty, just unused and abandoned, unloved. Ambrose went ahead into the kitchen and flicked a light.

I saw at once the unwashed cups and glasses piled in the sink and the empty liquor bottles standing on the draining board. There was a pile of unopened mail on the table, mostly with his wife's name on, like he'd left it there in case she came back.

Since his wife had left, Ambrose evidently hadn't kept a grip on his domestic situation. That was typical of men of his age and upbringing. They expected life to be ordered about them so they could get on with their affairs, and then, when one day it wasn't, they didn't know how to cope.

Ambrose put his bags down next to the sink, careful to conceal the bottle underneath his briefcase, before coming back to sit at the kitchen table, ushering me into a seat opposite him.

Then he caught my eye and smiled sadly.

"Who am I fooling?" he said, and he went back to the sink, rinsed a couple of glasses and reached into the bag for the bottle of whiskey. He twisted open the cap, all pretence gone.

"Can I pour you one?"

"Might as well."

What was another one after the day I'd had?

He seemed more at ease once he didn't have to put on an act, though he didn't have to put on any act for my benefit. Or perhaps it was simply the thought of whiskey which put him at ease.

"How did *you* get on in the mountains while all this was going on?" I asked as he poured.

"Magnificently," said Ambrose drily. "What better way to spend the weeks before Christmas than in the company of the dead? The conversation is so sparkling, so witty."

"Have you managed to identify the body yet?"

Ambrose shook his head.

"Since when are our lives ever that simple?" he said. "The body appears to be that of a man about the right age and height to be our Mr Fagan, and between you and me, of course it *is* him; but for now he remains officially unidentified. Just like his predecessor in the churchyard."

"Actually, that's what I wanted to ask you about," I said. "Yesterday I spent some time with Professor Salvatore. Have you heard of him? No? He's a theologian who used to work with Fagan; he pointed out a few interesting things to me. Thought I'd run them by you."

"I'm all ears," he said.

"Do you know who Jehu is?"

"Unlike most people in this modern world of ours," said Ambrose, "I happen to have had the benefit of a decent classical education, so yes, I know who Jehu is. Old Testament chappie, if I remember rightly. An avenger sent by God to kill the unholy."

"He killed Jezebel," I said. "That's where the quote came from. *Go, see now this cursed woman and bury her.*"

"I didn't know that," he admitted. "I can certainly see why it would excite your interest."

"Right now I'm more interested in the way Jezebel died. You remember that?"

"I'm afraid not," said Ambrose.

"Your classical education did leave some gaps then?" I teased. "She was thrown out of a window. I was wondering if that was a clue to how this woman died."

"You think, in choosing this particular quote, the killer was telling us that he threw this unfortunate woman out of a window?" said Ambrose.

"Not necessarily out of a window. Off a wall, down the stairs even. You said the injuries were consistent with a beating. Could they be consistent with a fall as well?"

"Intriguing." He reached over to refill his glass. "I hadn't considered that possibility, I must admit. I don't think so, alas."

"Why not?"

"For one thing, one wouldn't get the same pattern of injuries in a fall; for another, the injuries would tend to be more severe. One would normally expect some kind of spinal injury to be present. Transection of the thoracic, perhaps."

"And there was nothing like that?"

"Sorry. I'm not saying that it's impossible," said Ambrose, "but the injuries simply did not conform to any that I've ever observed in the victim of a fall before, accidental or otherwise."

"I needed to ask," I said dismissively to hide my disappointment. "I won't be happy, I think, till we know for sure whose body it was that was found down there. I don't suppose Susan Fuller's medical records have turned up yet, have they?"

"If I was an altogether less rational man," said Ambrose, "I might almost believe that the records had been interfered with. Her doctor can find no trace of the mysterious X-rays. We wait in hope. But what about you, my dear? What have you been doing all day?"

Strangely enough, I didn't mention sending the text message which had prompted his trip out to the mountains that afternoon. I told him instead about the symbol carved on the tree where Tara Cox died. I remembered that he'd identified the first one. He seemed impressed.

"Have you a pen and paper?" I asked. "I'll try to draw it."

"Of course I do."

On the fourth attempt, I got as near as I was likely to get.

"Lamedh," he said at once. "And you know, that means ox as well. At least . . . wait there."

He disappeared for a few moments and returned with a book. He pushed the glasses aside, and laid the book flat, pointing out the definition for me to read: *Lamedh, the twelfth letter in the Hebrew alphabet. Transliterated as L. Literal meaning: ox goad (from its shape).*

286

"What's a goad?" I said.

"A pointed stick," said Ambrose.

"An ox, a pointed stick, the first and twelfth letters of the Hebrew alphabet. One and twelve make thirteen. Is that it? Unlucky for some? This freak's certainly been unlucky for some." I could feel myself growing frustrated. "I wish I could work out what it means. Tillman reckons it's probably something so simple that we'll never even consider it."

"Occam's Razor," said Lynch. "He could be right."

"You mind explaining that?"

"William of Occam was a philosopher who formulated the principle that the fewest possible assumptions should be made when explaining a thing. It's called Occam's Razor."

"Is that right? And what principle would this William formulate to explain why someone kills innocent women then leaves little messages hidden all over town like the Easter bunny?"

"That I cannot answer," conceded Ambrose, "but what he would say to you, I'm sure, is that you are doing your best and it's not your fault if you have failed so far to put all the pieces together. You shouldn't beat yourself up about it, as I believe you Americans put it."

"Are you kidding?" I said. "Beating myself up is about the only thing I'm any good at these days. Well, that and poker."

"You play poker?"

"I play poker the way John Coltrane played the saxophone."

"That sounds very much like a challenge," said Ambrose, "and I hope you realise that I never could resist a challenge."

"Save your blushes and your money, Lynch. You haven't a prayer."

"That decides it. Where did I put those cards?" Ambrose rose to his feet and started searching purposefully through the drawers. "There's just one thing I need to ask you first."

"Fire away."

"Who exactly was this John Coltrane person?"

I think he was joking.

FIFTH DAY

CHAPTER
TWENTY-FIVE

Later, I learned that her name meant "belonging to God"; and she did now. She was Nikolaevna Tsilevich — not quite the Nikola that the letter-writer had promised, but close enough to have made it possible to identify her before she was killed, if only we had known her real name, if only anyone had. But Nikolaevna Tsilevich was known to those around her only as Sadie.

She came from Novosibirsk in Siberia, Russia's third largest city — an empty wasteland, so the travel guides said, of grey Stalinist apartment blocks and filthy factories, where the river was so toxic that it couldn't freeze in winter. There were coalfields to the east and vast mineral deposits to the west — and nothing in the middle for a nineteen-year-old girl like her.

She'd come to Dublin on a short-hop flight from London about six months ago and disappeared into the city like a diver breaking the water, never to emerge back into the air. She was equally unknown to Immigration and Vice. One more invisible woman.

It was a familiar story, and one in which Niall Boland became something of an expert in the coming days. The cops over in Vice explained to him how it worked. Employment agencies throughout Eastern Europe advertised jobs in Dublin for nannies, chambermaids, waitresses, then when the girls got here, lured by the promise of money beyond what they could ever hope to earn back home, they were coaxed, cajoled, intimidated, whatever, into prostitution instead.

They were told that the money which had brought them to Dublin was only a loan and they would now have to pay it back. And what other way was there? Anything they made on top, meanwhile, they got to keep, and for many that did represent a considerable sum.

As I looked through the wardrobe in Nikolaevna's Temple Bar apartment in the city centre about twelve hours after she'd been killed, and only half an hour or so after her body had finally been taken away by the city pathologist, I found it filled with expensive labels.

"She was obviously doing well," I said as I flicked through the hangers.

"There was about ten thousand a month going into her account," Fitzgerald said.

She was standing by the window, looking out. A small crowd had gathered below at the news of another murder. Why does a crowd always gather? What is it that they want to see? The dead borne out on stretchers in a public display?

"You've been through her bank records already?"

"No point hanging around," Fitzgerald said. "She was sending about two thousand home a month to her parents, saving some for herself, spending the rest. What her pimp cleared, we don't know. This isn't exactly a business where you keep accounts."

"Got any names there?"

"Stephen Clark's the name on the lease. Have you heard of him?"

"Is he the one who owns the lap-dancing place down by the docks? Last I saw of him was on the news a couple of months ago. Something to do with tax evasion, wasn't it?"

"That's him. He got hit with a one and a half million tax bill and three months to pay to avoid prison. Got off lightly too, from what I can tell from the Revenue Commissioners. He hasn't paid tax for the last ten years and, though of course he denies it, he was pretty heavily involved in prostitution that whole time."

"Now lap dancing."

"Proper little entrepreneur," Fitzgerald agreed. "A credit to freemarket capitalism. He'll probably try to offset this little loss to his profitability against his tax bill. The money for this place was paid through his personal account every month, has been now for two years. This Nikolaevna wasn't here all that time, though."

"Who was?"

"According to neighbours, there was another girl here for the first eighteen months. She called herself Violet."

"Violet?"

"So she told them. We don't know what happened to her."

"You think there's any cause for concern?" I said.

"Well, she was never reported missing, so who knows? I'm going over to Clark's after I've finished up here. If he knows what's good for him, he'll be cooperative."

"I wonder if Mary Dalton worked for him as well," I said, remembering the report we'd heard yesterday morning on *her* equally shortlived career. "She worked as a lap dancer too."

I looked over at the bed where the body of the Russian prostitute had been found by the cleaner when she arrived that morning. I could still see the indentation in the sheet where she'd lain. I thought about her parents in the cold east, about the friends she'd known who'd watched her flying off to the west, envying her no doubt, entranced by the glamour of departure, the lure of possibilities; and what they would all think when they heard about this.

Nikolaevna had been naked when she was found, face down, hands tied behind her back, one foot trailing on the ground, half on, half off the bed. Her neck was crisscrossed with post-mortem slash marks, and it looked as though she'd been raped, though whether this was post-mortem too would have to await the autopsy report from Ambrose Lynch.

And there was the quote we'd all been expecting. *He that is without sin among you, let him first cast a stone.* Which was exactly what the killer had done.

The back of Nikola's head had been all but obliterated by the force of a rock striking down, and the rock itself had been left on the pillow, on top of the scrap of paper with the typewritten message, weighing it down.

That, presumably, was his idea of a joke.

294

The differences between this murder and the previous three, not to mention between this and the murders carried out by Fagan, were so obvious I hardly needed to list them in my head.

In fact, apart from the quotation everything was different. The rape was different — Fagan had never raped any of his victims, nor had this latest killer so far. The use of restraints was different — that reminded me again of Monica Lee, the prostitute dumped in the mountains three years ago. There was the rock too. I wondered if it would turn out on analysis to be the same type of rock whose traces were found on Monica's body, and I knew in my heart that it would. There was no strangulation. Tsilevich was hardly a name connected to the investigation either, and there was no buried reference in where or how she died to Fagan's killing of Liana Cassidy.

He'd stopped pretending now. His self was coming through, as Tillman had said it would. And he was growing bolder, more assured. He had even stayed a while afterwards to take a shower. It made sense; Lynch said he'd have been splashed with blood. But there was something callous about it too. First you kill a woman, then clean yourself up in her own shower. He wasn't taking precautions against leaving traces of his hair in the plughole, that was for sure.

Because he didn't expect ever to be caught — or because he didn't care if he *was* caught?

I'd have liked to ask Tillman about that, for all I hadn't been impressed with his profile; but Tillman had been curt with me when I phoned earlier to tell him about the latest killing.

No, he didn't want to come down to the scene. No, he didn't want to look at photographs. And no, he didn't want the opportunity to review the evidence with a view perhaps to fine-tuning his initial findings. He'd agreed to provide a preliminary profile, that was all; his work was over. Now he was concentrating on his lecture, so would I kindly just leave him alone?

That Nikolaevna had been killed indoors wouldn't hurt the investigation, at any rate. There was no worrying what the weather would do to the physical evidence here, no worrying who had trampled through the scene or what was here that had nothing to do with the victim or the killer. This was her apartment. What was here was only what should have been here. Everything was evidence, and inch by inch the technical bureau would strip it bare.

"What did the neighbours hear?" I said, shutting the wardrobe door again and turning round, avoiding the sight of the bed, the blood on the walls.

"Dalton and Lawlor are still doing the door-to-doors," Fitzgerald explained. "There are about twenty other residents in this block, only half of whom claim to have been in last night when the killing happened. So far, most swear they saw and heard nothing. Goes without saying."

"You said most."

"Lawlor got something interesting a couple of doors down. I'll tell you about it later."

"Fair enough. Anyone else in the vicinity last night?"

"There's no doorman, you can see it's not that kind of place, but the caretaker is Joe Keogh," she confirmed. "He's told us what he knows, which isn't much. He seems on the level. He ran up when the cleaner started screaming. It's the same old story. He didn't see anyone he didn't expect to see last night. Though who knows, maybe it was someone who lives here or who comes here often, someone familiar who wouldn't be noticed."

"Like Clark."

"Or a regular client," said Fitzgerald. "But don't worry, we'll not let Clark slip through the net. I wouldn't mind getting a warrant to search his place anyway, just to see what turns up."

"Wouldn't be admissible if you weren't looking for it."

"To hell with admissible," said Fitzgerald.

I followed her out of the bedroom, glad to leave it, into a small sitting room where the fingerprint team were still dusting for prints along all the surfaces: windows, doors, handles, tables, chairs, cups. Nothing would be overlooked.

"You were missed yesterday," she said to me as we stood together in the silence, watching them work.

"In the mountains?" I said carefully. This morning was the first time I'd seen her since sending the message about Fagan, and I still felt awkward.

"The mountains, the office." She caught my eye. Held it. "You know, if this is all too much for you —"

"No!"

"If it brings back too many memories."

297

What was she trying to say?

"It's not that," I said quickly. "It's just . . . I needed to get away yesterday. I explained. It was all getting too much. I'm back now." I tried out a smile, though it didn't seem convincing even to me. "Besides, who was there to miss me? Dalton? Draker?"

"There was me," she said. "I missed you."

As if I didn't feel bad enough already.

"At least we know now it isn't Fagan we're looking for," she went on before I could think of what to say to cover my discomfort. "That's something, though Draker, can you believe it, is still refusing to make it official until we have a definite ID on the body."

"He would," I said. "Doesn't like admitting that he's wrong."

Fitzgerald shrugged. "Maybe he's right to be cautious. The simplest way to clear it up would be for Mullen to offer a DNA sample so that we can make a match to the father, but he's refusing. He's even got himself a lawyer to hide behind. You'll never guess who."

"Not Conor Buckley?"

"The very same."

Just what we needed. More ghosts.

"What does Mullen want a lawyer for?" I said. "He's not officially a suspect."

"He says he doesn't trust the police. He says they stitched his father up and he's not going to let them stitch him up too."

"Has something to hide, more like."

"Everyone has something to hide," said Fitzgerald.

298

And there was my paranoia hammering again.

Change the subject.

"So what next?"

"What's next is we get back to work," she said. "We've got more than enough to be getting on with. I heard about the information Lawrence Fisher brought over with him. If Mullen's picture is recognised by any of the women who were attacked in London, then we're going to have to put his alibi for Mary Lynch's murder under the microscope again. If this is the work of Mullen, that would certainly explain how the killer got hold of a knife belonging to Fagan."

"It definitely wasn't the same one that was used to kill Tara Cox then?"

She shook her head. "I sent Healy down to check out the old evidence stores, like you suggested. It didn't come from there. He's making enquiries now to see what happened to all Fagan's belongings after they were auctioned off; but it's a lifetime's work, if you ask me. Still, it was good thinking, Saxon. Good thinking too last night about the other scenes."

"Thank Fisher for that, not me. Has anything turned up there yet?"

"Nothing so far, but searches, as we often like to say to fob off the press, are continuing. Till then, Nikolaevna is what matters. Whatever the killer is playing at by revealing himself to us at this time, this apartment is what matters."

"How did he get in?" I asked.

"Well," said Fitzgerald, "there was no sign of a break-in."

"So she knew him, let him in."

"Looks like it," she said. "There were two glasses of wine on the kitchen table, half drunk. Two glasses suggests company."

"How did she find her clients?"

"How did they find her, you mean. Ads mainly. Here." She passed me a copy of a glossy magazine inside an evidence bag. *Dublin Today*. A listings magazine. I'd seen it sitting around on the shop shelves, even remembered some controversy in the papers about the ads it carried at the back. Ads for what, in that euphemistic way the vice trade had, were always termed massage parlours and escort agencies and health studios. Women for rent.

Nikolaevna's — Sadie's — ad was near the back. *Russian Lolita Wants To Play*, with a mobile phone number to call. There was a picture but it wasn't her. I recognised a teenage actress from one of the daytime American soaps that were shown over here on cable. Prostitutes often did that. Men saw the ad and called up, expecting one thing, then when the girl appeared, she looked nothing like the shot. What were they going to do — complain to the trading standards office?

"Is that her personal number?" I said.

"No. Vice have never been able to prove anything, but they think that's one of the lines run by Clark," Fitzgerald said. "Her services were advertised under the same number in some of the local adult magazines too. Contact mags, that sort of thing. She did have her own mobile, but that number hasn't appeared in any of the ads I've seen so far. Boland's going through each call to see what comes up, but the killer won't be stupid enough to get caught through his home phone records when he could pick up a mobile any day of the week and never be traced."

"You never know," I said. "You might get lucky."

"Other people get lucky," said Fitzgerald. "Me, I just get a headache."

CHAPTER
TWENTY-SIX

Stephen Clark's lap-dancing club was an old meat-packing warehouse down by the river. Apt home for it under the circumstances. The sign outside read *Pussy Galore's*.

It was switched off now for the day, but I'd seen it blazing at night often as I walked, like a year-round Christmas decoration, beckoning the desperate and the lonely.

"Charming name," I said. "Subtle."

Fitzgerald grunted as we climbed out of the car and crossed to the door. "I doubt the men who come here are looking for subtlety," she said. "Most probably couldn't even spell it."

The club wouldn't be open for business again until dark, but the door was wedged wide with a beer barrel. Awaiting another delivery of disposable women, perhaps.

Buy one, get one free.

Inside, no one was about. The reception was all pot plants and leather, like the foyer of a cheap hotel. The words *Pussy Galore's* were woven in gold into the red carpet. I'd never been inside a brothel, but this was what I'd have expected it to look like if I had.

"Hello!" shouted Fitzgerald.

"What do you want?"

We turned round to find one of Clark's minders squeezing out of both his suit and another door simultaneously. His face looked as if it had been chipped out from a block of rough stone; I swear I could still see the chisel marks.

"Mr Clark's not here," he said once Fitzgerald had explained what we wanted.

"That's funny," said Fitzgerald, "because his car is parked right outside. Unless you're the one who drives the Rolls?"

The stone face didn't flicker.

"Do you have an appointment?"

"Do you think I'd be standing here wasting my time talking to you if I had an appointment? I don't need an appointment." And she produced her badge and showed it to the minder. "Now why don't you just pick up the phone and tell him we're here, then you can go back to polishing your collection of antique knuckledusters, or practising your third-rate heavy's act, or whatever it was you were doing before we arrived."

He took one glance at the card, and shrugged dully with an admission of defeat.

Fitzgerald turned away as he picked up the phone and growled into it.

"Boss."

A moment later, he replaced the receiver.

"Follow me."

Squeezing through the same door out of which he'd emerged a moment earlier, Clark's minder led the way into the club itself.

Here was a place where daylight never entered, and air even less. Mirrors lined the walls in place of windows and our footsteps were loud, making the few members of staff clearing away the remains of another long night look up curiously as we passed, weaving among the tables and high stages embellished with brass poles. It was always amazing what turned men on. They were so mechanical. A bit of bumping and grinding around a pole in your G-string and that was them, they were hooked, zippers down and wallets out. The brave new world of adult entertainment.

Clark's office was at the back, hidden among the rooms reserved for what were euphemistically called private dancing sessions, though what really went on there didn't take much guessing. The minder rapped lightly on the door.

"Come in!"

And Stone Face left us to make our own way inside.

Clark's head was bent to his desk, checking papers, as we walked in. He didn't even look up, but then I hadn't expected him to.

"Be with you in a minute," he said.

"No hurry," said Fitzgerald. "It's only a murder case, after all."

His head jerked up at that, and he rose to his feet, pretending embarrassment. "I'm sorry," he said. "I was expecting someone else." Yeah, right. Less than a minute after being told we were here. "You must be Inspector Fitzgerald," he said.

"Chief Superintendent Fitzgerald, that's right."

He looked much the same as he had when I'd first seen him on TV a few months ago. Sharp suit, silk tie, teeth that would have dazzled oncoming drivers. He even had a pair of silver shark cufflinks, I noticed, as he reached out a hand to shake mine. Self-knowledge is a wonderful thing. And was that a Rolex? Of course it was.

His voice was different from what I'd expected, though. It was quieter, more refined. Educated even. Clark obviously hadn't come from that mythical place on the wrong side of the tracks. He'd come from the right side and just decided along the way that he liked being a sleazeball. In a way it made him even more despicable. He had none of the traditional portfolio of excuses.

For now he was all fake bonhomie and handshakes. "Can I get you some coffee, tea? I mustn't forget my manners. I could have Carl bring some in."

"Was that Carl who showed us through?" said Fitzgerald. "In that case, better not. We didn't exactly hit if off, if you know what I mean. I wouldn't like to think what he'd put in it."

Clark laughed that little bit too heartily.

"We're here to talk about Nikolaevna Tsilevich," she interrupted him, and the fake bonhomie vanished at once, to be replaced by an even faker regret.

"Terrible business," he murmured. "Terrible, yes. I was very fond of Sadie. We all were. It was shocking what happened."

He started gathering his papers together.

"How did you find out about it?"

"A police sergeant came round to my house this morning and informed me," he said. "They wanted me to identify her body."

"Did you?" Fitzgerald asked, already knowing the answer.

"No," he admitted. "I told them to ask one of the girls who works here to do it. I'd have found it too . . . upsetting."

Had something more profitable to do at the time, surely? And there went the papers into a drawer in the desk. Bye, boys.

"It was better that way," he said, turning to me as if he'd read my thoughts. "The girls knew her better than I did."

"Yet they didn't pay the rent on her apartment," I said.

The mouth smiled, but the eyes refused to join in. "She worked for me here on and off, she needed a place to stay whilst she sorted herself out. I offered her the apartment, yes."

"Do you often provide places to stay for women who only work for you on and off?"

"Occasionally."

"Sort of like charity?" I said.

"What can I say? I do my best."

"Did you do your best for Mary Dalton as well?" asked Fitzgerald.

"Who?" He frowned.

"Mary Dalton," said Fitzgerald. "The woman whose body was found two days ago in the market behind the Four Courts. Don't you follow the news?"

"I've been very busy lately," Clark said.

"So busy that you couldn't even spare a thought for the death of a woman who once worked for you? That is, I assume that Mary worked for you. There aren't that many lap-dancing clubs in the city, after all, and you have a hand in most of them."

"Oh, that Mary?" he said, like he had strippers dying on him all the time and how could he be expected to remember them all. "Yes, she worked for me briefly. And even that wasn't brief enough for my liking. The woman was falling apart. Completely unprofessional."

"Not like Nikolaevna?"

"I liked Sadie. Liked her a lot. She was a terrific dancer."

"You keep calling her Sadie," Fitzgerald said. "Didn't you know her real name?"

"I knew she was from Russia," he answered, "of course I did. But I'm not sure if she ever told me her name. She was calling herself Sadie the first time she came by here looking for work. She might have told me. I don't pry." He waved his hands in a small gesture of regret.

"Tell me," said Fitzgerald. "How much would Nikolaevna have earned here as a . . . what was the word you used? A dancer, that was it."

"Sadie? About three hundred a night," Clark replied.

"And how many nights a week did she work?"

"On average, about four."

"That makes just over a thousand a week. I suppose you'd be surprised then to know that she was putting about ten thousand a month into her bank account?"

I saw from his face that he was. Saw his busy mind calculating back from what she'd passed on to him to what she should have had left to bank. I realised then that she must have been keeping part of her earnings, possibly a substantial part, hidden from him. His thumbs started to twitch with annoyance. I saw the capacity in him for sudden anger. Saw him control it icily.

"I would be . . . very surprised," he said.

"And how do you think she made the extra income on top of her work here as a dancer?"

"Perhaps she had a paper round," said Clark.

Sarcasm now. Was that a sign we were getting somewhere?

"You don't think it more likely," said Fitzgerald, "that she was using the premises of your apartment for the purposes of prostitution?"

"She may have been. I really wouldn't know."

"You weren't taking a slice of Nikolaevna's earnings in return for providing the premises and arranging her customers?"

"No I wasn't," said Clark.

He was back in control now. He didn't even protest at being asked. He just answered with a faint air of sorrow, as if being considered such a person was a great affront to him but under the circumstances he wouldn't make a fuss about it. He was good at innocence. There was something almost priestly as he sat there at his desk, hands folded together.

"You know," said Fitzgerald, "right now I don't much care what goes on in this club or what arrangement you have with the women who advertise on the back pages of *Dublin Today*. That's between you, them and the vice squad. But let's get to the point, shall we? I am investigating the murder of a young woman by a serial killer who will undoubtedly strike again within days if he is not caught. So I'll ask again, now you understand that nothing you say will go further than this room. Were you aware of Nikolaevna Tsilevich's activities as a prostitute?"

"I was not."

"You didn't arrange clients for her via the mobile phone numbers in her ads?"

"Absolutely not."

"You wouldn't be willing then to provide, in complete confidentiality, a list of the clients that you *didn't* arrange via the mobile phone numbers that you *don't* control?"

"I would be happy to provide any information that might lead to the man you're looking for," said Clark, "but the truth is I don't have any. I don't know who killed Nikol . . . Sadie."

Fitzgerald paused to allow the slip to linger, like a struck bell taking an age to fall to silence. "Did you ever sleep with her?" was how she disturbed it eventually.

He shook his head. Irritated.

"She didn't pay off part of the rent that way?"

"I never even visited her there."

"You're sure about that? Be careful now," said Fitzgerald. "Because if any witnesses were to come forward to say that, for example, around the time of the murder they heard Nikolaevna arguing with a man with a well-to-do accent, an *educated* accent, it wouldn't look good for you."

I realised now what she'd meant earlier in Nikolaevna's flat when she'd talked about Lawlor getting something interesting from his interviews with the neighbours.

"As I said, I hardly ever visited the apartment. The last time was months ago. I don't really see how I can make that any clearer."

"I only hope your memory is better when it comes to your movements last night than it is about your activities as a pimp," said Fitzgerald nonchalantly. "Because either Nikolaevna Tsilevich's killer let himself in with a key, or she let him in because she knew him, because she was expecting him. And you potentially fit both categories. Plus the killer had to be someone who knew that Sadie wasn't her real name. You're an intelligent man. I'm sure you can appreciate that it wouldn't be a good idea to be caught lying at this stage."

"I do not tell lies," Clark said.

And like all the best liars, at that moment it was almost as though he believed it.

★ ★ ★

"*You're an intelligent man,*" said Fitzgerald again as we crossed the car park back to her Rover, the river grey at its side. "Did you hear me? For Christ's sake, the lies I have to tell."

"Flattery always works better than threats with a man like that," I said.

"No. Bribery always works better with a man like that. I, unfortunately, don't have anything to bribe him with." She stood by the driver's side door, searching her coat pockets for the keys. "What did you make of him?"

"Well, I wouldn't want him for a character witness."

"I wouldn't want him for anything," said Fitzgerald. "He's slippery right enough. The worst sort of villain. At least the old school didn't bother with the respectable businessman act."

She unlocked the car and we climbed back in. Sat looking across at the entrance to *Pussy Galore's*. I was trying to conjure up a picture of Nikolaevna Tsilevich arriving here for the first time, thousands of miles from home, into the protective custody of Stephen Clark, with his shining teeth and silver shark cufflinks.

A thought was struggling to take shape.

"Maybe he chooses them here," I ventured in the end.

"The victims?"

"It was a while since Mary Dalton worked as a lap dancer, but it *is* a link. Pretty thin one, I admit, but a link all the same. He might have spotted them here for the first time."

Did I say thin? Thin was putting it too kindly. Mary Lynch never worked for Clark.

Before I could try to fatten up the idea though, Fitzgerald's name crackled quietly over the police radio and she reached across to snatch it from its hook.

"Fitzgerald," she said. "Who's this?"

"It's Sergeant Boland, Chief."

"Boland, what is it?"

"We've been going through the mobile phone records of the Russian woman," Boland's voice explained. "The same number appears more than a hundred times in the last two months. Some days there were as many as six calls. We were going to try and get a match through records when Lawlor said he recognised it. Do you want me to tell you whose number it is?"

Fitzgerald rolled her eyes at me.

"That's the general idea, Sergeant."

"Sorry, Chief," said Boland. "I didn't know who was there with you, that's all. You see, it's Nick Elliott."

He must have been surprised by the silence that followed.

"The reporter," he crackled on. "You know?"

Oh, we knew Elliott all right. Knew him only too well.

Although perhaps not half so well as we'd once thought.

CHAPTER
TWENTY-SEVEN

It got better. Within the hour, a witness had come forward who could put Elliott at the scene of the crime last night and he was brought in for questioning. I watched him through the glass of the interrogation room, slumped in a chair, weary and unshaven, hands on the table, curling and uncurling his fingers repeatedly as if his body couldn't settle whilst his mind was making such panicked leaps. There was a cigarette smouldering in the ashtray next to his hands.

Fitzgerald sat opposite him, turning the pages of her notes slowly, taking her time, like Elliott wasn't there, like he hadn't even entered her thoughts. A uniformed officer stood watch by the door. A clock ticked loudly on the wall. That and the rustling of Fitzgerald's notes were the only sounds coming over the speaker connecting the two rooms.

I sat on the wrong side of the glass with Boland and Sean Healy, waiting for her to begin, as impatient as Elliott. She was making him sweat, but she was making me sweat too.

"Where's his lawyer?" I said when another minute had ticked by.

"He hasn't asked for one," said Boland. "He was told it was his right, but he passed."

"That surprises me," I said. "I'd have thought Elliott was the sort to go hide behind his rights at the first sign of trouble."

"Probably thinks he can talk his way out of it," said Healy.

He took a bite out of a sandwich, and it was only his sandwich which made me realise it was nearly lunchtime already. My stomach didn't even feel like it could cope with coffee.

"Or," Healy went on, his mouth full, "he thinks that not asking for a lawyer makes him look more innocent. I've seen that happen before."

Elliott didn't look like he had any kind of a plan at that moment, unless obsessively tapping his cigarette to shake off the dead ash could be called a plan, and it was a relief when Fitzgerald finally put down her notes and fixed him with a friendly smile.

Stephen Clark wasn't the only shark.

"So help me out, Elliott," were her first words. "More to the point, help yourself out. What was your relationship with Nikolaevna Tsilevich?"

"I didn't have a relationship with her," Elliott said. "I told you already. I . . . went to her a couple of times."

"For sex."

"Of course for sex. She was a prostitute, what do you think I paid her for — doing my gardening?"

Scared or not, Elliott obviously hadn't lost his talent for being bloody-minded.

"Did you pay for her services often?" she said.

314

"A couple of times."

"Elliott." She sighed. "You know why we've brought you in here. Because your number came up on Nikolaevna's phone records more than a hundred times in the past two months."

"OK. I was seeing her" — he considered — "a couple of times a week. Mondays and Fridays mostly."

"Always at her flat?"

"Yeah."

"She never came round to your place?" said Fitzgerald.

Elliott shook his head.

"You're sure about that?"

"Of course I'm sure. You think I'd forget?"

"I really couldn't say," said Fitzgerald. "I don't know how many prostitutes you have sex with. Maybe you stop remembering the details after a while."

"There weren't any others," said Elliott.

"Just Nikolaevna."

"That's right."

"This is just so you know we'll be checking out your house," she said. "Lifting prints. If she was there, we'll find out about it soon enough." She paused a moment, giving him a chance to rescue himself if he wanted to, but Elliott stayed silent. "Maybe find about any others too."

He gave an alarmed look.

"What's that supposed to mean?"

"Nothing," Fitzgerald said soothingly. "Like you say, you never had any other prostitutes round, so what do you have to worry about?" Her eyes slid to her notes for a second. "You never had sex with Monica Lee, for example. Or Mary Lynch."

"What have they got to do with it?"

"Nothing, according to you. That's fine. Forget about them. Forget I mentioned them. You never slept with them."

"No I didn't."

"Never paid them for their professional services."

"No."

"Then why are we still talking about them?" said Fitzgerald, and she gave him a look like she almost pitied his stupidity. "Back to Nikolaevna then. How did you first meet her?"

"I got her number through a friend," said Elliott. "He'd been to her before. He recommended her."

"Are you going to give us his name?"

Elliott hesitated.

"I don't want to get anyone into trouble."

"You're the one who's in trouble, Elliott. I wouldn't waste any energy worrying about anyone else right now."

He hesitated again, but it was obvious it was coming. "Brendan Harte."

"Sorry, Elliott, I didn't quite catch that."

"Brendan Harte," he said, louder. "He recommended her."

"The theatre critic?" said Fitzgerald. "Gave you a good review, did he? Of Nikolaevna's performance?"

"He knew my position. He was just being friendly."

"Is that what they call it nowadays?" Fitzgerald leaned back in her chair. "Just for the record, what exactly was your position?"

"My wife and I . . . it hadn't been going well. We'd split up."

"This would be the wife you only married four months ago?"

"Am I being interrogated about my marriage problems or about Sadie's murder?"

"I'm interested, that's all," said Fitzgerald. "Interested in why your wife would've left you only a couple of months after you married. Just wondering if it's relevant."

"You think I was violent towards her?"

"Who mentioned violence?"

"I know what you're doing," said Elliott. "You're putting two and two together and getting five. You'll have me down as a wife-beater first and say that's why she left me, and then you'll say I was some creep who went to prostitutes, and before you know it I'm a killer."

"But you've got nothing to worry about because it didn't happen like that, right?" said Fitzgerald. "So that's fine. Except," she added, "that you *were* paying Nikolaevna Tsilevich to have sex with you. That part of the scenario's right."

"It wasn't like that," said Elliott.

"It never is," she said wryly, but he didn't take the bait. "How long did you say you'd been going to her? Two months, was it?"

"Two, maybe three."

"It's three now? That would be before your wife left you," said Fitzgerald. "Was that *why* she left you?"

"Why don't you ask her?" he said.

"We will. When was the last time you saw her?"

"My wife or Sadie?"

"Whichever one you prefer to tell us about."

"My wife, two weeks ago. We had stuff to arrange. Financial stuff. We had lunch."

"No chance of a reconciliation then?"

"No."

"Sorry to hear it. What about Nikolaevna?"

Hesitation again. He hadn't been told yet about the witness. Fitzgerald was saving up that little surprise.

"I don't remember," he said.

"Two weeks, one week, three days?"

"I told you, I —"

"Don't remember. Yeah, you said." She raised her eyebrows. "You don't make this easy, you know that, Elliott? Every detail dragged out under duress. Doesn't look good."

"I've got nothing to hide. I didn't kill anyone."

"Think the jury'll agree?"

"Don't start that shit on me!" said Elliott, slamming his knuckles on the desk suddenly. It was the first time he'd really raised his voice, though now he'd raised it he didn't seem to know what to do with it. "Don't you even think of — fuck. A jury, Christ! You're not charging me with this. I didn't kill Sadie. You've got nothing says I did. I cared about her."

318

"You cared about her?" echoed Fitzgerald incredulously. "This isn't exactly Romeo and Juliet, you know."

"You can go to hell, Fitzgerald. I did care about her, she was good to me. I would never have done anything to hurt her."

Boland snorted next to me, but it wouldn't have been so unusual if Elliott *had* fallen for Nikolaevna. Men often fall for the prostitutes they visit. They convince themselves that what goes on between them is a sign of real affection rather than a mockery of it. They blind themselves to the mesmeric power of the money they bring with them to the room. I said nothing, though, because it would've taken too long to explain and Fitzgerald was speaking again.

"If you cared about Nikolaevna so much," she was asking Elliott, "why didn't you make it more than twice a week?"

Elliott breathed out hard with irritation.

"Twice a week was all I could afford," he said.

"She was expensive?"

"She wasn't some common street whore, if that's what you mean," he said.

"Have you got something against common street whores?"

"I don't have anything against anyone. I'm just saying there's a difference. Sadie was classy. I loved her."

"First you cared for her, now you loved her." Fitzgerald scratched her head with her pen and looked sceptical. "How did it make you feel then, that she slept with other men for money?"

Elliott shifted uncomfortably. "I didn't like it," he admitted reluctantly. "I asked her to come live with me. I asked her to give it up."

"On the salary of a man who could only afford her twice a week?" said Fitzgerald.

"Things change," Elliott said. "I'm going places. I had my book out, I had other things lined up, I —"

"Did you tell her all this?"

"I tried to."

A long pause.

"Elliott?"

"If you must know," he said, "she laughed."

Fitzgerald laughed too.

"I can imagine," she said. "That must've made you angry."

"Don't start those games again," Elliott sighed. "Not angry, just sad, just wishing it was different. She was better than that."

"Don't tell me. You wanted to take her away from it all."

"I did."

"That's very admirable. We've obviously misunderstood you." Fitzgerald smiled. "You're a hero, that's what you are. Nick Elliott — mild-mannered newspaper reporter by day, saviour of fallen women everywhere by night. I can already see the movie."

"It's easy to sneer," said Elliott.

"I'm not sneering," Fitzgerald said. "The only thing is, I can't understand why, if you cared about her so much and wanted to save her from herself and the cruel

320

world, you can't remember the last time you saw her. Does that make sense to you?"

He was looking down at his hands.

"What's wrong, Elliott?"

"I'm hot."

"You want a drink, I can get you a drink. Sergeant, see to that, will you?"

The uniformed policeman on watch went to the water cooler and filled a plastic cup for Elliott. He brought it back to the table and set it by the ashtray. Elliott didn't touch it.

"The fact is," Fitzgerald went on as Elliott lit another cigarette, "we don't need you to tell us when you last saw the woman you call Sadie, because we know. You were there last night. We have a witness."

"You're lying," said Elliott, but I could see the sudden fear in him.

"You don't have to say anything," said Fitzgerald. "It doesn't make any difference to us; we've got prints all over the apartment, her phone records show you clearly had some kind of obsession with her. Add in the witness who saw you arriving, and I'd say we nearly have enough to charge you already. You know a bit about the law. What do you think?"

Elliott sought out understanding in her eyes, but she stayed cold.

"I *was* there last night," he said at last, "but I didn't kill her, I swear I didn't kill her." He was still looking for that sign that she understood. "I phoned her earlier, about seven. The editor had called me into his office that afternoon, he was giving me a pay rise for my work on the Night Hunter case. So I called her. I wanted to celebrate."

"Celebrate," she said, like the word was alien.

"Celebrate," he repeated defiantly.

"And how did she react to your suggestion of a . . . celebration?"

"She said no, at first. She said she'd cancelled all her appointments for that night. Said she wasn't seeing anyone."

"Did she say why?"

"No, but . . . well, it doesn't take a genius to work out why now."

For once, Elliott was right. It didn't take a genius, as his own insight proved. Nikolaevna must have seen the killer's latest letter when it was leaked to the *Evening News* and realised she was a potential target. She'd cancelled her appointments because she no longer felt safe. Elliott's information only confirmed that the killer must have been well known to her, familiar enough for her to ignore her fears and let him in. As familiar as Elliott, perhaps? She'd obviously been comfortable enough with him to let him come round in the end.

"What was she like when you got there?" said Fitzgerald.

"On edge," Elliott said. "It wasn't like her. She kept asking about the Night Hunter, whether the police were close to catching him. She asked about the other victims too."

"It's understandable she'd be concerned," said Fitzgerald. "Prostitutes were dying."

322

"That's what I thought at the time. This morning, when I heard what had happened to her, I realised she must've been worried because she thought she might be next."

"She never said anything to you, though? You just went round, opened a bottle of wine —"

"We didn't have wine."

"No need to get touchy. I meant it metaphorically. You went round to her apartment, you indulged in a little pillow talk about the local serial killer, and then?"

"Then I screwed her and left, yes. End of story."

"You screwed her? You really need to do some work on the language of love, Elliott. You don't want to be disrespecting your beloved, especially now that she's no longer with us."

"Fuck you," he said. "I didn't kill anyone. Christ, I didn't even know she was called Nikola-whatever-it-is until I got a call this morning that another body had been found. Even when I went round to the building, I still thought it must be someone else the police were talking about. She never told me her real name."

"Sounds like you had one hell of a relationship," said Fitzgerald, "if you didn't even know her name. Someone certainly knew it."

"How many times do I have to tell you? It wasn't me," Elliott insisted. "Someone must have come round after I left. Isn't it obvious? You should be trying to find him instead of harassing me. I know she wasn't killed until after nine, and I was out of there by eight thirty. At the latest. You can check the CCTV at her apartment block if you don't believe me."

"There's a slight problem with that," said Fitzgerald. "There isn't any CCTV at her apartment block, so it'd be impossible for us to check *exactly* when you left. But then maybe you knew that already." She raised a hand to silence him before he could start protesting again. "Plus there's one other thing puzzles me. If you didn't kill Nikolaevna last night, how come you know so much about what time she died? Did I mention what time she died?"

"I have my sources," said Elliott.

"These sources have names?"

"I can't tell you their names. I have to respect their confidentiality."

"Like you did with Brendan Harte?"

"That was different. If I tell you this, my career's finished. People need to know they can trust me."

"And what do you think'll happen to your career if you're charged with murder?"

"I am not telling you my sources, Chief Superintendent. It's a matter of principle."

Before Fitzgerald could continue, there was a knock at the door of the interrogation room and Seamus Dalton walked in. He was smiling at Elliott with that lopsided, smug smile of his as he bent his lips to Fitzgerald's ear and whispered.

A raised eyebrow was all that his words drew from Fitzgerald till Dalton stood up straight again, then she clicked her tongue as if unsure how to break the bad news to Elliott.

"When the crime tech team came to lift the body of Mary Lynch," she began, "they found a bottle placed underneath her. A Coors Light beer bottle, just like the ones in Nikolaevna's fridge. We couldn't figure at the time what it was doing there, but we took it away anyway and checked it for fingerprints."

She waited until Elliott looked up before continuing. "Guess whose prints they matched?" she said.

Healy drew in his breath sharply. This was a risky tactic. There was nothing in the rules said Fitzgerald couldn't lie to Elliott, but she'd lose the initiative if Elliott realised it was a lie. And the reporter's immediate response suggested she'd blown it, she'd lost him.

"You found my *what?*" screamed Elliott. "How could you have found my fingerprints at the scene? I was never there. I didn't kill Mary Lynch. I'd never even heard of her before!"

"Like you didn't kill Nikolaevna?"

"Yes!" Elliott pushed back his chair noisily and made to get up, then changed his mind as Dalton stepped in to stop him. Fitzgerald hadn't flinched. "You're . . . you're setting me up!"

"Why would we set you up?"

"Well, someone is! I'm not going to sit here and let you do this to me. You're trying to sleepwalk me into incriminating myself. I can't believe I've been so stupid. I thought if I only explained to you what happened, that you'd see I couldn't . . . that I didn't . . ."

"You can still explain," said Fitzgerald. "Still make us see."

It was too late.

"This has gone far enough. I want a lawyer."

"Are you asking for a lawyer?" she said. "Because you know, Elliott, if you bring in a lawyer, then I'll not be able to help you any more."

"Get me a fucking lawyer. Now."

"Your call," Fitzgerald said, and she looked at that moment almost wearier than Elliott. "Just one last question. Will any lawyer do, or does it specifically have to be a fucking one?"

I made my way to the vending machine out in the corridor for coffee, but I couldn't find the right change. Fitzgerald came along just as I was kicking the machine to make the cup drop down.

"Here," she said, "I have change."

"No need." The coffee had suddenly started to appear, though now that I saw it I wasn't sure I should've wasted a kick on it. "Must be my woman's touch," I said. "You OK?"

"I blew it in there. I should've taken my time. I pushed him too fast."

"Don't be too hard on yourself. You did good," I said, taking a sip from the cup and wincing. "It's not like you have the time for niceties. It's not your fault that trying to pull a fast one on him about the bottle backfired."

"What do you mean?" said Fitzgerald. "That stuff about the bottle happens to be true. That's what Dalton came in to tell me. Elliott's prints matched."

I could hardly take in what she was telling me.

"But then why didn't they show up before? The staff at the *Post* all gave their prints to Boland to check against the first letter."

"No one thought of matching the prints with that sample until now. We haven't got our fingerprint records on computer yet, you know that, so unless someone thinks of cross-checking them manually, it wouldn't come up. We only took the prints from the *Post*'s staff to see if we could isolate the killer's prints on the envelope, not to get a match with the bottle."

"Elliott's prints," I said. "I can hardly believe it. And the worst of it is, I could've sworn Elliott couldn't believe it either."

"I know. I couldn't tell if he was looking so shocked because he realised he'd left incriminating evidence behind when he killed Mary Lynch, or because he couldn't figure out how his prints had ended up there when he was never anywhere near the place."

"It was beginning to make sense too," I said. "Elliott's book, the obsession with Fagan; he's still going on about it and what it could do for his career. Not to mention the split from his wife. Relationship breakdown's a classic stressor. If he was immersed in his book on Fagan, living with Fagan in his head all that time, while outside it his life was going down the toilet, maybe that'd be enough to send him over the edge."

"You still don't sound convinced."

"I'm not. That's the problem."

"And there was me hoping," said Fitzgerald over her shoulder as she made her way back towards the interrogation room, "that you could convince me I'd got the right man."

My mobile, which I'd finally got back from Boland after leaving it in his car the other day, began ringing as I watched her go. I didn't recognise the number that flashed up and thought about directing it to voicemail. I'd been getting calls from reporters all week, I didn't think I could bear another one. Perhaps word had got out that Nick Elliott was "helping police with their enquiries", as they put it. But there was something about this one. Call it a sixth sense.

I pressed the button to answer.

CHAPTER
TWENTY-EIGHT

Sebastiane's wasn't really my kind of place; and from the look he gave me when I walked in, the head waiter obviously agreed. "Madame is waiting for you at the table," he conceded when I told him who I'd come to see. He seemed disappointed that I had a legitimate reason for being there.

Madame indeed. He was no more French than I was.

It wasn't as if they were so busy they could afford to be rude to customers. The restaurant was practically empty as I followed him over to a huge arched window at the far end of the room, where a table had been set for two and a woman looked out at bare trees in a grey square.

For someone who was supposed to be dead, Susan Fuller looked pretty good.

She'd hardly changed a bit in the five years since I'd last met her. No, that wasn't quite true. She'd always been striking, always been well dressed, always had poise, but now she looked happier, more relaxed. Her skin glowed with health like she'd just stepped out of the sea after a swim. She looked years younger than her forty-two, and smiled warmly when she saw me; if she considered, like the waiter, that I'd taken dressing down a touch too far, she gave no hint.

"You don't know how relieved I was to hear your voice," I said.

"I'm just sorry I put you to so much trouble," Susan said as I took a seat opposite her and glanced out briefly at the winter trees shaking and stirring. Strange how such loveliness can continue whilst the world falls apart just out of sight. "I'm so embarrassed. If I'd known Tom was going to be silly about all this, I'd have been in contact sooner."

"He was worried."

"I told him I was going to leave him," she said. "I told him a thousand times. That night, when we quarrelled . . . well, I really don't know how much clearer I could have made it."

"When you didn't come back for your things —"

"I didn't *want* my things, I wanted to change my life; he's welcome to my things. I went round to Roy's house and left it all behind. I'd been seeing him again since the summer. A couple of days later, we left for France. Roy has a house there, a business."

I cursed. The police should have found all that out, tracked him down, and we wouldn't have wasted more time thinking Susan was the body in the churchyard.

"Didn't you even want to take your books, your papers?" I said as the wine waiter stepped forward to fill our glasses with the wine Susan had already ordered.

"I've had it with academia," she replied dismissively. "The pay stinks, the company's boring, there's too much pressure to publish. It was better when I started out. I just got on quietly with teaching my students. It's all different now." She shrugged. "It's behind me now."

"What are you going to do?" I said, reaching for my glass and taking a sip.

"Roy's in antiques. He's going to teach me all about it, we'll live in France. I'm not getting any younger. I need to get away. From Dublin, from my job, from the same old routine."

"From Tom."

"From Tom, especially. I know it sounds cruel, but he's stifled me for years."

"You kept going back to him."

"Only out of pity. I'm not blaming him. It was my decision. But I finally ran out of pity."

"Isn't this where you're supposed to say you gave him the best years of your life?"

"No," said Susan. "The best years of my life are all ahead of me, and Tom's not going to ruin them. We're only back now to put Roy's place up for sale and then we're going again."

"Out of Tom's orbit."

"Precisely," she said brightly.

I picked something at random from the menu, not really caring what I ate. By the time it came I'd completely forgotten what I'd ordered and picked through it unenthusiastically as Susan explained how she'd found out that the police were searching for her.

"We only got in this morning, went straight to Roy's apartment, and it was pandemonium. I've never seen so many messages on an answering machine. Friends, colleagues, reporters, all wondering what had happened to me."

"Did you call the police and let them know you were back, like I told you earlier?"

"Straight away. I think they were annoyed that I was alive. They made me feel like I'd been wasting police time."

"You can't blame them for thinking the body was you," I said. "First Fagan's back in the news, then a woman's body's found and your name comes up on the missing files. I thought it was you too for a while. It all added up, even the fact that you had a fractured leg."

"It's creepy," admitted Susan. "Too creepy. To be honest, I don't want to think about it. I just want to get everything cleared up then I can go again. I don't even want to think about that poor woman, whoever she is. I know that sounds awful. Have you any idea who she might be?"

"Not really," I said.

She giggled nervously. "I shouldn't laugh, but I was about to say I was sorry. Sorry it wasn't me, I mean. Then I realised what I'd be saying."

"Forget it. It's relief." I put out a hand to stop her refilling my glass. I'd had enough of drinking too much in the last few days. "Do you mind if I ask you a question?"

"Try me and see."

"What did you think when you heard someone was back claiming to be Ed Fagan?"

Susan took a deep breath.

"I could write a book about Ed Fagan," she said. "About my feelings for him. How did I feel? I felt sick, disgusted. Afraid too. It all seemed horribly plausible once I realised what people thought. Plausible that Fagan would come back for me, I mean."

"Why would he want to kill you?" I said.

"Why would he want to kill anyone? But he did." She was gazing abstractedly out through the glass again. The wind was up, though I couldn't hear it. The air was alive with leaves that had fallen weeks ago and now were whipped up again from the wet ground in some mad dance. On the other side of the square, a man in a raincoat struggled with an umbrella. Here it was like being inside an aquarium, looking out. "I wouldn't have been surprised if he *had* tried to kill me, put it that way. He always suspected me of tipping off the police about him."

"You never said anything the times we spoke."

"It didn't feel right to say anything," she said. "Fagan was out of jail by then, the police had admitted planting evidence against him, he was claiming to be innocent, I thought your book was going to take his side. I told myself my doubts were foolish."

"What doubts did you have?"

"You name them," she said. "I'd only started a relationship with him a few months before he was arrested and he seemed obsessed. He'd suggested himself as a consultant to the police, of course, and they listened to him up to a point, but he was never as much in on the investigation as he wanted to be, so all the time he'd be discussing it, insisting on silence when the news came on, reading the papers. Sometimes he used to take me out and show me the places where it had all happened. Down by the canal, you know, the cemeteries. I told him I didn't like it, but he just treated it like a joke. One time he picked me up, wanted us to go to the grounds of the Law Library to make love. He got angry when I said no."

"You didn't tell the police?"

"No. I look back now and can't understand why I didn't, but at the time I suppose I felt stupid." She mimed putting a phone to her ear. "*Excuse me, is that the police? Well I'm having an extramarital affair and I think my lover is a serial killer.* Come on."

"So you said nothing."

"So I said nothing, and don't think I haven't felt guilty about it every day since. It killed me for a while at first, after he was arrested, thinking that if I'd just been a bit braver, come forward, I might have saved some of those girls' lives."

"Fear of being thought stupid stops plenty of people doing what they want to do, what they know they should do."

"That's me," said Susan. "Always has been. That was the problem with Tom. If I told him I wanted to, oh I don't know, go skiing in the nude down the Matterhorn, he'd just have told me not to be silly, what would people think? What people would think, that was his moral compass. The result was I never did anything. We always went on holiday to the same place, ate in the same restaurants; he even bought me the same perfume every year for my birthday."

"Roy's up for skiing in the nude, is he?" I said.

"Roy's up for anything," she said, and arched her eyebrows meaningfully over the top of her wine glass and giggled. Then she stopped herself. "God in heaven, listen to me getting on and giggling like a horny teenager."

"Nothing wrong with that," I said.

"You should tell that to Tom," Susan shot back with sudden bitterness. She looked sombre all of a sudden. "Sorry, I always giggle when I'm nervous. Tom hated it, and that made me worse, knowing he was so disapproving. He used to say I was frivolous. That very word used to set me off again. Frivolous. Nasty, begrudging little word. So anyway, when I started to have doubts about Ed, I just thought I was being stupid again. That was supposed to be my speciality, after all. Only now I know it was *not* going to the police that was stupid."

"But Fagan thought you had?"

"He wrote to me when he was in prison," she explained. "Lots of letters, swearing he was innocent and would I wait for him, we could make a go of it, we could go abroad and start again. Then when I didn't reply, he started getting more aggressive, demanding I come and see him, saying it was all my fault that he'd been arrested, that I must have put the police up to it. And in his last letter, he promised that he'd make me suffer for what I'd done."

"You took it to mean he'd kill you?" I said.

"What else was I to think?"

"Did you tell Tom about the letters?"

"Hardly," Susan said. "Ed wasn't exactly a big topic of conversation between us. Tom always made it perfectly clear that he didn't want to hear Ed Fagan's name. He used to turn off the television if the news even mentioned the case."

"He showed no interest in the murders?"

"None that I ever saw. He'd have thought that was frivolous too. The closing stock market prices were all he cared about."

Except, of course, that he now had Nick Elliott's book about Ed Fagan in his collection.

"So what did you do?" I asked instead.

"About the letters? I told the prison about them and I never received another one. I don't know if Ed stopped writing them or they simply stopped sending them on. I was just grateful for the silence. Only then his trial collapsed and he was back out again, a free man."

"You must've been afraid."

"Terrified would be nearer the mark," she said. "Ed might have been insisting to everyone who'd listen that he was innocent, but I knew the police were still convinced he'd done it, and I didn't know what I thought. All I knew was I couldn't take the chance. I finally got up the courage to tell Tom about Ed's threats and beg him to take us away from Dublin. He said I was being silly. That one again."

"Did you hear from Fagan after he got out?"

"He phoned me at work once, a couple of weeks after he was released. He said he wanted to meet me. I asked him why, he said he wanted to explain things to me, he said he was sorry for writing those letters but prison had been unbearable for him. He said he knew I could never forgive him but he needed to know I understood he never meant it." She must have seen the scepticism in my face. "My reaction was exactly the same. I asked him why, if he was so innocent, he'd wanted me to go to the Law Library to make love where that girl Tara had been killed."

"What was his answer?"

"He said he'd only been joking. I told him he must think I was as stupid as Tom did if he expected me to believe that. Then he said —" She stopped, as if she'd already revealed too much.

"Said what?" I pressed her.

"Ed said a lot of things," she answered carefully. "I don't want to give them credence by repeating them now. He was good at lying."

"Just because you tell me what he said doesn't mean I'll believe him."

Still she spoke the next words reluctantly, as if she felt she was being used by Fagan to carry messages, as if she felt soiled by his words.

"He claimed to have been so obsessed by the murders," she said, "because he thought he knew who might have committed them."

"Did he say who he suspected?"

The pause was briefer this time.

"He said he thought it was his son."

Jack Mullen.

"It's crazy, I know," she added hurriedly. "Ed was always trying to pretend everything he did was for some higher motive. He reported one of his fellow lecturers once for plagiarism and said afterwards it was out of concern for the standing of the university. The fact that the man was also in line for a job Fagan wanted was beside the point. He was doing the same now, playing the concerned father, when really he was just trying to blame his own son for what he'd done."

I couldn't speak. I tried to think of something to say, but I was remembering what Lawrence Fisher had told me when I picked him up from the airport. An awful possibility had started hammering inside my skull.

"What did you say to him?" I managed to get out at last.

"I told him to leave me alone. I told him I never wanted to see or hear from him again. In the end, I slammed down the phone. Not long afterwards, he disappeared."

A huge gust of wind suddenly filled the trees outside. It was unnatural not to hear it. It must be roaring. Susan caught a glimpse of it out of the corner of her eye and shivered.

"Someone must be walking over my grave," she said.

I knew exactly how she felt.

CHAPTER
TWENTY-NINE

Back in my apartment again, I lay down on the couch, feeling dizzy. The room was spinning. One thought kept coming back to me. Ed Fagan wasn't the Night Hunter. It was his son.

I'd killed the wrong man.

As I lay there, I made a list in my head of those earlier deaths, tried to remember the dates. Julie Feeney, late October; Sylvia Judge, early December; Tara Cox, late January. After the first three deaths, a gap of six months before the final two.

Police had been intrigued by that gap at the time. Had the killer been out of the country during those months? In hospital or prison? Had he managed to stop himself temporarily for fear of being caught, or out of shame, only for the urge to kill to grow too intense again as the months passed? Then Fagan had been picked up and charged with two of the murders and the questions had effectively ceased. There were enough demands on everyone's time, enough other cases to be dealing with. The killer was caught, so why worry about the small details?

But what if the original hypothesis had been right? What if the killer had stopped killing during that time because he was out of action in some way? What if he'd been someplace where he had nothing to do but nurse his fantasies, watch them fester, until, able to act them out once more, he could unleash them in furious succession on Liana Cassidy and Maddy Holt?

Then it hit me with a jolt.

Fagan's son had been imprisoned once for — what was it? Stealing cars, that was it.

Next question. When?

Pulling myself to my feet, I dragged the box in which I kept the notes on Fagan out once more, tipped it upside down and ransacked the scattered papers till I found what I wanted.

There it was.

For four of those six months, Jack Mullen had been behind bars in Mountjoy Prison serving a sentence for car theft.

The room was spinning again. I needed to sit down. I laid my head against the arm of the couch and closed my eyes and cursed myself for a fool. I'd been so convinced Fagan had killed those women, I hadn't even given a thought to Jack. How could I have missed that the dates tallied?

Now Jack Mullen's name was staring out at me from my own notes like an accusation. In the clockwork of my head, the cogs started locking together. The dates. The forensic traces in Fagan's car: Mullen must have been using it. What if Fagan had been unable to account for the presence of the green twine in his car because of the simple fact that he didn't know it was there?

Even if I *had* killed the wrong man, of course, I'd still done so in self-defence. Fagan was going to kill me that night. Not because he feared I was about to expose him as the killer, perhaps, but because he feared I was about to expose his son.

I remembered him coming at me, I remembered the flash of the gun. I knew I'd done the right thing, or it would have been me buried in a shallow grave in the mountains for the past five years, not Fagan. Me or him: simple as that. I'd made the right choice.

But that wasn't making me feel a whole lot better. Instead I felt soiled. I felt wicked.

I felt —

Wait.

Why would Fagan want to take Susan to where Tara Cox had died for sex if his only interest was in protecting his son? Why had the eyewitnesses described seeing someone of Fagan's age and build? Why had he persistently inveigled himself into the investigation from the beginning? That was more likely to draw the police's attention in his and his son's direction. And why — Christ, why did I have to keep remembering that night? — had he said to me when I came across him in the wood: "You know, Saxon, I think I'm going to enjoy you best of all"?

His last words. Not quite up there in terms of poetry with "this is a far, far better thing I do now than I have ever done", but they were seared into my memory all the same.

Most of all, if Mullen was the killer, why would the killings have stopped for seven years? And that was when the next thought started to take shape.

The thought which said: what if father and son had been in it together? What if they murdered together? It wasn't so rare to find potential killers needing one another's encouragement in order to fulfil their shared fantasies, to become what they each dreamed of being. Without that encouragement from Fagan any more, that fatherly nurturing, maybe Mullen simply didn't have it in him to carry on alone — till now. And the more I thought about it, the more the theory that Fagan and his son had been working together made sense.

Take that night. I remembered shooting Fagan and burying his body; I remembered the dark wood; I remembered a car revving up and the sweep of headlights through the trees.

Who had that been?

Some innocent passer-by had been my thought at the time. But what if it had been Mullen? Mullen waiting in a stolen car to take his father home. He was good at getting hold of cars. Not so good that he didn't get caught now and again, but good enough.

That would explain at least how Fagan had got into the mountains that night. That was one thing I'd never understood. When police went to follow up reports that he'd gone missing, they found his own car parked outside his house where he'd left it. At the time, I'd just presumed he was being clever. Of course he wouldn't have taken his car with him. I was scheduled to die, and Fagan wouldn't take the risk that, if my body was ever found, his car could be placed in the area on the night it happened. I wouldn't have taken mine if I'd known what was to happen that night either. But then how did he get into the mountains? Police had never managed to trace Fagan's movements that night. No taxi drivers came forward with memories of having taken his fare; none of the bus drivers recognised his picture as one of their passengers — and there weren't so many people travelling into the mountains after nightfall that they were likely to forget.

Five years ago, I'd come to the unsatisfactory conclusion that he must have made his way there on foot from the nearest train station, or else hitched a lift and the driver, luckily for me, had not seen the appeals for information about the whereabouts of his passenger that night. Now I saw that it was more likely to have been Mullen. Mullen drove him there, then waited out of sight whilst Fagan went into the woods to kill me. Waited till he heard the shot and realised what must've happened. Fagan never owned a gun, after all. At which point he fled, panicked, afraid.

True, the theory didn't make complete sense. If Mullen knew what I'd done, why had he never come after me himself? I wasn't the hardest target to get at if he wanted revenge. Or why hadn't he tipped off police anonymously about what I'd done?

But for all its faults, I kept coming back to those same basic facts: a car revving up, Mullen's four-month stretch in jail to account for the gap in the first sequence of killings, his time in London when Fisher told me more prostitutes had been attacked, the return of the Night Hunter motif since Mullen had returned to Dublin. It was too many coincidences to be coincidental, and certainly too many to ignore. I needed to talk to Lawrence Fisher. Now.

My first mistake was to call his house in north London. The phone was picked up by his au pair.

She was from the Far East somewhere and sounded like English wasn't even her second language, never mind her first, but she understood well enough that I wanted to speak to Fisher and communicated well enough back that he wasn't there.

I tried his office next. His secretary told me that Dr Fisher was out of the country. I knew that, I explained, because it was me he'd come to see, but he ought to be back by now.

She said she didn't know anything about that.

Was there a number where he could be contacted?

She said she didn't know that either.

Anyone I could speak to?

No.

Did she ever wonder, I asked finally, how she managed to keep her job despite obviously having the intellectual capacity of an amoeba?

She said she didn't like my attitude.

I said I didn't like that she was an idiot but we were both going to have to live with it.

The line went dead.

Scotland yard next. Inspector Neil Taylor was the name Fisher had given me, and he proved easier to track down, at any rate.

"I recognise your name," he said once I'd introduced myself. "Lawrence told me all about you. He said you wrote books, isn't that so? Maybe I should pick one up, eh?"

I tried not to sound too impatient, but my words came out quickly as I tried to stop him starting a conversation. "Is Fisher there now, Inspector? I really need to talk to him."

"You'd have more idea where he is than I would," he said.

"Me?"

"Fisher's not going to be back here for a few days. He called me last night, said he was staying on in Dublin a while longer. He had the photographs couriered over to me this morning; you just caught me as I was heading out the door to show them round." He paused as if not knowing what else to add. "Did he not tell you?"

"There must've been . . . a misunderstanding." It sounded feeble, but I couldn't think of any word right now that would cover the fact that Fisher hadn't been straight with me.

Why hadn't he told me he wasn't going home?

And more to the point, where the hell was he?

I extricated myself from the call as quickly as I could and sat staring out beyond the terrace to the tempered steel of the sky, a coldness creeping over me. Eventually

I phoned the airport and asked to be put through to the British Airways desk.

"Hello, how can I help you?"

"I want to check whether a passenger made a connection to London Heathrow last night."

"And you are?"

I explained about the investigation, dropped a few names and a few hints without quite admitting that I didn't have the authority to be delving after Fisher's personal details.

"It's important," I added as a footnote.

"Hold on a moment."

I heard the rattle of a keyboard in the background and a tannoy announcing the last call for a flight to Dusseldorf.

"What flight did you say he was on?"

I gave her the flight number. "It was scheduled for take-off last night at twenty-two hundred hours."

"Yes, I have it here. What was the name again?"

"Fisher. Dr Lawrence Fisher."

"I'm sorry," she said, "there was no one on the plane by that name."

Maybe he'd used a different name.

"Could you try the night before?" I said. "A flight came in from Heathrow at twelve fifteen, I met him off the plane."

More rattling.

"Yes, according to the records a Dr Fisher was booked on to that flight."

"Does it say when he was due to return?"

"I'll check." She checked. "It was a one-way ticket."

"A one-way ticket?"

"That's right, madam."

"Right, I'm going to ask you to do something for me."

"I'll do my best."

"I want you to check all the flights that left Dublin last night for London. All airports, Heathrow, Stansted, Luton, see if Dr Fisher was booked on to any flight. Can you do that?"

"It may take some time."

"Quick as you can. I'll give you my number."

Nothing made sense any more, I reflected bitterly after I hung up. The only reason Fisher would have me take him all the way out to Dublin Airport when he had no intention of making a flight was to fool me into thinking he'd left the city when in fact he was still here.

But why would he want to do that? He'd got what he'd come for; at least he'd got what he'd told me he'd come for. I couldn't suspect him of being involved in anything sinister, I simply couldn't, but it was difficult to imagine any benign reason why he would have lied to me.

The one thing I had to cling on to was the hope that I'd misheard him when he told me he was on the 2200 flight, or that he was the one who was mistaken and he'd actually been booked on a later plane. That still wouldn't explain the one-way ticket, but one step at a time.

Half an hour later, the girl from British Airways called back. Fisher's name had not appeared on the lists for any of the flights leaving Dublin for England last night. He was still in the city somewhere. And he obviously didn't want me to know where he was.

CHAPTER
THIRTY

It didn't taken long to find out where Jack Mullen was living. A quiet call to someone I knew in Probation and I had an address. He was back near his father's old haunts, in a couple of rooms in a crumbling terrace off the North Circular Road in the dark shadow of Mountjoy Prison. Perhaps he missed his old home. Perhaps it contained some malevolent spirit that soothed him. It certainly seemed to pervade the streets as I drove through the rain to get there.

Most of the houses in the area had been converted into apartments and bedsits. A few remained in the hands of the old and the stubborn, but once they died, the battle would be lost. It was one of those city districts which had made the all-too-common passage from grandeur through slow neglect and indifference to final despair, with few stops on the way.

I parked at the dead end of the narrow street, so that if Mullen did come out any time soon he wouldn't walk this way and see me. I had no doubt now that he'd remember me.

The rain made the day darker than ever, hammering on the roof of the Jeep with a lonely, metallic, empty sound, and the houses, black with soot and damp, didn't help. Even the windows were black holes, curtains drawn, as if everyone was still in bed, late afternoon though it was, with nothing to get up for. There was no sign of Christmas. Occasionally a figure emerged from a door to trudge down to the corner store for cigarettes or milk or evening paper. I could see the warm glow of it at the end of the street, beckoning like a campfire in a hostile wilderness.

I'd lost my taste for this sort of waiting and watching work. I didn't even know if Mullen was in. All that kept my impatience in check was my need to know, after speaking to Fisher and Susan Fuller, whether Mullen really was measuring up to fill that offender-shaped hole.

After a while, I rummaged round for a cigar, and eventually found one, slightly bent, in the glove compartment. I was about to light it when I saw . . . was it him? Was that Jack Mullen?

Someone had appeared at the door of the address I'd been given, just as the rain started to ease. He must have been waiting for it to stop. He had no coat on, just a thin jacket wrapped about a shirt, and he had the familiar hunched, secretive, evasive stance of a man who spent his life waiting for the hand on his shoulder telling him that he was finally caught.

I felt sure it was Mullen; there was something unmistakable in his eyes, about the way he carried himself. The only difference was that this man had a thick, unkempt black beard.

I realised my mistake at once. The picture I'd shown to Jackie to test whether Mullen was the man who'd

350

raped her down by the canal had been taken more than five years ago, when Fagan was still alive. He didn't have a beard in those days. What a fool I was. Of course Jack Mullen would have changed.

I recalled Jackie's hesitation when I asked if she recognised him. There was something she said, but no, she couldn't be sure. But what if I could show her a more recent picture?

I watched as Mullen shuffled down the steps of the house where he now lived and along the road. Now was my chance. But how long would he be gone? I'd have to follow to see where he went. I opened the door of the car, climbed out and closed it behind me. The door shutting sounded like a shot in the still air, but miraculously he didn't turn round.

By the time I got to the end of the street, I thought I'd missed him. There were more people here. The North Circular Road was busy. The traffic rumbled by. Then I saw him, stepping to the kerb as a bus approached and flagging it down. He must be going into town. Couldn't be better. I saw him hop on and take his seat on the lower deck as the bus pulled away.

I watched till it disappeared. Then I turned round, and nervously made my way back towards his house, pulling on my gloves as I went. Here's hoping I hadn't forgotten all my breaking and entering skills. Though hold on, no need. The door had been left ajar.

I was suspicious at once. It was too easy, almost as if Mullen had known I was outside and was luring me in; but screw it, I didn't have time for hesitation. He'd no reason to suspect me of being here. I made up my mind, pushed open the door and stepped inside.

Closed it.

Steadied my breathing.

I was looking down a narrow corridor with three doors on the right, all thankfully shut. Behind them I heard hammering; the sound of fake laughter on daytime TV; a kettle shrieking.

Probation had told me that Mullen's place was second from the top, so I hurried up, stairs creaking. The carpet was worn and thin, and sticky underfoot; there was a bad smell in the air, like drains and fried food; the wallpaper curled with damp.

At his door, I paused once more to make sure no one was coming. Then I took out my credit card, slipped the lock, waited for the click, and I was in. Easy as that. I shut the door behind me and listened for any noise outside . . . no, all was quiet . . . before turning to inspect Mullen's mean domain.

It only occurred to me then that Mullen might have had someone in here with him, and that I might've disturbed them. That was careless, but fortunately it was obvious at once that he had been alone. The silence was too intense, the air too stagnant.

There wasn't much to his home at all. One main room, a kitchenette along the back wall with dishes thrown in the sink, the remains of a chip supper wrapped in greasy paper, a lingering smell of fish, used tea bags clogging the plughole, spoons stained brown, stale bread; in the fridge, some tins of lager, sliced ham, cooked sausages in a dish, milk gone off.

352

In the middle of the room, an armchair and sofa that had seen better days, a small gas heater, a table on which dirty clothes had been piled. The only things that looked like they were worth anything were a TV and video. And a computer, looking new. Stolen? Probably.

Two doors led off from this room. One into a tiny bathroom, with a towel heaped wetly on the floor and a toilet with no seat. The other led into a bedroom, almost as small, where —

I stopped.

All around the walls were pasted religious pictures, cut from newspapers and magazines or torn from the pages of books or downloaded, from the look of them, off the Internet.

There were pictures of the Crucifixion, and of Christ in Gethsemane weeping tears of blood; of Thomas with his hands thrust into Christ's wounds, and Christ in a crown of thorns, and Judas hanging from the tree in a field of blood. And there were pictures of the Virgin Mary too — perhaps the name Mary *had* been important, after all. A calendar of saints hung above the filthy mattress on the floor that served Mullen as a bed.

It was all exactly as Fisher had described the room of the offender in London.

Next to the mattress was a small heap of magazines, and they weren't back issues of the *New Yorker* either. I flicked through them quickly. It was the usual hardcore bedtime reading of dysfunctional loners everywhere. Many of the magazines came from the Far East and featured girls who looked barely out of puberty. I was glad I was wearing gloves.

Among them, too, a copy of yesterday's *Evening News* open, surprise, surprise, at the page with the leaked last letter from the killer. There was no law against taking an interest in crimes supposedly committed by your dead father, but even so.

And what was this under the pillow? A Bible, leatherbound, with an inscription inside — *To Jack, my beloved Son, in whom I am well pleased. Your loving father EF* — and a photograph, used as a bookmark, of Mullen's late mother in the garden of their old home, cotton pattern-print dress, shielding her eyes from the sun, looking far too lovely to have deserved either of them.

Apart from the mattress, the only other furniture in the room was a wardrobe. Inside that, more magazines, some clothes. A jacket, cellophane-wrapped, just back from the cleaner's. An extra pair of shoes, spotlessly polished. Unusually clean for this place. To wipe away any identifiable traces from Nikolaevna Tsilevich's flat? No, I was going too fast, I was letting my own desire to bring this game to an end get the better of me. Mullen could simply have had them cleaned for a job interview. Or a date. Stranger things had happened.

Back in the main room, I noticed for the first time the pile of videos on the carpet next to the TV, cheap pirate porn films, I saw from the labels, picked up in what were laughingly called the adult shops round Capel Street. Stunted adolescence shops would be a better description. That was probably where he was off to now.

354

There were some blank videos among the pile too. I switched on the TV at the socket, turned down the sound, and slotted one into the video to check what was on it.

At least he was consistent. Mullen had recorded something off one of the cable porn channels. It sounded like German, though there wasn't much actual dialogue to go on.

I fast-forwarded impatiently to see if anything else was there.

I don't know what I expected to find. Shots of the murdered women, perhaps. The killer had watched them so closely before their deaths I wouldn't have been surprised to find that he'd filmed them too. It would be a way for him to keep alive the memory of what he'd done to them, of sustaining the fantasy. But it was a long shot. I hadn't even seen a stills camera in the bedsit so far, never mind a video camera, and this tape spooled to its end with no surprises.

I tried the second video, then the third. Nothing more sinister there than the same young women with the same silicone breasts and the same absence of inhibitions cavorting on screen.

I switched off. The computer next? For a man with Jack Mullen's appetites, the Internet would be a door to an infinity of forbidden, suffering flesh. But no, it would take too long, and like I'd said to Salvatore, I was useless with technology. If Mullen had encrypted the contents of his computer, I'd be sunk. Besides, there'd be time enough for that if the police in London got Ellen Shaw or one of the other two prostitutes who'd been attacked to identify him.

I certainly had no doubt now that Mullen was the man they were looking for.

But was he the man *we* were looking for too? I had to admit that there was no evidence here of the highly intelligent, sexually competent offender with his own car and house and steady job that Mort Tillman's profile had spoken about, nor of one who was only using religious symbolism because it was part of some intellectual game. Mullen, worryingly, was far more like his father in that respect. He wasn't faking anything. Which left us where exactly?

I made one last circuit, trying to ensure everything was the way I'd found it and wishing there was someone I could tell about what I'd found — I could have told Fisher if he hadn't decided to play hide and seek — then I tiptoed back to the door and readied myself to leave.

And that was when I heard the front door below slam, as someone came in.

It's Mullen, I thought at once. I checked my watch. I'd been in here more than half an hour; he could easily have returned in that time.

Anxiously, I pressed my ear to the door and listened.

The someone was climbing the stairs.

I hurried back as silently as I could to the kitchenette, slid open the drawer, lifted out the sharpest knife I could find, and returned.

The footsteps were nearer now, but slow. It was almost as if the someone was deliberately trying not to be heard, or was trying to frighten me, knowing I was here. My heart was pounding; I needed to take deep breaths, but didn't want to in case I was heard.

The footsteps came closer and closer . . . was this it? Then they went on — on up, to the flat above. I heard a door click, a muffled cough, silence.

Only then did I realise how much I was sweating and how terrified I'd been. I wanted to get out of there and never come back, but I had to wait a while longer, not least to calm down. I couldn't believe what a fool I'd been, how easily I might've been caught.

I planned on waiting another five minutes, but managed three before opening the door and slipping out. Relief. No one there. I shut the door as gently as I could behind me, skipped down the stairs to the front door, and a moment later I was out in the air again.

It was dark, and the street was still deserted and the rain hadn't returned, and I got back to my car and climbed inside; lit that cigar I'd wanted earlier, hands shaking. I drew in deeply, relishing the scent that filled the Jeep after the fetid oppression of Mullen's place. Gradually I calmed down, and my hands stopped shaking enough for me to think about driving home.

My own apartment had never seemed such a haven.

It was only when I reached into my pocket for the car keys that I realised what I'd done.

My fingers touched the cold edge of the knife, the one I'd picked up for protection when Mullen's neighbour disturbed me. I'd forgotten to replace it in the drawer.

So much for not leaving any clue to my visit, but I wasn't going back in there to put it right. I simply had to hope that Mullen wouldn't notice the missing knife, or, even if he did, wouldn't have sufficient imagination to figure out why it was missing.

I started the car and made my escape.

CHAPTER
THIRTY-ONE

Six o'clock. Fitzgerald had asked me to call in at Dublin Castle as soon as I was free again. I was one of the last people to see Fagan alive, was the way she put it, and I could hardly deny that, so I'd have to make a fresh statement to the police detailing what I knew of his last movements.

I wasn't worried about it; I'd been rehearsing my lies about Fagan for five years. Besides, now that my head was buzzing with angles and possibilities, I was desperate to know what the crime tech team had uncovered at Nikolaevna Tsilevich's apartment; and whether anything had been found during the search of the older scenes that Fisher and I had instigated the night before.

All the same, I couldn't face it straight away, not after the fright in Mullen's place. I decided to head back to my own apartment first to see if Fisher had called in my absence.

I'd barely got inside and thrown the car keys on to the table by the door when the buzzer went and Nick Elliott's voice came through the intercom. That was the last thing I'd expected.

"Saxon, can I come up?"

I ignored his question.

"When did you get out?" I demanded instead.

"Half an hour . . . an hour ago . . . Christ, I don't know. I've lost track. Can I? Come up?"

"That's not such a great idea, Elliott. I'm still connected with this case; you shouldn't be speaking to me."

"I need to talk to you, Saxon. *Please*."

That *please* was so pathetic, I could hardly refuse; but there was no way Elliott was getting into my apartment.

"Saxon?" he whined again.

"Wait there," I said. "I'll come down."

A few moments later, I was in the front lobby again. There was no sign of Elliott on the other side of the rain-streaked glass, just traffic swishing by on its eternal journey, headlights glaring in the dark like the eyes of hungry predators.

I stepped out into the wet. The noise of the city, dulled by the glass, assaulted me at once. Evening sounds. The unremarkable sounds of people winding their way home. Tyres turning on a wet road. But no sight or sound of Elliott. Was I imagining him now? That was all I needed.

I looked up and down the street a couple of times, and was about to go back inside when I caught sight of him attracting attention to himself at the edge of the building, beckoning me clumsily, before ducking out of sight again. I followed with a weary sigh, and found him waiting round the corner. He looked tired. He'd had a long day. Hadn't we all?

"Is this your idea of being discreet?" I said.

"What do you mean?" he said, looking hurt.

"You couldn't have made yourself more conspicuous if you'd put out a press release announcing when you'd be visiting me," I said. "And if the DMP see me with their prime suspect" — he snorted at the description and I didn't blame him; if he was their prime suspect, he wouldn't be standing here talking to me — "I won't be on the investigation longer than it takes to say conflict of interest."

"Thinking of yourself again?"

"You're the expert at that, Elliott."

He was starting to look sulky now as he turned up his collar to take shelter.

"I was only —" he began to explain, but I stopped him right there.

"Save it," I said. "Let's walk."

Before he could object, I set off against the flow of the traffic as it streamed towards me, dragging lights, pricked by rain, making my way to the darker streets off St Stephen's Green.

"How did you get out, anyway?"

"I dug a tunnel," said Elliott, "like they did in Colditz."

"Is that supposed to be funny?"

"I got an alibi, if you must know."

"Lawyers are good at providing those. I hope it didn't cost you too much."

"My alibi was genuine, like I told Fitzgerald when she questioned me this morning," Elliott said. "My lawyer had nothing to do with it. It would've saved everyone a whole lot of trouble today if you'd just listened to me from the start."

"Who was it then?" I said.

"Ray Lawlor. I was having a drink with him last night after I left Sadie's place ... Nikolaevna's place, I suppose I should call it now. The time on Lynch's autopsy report puts me in the clear. Not even I'm gifted enough to have killed her and met Lawlor at the same time."

"So you split on Lawlor?"

"Didn't need to," said Elliott, putting his head down as another gust of wind, heavy-bellied with rain, flung itself at us. "He came forward and told Fitzgerald he was with me from nine onwards. I think he felt guilty that I was on the rack when he knew I was innocent."

Innocent wasn't exactly the word I'd choose.

I held my tongue, though. For the first time in his life, Lawlor had done something noble. It almost made me feel guilty for disliking him so much. "He saved your skin," I said, stepping back to avoid a car before crossing the street and forcing Elliott to trail in my wake.

"If he hadn't come forward, I was going to tell them anyway."

"Tell them about your little arrangement with Lawlor?" I stopped and stared at him for a moment in disgust before walking on. "So what was all that about protecting your sources?"

"There are limits," said Elliott.

"A matter of principle, you said it was."

362

"Fuck principle," he said. "I'm not being landed with Sadie's murder on a matter of principle. Lawlor knew the rules. Especially as he'd stopped being any use to me since this whole thing started. He wasn't giving me a scrap. Even that first night when Mary Lynch got herself killed and I followed him to his car, he just blanked me. Said things were different now. Last night when we met he even tried to palm me off with some leftovers about a drugs hit on the Northside. He knew what I wanted was information on this case."

I was getting more respect for Lawlor with every word.

"What's happening to him now?" I asked.

"Suspended pending an enquiry," said Elliott. "Probably drowning his sorrows somewhere in the soulless city as we speak."

"You're all heart."

"I've got troubles enough of my own without wasting my energy worrying about Lawlor. Do you have any idea what this has been like for me? The editor won't even return my phone calls. I went round there tonight and they told me I couldn't come in. They called security."

I couldn't help smiling at the picture that conjured in my head.

"What did you expect them to do?" I said. "Throw a party?"

"Some thanks is what I expected," said Elliott. "I brought them the biggest story the paper's ever had and they go and dump on me. They could at least have been glad I'm in the clear."

"Just because your lawyer pulled some strings and got you released a few hours early doesn't mean you're in the clear. You might still be charged if your alibi falls apart, or Lynch changes his autopsy report. Maybe he got the time of Nikolaevna Tsilevich's murder wrong. The *Post* might not be the *New York Times*, Elliott, but even they don't want murder suspects on the staff."

"But I didn't kill anyone. An idiot could see that the bottle was planted to make me look guilty. I don't know how yet, but you do see that, don't you?"

"It doesn't matter what I see," I said. "What matters is what your editor thinks. He's the one who pays your salary."

He thought about that.

"This is still my story," he said at last, "whether they believe me or not. I'll go somewhere else if I have to. The killer will come with me, I'm sure of it. I think he trusts me."

"In case you've forgotten, the first letter that came made you out to be an idiot. And for another thing, it looks as though your boyfriend has switched allegiance to the *Evening News*."

"You don't know that information yesterday came from the killer. It could have come out of your girlfriend's department. And even if it was the killer, he could've simply been pissed off with us because we didn't print his letter when it came in. But when the next letter's ready, he'll come to me, I'm sure of it. Then the *Post* can either bring me back on board or I'll go elsewhere."

364

"You almost sound like you can hardly wait for him to strike again, just so that you can get some action out of it."

"That's uncalled for, Saxon. I'm just looking out for myself. No one else will."

"Then you'd better find another way of doing it," I said, "because the *Post* won't touch you whilst you're still a suspect and nor will any other newspaper, no matter what you bring them. And the police warned you to tell them each time you get something else. Not even you're stupid enough to go and hack them off whilst you're only out on sufferance."

"I have the rest of my career to think of," he said.

"What do you mean, the rest of it?" I said. "That *was* your career and you blew it."

"But that's not" — he struggled for the right word — "fair."

"What are you — eleven years old? Life isn't fair, Elliott. You just got unlucky picking a prostitute to screw who then goes and gets killed. Life was a hell of a lot more unfair for her."

"So because she got cut up, I have to suffer for it?"

"You should have thought of that before." I looked at him. "Look, I don't hold it against you that you were seeing Nikolaevna. None of my business. But it's always a gamble; you could've been arrested any time just for being in her apartment and the same thing would've happened to your career. The gamble didn't pay off. You'll just have to deal with that."

"What am I supposed to do?" he said. "I've got no job, and no chance of one again according to you, and now you tell me I just have to accept it?"

"I'm not a career guidance counsellor," I said. "It's your problem what you do next. Maybe once this psycho's caught and everything calms down, you'll get your chance to tell your side of the story. You can do the Romeo and Juliet act about Nikolaevna, make it seem like you were trying to save her from herself, and they might let you have your old job back."

"You can sneer, but I did care about her," he insisted. "I can't wait that long, that's all."

"So what are you going to do?"

"I'll think of something."

"Just make sure what you think of doesn't include trying to make contact with the killer," I said. "For what it's worth, I happen to agree that the bottle was planted to make it look like you're guilty. Finding it at the scene of Mary Lynch's death was too convenient, too obviously staged. But the killer's not stupid. He'll know it wasn't going to fool anyone for long. So you have to start asking yourself why he's chosen you as his outlet to the world, only to then get you arrested. Ever wonder if he's building you up for something other than stardom?"

"Like what?"

"Gee, I don't know, Elliott," I said artlessly. "What is it he does best? It sure isn't flower arranging."

He stared at me a moment as the realisation of what I meant sank in. A shadow crossed his face, then he laughed unconvincingly to erase it.

"I can look after myself," he said.

"That's probably what Fagan thought too," I said, "and look what happened to him."

We had come to a halt outside a pub, and Elliott looked to the door as if for refuge. The light was warm within, beckoning.

"You want a drink?"

"No, I don't," I said firmly. "Not with you. I don't like you, Elliott, I never have, and this coming round here playing the victim hasn't exactly endeared you to me further. I still don't see why you wanted to come round and needle me at all."

"I wanted you to know that I'm innocent."

"Why do you care what I think?"

"It just bugs me," he said. "Bugs me that you think I'm such a lowlife when you've got this blind spot about things a lot closer to home." He turned away and shifted awkwardly inside his coat like he'd said too much but I'd driven him to it.

"You want to elaborate on that comment?" I said.

"No," said Elliott, but it was plain that he could barely keep from giving me the whole ten chapters, together with footnotes and illustrations. "Maybe you should ask Boland."

"Here's a better idea. I'll ask you. You're the one who seems to have all the answers. About Boland especially, it seems."

"I don't have answers. I just have questions. Questions like, who leaked the Nikola letter to the *Evening News*? I know, I know, you think it was the killer, but what if I'm right and it *was* someone in the murder squad? It wasn't Lawlor, I can guarantee that. He'd gone all saintly since the investigation began. Questions like, how did Boland know how Mary Dalton died before Lynch's autopsy? Boland was the one who called me from the market to tell me another body had been discovered so that I could get down there ahead of the competition. He told me the cause of death was loss of blood caused by a severed jugular. How did he know that? She was still lying in the shed when I got there; she hadn't even been carried to the mortuary, never mind opened up by Ambrose Lynch."

"You're not trying to tell me you think Boland's involved in the killings, are you? Because if you are, that's —"

"I'm not saying anything," Elliott said with the same infuriatingly artless air I'd used on him earlier. "Like I told you, I'm just posing questions."

I stood there, thinking. Thinking about the day I'd let Boland drive me from Tom Fuller's house over to the National Library and we'd found ourselves at the scene of Mary Dalton's murder. At the time it had seemed a strange route to have taken; it just hadn't been important enough to quibble about at the time. Now I wondered. Could he have taken us by that route because he'd *known* what we were going to find behind the Four Courts on the way?

No. It was ridiculous. Fantastical. I couldn't allow Nick Elliott to start manipulating my thoughts so easily. And yet I knew, as I watched him flash me a final smug smile of triumph and disappear into the comfort of the bar, that it was already way too late for that.

368

CHAPTER
THIRTY-TWO

The lights were out in Fitzgerald's office and the door was ajar.

I didn't even knock, just put my head quickly round the door, expecting her to be gone already — but there she was, sitting in the dark, chair turned to the window.

"You're late," she said when she caught sight of my faint reflection in the glass and realised who it was.

"Sorry. Dalton kept me longer than I expected."

"You gave your statement to *Dalton*?"

"He insisted. Gave me the full nine yards about what I knew of Ed Fagan's final movements. Like it's going to help catch the killer. That man has a genius for being obnoxious."

"Do you want me to pull him up about it?"

"Dalton doesn't bother me. I've dealt with enough of his sort in the past. What are you doing here in the dark anyway?"

"Facing facts, losing hope."

"Facts like what?"

"Facts like we'll never find him," Fitzgerald said bluntly. "Look how dark it is. That's another day gone, another day wasted; we've got nowhere."

"Not nowhere," I said, though even as I spoke the words I wondered if they were true. "Just not far enough. We'll get there."

"It'll be too late even if we do," Fitzgerald said. "Four women are dead already. There's only one to go. *If* he stops."

If he stopped. That was what had been bothering me too. There were only five victims promised at the beginning because he wanted us to believe that he was Fagan. Now no one believed he was Fagan any more, there was no need to keep on obeying the pattern.

And who knows how he'd react to the discovery of Fagan's body. The police and media might be blaming him for it, but he'd know that someone out there was playing a game of their own; and what if that only enraged him? What if it only made him worse?

It was a risk I'd had to take; the police needed to know Fagan wasn't the man they were looking for, and nothing else but Fagan's body would have convinced them; but my fear now was that my intervention might have changed the template for the killer. Part of me had already begun taking refuge in the hope that, when the killer spoke of disappearing after the fifth death, he meant that he himself would die. Suicide was often the logical outcome of such short-term killing sprees. A fume-filled car, slashed wrists, a rope; a written confession; fingerprint and DNA samples to wrap up the case. An unsatisfactory end, but at least it would be an end.

What, though, if this was only the beginning? If freeing himself from the shadow of Fagan simply gave him new energy? How many more victims would there be then?

"You've been in the dark too long," I said suddenly to break the spell of despondency I could feel creeping over me, and I reached down and turned on the desk lamp.

Outside vanished immediately, and the window was another office with another Saxon and another Fitzgerald staring back.

If only it was so easy to step outside yourself.

I looked down and caught sight of a folder on her desk.

"What's this?"

"That?" Fitzgerald glanced across at it, still blinking in the light. "That's a list of what the search teams found at Fagan's last two crime scenes. Here, take a look."

She handed me the report which Sean Healy had compiled on the search and I flicked through it quickly whilst she withdrew into the building somewhere to get coffee. Had she eaten? Maybe we could go somewhere afterwards for supper.

My eyes glided over the usual lists of everyday detritus that had been picked up and meticulously logged by the search teams.

Scraps of newspaper — none of it relating to the case. Empty plastic cider bottles. Wrappers from tins of cat food. Broken glass. A few rusted coins. Just like at the Law Library, there was nothing that could possibly have any relevance to the investigation.

Except . . .

"A chess piece," I said aloud.

"Not exactly what you'd expect to find in a graveyard," agreed Fitzgerald, coming back into the room at that moment and depositing a cup hastily on the edge of the desk.

The coffee had burned her fingers and she put them now up to her lips to blow them cool again before resuming her seat.

"And they found this where?" I said, skipping back through the sheets.

"Near where Liana Cassidy was killed."

"It doesn't say what piece."

"You want to take a guess?"

I remembered what Ambrose Lynch had told me about the leak to the *Evening News*.

"A bishop," I said.

"Congratulations, you win a year's supply of washing powder. Our friend Gus Bishop has a sense of humour."

"At least we know now it was the killer who told the *News* all the details of the killings."

Fitzgerald looked puzzled.

"Who else would it have been?"

"Elliott came round to my apartment a couple of hours ago — don't worry, I didn't let him in. He tried to make out that it was someone in the department who'd leaked the information."

"Not Lawlor again?"

"It looks like Lawlor was behaving himself for once."

"Who then? Did he offer any names?"

Should I tell her about Boland?

372

"No," I said.

"Well then. I don't think Elliott's exactly a reliable witness," she said, and it was hard to disagree with that. "There was something else there," she added. "Have you seen it?"

She leaned over and found the place for me with a finger.

Healy had suggested taking a look at Liana Cassidy's grave, in the same cemetery, in case the killer had been there too — good thinking — and there they'd found words scratched lightly on the smooth nameplate on the front of her memorial stone.

I know of no bishop worth the name.

At the foot of the gravestone was an old fountain pen which, from the scoring of the nib, looked to have been used to engrave the message.

"More riddles," I said irritably.

I don't know what I'd expected from the searches, but right now I had little patience with the string of enigmatic hints this killer had left for us to find. The very fact that we were chasing after these shadows only showed how little else we had of substance to pursue. It also showed how easily he'd drawn us all into the game. Even our attempts to unravel what he was about only served to make him feel more powerful, more in control.

I resented the questions which pricked now at my mind, but prick at it they did. Why the name Bishop? Simply because of the religious connotation, or did it have a more specific meaning? Was it a pointer to his identity? And why Liana Cassidy's gravestone? Was the fact that it was hers significant?

Tillman had warned us against becoming too enraptured by the scraps the killer had left us, but it was hard. Especially when there was nothing else to go on.

In the end I pushed the report away and reached for my coffee, and for the next hour Fitzgerald and I sat in her office reviewing the case so far.

Everything, we quickly realised, went in circles.

Monica Lee and Gus Bishop, Mary Lynch and Gus Bishop. Aleph. Lamedh. *I know of no bishop worth the name.* Nikolaevna and the stone. Lynch said it was of a similar sort to the one found on Monica Lee's body. The knots used to tie up Nikolaevna were the same too, photographs showed. But the name Bishop hadn't come up in relation to the Russian woman, nor was there a Gus Bishop, or any of its possible variations, in the Dublin phone book.

There was plenty of fingerprint evidence, especially from Nikolaevna's apartment, but the only matches so far led to Fagan, who was dead, and Elliott. And Elliott had an alibi. Nor was there anything in the background check on him to rouse suspicion. Elliott didn't have so much as a parking ticket for speeding, and colleagues claimed to be surprised that he'd been seeing a hooker. They didn't think there were any skeletons in his closet. They didn't think he had it in him to be that interesting. Brendan Harte, the theatre critic, was embarrassed and furious with Elliott, but confirmed that he had told him about the Russian prostitute. He himself had been at a theatre festival in town on the night she was killed. No, he had no idea who might have killed her but he'd be sure to let the police know if anything came back to him. That was nice of him.

Seamus Dalton had tracked down Elliott's wife too. Estranged wife, isn't that the word they use? It sounds almost exotic. She confirmed the basic facts of the story as told by Elliott in the interview room. They'd been together about a year, got married at a registry office in the summer. Things went wrong shortly after they came back from honeymoon. The only new information she had to offer was that Elliott had started getting mood swings round that time; he was unpredictable, volatile. He started staying out late, drinking, sometimes didn't come home at all. She thought he might be seeing another woman and he didn't deny it. Eventually she left him. He tried to coax her back, claimed it was only putting the finishing touches to his book that had made him act so strange, but she didn't buy it. She didn't like how he'd changed. She got her own apartment and filed for divorce. Elliott would've received the papers about two weeks ago.

Perfect trigger for the killings — if he didn't have an equally perfect alibi from Lawlor. Unless Ambrose Lynch could be swayed from his estimated time of death? It was worth a call.

Meanwhile, the woman who it had been assumed was the body in the churchyard had turned up safe and well after spending the last few weeks in France, and further cross-checking of the missing files had failed to find anyone who fitted the bill even half as well.

"Fuller wasn't exactly overjoyed to learn his wife had run out on him again either."

"He'd rather his wife was dead than with another man?"

"Till death us do part," said Fitzgerald. "As you said to me: Who are we to argue with the word of the Lord? He's obviously a man who takes his vows seriously."

"The marriage vows also say something about love, as far as I remember. It's a strange sort of love to want your wife dead."

"Strange, but not technically illegal. At least it means we can rule Fuller out as a possible suspect." She sensed a reluctance in me. "Doesn't it?"

"You know me, I hate losing potential suspects. We're not exactly overrun with them."

"You can say that again. What the —"

Both of us jumped as the door opened unexpectedly.

"Healy, for Christ's sake —"

"Sorry, Chief," said Healy, stopping dead with his hand still on the door handle and looking embarrassed. "I thought you'd gone."

"If you thought I'd gone, what are you doing in my office?"

"I had to leave this."

He stepped forward and handed Fitzgerald a large brown paper envelope, sealed, with her name and an official DMP stamp on the cover. Fitzgerald looked down at it curiously.

"Who gave you this?" she said.

"Donnelly sent it over from Surveillance," answered Healy. "He said you'd want to look at it straight away. I told him I'd drop it in on my way out. Help me kill another five minutes before finding out if I still have a wife waiting for me at home. I've not seen much of her lately. She'll be running off with the milkman if I'm not careful."

"That's not such a bad idea. You'd be able to work more overtime then."

"Not unless they put more hours in the day, I wouldn't."

Fitzgerald waited until Healy had closed the door behind him again before she opened the envelope. She held it up to shake it and a small note fell out on to the desk.

"*Thought you'd want to see these before I entered them into the report,*" she read aloud. "*Tell me what you want me to do.* What's Donnelly up to now?"

She reached into the envelope and pulled out a small handful of photographs. I couldn't see the pictures, but I saw the exhausted look that came into her face when she looked at them.

"Grace?" I said.

She didn't look at me, just slid the photographs over. I felt cold when I saw them.

The first picture showed me hurrying back down the street towards Mullen's house that afternoon after following Fagan's son to the main road to see where he was going. I was framed by the curve of the car window through which the surveillance team had taken the shot. In the next, I was slipping into the house where Mullen now lived. The third and fourth showed me hurrying out and down the steps half an hour later. In the last one, I sat in my Jeep smoking a cigar.

I hadn't even noticed them in the street.

Another triumph, Special Agent.

"I can explain," I said to Fitzgerald quietly.

"You'd better," was all she said in return.

SIXTH DAY

CHAPTER
THIRTY-THREE

Sleep and strong coffee. Cure for anything. I had to make do with coffee, for sleep had been hard to come by. Each time it seemed that I'd fall into unconsciousness at last, panic would grip me at how stupid I'd been by breaking into Mullen's place. Either that, or another memory of Fagan would assault me each time I closed my eyes. The memories were multiplying like viruses this week. I didn't even need to close my eyes any more to see him as he had been five years ago, melting out of the shadows between the trees and materialising before me. Smiling.

"Did I make you jump?" he'd said.

It was as well for me, at any rate, that Finbar Donnelly, head of the surveillance unit with the DMP, was a friend of Fitzgerald's from her early days in the force, or I would have been out in the cold already, like Lawlor, like Elliott. He'd agreed to keep the photographs of me doing a little freelance breaking and entering out of his official report into the watch on Jack Mullen. I owed him. There were plenty of people who would have loved to see me take a fall.

As for what it might've done to Fitzgerald's career — what it *still* might do if it came out — well, that didn't bear thinking about.

She'd ordered the surveillance on Mullen, she'd told me in her office last night, once she heard the information Fisher had brought over from London. I'd gone walkabout shortly after that and had scarcely been alone with her since long enough for her to tell me about it; and so much else was happening besides. As it was, there'd been little enough to report before my intervention.

I didn't tell Fitzgerald about the knife I'd taken from Mullen's kitchen drawer, and I certainly didn't tell her that I'd thrown it in the river. She was wounded enough at my keeping the break-in from her. Instead I detailed quietly what I'd found in his rooms and she listened carefully, making occasional notes. What she made of what I'd done she didn't say; she didn't need to. We'd driven late back to her place without speaking.

Now it was early morning and I was standing at the window of her kitchen, exhausted after counting each passing hour, and idly drawing spirals in the condensation on the inside of the cold glass that only trickled down and spoiled themselves before they were even complete.

Self-destructive impulses. I knew all about those.

The light outside was grey like a sickness as the day ground clumsily into gear.

You could see the sea from the kitchen window, weather permitting. It was in view from most of the windows this side of the house. This was the main reason why she'd bought it. That and the fact that it was new, part of a small, functional development just across the busy Strand Road from the seafront, which meant she didn't have to pay it any attention.

In other circumstances, Fitzgerald was much more the sort of woman who'd like to spend time putting homely touches to her surroundings than I was. I could see her up ladders hanging blinds and painting window frames or repairing cracks, hair tied back; or scouring antique shops and flea markets for ornaments. But her life left little space for incidental pleasures like that. Left little space for anything at all, if the truth be told. All she needed at this point was somewhere she could unlock the door at the end of the day, fling down her coat and papers, and be sure there was hot water in the tank and something in the freezer for the microwave.

This place is like a hotel, she often said. Not resentfully; she'd accepted that was the way her life was. But she liked being in my place all the same because, though I paid little attention to my surroundings — as long as they were at the heart of the city, where a glance out of the window could reassure me that everything was still as disconnected and chaotic as ever, that was enough for me — she knew at least that my apartment was lived in, was real, that my thoughts and breath inhabited that space and gave the air some unique quality that it wouldn't otherwise have had.

"This place would miss you," she'd say to me when we were there. "Mine probably doesn't even notice when I'm gone."

She hardly ever saw her neighbours and doubted they even knew who she was. No doubt they thought of her as some anonymous businesswoman, out before dawn, back after nightfall.

At least there was the sea at hand for those rare times when she was in her house with no other claims on her hours. She liked walking there, along the shore, when she needed to think. She loved the sea. Sometimes she even spoke about getting a place in the country where we could spend weekends, though she knew how I felt about the countryside, and since when did she ever have weekends to spend anywhere out of range of the Dublin Metropolitan Police?

I heard her, as I stood there, moving about upstairs, and went to put the coffee on and lift out some of yesterday's bread rolls from the cupboard.

I put them into the oven to coax some semblance of life back into them, and by the time Fitzgerald appeared in the doorway, wrapped in a dressing gown, hair tousled from what little sleep she'd managed, eyes still unfocused by dreams, the bread was resting in a basket on the table, heat rising sluggishly from the crusts as though it was half asleep itself.

I reached for one and broke it open, took a bite.

"Here, let me," she said.

She reached over and took the other half of my roll and raised it to her own mouth to share. A peace gesture — but all I saw was the white flour brushing against her lips like dust.

Dust to dust. Ashes to ashes.

So little time.

Fitzgerald went to take a shower and I turned on the radio to listen to the news. The hunt for the murderer of four women wasn't even the main story that morning. That's what happens. A killer takes a break one night and he loses top billing. The public is so demanding. The ads in between the headlines piped out Christmas music. *Hark the herald angels sing . . . Silent night . . .*

I switched it off.

Almost immediately, there was a knock at the door.

My instinct was to ignore it. Fitzerald had been badgered by reporters as much as I had myself. They were on the line all hours for interviews. Had they started calling round too?

Last night in her office, I'd even seen a list of questions which the *Evening News* had faxed through to her for prior approval for an interview they'd lined up.

How tough has it been for you, making your mark as a woman in a male-dominated world? Not that one again. *What special qualities can you as a woman bring to the job of chief superintendent of the murder squad? Does the fact that you are a woman make you even more determined to catch this killer?* The *News* was obviously determined to ask all the questions she hated most. I remembered having to answer the same ones after writing my book.

Couldn't they see that it was only by ignoring moronic questions like those, by refusing to let them eat up the valuable space in her head, that Grace had got anywhere? She had nothing to prove. She just did her job. And if other people had a problem with that, with *her*, then she wasn't going to waste time trying to gently bring them round.

I wouldn't have cared about her so much if she did.

The knocking wasn't put off, however, and soon Fitzgerald's voice echoed down from the shower.

"Saxon, will you get that?"

Irritably, I went to the door.

A young man stood outside wearing leathers and a motorcycle helmet with the visor pushed up. Not a reporter, anyway; at least that was something. He was holding — what was it? — an envelope. A courier then. I looked over his shoulder and saw his motorcycle parked by the path. The road was wet, beginning to flood. Another miserable day was in prospect.

He was glancing at the envelope as I pulled back the door.

"Grace Fitzgerald?"

"Right door, wrong woman."

"The right door's all I'm paid to find," he said. "Here, it's all yours. Just sign here."

I signed, took the envelope from him and closed the door before he'd even turned away. I tossed it on to the hall table and walked back to the kitchen, listening to the rising roar of the motorcycle engine as he kicked it into life. Fitzgerald's mail was none of my business. I simply sat down again and reached for another bread roll.

Then I stopped.
That typeface.
It couldn't be — could it?

At least that's over. You people cannot imagine how hard it is keeping up the religious fruitcake act. "I have seen the ungodly in great power and flourishing like a green bay tree."

Who talks like that?

Not forgetting: "One must be on one's guard with every woman, as if she were a poisonous snake and the horned devil."

Though I suppose that part's true enough.

In one way I am quite annoyed that the deception has to end. I really did have some interesting material for my next letter. My theme was to be the impertinence of the Dublin Metropolitan Police in believing they had any right to interfere with the work of the Lord. Scripture teaches that death is not so bad, after all. Death is to be embraced, welcomed, yearned for. So who are you to prevent what Scripture says cannot come soon enough? Now all that will have to be scrapped and I must start again. What a waste. What an inconvenience.

Speaking for myself, as I now can, I always preferred the wise words of Noël Coward rather than those of the Good Book. "We have no reliable guarantee that the afterlife will be any less exasperating than this one, have we?" he once said.

How true that is. The next world might be exactly like this one, only without those glorious distractions of wine, women, song, murder. And what would be the point of an eternity like that? One would surely die of boredom — if one wasn't dead already.

388

I couldn't have said so, of course, if I was still being Ed Fagan; if I was still the offerer-up of sacrifices of the ungodly on the altar of . . . well, I forget the details now. But I am not Ed Fagan any more, because what is left of Ed Fagan lies on a mortuary slab having been disturbed from a dreamless five years' sleep in his shallow soily bed in the mountains.

You cannot honestly believe that I put him there? If I had made Ed Fagan's acquaintance, I would have offered him my congratulations and admiration for a job well done rather than giving him the chance to fertilise some patch of barren earth with a half-inch hole in his skull and a bellyful of worms.

So who did kill Ed Fagan? Who saw fit to reveal that Ed Fagan was dead? It was hardly in my interests to have him emerge from his grave to prove me a liar. In whose interests was it then? Who had motive? Who had opportunity? Who had means?

These, it need hardly be said, are meant to be matters for the Dublin Metropolitan Police — for Chief Superintendent Grace Fitzgerald and her motley crew of ne'er-do-wells and rejects and second-rankers in the murder squad — but the city would wait a long time for them to disentangle the web they have woven about themselves in the past few days. They seem no closer to catching me now than they ever did. Further, in fact? They blindly follow every lead, every red herring that goes swimming by. One flick of its tail and they dive into dark water after it.

It is embarrassing. A display of ineptitude and incompetence that would be shocking were it not by now such an accepted pattern. Monica Lee, two years ago. Unsolved. Sally Tyrrell. Where is she? Helen Cranmore, credit for whose demise Nick Elliott in his absurd book sought to give Ed Fagan. She was another of mine. And what was the name of that syphilitic bitch that I ran down on the corner of Fitzwilliam Street and Merrion Square one night some years ago on my way home from work? I forget now. As if it matters. And there were more. So many more. Perhaps one day I shall tell you all about them. But you will have to catch me first.

It will be too late for Jackie, poor thing (I promised five when I was Fagan and, having come so far, I should see it through to the end), but perhaps you'll be in time for the next one.

Or the one after that. Or the one after that . . .

CHAPTER
THIRTY-FOUR

Fitzgerald had thought my presence might calm Jackie down, but it wasn't working so far. "Why?" she kept asking, her voice rising to a wail as she struggled to control herself. She'd barely stopped crying since we arrived. "Why would he want to kill me?"

Why, I thought, would the creep want to kill anyone? Because his heart was poisoned by evil; what other reason did he need? But I didn't say so to Jackie.

"We don't know if he wants to kill you, Jackie," I said flatly instead. "But you've the letter. We just want to take precautions."

Yeah, right. Precautions. We'd been through all the lists of known prostitutes, even contacted the Blessed Order of Mary for help, and she was the only Jackie whose name had come back. There might be others the police didn't know about, or the name might be only half right, like with Nikolaevna Tsilevich, but there wasn't any serious doubt in my head that Jackie Hill was the target the killer intended to go after next. The search had narrowed down quickly and it had narrowed down to this one mean room in her tiny terraced house not far from the canal.

The letter had taken us all by surprise. I couldn't even remember when Fitzgerald asked me which courier company it was had delivered it. Another slip-up — or another sign, perhaps, of how luck was shining on the killer. She hadn't said anything yet about the letter itself, and I was grateful for that. I dreaded her asking me why the killer was denying having killed Ed Fagan.

Is it part of the game? Is he telling the truth? It would just be more riddles to her, and I wasn't sure I could keep up the pretence any more.

Though what had I expected? Had I really thought the killer would just sit quietly in his hole as the newspapers, finding out about the discovery of Fagan's body (still officially unidentified, though when did that ever hold back the press?), drew the obvious conclusions and immediately blamed the killer of Mary Lynch for the Night Hunter's death as well?

At that moment, I didn't know what I'd expected, and I certainly didn't know what would happen next. I couldn't think more than a few hours ahead. That was how I kept going.

One step at a time.

Again, I found myself wishing that I knew where Fisher was. I needed to talk to him. Needed his advice. He sure picked his times to become secretive.

I stared now at Jackie as she reached nervously for another cigarette, lighting it from the end of the last one, which she'd smoked down till the hot glow of it was almost touching her fingers. The proximity of danger, of pain: my eyes were transfixed by it. It was too symbolic.

Her eyes were black-ringed, bloodshot. She'd been working late last night, she told us. She'd only had a few hours' sleep, and it showed. The room stank of alcohol, stale food, stale bodies. Jackie's hands were shaking as she raised the cigarette to her lips. She wasn't dressed.

"And even if he does mean you," I went on, trying to free my attention from the sight of her disintegration, "we're here now."

"What can you do?" she said bitterly.

"We can protect you."

"Like you did with Mary, you mean?"

"We weren't able to find Mary Lynch in time," said Fitzgerald from the doorway, where she was listening to Jackie and me talk. She was leaning against the door frame, arms crossed, foot tapping quietly but impatiently against the carpet. "It's different now. You're here, we're here, and we'll not be going anywhere until we're sure you're safe."

Saying all the right things like they were true.

"Fitzgerald's called up support from the Armed Response Unit," I tried to explain to Jackie. "They'll be here soon. They're going to stay here with you whilst we get this sorted."

"And how long's that going to be? I can't have her fucking Armed Response Unit out with me when I'm working, can I? That'd really help business."

"How long it takes depends on you," said Fitzgerald.

"What do you mean by that?" Jackie demanded of her, and when Fitzgerald didn't answer she turned to me. "What does she mean?"

"The man who killed Mary names those he wants to kill. This time the name fits you. Might be a coincidence, but if not then it means we have a good chance, maybe, to get him."

"You want me to . . . what? Sit here and wait for him to climb in the window to kill me, just so that you can *maybe* catch him in the act? You must think I'm as crazy as he is."

"Not crazy, Jackie. Realistic. I think you'll try and help us so this doesn't happen to any other woman out there."

"Right," said Jackie, stabbing out her cigarette on the table before getting up and walking about angrily. "So now you're trying to tell me it's up to me to catch this bastard? That if I don't let him come and get me, it'll be my fault if anyone else dies, is that it?"

"You can help bring this to an end," I said. "I'm not pretending it's easy —"

"You're damn right it isn't easy," Jackie answered, raising her voice and pointing a finger at me like an accusation. Her head as I looked up at her was framed by a picture of the Sacred Heart. Some protection that was. "I can't. I can't do it. I'll go away."

"You can't go away," I said.

"Don't tell me what I can do! I can do what I like, you fucking Yankee bitch. I'm going to pack my bag right this minute and get out of here."

"Where you going to go?"

I saw her stop as she considered her own words, trying to put flesh on the bones of the idea she'd just thrown into the conversation without thinking what it really meant.

"I'll go to London," she said eventually. "I know people there."

"You went there once before," I said.

"I did."

"You were back within two weeks."

That was the thing about people like Jackie: they lived in an enclosed world, it wasn't possible for them to break free of it, it kept drawing them back, their nerves would never allow them to settle too far from where they'd spent all their lives. She probably couldn't even cope on the other side of the city, never mind another city, another country, unfamiliar streets.

I watched her face as she remembered, saw the truth settle on her features like a shadow. She knew herself well enough.

"What are you going to do?" I went on before the possibility of escape could truly penetrate her head. "Spend the rest of your life wondering if this monster is going to find you one night?"

I was being cruel again, playing on her fears. I had to.

"Each punter, each car that slows up to the kerb and winds down a window, you're going to think it's him. Every stranger who walks past and catches your eye, every man you find walking behind you at night. Are they on their way home from the bar, or is it *him*?" I glanced over at Fitzgerald. She gave a sharp approving nod.

"And even if you do get away to London," I said, "what are you going to do? Never come back to Dublin in case he finds out you're back and comes to finish the job? You don't even know he won't follow you there. We can't protect you if you go to London, Jackie, no one can."

That was it. I saw the last trace of a fight go out of her eyes. I didn't exactly feel delighted with myself, but what was happening here was too important to risk failure by sparing Jackie's feelings; and to be honest, she didn't seem too disappointed by defeat.

She didn't have the resources to manage her own life, that was how she'd ended up where she was. Sure, she'd whipped herself up into defiance to show that she could get away and take control if she wanted, but she'd never truly believed it. Now I saw the relief in her as she realised she could just submit to someone else's bidding again.

"So what am I supposed to do?" she said.

"Like I said, the Armed Response Unit will be round here soon. Everything will be kept quiet. Low key. A few minutes' time, they'll arrive in an unmarked car, plain clothes, and they'll stay here with you. There'll be others outside the house too, front and back. No one will know they're there. And if he does come to the house to find you, it's us who'll find *him*."

Simple as that.

Though I wish I felt sure it would be that simple.

"You just tell people you'll not be about for a few days so that they don't get suspicious."

"Tony'll be round."

She meant the boyfriend who'd been waiting for her the night after Mary Lynch's death, when I'd picked her up in the Jeep.

"To hell with Tony, Tony can look after himself for once. It might even do him some good. Anything *you* want in the mean time, just ask."

"There is something I want," she said. "Two things."

"Shoot."

She glanced at Fitzgerald, half defiance again, half uncertainty at what she was about to say. "I'll need some gear. I'm not staying here without it."

"Fitzgerald?"

"What you're suggesting is illegal," Fitzgerald said. "I couldn't sanction it. But if you need to go out later to pick up anything, fettucine, olives, whatever, no one will be searching your bags when you come back in. It's your house."

Jackie frowned, but I think she understood.

"What else?" I said.

"I want you to stay with me," she said to me.

"Me?"

"I don't know any of these people," she said. "Please, Saxon. This is bad enough without being left alone. I want someone here that I know, that I can trust."

"You OK with that, Chief Superintendent?" I said.

I could see in Fitzgerald's eyes that she'd rather I wasn't there if the killer came calling, and Jackie must have sensed something too.

"I'll not do it otherwise," she said quickly.

"Your decision," Fitzgerald said to me.

"Then," I said, "the Yankee bitch stays. But only at night, Jackie. There are things I have to take care of during the day."

"It's the nights I'm afraid of," she said.

A Volvo pulled up a couple of hundred yards down the street about ten minutes later, and a man got out, jeans, sneakers, baseball cap, baggy jacket, carrying a parcel and a clipboard like he was making a delivery. He came to the door and rang the bell.

"That's the Armed Response Unit," said Fitzgerald. "Jackie, go answer the door and let him in. And try to act normally."

Jackie had put on some clothes in the mean time, splashed some water on her face. You could tell she'd been crying, but she was trying hard to stay calm. Doing what she was told was part of that. She got to her feet and went to the door.

"John," said Fitzgerald when the new arrival walked in. "Good to see you here so fast."

"Wouldn't miss it for the world," he replied.

Fitzgerald introduced everyone quickly. This was John Haran, only about thirty but already one of the DMP's most experienced Armed Response Unit officers. He was going to be staying in Jackie's house whilst the stakeout continued.

The Volvo in the street, he explained, contained another officer by the name of Dean Welling, and others would be moving quietly into position around the house over the next few hours. A derelict house across the street had already been checked out and given over to the ARU as well. There were signs inside that it was used by drug addicts, though not recently; it would do. Plus they'd have people in the entryway out the back. In all, there'd be between ten and fifteen armed police guarding Jackie at any one time, and others cruising the streets around.

It was a small enough number that they wouldn't make themselves known to the offender, unless he knew what to look for, but large enough to make Haran pretty confident that no one would be able to get through to Jackie without being picked up.

"Just *pretty* confident?" I said.

"No one will get through," Haran said firmly, but there was a smile there too. He was enjoying this. He looked younger than his thirty years in that moment; I only hoped his reputation was earned. In a city where so few police went armed, it was always a matter of trust, and I'd never trusted anyone but myself.

When he'd finished explaining the arrangements outside, Haran checked over the interior quickly, entrances and exits, windows. It was only a small house and it already felt crowded.

Still he seemed satisfied with what he saw. Upstairs he glanced out of the window at the front to the derelict house across the street that the ARU would be taking over. The windows were boarded up, but they'd drill holes for looking through.

People walked by on the street below like nothing was more awry than the weather.

For them, nothing was.

Haran left a few minutes later, started the car and drove away. Five minutes after that, he was knocking at the rear kitchen window and stepping back inside, the charade of leaving complete. He was now in place for the night.

Then it was our turn to leave. I managed to slip Jackie some money before we went, for later when she went to get what she needed; there wasn't much point worrying about her health or her lifestyle right now. She didn't say thanks, just put it in the pocket of her jeans, but that was her way of showing defiance and I didn't begrudge her it. She didn't have much else.

CHAPTER
THIRTY-FIVE

I decided to skip the crime team meeting, partly because I felt increasingly isolated in there, partly because there seemed no point to it with so little progress to report.

Fitzgerald didn't press me. I was a big girl, she probably thought, I could make up my own mind. I stood in the street and watched her car ease round the corner and disappear.

She'd barely gone when the sound of another car turning the corner at the other end of the road made me look back.

"Boland," I said aloud in recognition. "What's he doing here?"

Boland pulled into the space Fitzgerald had left only seconds before and got out.

"Aren't you supposed to be at the morning briefing?" he said to me.

"I was about to ask you the same question, Sergeant."

"I've got an excuse. I've been running round chasing up leads, orders of the Chief. Don't tell me I've missed her?"

"Afraid so. Want to share your news with me?"

"I suppose it can't hurt. I managed to track down the courier firm who delivered the letter to the Chief's house this morning. They weren't too much help; the guy on duty last night says he can't remember who left the envelope to be delivered. Said how was he supposed to remember? People are coming and going all the time."

"I don't know which is worse," I said. "The witness who claims to remember too much or the one who won't commit to saying anything in case they might be wrong."

"It's like keyhole surgery sometimes. Every fragment of information has to be fished out of them with tweezers."

"Another dead end then," I said.

"Not quite," said Boland. "They have CCTV."

"From last night? But that means we'll be able —"

"To see who dropped off the letter," Boland interrupted me. He was smiling. "Exactly."

I felt a smile coming to my own face, but brought it sharply under control. It was too early to allow myself to get excited.

"It's too easy," I said. "He won't be on CCTV."

"You sound sure."

"I am sure. He managed to avoid the security cameras round the canal when he killed Mary Lynch. Knew exactly where they all were. Why would he suddenly slip up now?"

"I don't know," said Boland. "But can we afford not to find out?"

★   ★   ★

It was Boland who eventually broke the silence.

"Are you all right, Saxon?" he asked as we drove.

We were heading towards a narrow street near Pearse Street Station where the courier firm was located. It was the same firm I'd used to send the case notes over to Tillman after hours a few nights ago.

"Why wouldn't I be all right?" I said.

"You seem distracted, that's all. You haven't said much since we set out."

"I guess I didn't get much rest last night," I said, sidestepping the question. "It's hard to sleep when every moment seems so vital and your thoughts are going at a hundred miles an hour. And then if I do sleep for half an hour, I feel guilty."

"Even the killer sleeps," said Boland.

"He can afford to sleep. He has this all mapped out, he knows where it's going. He's known a long time."

We were snarled in traffic by the hospital in Holles Street. The road ran straight here down to the river. The morning blared with horns and the sounds of construction. Scaffolding laced the sky, shutting us in.

"Elliott came round to my place last night," I said after a pause, glad I'd finally said the words that had been on the tip of my tongue from the moment I saw Boland's car approach.

"Did he?"

He sounded like he was wondering what Elliott had to do with this conversation.

"He wanted me to know he didn't have anything to do with the deaths. At least that's why he said he came round."

"Did you believe him?"

"Doesn't matter what I believe," I said.

"It obviously mattered to Elliott," Boland pointed out. He waited for me to continue, and when I didn't he said: "Did he tell you anything he didn't tell Fitzgerald yesterday?"

"No. In fact, he talked about you mainly. You never mentioned you were friends."

"Friends would be overstating it," said Boland. "I told you the other night I'd seen him around the bars. We used to have a couple of drinks now and then when I was in Serious Crime."

"You didn't hit it off."

"I always got the impression that any friendship we ever had would come on the back of what he could get out of me, nothing else."

"He wanted you for a source?"

"He wants everyone for a source," said Boland. "He never stops thinking about the next story. Every time you talk to him, it's like he's picking through the bones of what you're saying to see if there's anything in it for him."

"So you never gave him a story?"

"Nothing major, no state secrets," he said. "I threw him a few scraps, just to be friendly, then I stopped returning his calls." He cast me another sideways glance. "I hope you don't think I gave him anything on *this* investigation."

I didn't answer him directly.

"I just wanted to know what your relationship was," I said.

"Then you've got it. That's all there is."

"He said something else," I went on before I could persuade myself out of it. "He said you told him how Mary Dalton died before Lynch did the autopsy."

He gave a laugh, but there was no amusement in it.

"I'm beginning to see how it works," Boland said. "He's under pressure so he just shifts the suspicion on to me. Like pass the parcel. The one left holding the bundle when the music stops gets the blame. You mentioned your technique was similar that day at Tom Fuller's house."

"Who said anything about suspicion? They're just questions."

"There's no such thing as just questions. You know that."

He stopped suddenly at a red traffic light and jerked the handbrake roughly into place. He wiped his palms on his trousers.

"If you must know," he said, "Elliott called your mobile at the scene of Mary Dalton's murder, not long after you left to go to the library; remember how you'd dropped it in the car? I answered it in case it was important. Elliott didn't sound too surprised when he realised it was me. He'd just heard, he said, about the latest victim. He asked me how she died. I told him."

"But how did you know?"

"I'd just spoken to Lynch is how. He told me."

"Before he'd done an autopsy? That's not like Lynch."

"We're all doing things this week we wouldn't normally do," he said.

Again I felt that tinge of paranoia I'd experienced as I spoke to Fitzgerald about the discovery of Ed Fagan's body, but I pushed it back down. Boland couldn't know about *that*, or about my trip out to Mullen's place. Not unless someone in the surveillance team had talked . . .

Or had Healy seen the pictures before he dropped them off on Fitzgerald's desk? Would he have shown them to Boland if he had? Stop right there, I told myself sharply. I didn't have time to be tormenting myself with these senseless thoughts.

"I needed to ask," was all I said.

He was still shaking his head.

"I can't believe you let Nick Elliott in your head like that. Nick Elliott, of all people."

He seemed as if he was about to say more, but a horn sounded behind him.

We were green again.

Nearly there now.

There is something unmistakable about the look of a police officer, even out of uniform. The sullen young man behind the counter at the courier firm recognised it as soon as he looked up and saw us walking in. He knew what we were here for all right.

A sign flashed behind his head: *24-Hour Delivery Anywhere*. Anywhere? He was pale, like sunlight was only a rumour he'd heard about, not something he ever encountered for himself.

"You want the tape from last night, is that right?"

"That's right," said Boland.

"I got it out for you. I put it here somewhere. Wait."

He knelt down and searched under the counter.

"Here you go," he said, standing up again and holding out the video. "That's everything from ten till midnight. The entry for the letter you mentioned was in that list, marked for delivery first thing this morning, so whoever brought it in must be on there. Are you taking it with you?"

"If it's no trouble, we'd like to look at it now. Is there somewhere we can go?"

"There's a machine in the back here," the young man said reluctantly. "Will that do?"

"As long as it works," said Boland.

We followed him through to a small room behind the front office, where a kettle sat on a tray next to mugs that needed rinsing and coats hung over the backs of chairs; and there — a TV and video, left for the night shift in case they got bored.

"It's a good job you came by now," he said as he crouched down once more and switched on the video. "If you'd left it a couple of days, it would've been taped over. We have them running on a rota system, you see. Once one's done, we put it to the bottom of the pile and use it when its turn comes round again. Here, that's the right channel. This won't take long, will it?"

"We'll be as quick as we can," said Boland.

"Oh. OK. I'll just . . ."

He trailed off lamely, hoping maybe for an invitation to stay and watch.

"If you wouldn't mind," said Boland, and he held open the door as the young man left.

Boland sat down as soon as the door was closed and pressed the play button. A grainy picture came into something approaching focus. It showed the view from a camera above the door looking down into the street. A dark-haired woman with a headscarf shrouding her face was frozen as she reached out to the handle. The time at the bottom of the screen said 22:02.

My stomach danced lightly, for all I'd said to Boland about the killer not allowing himself to be caught on film.

Could this be it?

"I'll fast forward," said Boland, "and pause when anyone appears."

He pressed his finger to the fast forward button, and in a moment the woman had jerked out of shot, and another figure had appeared to take her place.

For much of the time there was nothing, disconnected people coming and going too fast, like they were trapped in an old Keystone Kops movie, everything speeded up. The quality of the videotape was poor too. It had been used so often it seemed people kept bumping into ghosts of others who'd been there before, and even behind the clock there was a faint image of other clocks. Faces were indistinct even close up. Figures farther away always seemed to be at the point of breaking up. We took what notes we could of the shadows who came and went.

There were quite a lot of people, considering the lateness of the hour. Motorcycle couriers parking outside as they came in to pick up packages. Office workers dropping off parcels on their way home from working late.

Other figures passed without stopping. A woman came to the window, peered in, then left. A boy who couldn't have been more than ten kicked the glass and ran away.

"Do you recognise anyone?"

"No one yet," said Boland.

Time ticked on.

A police officer in uniform. A woman wrapped in a fur coat. A shuffling teenager who looked like he might be on drugs. A woman in a short skirt and high heels carried two boxes precariously to the door and turned her back to push it open. A tall man with grey hair held it open for her as he left. How long would it take to identify and eliminate all these —

"Stop the tape," I said sharply.

"What is it?" said Boland.

He jabbed a finger to pause the film, but the moment had passed.

"Rewind it slowly," I said. "Stop when I tell you."

He pushed the video into rewind and the tall figure of the man I'd seen with grey hair walked backwards in time into sight.

The clock said 23:21.

I waited till his face was in shot.

"There."

"Jesus Christ," whispered Boland.

"Not quite," I said, "but at least this one'll be easier to get in touch with."

CHAPTER
THIRTY-SIX

Tillman didn't see Boland and me arriving. He was crossing the courtyard of Trinity College, deep in conversation with one of his students — Tim, wasn't that his name?

"Mort, wait up!" I shouted.

Tillman halted, irritated by the shouting, and he was even more irritated when he realised it was me. He looked tired.

"Good afternoon, Sergeant Boland," he said.

No greeting for me then.

"We need to talk," I said.

"Saxon, I already told you I want nothing more to do with this case. I'm busy. I have other things to do."

"Like finishing your lecture for tonight?"

"That's one of them."

"And is that what you were doing at the courier's office near Pearse Street Station last night at eleven twenty-one p.m.?"

His surprise was too obvious to hide.

"How did you —" He broke off. "No, forget it, I don't *want* to know how you seem so knowledgeable about my movements all of a sudden. I'll just make one thing clear. What I was doing last night, or any other night, is none of your business. Now if you'll excuse me, I have —"

"Tillman, I really don't give a damn what you have," I said. "We need to talk and it won't wait. How we do it is up to you."

He stared at me a long time, trying to read what was in my head. He must have sensed something, for he turned to Tim apologetically, opening his hands.

"I'm sorry," he said.

"I understand," replied Tim. "Another time. It was good meeting you again," he said to me and then he was gone, walking off quickly in the direction of College Green.

Tillman watched him go before turning back to me.

"Are you going to tell me what this is about?"

"The killer sent another letter. To Fitzgerald's house this time," I said. "He sent it last night from the same office and round the same time that you entered the building. Boland and I just watched you on CCTV."

That was one thing I liked about Tillman. He didn't go through the usual pantomime of astonishment, disbelief, ultimate acceptance. He just stood quietly for a moment, putting the pieces together in his head. The anger had gone out of him now.

"Did the letter name the next victim?" he said.

I nodded.

"Did he say why he killed Fagan?"

"He said he didn't do it."

"Interesting," said Tillman, and he stood thinking for what felt like a long time, seemingly unaware of the students who were drifting past offering greetings on the way to lunch.

"I got a call from the college switchboard last night about seven," he said eventually. "It'll all be down in the log if you need to check it out. They said they'd received a call from a courier firm near Pearse Street Station, saying there was a parcel waiting for me to collect. Whoever it was who called didn't want to speak to me directly, he just wanted the message passed on. He said I could pick it up from the office any time that evening."

"Why did you go?" I asked.

"Why wouldn't I go? For all I knew, it could've been important. My lawyer — not that this is any of your business either — is supposed to be sending me over some papers from Boston to sign." Papers relating to the sexual harassment suit that Lawrence Fisher had told me about? Possibly. "Naturally, I went to pick up the parcel the first free space I had. I knew it was open twenty-four hours because you'd sent me over files with the same company a few nights ago."

"And *did* they have a parcel for you?"

"They said they didn't even know what I was talking about. I was pretty sore about it, but what could I do? It wasn't their problem that someone was calling me up using their company's name as bait. So I came home again. End of story."

"Didn't you wonder who'd made the call?" Boland asked.

"I wondered, but what good is wondering? It could've been anyone. Someone who'd seen my name in the paper. One of the students fooling around. I put it out of my mind."

"And what about now?" said Boland. "Looking back, can you remember seeing anyone or anything in particular at the office last night when you got there?"

"You mean, did I notice any serial killers hanging around in the street?" said Tillman coldly. "Afraid not. Whoever it is obviously made himself scarce. Wouldn't you?"

"He still managed to send a letter."

"He managed to make sure that a letter was sent," corrected Tillman. "That doesn't mean he did the sending. He could've paid any passerby to deliver it for him; he wouldn't even have to go near the place. And I can see from your face, Saxon, that you'd already considered that possibility. Have you started tracing everyone else who appears on the tape?"

"We only just got it."

"Then the quicker you start, the better," Tillman said. "You don't have much time left, according to the killer's first letter. Not that he'll be on the tape," he added. "He's not that stupid. He'll have got some dupe to send the letter for him. Find the dupe and you might get an ID."

"What makes you so sure he won't be on the tape himself? Your profile said he'd engage in that sort of risk-taking."

"There's risk-taking and there's idiocy," said Tillman. "Just because he might secretly want to be caught doesn't mean he's going to hand himself to you on a plate. That's not the way the game works. He'll still make you work for it. Earn it."

"Is that what you'd do?" I said.

Tillman let out a laugh of contempt.

"Don't give me that, Saxon," he said. "You don't suspect me. You're too intelligent not to see what's going on here."

"Which is?"

"Your killer obviously knows that I dropped out of the game," Tillman said. "He doesn't like it, so he tried to draw me back in. One phone call and he has me roped in as a suspect, just like the hapless Nick Elliott. He's playing us all like chess pieces on a board. It must've left him really pissed that I didn't want to carry on being a part of it. Threatened his self-esteem. He's trying to remind us who's in charge. Remind us that it's up to him who makes the entrances and exits; no one else."

"Does that mean you *are* interested again?"

"No. I won't be picked up and put down like a toy. *I'm* in control of me and I don't want anything more to do with the case, I've made that clear. I gave you a profile. My job is done. Anything I do from now on, I do for myself. I'm strictly freelance now."

"So you're just going back to doing what you were doing before like nothing has happened?"

"Whatever plans your killer has for us all, I have plans too. I can't change them any more than I can change this filthy weather."

414

I looked up involuntarily. Tillman was right. Dark clouds were looming high; rain was starting to fall. The weather was trying to shut down the day early again.

"First and foremost, I have a lecture to deliver at eight o'clock and that's what I intend to do," he said. "Unless, Sergeant, you're planning on arresting me for being in a courier's office after dark without permission of the Dublin Metropolitan Police?"

"Of course he isn't going to arrest you, Tillman. Stop playing the wounded innocent. But what did you expect us to do after we saw you on the tape — pretend you weren't there?"

"I expected nothing, Saxon," Tillman said. "I stopped expecting anything of you eight years ago when you wrote your book. I stopped expecting anything of anyone."

When we got back to Dublin Castle, Fitzgerald was standing in the parking lot talking into a mobile phone, one hand covering her other ear to shut out the eternal white noise of the traffic. She signalled to us to wait before going in, then signalled again for silence when I tried to speak.

"No . . . no . . . definitely not. Just stay in touch. Anything that happens, *anything*, I want to know about it."

"Bad news?" I said when she'd finished.
She paused briefly whilst she put away her phone.
"I honestly don't know."

"It's not Jackie, is it?" I said, suddenly worried and feeling guilty for not having called to see how she was coping.

"Jackie's fine," said Fitzgerald. "I talked to Haran less than ten minutes ago. Everything's quiet there. Everything's in place. Jackie's spent most of the time asking for stuff to be delivered." That sounded like Jackie. "No, that was Donnelly on the line. The problem's with Mullen."

"What's he done now?"

"Nothing, that's the problem. The only time he left his bedsit since returning there early yesterday evening was to buy cigarettes from the shop on the corner. He certainly wasn't near any courier's office last night. He couldn't have sent any letter."

"That doesn't put him in the clear," I said. "Tillman reckons the killer probably used a patsy to send the letter so that he didn't appear on the tape. Mullen could easily have had it all arranged for someone else to drop off the letter for him without even crossing his front doorstep."

"What tape?" said Fitzgerald, frowning. "And what do you mean, Tillman? I thought you two weren't talking again? You said you hadn't heard from him for days now, that he wasn't returning your calls?"

"Tillman and me not talking? Whatever gave you that idea?"

Two hours had passed since then and Fitzgerald now had everyone focused on identifying the people in the

416

CCTV footage. They were as close as we'd come to eyewitnesses all week.

Even Seamus Dalton was helping out without complaint, but then he'd been uncharacteristically quiet, Boland told me, ever since the Assistant Commissioner had hauled him in that morning and taken him to task over Lawlor's suspension. Of course it wasn't his fault that Lawlor had been feeding stories to reporters for years. He'd known about it, naturally — who hadn't? — but had turned a blind eye to it rather than encouraged it. Still, Lawlor's fall was bound to reflect badly on him. Lawlor was in his orbit, under his planetary influence.

Frankly, I think I preferred Dalton obnoxious.

Already three of the people seen on the film had been identified and spoken to. They were regular clients of the courier firm so it hadn't been too difficult. Uniformed officers had also been sent to do spot checks on cars in the lanes round Pearse Street Station to find who'd been in the area last night. There'd even been an appeal for information on the lunchtime news which had produced nearly a hundred calls. Now all that was needed was to get through them, one by one, painstakingly. And how long would that take?

That was the point. He was sending us off into another maze. Boland's excitement when he realised the killer might have been captured on CCTV; the dash round there; the listing of each face, each figure, each passing car — it was all part of the illusionist's sleight of hand, making us look one way whilst the real action went on elsewhere. And I was growing weary of it. All we were doing was fighting amongst ourselves over what would probably turn out to be worthless scraps. And it didn't make matters any better that the more up-to-date picture of Mullen which Fitzgerald had sent round to Jackie's house on my suggestion had still not drawn a positive ID out of her. I was starting to doubt she'd ever remember who attacked her that night by the canal.

The day was turning into a chasm. Phones rang distantly down long corridors, sounding urgent. The clock was making us fraught. The ticking sounded louder than normal, insistent, an unnecessary reminder that time would not stop or slow for our benefit.

In the end, I left Dublin Castle and walked round to my apartment to pick up what I needed for the night ahead at Jackie's place. I didn't wait around; I didn't even call in at the porter's office to pick up my mail. I was beginning to understand how Fitzgerald felt about her own house. Like a stranger. How long had I spent here in the past few days?

I was halfway to the door again, having done what I came for, when I saw a copy of one of Lawrence Fisher's books lying open on the table next to my couch. I'd started reading it again this week to get me through the sleepless hours, when I was restless, agitated, searching for inspiration.

Fisher was who I needed now.

But where was he?

Seeing it again in daylight, I recalled again suddenly one late-night drinking session in London when I was researching my book on profiling and Fisher was not yet the celebrity he was about to become. We'd been talking about the black humour cops often used to deal with what they had to deal with. Laughing at death so that death, briefly, lost its terror.

Fisher had admitted that night that when he was called in by forces round the country, he sometimes booked himself into hotels under the names of various obscure serial killers. They had to be obscure so that he didn't terrify the receptionists.

"It used to be the prime ministers of Canada," he'd said with a laugh, "but I started running out."

And there was never any shortage of serial killers.

The only question was: did he still do it?

It had to be worth a try.

I put down my bag again and started ringing round hotels in the city to ask about recently arrived guests. I kept to the five-star hotels, because Fisher was never one to skimp on luxury. I could always try cheaper ones later if I drew a blank.

As it turned out, I didn't need to.

Third hotel I rang, I hit paydirt.

Three nights ago, a man calling himself Paul Nado had booked into the Imperial, a new, ugly, anonymous steel and glass business hotel down by the river, on an open-ended reservation.

The White Monk.

Fisher certainly had some gall.

CHAPTER
THIRTY-SEVEN

Paul Nado was in his room. I checked with reception. The room was at the front — probably a suite, knowing Fisher — overlooking the river. All I had to do was take a seat on a bench by the railings next to the water and wait. He'd see me. He'd come.

So that was what I did. I sat with my back to the hotel and my face to the river and lit a cigar, and let the smoke and the water passing sluggishly below mesmerise me.

The river was grey today, and heavy, like it had gathered so much of the darkness of the city as it went on its way that it was slowing under the weight and might stop. A solitary seagull sat bobbing on the surface. The wind was strong and its edge would have sharpened iron. On the far bank brooded the Four Courts. Clouds weighed heavy on its shoulders. Along the waterfront, the buildings were drained of colour.

I loved the river. Sometimes if I watched it long enough, it merged and faded and then it might have been the Charles and I might have been home and I could close my eyes and imagine that when I opened them Boston would have risen round me, like the forest growing round a sleeping princess in some fairy tale. Only then I opened my eyes and Dublin was still there.

Today I didn't close my eyes. Instead I waited, eking out the time in cigars, until the voice I was waiting for spoke.

"Not going to throw yourself in, are you?" it said.

"And waste a perfectly good cigar?"

I hadn't even heard his footsteps but I didn't turn round.

Fisher sat down heavily at the other end of the bench. He was a presence at the edge of my vision, that was all, because I didn't turn my head to see him. I knew what he looked like.

"Do you know how many bodies were fished out of there last year?" he asked. He didn't wait for me to guess. "Eighteen. I looked it up."

"Enough for two baseball teams."

"There used to only be one or two every year, and that was when the city was falling apart. Now it's meant to be buzzing, and they're lining up to take a dive. Why is that?"

"You're the expert in psychology," I said. "You tell me."

I sensed Fisher shrug his shoulders beside me.

"Who knows?" he said. "Sometimes other people's success only makes those at the bottom feel worse. It's a perpetual reminder of what they're missing out on. Of what they can't quite reach."

"Is that so?"

"It's an idea."

He was silent for a moment and I let him be silent.

This was up to him.

"I was going to call you," he said at last.

"Sure you were."

For the first time, I turned my head and looked at him. The same old Lawrence Fisher stared back, watching me warily as if trying to assess whether or not I was in a dangerous mood. He was out without a coat and sat tightly, shivering as the wind off the water jabbed its fingers into him, and he was smiling nervously, shamefaced, like a schoolkid who'd been caught stealing candy.

"I spoke to my office," he said. "I knew all along you'd been looking for me. I knew you'd figured out I was still here in Dublin."

"If you knew I was looking for you, do you mind explaining why you kept up the now-you-see-him-now-you-don't act? I needed you the last couple of days."

"I was *doing* it for you," said Fisher.

I laughed sharply.

"I've heard it all now."

"Saxon, listen. Give me a chance. What did you come down here for if it wasn't to hear what I had to say?"

I drew a mouthful of smoke from the cigar and arched my head back to release it. It was another cloud, grey as the day.

"I'm listening," I said.

"I told you I didn't want you to give me a lift out to the airport that night," he said, "but you were so insistent. I knew I couldn't say no without rousing your suspicions, and I didn't want to tell you I was staying

422

because you'd only have started asking questions. Questions I wasn't in any position to answer. I know what you're like. So I let you take me out and then caught a taxi straight back, What else was I to do? I needed time."

"Time for what?"

"To check a few things out. I wanted to be sure of where I was going before I told you I was going anywhere. I needed some answers. The plan was that if nothing came of my trip, you need never know. Though that plan certainly didn't last long."

"If you want to tiptoe incognito round a small place like Dublin," I told him, "you'd better make sure you do it properly next time."

"I realise that now," Fisher said. "Not all of us, unfortunately, have your gift for stealth."

"You're being sarcastic now. Things are looking up," I said. "So tell me. Did you find what you were looking for?"

"I'm not sure," he said. "That's the problem."

"Not good enough, Fisher. If you have any ideas about this case, you'd better start sharing them. Our seven days are almost up. There's another victim in preparation. We don't exactly have the luxury of sitting around waiting for your suspicions to turn into certainties. Suspicions might be all we have."

Fisher didn't answer right away.

"Look," he said, "let's take a walk along the river. It's cold sitting here. Just give me a moment to go back for my coat."

"You'll get by without a coat," I said.

At first it looked like he was going to insist, but I just turned away and started walking and he had little choice but to follow.

"I'll catch my death," he complained as he fell into step.

"Stop whining. Walking will keep you warm enough."

Fisher wasn't convinced, but he obviously didn't feel he was in any position to be demanding consideration when I was still sore with him. He simply took a deep breath as we walked, the quays unfolding beneath our feet, like he was a diver preparing to plunge into cold water.

"I was checking up on Tillman," was what he said when he was ready.

That floored me.

"What the hell does this have to do with Tillman?"

"You remember that student of his I told you about the other night?" Fisher asked. "The one who accused him of sexual harassment?"

"I remember. He gave her an F."

"I've been badgering some people at his old college for more background about what happened. It seems there were a couple of details that didn't emerge at the time. I managed to get the full story from one of his former colleagues. It turns out that her name was Mary, for starters. Like Mary Lynch. Like Mary Dalton."

"Mary's a common enough name," I said.

"I said there were a couple of details," Fisher pointed out. "She was Jewish as well. According to her, that was part of Tillman's problem with her. That was another

424

reason why the college was so quick to dump on him. You know how sensitive they are about any suggestion of a racial slur."

"I don't believe it," I said. "Tillman's no anti-semite. He must've had thousands of students before who were Jewish. He's taught his whole professional life on the East Coast, for God's sake. How come he never had a complaint from any of them?"

"I didn't say it made sense," he said, "but it would certainly help explain a few things."

"You're talking about the writing on the body?"

"And on the tree where Tara Cox died. Aleph and lamedh," he said. "Tillman just dismissed it in his profile, he flatly refused to accept it had any symbolic significance. Why would he do that unless he's trying to downplay a possible anti-Jewish motivation?"

"You're wrong. Tillman *did* address the significance of the writing. He just concluded that it was there to confuse us, that it was part of the game."

"Not so fast. It still matters why the killer chose that game rather than another. However you look at it, the writing is a major difference between Fagan's killings and these killings, and differences call for explanation. *All* differences. At the least it needed to be asked why a Jewish symbol rather than, say, an Egyptian or a Chinese one; but Tillman wasn't even interested in exploring what that difference meant. Even when I called him again this morning on a pretext of asking how preparations were coming along for his lecture, he still wouldn't discuss it."

"Tillman's stubborn."

"Not as stubborn as you, if you refuse to admit that I might be on to something here."

I didn't answer. We were coming to the brewery now and the city was breaking up into roughness. Seagulls circled, squawking, over empty ground, descending in turn to peck at the garbage below. It was bleak here and Fisher was making it bleaker.

"I'm not saying it *is* Tillman," he continued as we stood there watching the birds. "Even thinking it frightens me. I'm just saying let's be careful. You especially."

"Me?"

"Don't you get it? Tillman never ceases talking about you, about the way you betrayed him after the White Monk case."

"I never betrayed Tillman."

"Try to see it from his point of view," Fisher said. "One minute he's a respected criminal psychologist, the next he's what? A criminal psychologist with a big question mark next to his name, and it's all thanks to you."

"The question mark was there already because of his handling of the White Monk case. People were talking. The FBI were furious. All I did was write about it in my book."

"You say that was all you did as if it was nothing, when that's exactly what made it worse. He could take it that the FBI were furious and a few people were talking behind his back. He could overcome that. To have the whole world know about it too was something else."

426

I had no reply. Perhaps for the first time, I was starting to see how I might have done Tillman an injustice. I didn't have to write my book. He knew he'd screwed up on the White Monk case. He didn't need me spelling it out to anyone with a few dollars to spare for a paperback. Honesty was a poor excuse for abusing a friendship.

"The first time I spoke to him when he arrived here," Fisher was going on, "he said he'd show you he wasn't such a loser. I thought he just meant he'd make something out of being here, start to put his life back in order, make you rethink your ideas about him. Now I'm not so sure what he meant. He's been acting strange all week. There's something inside his head."

What had the letter said? *There are nine things I have judged in my heart to be happy, and the tenth I will utter with my tongue: A man that hath joy of his children and he that liveth to see the fall of his enemy.*

"Why didn't you tell me all this the other night?" I said bitterly.

"Because I didn't have all the pieces then and I didn't want to send you down the wrong track," Fisher said. "Tillman's had a tough time. I had no right to add to that by making you suspicious of him as well."

"*You* were suspicious of him."

"My suspicions were in my own head. They were containable there. And that's where I wanted them to stay until I could be sure that they amounted to anything more than paranoia. I'm still not sure whether they amount to anything. I'm just telling you because I think you have a right to know. If Tillman did want some kind of revenge on you, what better way than to play about with all the pieces of your past, rearranging them, disordering them, so that you're forced to revisit your failures as well, the way he was made to confront his?"

"My failures?"

"The failure to get Fagan. The thing that eats at you the same way his failure to get Paul Nado eats at him."

"Is that what people say about me?" I said.

"They say that's why you haven't written anything since."

I almost laughed again. It was the last thing I'd expected. I never gave much thought to what other people thought of me. I'd forgotten that thoughts and memories were two-way roads.

Now I knew how Tillman felt after my book came out.

Under scrutiny.

Judged.

"I still can't believe Tillman would be involved in anything like this," I said. "To get back at me? Being resentful's a long way from being a murderer. And besides, he wasn't to know I'd even get involved in the investigation. For all we know, the killer could simply be setting him up, like he tried to with Elliott. He suggested as much this afternoon."

"Elliott did?"

"I meant Tillman."

"You've seen him?" said Fisher.

There was no point keeping information back from Fisher now. I told him about the courier's office, about the videotape.

He whistled softly.

"The guy on duty swears Tillman didn't leave any letter in to be sent," I said. "Though like Mort said himself, the killer wouldn't be stupid enough to be caught on tape."

"It's classic risk-taking behaviour," Fisher said. "Fits the profile perfectly. He arranges for a letter to be sent, then turns up at the same time in order to prise himself into the investigation again when his role was meant to have ended."

I sighed.

"What are we going to do?" I said.

"There's nothing much we can do before this evening," Fisher replied. "Look at the time. There's only a couple of hours to go before Tillman gives his lecture."

"We should go to that."

"Of course we should go," said Fisher. "We'll go together. We can talk to Tillman afterwards, perhaps even clear this whole mess up. Either we put our minds at ease, or . . ." He paused. "No, I don't want to think about the alternative."

"Till then?"

"We can bring one another up to date over dinner," said Fisher. "I'm buying. It's the least I can do after playing hide and seek with you for the last couple of days."

"Sounds good to me," I said. "But don't think this means you're off the hook, Fisher. I've had thoughts these last few days I don't ever want to have again. It's made me wonder who I can really trust. Made me wonder if I can trust anyone."

"Give me another chance," said Fisher. "It's all I ask." He stopped. "Actually, no. There is one other thing I have to ask."

"What is it?"

"Can I please go back and fetch my coat before I freeze? I had no idea the city was going to get this cold."

"Cold in December," I said. "Who'd have guessed it?"

CHAPTER
THIRTY-EIGHT

By the time Fisher and I arrived at Trinity, there was hardly an empty seat left in the hall. A murmur of conversation rose like an orchestra tuning up, awaiting the soloist; and looking round as we took our seats near the back, I saw some familiar faces.

There was Tim seated near the front, and Tillman's other students scattered about. Academics huddled together for safety on the edge of the room. There were even some people I recognised from the DMP, including Healy with a woman I took to be his wife.

So she hadn't left him. It wasn't all bad news.

And was that Assistant Commissioner Draker? Of course it wasn't. The trees on St Stephen's Green would grow leaves of gold before Draker would be drawn to a lecture on criminal psychology. God forbid that he should ever learn something new, after all.

Reporters were out in force too, eyeing one another warily. A lecture by a well-known American profiler with inside knowledge of the week's murders was bound to attract their attention. There was no sign of Nick Elliott, though. He must still be keeping his head down.

No sign of Fitzgerald either. She'd said she would try and make it, but perhaps she'd been held up at Dublin Castle.

And what about Gus Bishop? Was he somewhere, sitting unobtrusively among the rows, enjoying his anonymity, nursing his secret? I searched the ranks of faces for clues, contemptuous of myself for being so foolish as to think I might see something. What did I expect — a guilty look, a bloodstained collar? And maybe Gus Bishop was out in the back of the hall instead, drinking sherry with the college bigwigs and making small talk, preparing for his grand entrance. The podium where Tillman would give his lecture was lit already with one bright spotlight.

Ladies and gentlemen, we present — well, who?

Who *was* Tillman any more?

"If I'd known so many people would turn up for a mere lecture," said Fisher quietly, "I'd have started giving them myself years ago. Fiver a ticket and I'd be rich by now."

"You're rich already," I reminded him, "and half these people are only here because of what they've read in the papers all week. It's just some cheap second-hand thrill for them."

"You're too hard on people," he said. "Maybe they're trying to understand."

"More like trying to give themselves something gruesome to talk about in the bar later."

I checked my watch. Tillman was due to start speaking at eight.

Still another ten minutes to go.

I wondered if I had time to call Jackie again. I'd rung her after meeting up with Fisher and told her something had come up and I'd be later than I'd promised. She hadn't sounded too pleased, but then I wouldn't be too pleased if I was her either. The night was what she said she feared and the night was here. The time for shadows. "What about me?" she'd said.

"I'll be there. I need a little more time, that's all. You've got Haran."

"I want *you*. You promised."

And there was no denying that. I had.

I'd made up my mind to call her again, though I doubted it would do much good, when a figure stepped up purposefully to the end of the row where Fisher and I were sitting.

I made to get up and let the newcomer through until I looked up and saw that it was Tim. He was wearing a T-shirt with the name on it of some band I'd never heard of.

"I thought it was you," he said.

"So we meet again," I answered. "Fisher, this is Tim — I'm sorry, I don't know your second name."

"It doesn't matter. No one knows yours either," said Tim brightly. "You're Lawrence Fisher, aren't you? I've read your books. I found them intriguing."

"Is *intriguing* a compliment?" said Fisher. "I'm never sure."

Tim laughed, but Fisher didn't get his answer.

"Have you come to hear the lecture or to speak to Mort?" he asked me instead.

Mort now, was it?

"A bit of both," I said. "But what about you? I thought you didn't believe in psychological profiling. At least you didn't the first time I saw you. Has Tillman made a convert out of you?"

"Not yet. I'm still on the side of real science," said Tim. "But I never said I wasn't open to alternative ideas. Do you think he'll talk about the Night Hunter killings tonight?"

"I have no idea," I said. "You'd probably know better than me. You were friendly enough with him when I saw you both at lunchtime. *I'm* not someone he shares his intentions with that closely."

"He doesn't like you."

"Are you asking me or telling me?"

"Just making an observation," he said.

"Is that what you call it?"

Tim leaned forward slightly and lowered his voice.

"Don't you want to know what he says about you?"

"Not really," I said. "What I want is for you to go back to your seat like a good little boy so that I can listen to Tillman's lecture."

"No rush," said Tim, straightening up again. "There's no sign of him yet."

It was the first sensible thing he'd said. There wasn't.

Now I realised it, I also began to notice that the conversation in the hall had taken on a different tone, a higher pitch, shot through with impatience.

I looked at my watch again.

Ten past eight.

Fisher didn't seem to have noticed the change in the mood of the hall. Some psychologist he was. Rather he

434

was watching Tim as the student made his way slowly back to his seat.

"He was a bundle of laughs, wasn't he?" he said with a glance at me. Then he stopped. "What's wrong? What is it? Don't say you let that boy needle you?"

"Screw Tim. Look."

A door had opened at the far end of the hall from where Tillman should have emerged ten minutes ago. Now a woman came out and walked briskly up the side of the hall to the exit.

"Something's going on," I said. "Come on."

I left Fisher to fumble for his coat whilst I made my way towards the exit in pursuit. He had to hurry to catch up.

"Do you have the faintest idea where you're going?" he said as we stepped out into the corridor again and the door closed and the voices fell away to a hum again behind us.

"No," I said. "But they'll do as a first stop."

The woman who'd appeared from the door at the far end of the hall was standing about a hundred yards away in front of three men who, from the look of them, must have been part of the college, her hands upturned and outstretched in that universal gesture of bewilderment. One of the men looked up sharply as he saw us approach.

"Whatever you want, this isn't the time," he barked.

"I'm a friend of Tillman's," I said. "I'm with the murder squad." And I wondered which of the statements was the greater lie.

"Then perhaps," he said with a look half of relief and half irritation, "you wouldn't mind telling us where the hell he is."

"Tillman isn't here?"

"Don't say you don't know either?"

"I came out here to look for him," I said.

"Then as you can see, he isn't here. He called about an hour ago, saying he had to go somewhere but that he'd be back in plenty of time for eight o'clock. Since then, nothing. There's no answer at his rooms, he's not responding to his pager. We have hundreds of people in there waiting to hear him speak and for all we know he's decided to go and do his Christmas shopping."

"What's the problem?" asked a new voice.

We all turned and there was Sean Healy. I was glad he'd followed us out. A badge worked wonders sometimes. Quickly I explained to him that Tillman hadn't shown up.

"Maybe," he said, "one of us had better go to his rooms to check that everything's OK."

"Take you over? You're not saying —"

"I'm not saying anything. Just get the key."

A couple of minutes later, the woman was leading Healy and me out into the rain and across the courtyard to the accommodation block where I'd been three nights ago to hear Tillman's profile with Fitzgerald. Fisher hung behind at the lecture hall in case Tillman turned up in the mean time, though it was obvious from his face that he didn't expect it.

The cobbles were wet with rain and shone with reflected light from the windows. Everything seemed restful and festive, the night at ease with itself, but that was only another lie.

Healy was talking into a mobile phone and the phone was replying in crackles.

Briefly I heard Fitzgerald's voice fill the silence, then it was crackles again.

"She's on her way," Healy said.

A moment later, we were climbing the stairs and there was Tillman's door. The sign on it still bore the name Dr Murray after the previous occupant. Healy stepped forward and knocked.

"Dr Tillman?" he said. "Are you in there? Open up. It's the police." Silence. "Dr Tillman, can you hear me?"

The air held its breath, but there was no answer.

"Open it," he said to the woman.

Her hands were shaking as she found the right key from the bunch in her hand, slipped it into the keyhole and turned. The click was as loud as the tap of a hammer.

"Stay here," Healy said to her. "You too."

"No way," I said. "I'm coming in."

He didn't bother objecting, or maybe he didn't hear. He simply turned the handle, pushed open the door and stepped carefully into the dark. Or not quite dark. The faint glow of the city through open curtains took the edge off the blackness.

"Tillman?" I said quietly as I came after him, but I knew now that he was gone. Empty rooms have their own atmospheres.

Healy reached to the wall and pressed the switch. A dingy light like I remembered from the other night replaced the city's glow and the room swam into relief.

Tillman's coat lay draped across the back of one of the chairs. On the other lay a thin sheaf of papers. His lecture. *The Science of Murder — A Few Practical and Impractical Suggestions*, I read at the top of the page. The floor was littered with books — some taken from the library, others with barely a crease in the spine that might have been only days old.

I squatted down to take in the titles. They were books of theology mainly. Histories of the Church Fathers. The *Confession* of St Augustine.

I picked one up at random and flicked through it. Tillman had scribbled copious notes in the margin in pencil. He'd written so quickly, as though he was excited, that I could hardly decipher it. *Ox/pen/dove* said one scrawl, and that reminded me of the pen which had been found at the grave of Liana Cassidy. What did it mean?

"Hello, what's this?" I said quietly.

For the first time, I noticed that there was a large cardboard box sitting on Tillman's table with a sheaf of Christmas paper laid to one side, like it was waiting to be wrapped up as a present. The lid sat slightly askew on top of the rim. Without thinking, I nudged it aside with my finger and looked inside.

The breath caught in my throat at once, but it was in expectation of a familiar stench rather than at the stench itself. The only smell was one of disinfectant and the hands were perfectly preserved, with no trace of decay. I'd seen pictures of Iron Age bodies that had spent centuries encased in ice and looked much the same; you almost expected to see them twitch, though *they* hadn't been shorn off at the wrists or come with fingers folded neatly together.

"Healy," I said, louder, "I think you'd better call Ambrose Lynch."

CHAPTER
THIRTY-NINE

I took a taxi, made a couple of stops, then ordered the driver to drop me three streets away, outside the sort of bar that even I might think twice about entering. Minutes later, I was letting myself in through the back door of Jackie's house after checking that the entryway was clear. The Armed Response Unit was good. I hadn't picked up a sign of them at all.

Jackie was sulking when I walked in. She was playing cards with John Haran, staring at her hand through glassy eyes; she didn't even look up. No need to ask whether she'd got the gear, as she called it. "The wanderer returns," was all she said to me.

"I told you I'd be here," I said, nodding to Haran and taking a seat across the table from Jackie.

"You told me a lot of things."

I didn't bother arguing.

"I brought you cigarettes," I said instead, digging into the pocket of my jacket and tossing two packets across towards her. "And I put some more beer in the fridge."

A smile. At last.

"Why didn't you say so?"

Jackie rose to her feet to go get it, walking carefully like she was afraid of falling over.

"I heard what happened with the profiler," Haran said when she was out of earshot. "Do you really think it was him all along?"

Where could I begin?

"Later, yeah?" I hedged as Jackie reappeared, carrying two bottles of Bud. She tossed one to me. Looked like I was forgiven, and that only made me feel worse. Jackie was so used to being let down that she'd learned to be easily bought off.

"Rambo isn't drinking," she explained.

"I have to keep my wits about me," Haran said, "to beat this woman at cards."

"What are you playing?" I said.

"Gin rummy. It's the only thing I know," said Jackie.

"Then deal me in and prepare to lose all your money."

"Think you're good, do you?" said Haran.

"Ask Ambrose Lynch. He played poker with me a couple of nights ago and had to take out a loan with the International Monetary Fund to pay me my winnings . . ."

It was like any ordinary night playing cards and drinking beer, except for why we were there, what we were waiting for. Jackie had the radio switched to one of the rock music stations I hated so much. I tried to tune it out of my brainwaves, but it kept sneaking in and invading my thoughts. She was singing along absently.

She was flirting with Haran too, making suggestive remarks and then laughing, and not at all put off by his unresponsiveness, especially now that she'd started on the beer. Maybe it hadn't been such a great idea, but I'd hoped it would put her to sleep, make her easier to handle.

Now and again Haran got up to make a circuit of the house, checking everything was as it had been before. Couple of other times his pager went off and he retreated somewhere quiet to make a call. Each time he returned, he gave me a look to say there was nothing to report. He always took care not to walk between the light and the windows so as not to cast a shadow there that anyone watching Jackie's house would have known was a man's.

Close to midnight, Jackie excused herself and sneaked off upstairs to the bathroom, and Haran and I exchanged glances, knowing what she was up to. A few minutes later she returned but the light had gone from her eyes temporarily and she was staring at nothing.

She lay on the filthy sofa and shivered.

Gradually she fell asleep.

"What's she been like?" I said.

"Jumpy," he said. "All over the place, never sitting still for a minute. I don't know if it's the drugs or she's like that all the time, or whether she's just afraid."

"She have any calls?"

"Only one. Some man. Tony. Is he her pimp?"

"Boyfriend, pimp, same difference."

He snorted agreement.

"She was trying to calm him down about something. I didn't hear too much, but it didn't sound like he was in the mood to be calmed down."

"He's probably wondering where his next fix is coming from with her out of action for a couple of days. She tell him anything?"

"Not that I could hear. She was whispering though. The Chief should have put a tap on the phone just to be sure." I saw his hand go to his gun, where it was hidden next to his shirt.

"Do you mind if I take a look?" I said.

"At my gun?" He seemed unsure. "You know how to handle one?"

"Full ballistics training with the FBI. I carried a gun every day for the five years I was with the Bureau. Once took out a roomful of armed terrorists singlehandedly."

"You did what?"

He didn't know whether to be impressed or dubious.

"Yeah, seven of them. They were all made of cardboard. It was an exercise we did during my weapons training, and unfortunately I never got the chance to do it for real afterwards. Still, I don't think I've forgotten how to handle one. You'll be safe enough."

He smiled and took out the handgun and handed it to me. It felt good to be holding one again, testing its weight. I'd always liked guns, always felt safe when I had one. I didn't know a woman who wouldn't. That was always my standard response when people asked me, as they often did when they realised I was an American, whether I believed in gun control.

"Only for men," I'd answer.

I hadn't held one since . . . well.

"I wish I had one now," I said. "Sitting here waiting for who the hell knows who to show, it'd make me feel a whole lot better." I handed it back. "Let's hope you're as good as Fitzgerald says you are. There's three of us to protect and only one gun."

"Soon as anything happens, there'll be a swarm of armed officers here in two seconds," he reassured me.

"It's those two seconds that do the damage," I said.

I went to the bathroom, ignoring the dirty needles I could see in Jackie's wastebin, and stared at myself in the mirror. Through the thin glass, I could hear cars, voices, music drifting from open windows down the street.

Tillman was out there somewhere. The killer was out there somewhere. Both statements were true, but however I picked at them I just couldn't figure where they intersected.

Downstairs again, I went to the kitchen and opened another beer.

Jackie was still sleeping.

"You want to play some more cards?" said Haran. "Let me win back some of my money?"

I shook my head. The mood had changed as the night grew older. If he was coming, now would be the time. My nerves were aching tight with the strain of anticipation.

I shook Jackie awake and told her to go to bed.

"Promise you'll stay?" she said reluctantly.

"Jackie, trust us. We're not going anywhere."

She wasn't convinced, but made her way to the door anyway. Like I said, she was used to doing what she was told.

"Wait. We have to hit the lights first."

Jackie walked from room to room of her small house, switching off lights, then climbed the stairs, catching my eye as she went. She looked terrified and I didn't blame her.

Upstairs we heard her moving about, heard the pull of the drapes, the creak of floorboards, followed by the squeak of the bed as she climbed into it, a light switched off.

The charade of normality for any possible audience.

Haran and I sat in the dark, and I pictured Jackie lying there in the dark too, trying to sleep, hearing noises.

He asked me in a whisper about my time in the FBI, but I brushed him off, shifting the talk to him instead. He gave me some of his favourite anecdotes about his time in the ARU. I got the impression he'd told them plenty enough times before.

Truth was, I wasn't much in the mood for talking.

It was getting cold. Jackie had a gas fire, but we'd let it go down to make things seem as they should be, and also because cold kept you alert, and alert was what we needed to be. All I could see in the dark whilst we waited was the green glow of the digital clock that Jackie had in her sitting room, tracking the hours. One a.m . . . two . . . Jackie coughed faintly upstairs.

Outside was all quiet now, barely any traffic; the music of parties had died. Footsteps intermittently alerted my senses, but they had places to go and went to them without disturbing this house; and once they were gone, the night dragged again. Dark took on its own presence and sentience. My eyes became attuned to it, so that I could look round the room and see as well as if I had switched on a light. John Haran's eyes glinted in the dark.

At some point, I must have nodded off, for I was back in my own apartment and I didn't know how I'd got there. I knew at once that it was a dream and that I shouldn't be sleeping, but I stopped myself from stirring because I was curious to know why I was here, *what* was here. The door out to the terrace was open, and an icy draught was snaking round my feet. Outside was no city, only trees, a dark wood like the one where Fagan had died.

There was someone in here with me. I knew it instinctively, like the particles in the atmosphere had been altered by a stranger's breath, so that they felt desecrated.

As I stepped through the shapes of my furniture, down the hallway to the bedroom, I could hear a breathing that wasn't mine. The door was closed. I touched it and it swung open.

There on the bed lay Jackie. She was face down on the sheet, naked, a length of green twine twisted round her neck, her wrists and ankles tied with the same, only she had no hands. And there, sketched on to her back in blood, were two letters. Aleph. Lamedh.

And Tillman stood by the bed, pointing at them.

446

I started awake, only just managing to prevent myself from crying out, taking short, shallow breaths to compose myself.

Then I noticed.

Haran was gone.

I was out of my chair in an instant. Quick look round the room. Into the kitchen. Check the time: shortly after three. He wasn't there.

Into the hallway, careful not to make too much noise. Not there either. Then the stairs, climbing them slowly, remembering Haran's gun and wishing it was mine. Though what did I need a gun for? Haran had probably only gone to the bathroom. Hadn't he?

If he had, he wasn't there now. Nor in the second bedroom. That only left — Jackie's room. I was alarmed now as I stepped, quicker, quicker, down the hall to the front of the house.

Stop.

Jackie's door was ajar.

"Haran?"

I saw him at once, standing close to the window nearest the door, peering out through a narrow crack.

"Haran, what the —"

He raised a finger to his lips to silence me, though without taking his eyes off the window, and I saw he'd taken his gun out and now had it balanced lightly in his other hand.

"There's someone here," he whispered.

"You should have woken me."

"You fall asleep, this is what happens. You miss all the fun."

"You call this fun?"

I stepped over to his side lightly, sparing a quick glance to the bed where Jackie lay. I couldn't see her face, but I heard her breathing faintly. Dead to the world. No, don't say that.

"Why hasn't he been closed down yet?"

"Just waiting for the right moment. There. See him?"

Through the crack, I saw a shadow stir.

I looked over to the derelict house. I knew there was back-up there, but right now I felt like the city had emptied itself of possible aid and we were alone. One gun. One killer.

Was this him?

"Come on."

Haran crept back out to the top of the stairs. The door below was rattling faintly as the shadow tested the lock.

"Soon as he comes in, you take cover," he said.

Haran levelled the gun patiently as the door began to open slowly and the shadow stepped over the threshold. How had he got past the lock?

There was no time left to ask. This was it.

"Freeze!" shouted Haran — and at that moment there was a scuffle outside and I saw two more shadows appear.

The figure in the doorway turned in alarm, and a shot rang out. Not one of Haran's. There was a flash like lightning as he was hit, so bright that I could see his face. Not Tillman's face, but familiar all the same. Where had I seen it before?

He fell to the ground with a cry of pain, and from upstairs I could hear Jackie shout out too as she woke to the noise.

Haran took the stairs two at a time on the way down as another voice shouted at the injured man: "Stay where you are!"

Haran bent down and started to frisk the figure on the ground.

"Who fired?" he demanded. "Was it you, Baily?"

"I thought he was going to shoot."

"He hasn't got a fucking gun; what did you think he was going to shoot you with — a mobile phone?"

"I thought —"

"Wrong, Baily. To think, you'd need a fucking brain."

"Tony!"

The last cry made me turn, and there was Jackie at the top of the stairs, hand over her mouth, shaking.

Tony. Of course. I remembered now where I'd seen him, hopping from foot to foot in his baggy pants, waiting for Jackie at her usual pitch the night I'd gone out in the Jeep to find her.

It was the end of another malignant day.

And tomorrow didn't look like being much better.

SEVENTH DAY

CHAPTER
FORTY

"But he *is* going to be all right?" said Fisher.

"There's nothing wrong with him," I said. "He only got hit in the shoulder — though to listen to him whining, you'd have thought he was being tortured by the Vietcong."

"What about the officer who shot him?"

"Baily," said Fitzgerald, "will be shunted off into official purgatory for a while to await the findings of an enquiry."

"A bit harsh," I said, "considering his only mistake was not finishing the job properly."

"You don't mean that," she said, but at that moment I almost did. Probably nothing would have happened at Jackie's house if Tony hadn't turned up, the night was running out as it was; but we'd never know now. It could have been over. Instead . . .

"Look, forget about Tony," I said gruffly. "What about breakfast? Have you decided what you want yet?"

It was just after eight and we were sitting in the same café where I'd been that first day when Nick Elliott walked in and the world went dark. Same table, same view out the window, same rain. Margaret had welcomed me back like she hadn't seen me in years

453

instead of days. It was good to realise some people would miss me if I was gone; I was strangely touched. Or maybe she was just glad I had company for a change. Company meant extra orders.

Apart from us, there were no other customers.

"I'm not hungry," Fisher said, laying down the menu which he'd been peering at without taking in the words for the last ten minutes. He looked beat. "I'll make do with a coffee."

"You don't make do with a coffee here," I told him. "You have to eat something or they take out a professional hit on you. The owner's Italian. It's an honour code thing."

"In that case," he conceded with a sigh, "I'd better have the scrambled eggs."

"Fitzgerald?"

"My usual."

Margaret, who'd been waiting patiently for our order, stepped over to the table, pad and pencil at the ready.

"Scrambled eggs with extra toast for Fatty Arbuckle there," I told her, "and we'll just have a couple of coffees. Black."

"Coming right up."

"But you said — oh, never mind," said Fisher. "I'm too tired to resist. I hardly got a minute's sleep last night. I was tied up at Trinity till all hours, then when I eventually got back to my hotel my mobile hardly stopped ringing with reporters looking for information on Tillman — where he'd got to, whether it was true that he was a suspect. Your department's leakier than the *Titanic*."

"You should have switched it off," said Fitzgerald.

"I couldn't in case either you or my wife was trying to contact me. I don't even know where the vultures got my number from. They wouldn't take no for an answer."

"Tell me about it," said Fitzgerald. "I just fob them off with the usual lie about following a definite line of enquiry."

Lie was right. The police were as bemused as the press about what had become of Mort Tillman. He certainly hadn't turned up at the airports or ferry docks trying to flee the country, and there hadn't been a single sighting of him. From what they could reconstruct of his movements, Boland and I were among the last people to see him when we turned up yesterday lunchtime to ask about his visit to the courier's office the night before. He'd been seen returning to his rooms half an hour later by two witnesses in the college, and then nothing more.

Now, twenty hours later, here we sat, none the wiser, waiting for some sign, some portent that would make the shattered fragments of the last six days repair themselves into the semblance of a shape — though that was looking even less likely to appear than Fisher's breakfast. In the end, he got tired of waiting for it to arrive and said he was going to the men's room.

"What's wrong?" I said once we were alone.

Fitzgerald had been frowning ever since we came in and now she lifted her hand to pinch the bridge of her nose.

"Is it your head? I've tablets somewhere if you want one."

"My head's fine," she said. "Or no worse than it's been all week, at any rate. I still can't believe it about Tillman, that's all. Why? That's what I don't get. Why would he get involved in something like this? It doesn't make sense."

"You heard what Fisher had to say. That he's seeking revenge on me for ruining his life over the White Monk case."

"You don't exactly sound convinced."

I didn't answer her directly.

"It adds up, I can't deny that," I said. "Say something was building inside him, some kind of breakdown. For the first time in his life he loses his self-control and he's suspended with nowhere to turn, no family, no partner, old friends and colleagues all keeping their distance. It's one stressor after another. Textbook stuff. Next thing is, he gets invited to Dublin and the gears start clicking and slotting together in his head. He knows I'm here, he knows about Fagan."

Or he thought he did.

"And where does that leave all our theories about Mullen?"

"Mullen attacked Jackie that night at the canal, I'm sure of it," I said, "and he attacked those prostitutes in London. And the more I go over it in my head, the more convinced I am that he was part of what Fagan did as well. I don't know how, we might never get to the root of it, but they were in it together. But maybe he *didn't* have anything to do with this. Maybe it only looks like he did because Tillman was playing games with all the bits and pieces of Mullen's past too, just like he was with ours, and Fagan's son being back in town was only a coincidence."

"You once told me there was no such thing as coincidence."

"You should know better by now than to listen to anything I say," I reminded her with a smile, and I would've said more, only at that moment my mobile began to ring from deep inside my jacket and I had to fumble through my pockets to find it.

I didn't recognise the number but took the call anyway. I could always cut the connection if it wasn't important.

"Yeah?" I said.

"*That's no way to answer the telephone,*" a voice said back. "*Didn't they teach you manners in the FBI?*"

I remembered how Elliott had described the call from the killer he'd received at the start of the week. Obviously it was some sort of electronic device attached to the phone. The voice sounded slowed down and robotic, like a tape in a Walkman when the batteries were low.

I mouthed to Fitzgerald: *It's him.*

Quickly, she got up and stretched across the table and put her ear as close to the phone as she could.

"It's hard to be polite," I said once she was in place, "when I don't know who I'm speaking to."

"*But that's exactly the way I like it,*" the voice said with a short stab of a laugh. "*As Scripture says: Without a parable spake he not unto them, that it might be fulfilled which was spoken by the prophet, saying, I will open my mouth in parables. The Gospel of St Matthew, Chapter Thirteen, if memory serves me right.*"

"I thought we'd given up all this religious play-acting."

"*I know, I know, but I've sort of gotten attached to it. I find it comforting. And isn't consolation one of the great benefits of religion? Besides, you know very well who I am.*"

"Is that you, Tillman?" I said. "Because if it is, just tell me what you want. Do you want me to say I'm sorry? Do you want me to admit I was wrong about you? Is that what you want?"

"*It's way too late for apologies. I simply called for a friendly chat. The seventh day is here. Time we talked freely.*"

"We can talk as freely as you like. How about it? Why don't we meet somewhere right now?"

That laugh again.

"*One step at a time, Saxon,*" the voice said. "*There's no hurry. No rush. I've looked forward for so long to being able to talk with you without pretence. I think we understand one another. I certainly have a great deal of respect for you.*"

"You don't say."

458

"That's why I'm disappointed in you. The others — well, I expected nothing from them. Draker. Dalton. Obedient little Sergeant Boland. Not forgetting Chief Superintendent Fitzgerald. No doubt Grace has her attractions for you as a playmate, but as an investigator she leaves a lot to be desired, wouldn't you say?"

"Seems to me like I'm not saying anything," I pointed out. "It's you doing all the talking."

"See what I mean? That's the spirit. That's why I had such high hopes of you. Now I'm beginning to wonder if I was wrong. What do you say? Shall I give you another chance?"

"That depends on what you mean by another chance."

"I mean Jackie," the voice said. "Don't worry. I'm not talking about your trashy friend from the canal. I actually find it insulting that you thought I could be snared so easily. Still, I promised you a Jackie and I always keep my promises. Those are the rules of the game. Are you ready to play your part?"

"Listen," I said, my voice rising, "don't even start that bullshit with me. There *is* no game, do you hear me?"

There was silence.

"Are you listening, damn it?"

"You know, Saxon," the voice returned, "you should really try and control that temper of yours. It is most unladylike. And how are you going to get anywhere if you fly off the handle at every setback?"

"According to you, we're not getting anywhere as it is."

"That's where I come in. Think of it as a helping hand from an old friend. To start, I have directions to something I think you'll find interesting. Do you have a pen and paper?"

"I'll remember them."

"Are you sure? They are rather complicated and I know how useless women are at finding their way around. Remember that winter we were travelling in Vermont and you nearly took us over the border into Canada? You didn't put that in your book, did you?"

My God, it was him.

"I swear, Tillman, I'm going to kill you."

"You'll have to find me first. Tell you what. Do you know the phone booth at the corner of Exchequer Street?"

"Of course I know it."

"Of course you do, because that's where your favourite café is. The one you're in right now. The one I watched you going into with Grace and Fisher earlier. Quite a cosy little party you have there. All for one and one for all. Like the three musketeers. Well, that's where I am right now. I'm going to leave something for —"

I didn't wait for him to finish. I dropped the phone and ran for the door. Out of the corner of my eye, I saw Fisher emerging from the men's room, heard him shout, but I couldn't wait.

I pulled the door open and ran out, nearly colliding with some old man who was reaching out a hand to the handle to come in. I yelled at him to get out of the way and went on running. There were steps running behind me too, but I didn't look back or slow down until I came to the end of the road and turned out of Exchequer Street.

The phone booth was less than twenty feet away.

He was gone. Of course he was gone. That was the point. That was the fun of it for him. I glanced left and right a few times, but the street was empty. My chest felt like it would burst.

"He was here all the time," I gasped to Fitzgerald as she caught up with me. "He was calling from that booth."

Tillman had even replaced the phone neatly back on its cradle before leaving, I noticed. There was no rush, like he said. No hurry. And there, taped to the inside of the glass, was a scrap of paper torn from some tourist map of the city, with a scrawled X marking the spot in pencil.

CHAPTER
FORTY-ONE

Fitzgerald drove fast, cursing the traffic, fingers drumming on the wheel, her palm striking the edge hard every time a light was against her. Third time it happened, she just nosed through and went on anyway, ignoring the blare of horns that followed.

"Take a left here," I said. "I know a short cut."

"My own town and I'm taking directions from a foreigner," she said wryly as she knocked down the indicator to signal left.

"Now a right."

"I know the way you mean."

As we drove, she called through on the radio to Dublin Castle to tell them what had happened and to send a team out to the place Tillman had marked on his map, and I explained to her about the incident he had reminded me of in his call. It was during the White Monk investigation. I'd been sent up to a nowhere, nothing kind of place in the north of Vermont, where Paul Nado's mother had retired. The agent in charge of the case had a hunch that the woman knew where Nado was; he was on the run by this stage, just like Tillman now. History repeating itself.

As it happened, he was right; she did know, though it wasn't thanks to me that she was caught out. That came much later.

I'd invited Tillman along for the ride, thinking he might be some help, and somewhere along the way, during a snowstorm, whilst Tillman slept in the passenger seat beside me, I'd lost my way completely and ended up just about halfway to Montreal.

Tillman hardly stopped laughing for the whole two days we were up there, and I'd made him swear he'd never tell anyone what I'd done. I'd never have lived it down. Agents were always quick to latch on to mistakes like that with which to taunt one another.

"Are you sure he never did tell anyone?" said Fitzgerald.

"Not to my knowledge," I said. "That's why I'm sure it was him on the phone. We're the only ones who know about it."

I checked one more time to make sure we were headed in the right direction and then we were passing through the pillars at Park Gate into the killer's latest playground.

Phoenix Park.

Twice the size of New York's Central Park, at night this place gouged a huge black hole in the north of the city, swallowing light; but it was day now and almost beautiful, with thickets of bare winter trees materialising like ghosts on either side of the road as we passed. A mist trailed rags among the trees, and the air between the branches was smudged with drifting, restless birds.

Now and then I even thought I could see a glimmer of silver deer darting, hiding, watching.

Tillman had marked an area on the map not far from Oldtown Wood. The park was full of such evocative names. Furry Glen, White Field, The Hollow, The Wilderness, a reminder to the city of what it had risen from — though had it really risen so far? The wild still clung on stubbornly; I'd never really doubted that it did. The trees huddled close like conspirators.

After a while, I told Fitzgerald to pull in.

"Is this the right place?"

"I think so."

Without a more detailed map it was impossible to tell exactly, but here would do, here was close enough.

Fitzgerald promptly pulled in and we climbed out.

The silence around us was incredible. There was only the dragging of wind through the branches over our heads like surf through stones, and somewhere far off a dog barking.

Fitzgerald scarcely noticed. She was reaching back in and lifting something out of the glove compartment, dropping it into her pocket before I could see what it was.

"Let's split up and search the trees," she said.

"Let's not," I answered, and something in my voice made her stop and look at me for what felt a long time before nodding.

"You're right," she said. "Let's not split up."

For how could we be sure that *he* wasn't in there now, waiting, like Fagan had been waiting for me that night five years ago?

464

Together we began to walk slowly down the road instead, scanning the edges where the ground was strewn with wet and rotting leaves for signs of a body, though we didn't put that thought into words. We didn't need to.

What was that?

I felt dizzy, but it was only a log.

A couple of hundred yards down the road, the trees on our right thinned momentarily and a track — fairly wide, though overgrown with weeds — snaked off into the shelter of the trees.

"This is it," I said at once, and I could tell from the look Fitzgerald returned that she thought so too.

He'd been here.

"Come on," she said.

In no time at all, we were moving deeper into the wood until there was no sight of the road behind us when we turned our heads, and ahead of us nothing moved and no birds sang. We were probably no farther from the road than the start of the track had been from the car, but each step felt like it was leading us deliberately astray. The city beyond us had ceased to exist.

Fitzgerald saw the car first.

It was parked up ahead a little way off the track. A metallic silver Daihatsu, only a couple of years old. Not the sort of car to be lightly abandoned, at any rate.

She didn't break her stride, only reached into her pocket as we drew nearer and pulled out a new pair of latex gloves. That was what she'd lifted from the glove compartment earlier.

"I'm going to take a look," she said.

We were only a couple of yards away by this point, and if the light had been better we'd have been able to see the inside of the car from where we were; but the trees wouldn't allow it. We had to come to a point almost adjacent to the driver's side door before we finally saw what we'd feared seeing from the moment we passed through Park Gate.

There, on the other seat, a blanket draped over the head and falling to the knees so that the face and upper body were invisible, was the next offering in the game.

Fitzgerald circled the car carefully, peering in at each window, checking each door. The keys were still hanging from the ignition — a gaudy little plastic toy in the shape of a bee and a tag saying Cassidy's Car Rentals alongside them; but only the passenger side door was unlocked.

It would have to be that one then.

She could have left it for the crime scene technicians to deal with, but I understood how she felt. She needed to know who it was.

Gently, she reached out to grasp the handle.

Pressed it down.

Opened the door.

Whichever way the body was sitting (whichever way it had been arranged?), the door was the only thing providing support, and as soon as she opened it fully the body fell out heavily.

Fitzgerald leapt back out of the way and nearly fell over, and I immediately made to rush forward to help

466

her; but she waved a hand abruptly and shouted at me to wait.

She was stooping over the tumbled figure at her feet. "Grace, what is it?"

She straightened up and walked back round towards me.

"Do you know who she is?" I said.

"It's not a she at all," she told me.

By the time we got back to the road, two patrol cars had already arrived and three uniformed police were standing round Fitzgerald's Rover, squinting inside, wondering what to do. They looked alarmed when they saw us stepping out from the trees — they'd obviously been sent out here without knowing what to expect — then simply embarrassed when they realised who it was.

Fitzgerald quickly told them about the car and the body, and ordered them to secure the scene. "And don't touch anything," she warned them again as they headed off towards the track.

Another car appeared from the direction of the city as we stood by the road. Seamus Dalton. Terrific. He pulled to a stop with a crunch, opened the door roughly and climbed out. He put on a look of contempt when he saw me and popped a stick of chewing gum into his mouth.

"You know something?" he said loudly to me. "You could have saved us all a lot of trouble if you'd just told us from the start that your friend from back home was a psycho."

"Unlike you, Dalton," I said, "I try to wait for the evidence first before closing a case. You should try it sometime. Make a change from your usual method of deciding beforehand who did it and then seeing if you can make the evidence fit."

"What can I say?" he said dismissively. "It works for me."

"Sure it does. That's how, a couple of days ago, you were trying to pin all this on a guy who's been dead five years."

"If you're trying to annoy me —"

"Dalton, I haven't even started."

"That's enough," said Fitzgerald. "Both of you."

But Dalton didn't wait for more. He shouldered past me pointedly without waiting for another word from Fitzgerald, and went instead to make himself unpopular with the uniforms.

"He's back to his usual form," I said.

"Probably just as well," said Fitzgerald. "Behaving like a decent human being for once didn't suit him. Here."

She handed me a scrap of paper on which she'd written the registration number of the Daihatsu, together with her car keys.

"When you get back to Dublin Castle, tell Boland or Healy to call Cassidy's Car Rentals and see if this really is one of theirs. Tell them if it *is* to find out who hired the car from them and when, and see if they have a contact address."

"Are you not coming?"

"I should stay here until Lynch and the others arrive," Fitzgerald said. "Just call me as soon as you have anything."

"And if I don't have anything?"

"Call me anyway."

CHAPTER
FORTY-TWO

I drove back out of Phoenix Park, my head aching with questions. I certainly couldn't help wondering why Tillman was making life so easy for us. First the map, now the car, and the keys. The best explanation I could come up with was that he knew he couldn't stay hidden in the city indefinitely and wanted to bring the seven days to their endgame on his own terms.

But why bring the car all the way out here, only to abandon it and leave himself with a risky journey back into town?

Come to think of it, how *had* he got back into town? Taxi?

And more important than all that, who had died last night, this morning, whenever it was it happened, back there among the trees? A rent boy was my immediate guess. Phoenix Park was notorious for being haunted after dark by male prostitutes and those who paid and preyed on them. It would've been easy for Tillman to pick up a potential victim without being seen.

But why this one?

"I promised you a Jackie and I always keep my promises . . ."

Was that it?

First thing I did when I got back to Dublin Castle, drawing a few hostile glances as I reversed the Rover into Fitzgerald's parking space, was head for the canteen, where I found Boland eating bacon and eggs and reading the morning's *Post*.

US Profiler In No-Show Mystery, read the headline.

Poor Elliott was missing it all.

"Where's Healy?" I said.

"Some down-and-out who lives along the railway line near Pearse Street Station called the hotline to say he'd been approached by a stranger the night the last letter was sent to the Chief," Boland said. "According to him, he was offered money to drop a package off at another courier firm, but he was pretty drunk so the operator couldn't get much sense out of him. Healy wanted to go down for himself and see if there's anything in it."

A possible ID at last, but only when it wasn't needed.

I guess that's what they call irony.

"What did you want him for, anyway?"

"Never mind," I said. "Will you do me a favour?"

"Name it."

I told him about the body. From his face, it was clear that he hadn't heard about it yet. When I also told him it was a young man we'd found, and that it looked like he'd been suffocated with a plastic bag over his head, he was even more surprised.

"You want me to check the files for male prostitutes?"

471

"That's what I was thinking. No one checked them when the letter came in yesterday because we just assumed Jackie would be a woman; but Jackie can be a man's name as well. He might be playing about with the names again, like he did with Nikolaevna."

"I'll get on it right away."

"Thanks. And Boland? About yesterday, when I gave you the third degree —"

"Forget it," said Boland. "I already have. We've all been running on our nerves lately. I shouldn't have taken it so personally. I just hope you're not going to make a habit of it, that's all."

I found an empty desk upstairs and dialled Cassidy's Car Rentals on the South Circular Road. Making the call myself might stop me feeling so restless. Soon as they picked up the phone, I said where I was calling from and asked to speak to whoever was in charge.

Presently, Cassidy himself came to the phone — or someone who called himself Cassidy, at any rate. Maybe they were all called Cassidy to make things easier.

He immediately confirmed that the car belonged to them. It had been hired out three weeks ago and was due to be returned in another week's time, though I didn't have the heart to tell him that it would be a lot longer than that now it was in the hands of Forensics. They hated handing anything back to its rightful owner too fast.

"Who hired it out?" I said.

I heard a rustle of pages as Cassidy checked the log.

"Someone by the name of M. Tillman," he answered.

"And how did you first hear from this M. Tillman?"

"He called us. I took the call myself. About a month ago it was. He was calling from the US. He was an American, like you. He said he was coming over to Dublin soon on personal business and needed a car. I ran through the price list with him, he picked out the car he wanted and asked for it to be there at the airport when he landed."

"Why didn't he just hire a car in the terminal on arrival?"

"I didn't ask," said Cassidy. "I didn't want to lose a customer to the opposition, after all."

"Did he specify the colour?"

"Not in so many words. He said he wanted a light-coloured car — white, yellow, silver, he wasn't fussy — but it had to be light-coloured. He said he didn't want it to look like he was driving round the city in a hearse."

What did the profile say? What do killer profiles always say? Look for a dark-coloured car. Orderly, compulsive people prefer dark-coloured cars. Tillman had it all planned from the beginning so that he could mock any likely profile. Even his own.

By the end of the call, I'd managed to confirm that, on the day of his arrival, one of the garage staff had driven the car out to the airport to meet Tillman, checked that his licence was in order, got him to sign for the car, and then taken the full payment from him for the four weeks.

"Cheque? Credit card?"

"Cash."

"Is that usual?" I said.

"We don't ask questions," replied Cassidy. "Like I say, I didn't want to lose a customer. He paid part of the money that was owed in dollars because that was all he had on him."

"One last thing. What address did he put down that he was staying at while he was here in Dublin?"

The rustling was back and it took longer this time.

"I don't have that here," Cassidy admitted eventually. "It'll be on file somewhere. Buried away, you know how it is. Why don't I have my secretary dig it out and I'll get back to you?"

"You do that," I said.

Boland walked in while I was waiting for Cassidy to call me back, and I was growing more impatient with each passing minute.

"You were right," he said. "Jackie Callaghan, seventeen years old, homeless, no family to speak of. He was in and out of children's homes up until about six months ago, when he was thrown out to make his own way in the world. He had numerous offences in the juvenile courts for petty crime, shoplifting, peddling dope. None for prostitution, but he *was* reported missing this morning by another homeless kid who said he'd been out with Jackie in the park until about four a.m. He didn't spell out what they were doing there, but it doesn't take a genius to guess."

"He must've been worried if he called the police."

474

"He didn't call the police. He called a gay helpline downtown and they passed it on anonymously. The boy who contacted them said it was completely out of character for Jackie to go AWOL, even for a few hours. He'd never done it before."

And he wouldn't be doing it again, I thought sadly. How the hell had Tillman found him? A random pick-up was one thing, but to know where to locate probably the one rent boy who shared a name with that other Jackie in order to send us off track needed time, it needed contacts.

How had he done it?

I was glad when the phone finally rang and gave me something to do besides asking what felt increasingly like unanswerable questions.

"Cassidy?" I said, snatching it up. "Did you find it?"

"*You've spoken to Cassidy already? Then you are moving fast,*" said the same dull, dragging, robotic voice I'd heard for the first time in the café that morning. "*I'm impressed.*"

Boland was standing now at the water cooler. I scrunched a piece of paper and threw it at his back to draw attention.

He turned round.

"Are you going to make a habit of this, Tillman?" I said.

Tillman? said Boland's face.

"*One final call, that's all this is, and then I'll be gone. Into — how shall I put it? Retirement. That'll do. The undefeated champion stepping down from the podium.*"

475

I wrote down for Boland: *Put a trace on the line.*

"What do you mean — gone?" I said as he ran out of the room to get help.

I heard him hammering on doors down the corridor and put my hand over the mouthpiece so that Tillman wouldn't suspect.

"*Sorry. No more helping hand,*" the voice went on. "*You're on your own now. I gave you the boy. I gave you the car. But don't worry. You can't be too far off if you've spoken to Cassidy.*"

"Won't you even tell me what this was all about?" I said.

"*I hate reducing motive to some mechanistic checklist. A broken home, a defective gene, a knock on the head. It's insulting. You know that better than anyone. Remember Paul Nado? He said he did what he did because he'd been rejected for a job and wanted to punish society. Did you believe him?*"

"Of course I didn't believe him."

"*Then why would you believe me if I gave you a reason?*"

"I didn't say I'd *accept* your reason," I said. "I simply wanted to know what you'd say. Why you thought you did it."

"*In that case, it's because I was rejected for a job and wanted to punish society,*" the voice said. "*No, I tell a lie. It was because I fell in love with a brilliant and beautiful but obstinate FBI agent who betrayed me for money and fame.*"

"You're breaking my heart, Tillman."

"Or was it because I got tired of always being in the shadows whilst the killers got the glory? I forget. Have you noticed that, by the way? We spend our entire lives catching killers and they end up more popular and renowned than we are. They have websites, for Christ's sake. They have fan clubs. They even have books written about them." He laughed. "Of course I had a book written about me once. You may have heard of it. Last I heard, the author was reduced to sleeping with some second-rate police chief in some second-rate city whilst trying to persuade herself that her second-rate life was sufficient to stave off dissatisfaction. Still, it serves her right, don't you think?"

I ignored the jibe.

"Where will you go?" I said instead.

"Somewhere you can't follow. Not yet anyway. Shame to break up the game just when it was getting interesting, but it can't be helped. The net is closing in. It's too tight now for my liking."

"It's only closing in because you allowed it to."

"True, but I would rather bring this to a close now on my terms than allow the pleasure I have to be sullied subsequently by failure. I'd rather keep it all as an exquisite memory."

"I'll not give up," I said. "I'll find you."

A laugh again.

"You're welcome to come with me if you like," he said, "though I'm not sure you'd like the journey. Another time, perhaps."

There was a click and the line went dead.

"Tillman? Tillman? Damn it."

"Has he gone?" said Boland.

I looked up to see him standing in the doorway. I didn't answer him because I didn't need to.

"Did you manage to trace it?" was all I said.

He shook his head.

What did it matter? He wouldn't have been there anyway.

Ten minutes later, the fax began to whirr and I waited anxiously as it printed out the single sheet on which Cassidy's secretary had written the promised address.

I recognised it at once.

The house had once been owned by Ed Fagan. He'd rented it out to students at University College where he taught. One of those students had been Sylvia Judge, his second victim.

Was this where Tillman had been hiding out? And if we were fast enough, was there still time to catch him before he fled?

CHAPTER
FORTY-THREE

The house had been leased on a twelve-month contract in the name of Gus Bishop, but the agency who handled it couldn't tell police anything about the man who'd leased it. He'd simply answered an ad in the evening newspaper that September, saying he wanted the house for his daughter, who was starting college in October. A couple of days later he walked into the office, paid in full — in cash again, though no dollars this time — and took the keys away with him. He hadn't even wanted to look at the house first, and, according to neighbours, it had been empty ever since. They hadn't seen so much as a light switched on inside.

Police showed the letting agents a photograph of Tillman, but how were they to remember what Gus Bishop looked like? It was two minutes of their life, if that; it meant nothing to them.

"How long are we going to sit here?" I snapped eventually.

We were in Fitzgerald's Rover again, a few hundred yards from the door of the house, waiting, watching. The repetitive swishing of the wipers to clear away the rain from the windscreen was starting to take a toll on my nerves.

"We should just break down the door and go in there."

"Slow down, Saxon," said Fitzgerald. "The armed response unit has to be in place before we move in. God knows what he's got in there. No one's going in until we're sure it's safe."

"Nothing's safe with the ARU around," I said. "They'll probably shoot up half the street."

Fitzgerald smiled, despite herself.

Outside was growing uncharacteristically quiet as the traffic was diverted away from each end of the narrow road and plainclothes detectives moved from door to door telling residents to stay inside. I wondered whether Tillman would notice as the street fell still.

If he was still in there. An officer posing as a postman had approached and left a listening device on the door, but it had failed so far to pick up any sound of movement.

"I almost forgot," said Fitzgerald as she watched the road gradually being taken over by police. "I brought you some food, seeing that you missed breakfast. It's in the back there."

I reached round for the bag that had been left on the back seat, and took out a sandwich, made from thickly cut dark bread.

"I don't know whether to eat this or keep it in case I need an offensive weapon later on," I said, lifting it up and sniffing it. I took a bite. "Actually, it's not bad. You want some?"

"I already ate."

"Liar."

A burst of white noise from the police radio stopped her from answering. She leaned over and turned it up to follow the crackle of commands and whispers as more officers moved in. I recognised John Haran's voice making sure everyone was in place. At least there was one person here who knew what he was doing.

"Jackson, you take the rear. Blake?"

"I'm in place."

"Any sign of movement?"

"Negative."

"McCabe, have you got that thing working yet?"

"It's working," came back McCabe. "No sound, that's all."

"Chief?"

"Go on, Haran," said Fitzgerald. "I'm listening."

"We're set. Just give the word."

She stared ahead at the street, gathering strength.

"Do it," she said.

So much for my sandwich.

Through the wipers, I saw Haran climb out of a parked car at the end of the street and start the walk down to the gate. As he did so, another man appeared from the other direction, moving slightly slower, and three more edged forward from their hiding places opposite. An unmarked armed response unit van waited, ticking over, a short distance away, in case back-up was needed.

Haran was first to the gate. Soon as he went in, we lost sight of him; but we heard the knock that immediately followed.

And the silence following that.

"McCabe," said Fitzgerald into the radio. "Are you picking up anything at all on the listener?"

"Nothing, Chief."

"One more chance then, Haran," she said, "and if he doesn't answer this time, get rid of the door and go in."

Her words crackled back through the air to Haran's earpiece.

A slight pause — then the second knock.

The second silence.

"Go!"

We couldn't see what happened, only hear the crash as Haran drew his weapon, stepped back and kicked open the door, and the remaining ARU officers surged forward through the gate and into the house. There were muffled footsteps echoing on what sounded like bare floorboards, and shouting, though it was difficult to make out the words through the screech of tyres as the unmarked van rushed forward to the gate and the doors at the back opened, spilling more armed officers out.

I reached for the door handle to get out.

"Wait till it's clear," Fitzgerald said, grabbing the arm of my jacket, but I couldn't. I shrugged off her hand and climbed out.

I heard a cry on the radio.

"Fuck!"

"Get the Chief!"

"Now!"

No one tried to stop me as I ran across the road and through the gate, Fitzgerald close behind, into the house, where the sound of hard boots on the floorboards upstairs filled the air.

Inside there was scarcely any light, for the windows were smudged grey with dirt and dust; but ahead of us, down the long hall, the light from a torch was picking a path through the gloom, sweeping like the beam of a lighthouse, and that was what we followed.

"Haran?" said Fitzgerald.

He was standing in the centre of the back room, which was even darker than the rest because a blanket had been nailed over the window; it was Haran holding the torch. He said nothing as we entered, simply pointed the light to the floor, where a pair of stepladders lay toppled in a huge pool of blood.

Then he swept the beam upwards.

A man's body dangled from a loop of electric flex attached to a hook, twisting gently round and round as if in a wind, shoes kicked off to show bare feet, left wrist slashed deep to the bone, crucifix dangling from the right; and his features were pulled so tight by the weight of the body beneath that he seemed to be almost smiling, nursing a secret.

Mort Tillman.

And behind him on the wall, a message written in the same blood. *The last enemy that shall be destroyed is death.*

Later, I retreated to the front steps and watched the cars crawl by as drivers, permitted down the road again now the armed response unit had dispersed, slowed to see what was going on.

I lit a cigar and listened, at the back of it all, to the customary cries of the city. It was a soundtrack that could never be turned off or the volume down; either you accepted and became part of it or you got out. There was no middle way, no compromise. I had always accepted it, but then I wasn't the sort for making compromises either. Right now, though, I wasn't so sure.

Thinking about Tillman was making me hollow. I shouldn't have cared about him, not after all that had happened; but I couldn't help remembering that, save for Fitzgerald, he was still the person I knew best in this whole city. Or thought I had. It spoke wonders for my ability to form meaningful relationships, but there you go.

Besides, I couldn't shake the feeling that I was why he was dead now, that I was why too many people had died. I didn't know how I was to blame, but I was. If it wasn't for me, he wouldn't be hanging in there now — or rather lying in there, for Ambrose Lynch had come to examine the body in the hour since the house had been entered and he'd immediately ordered Tillman cut down.

Sometimes it didn't do to know too much, to know what Lynch would do to Tillman once he was on the mortuary slab: how he would lift out each organ and weigh it carefully; how he would collect a sample of stomach contents to be sent for analysis if needed; how he would drain and store all fluids. The real Tillman had fled from the flesh, but it didn't make the knowledge of what would be done to that flesh feel any less like an affront.

I sensed Fitzgerald was there beside me before she spoke, leaning against the doorway and watching me smoke.

"Maybe that's what I need," she said.

"You?"

"Why not me?"

I passed her the cigar and watched her lift it to her lips and take a mouthful of smoke.

She coughed, like she always did, then raised a finger to pick a fragment of tobacco from the end of her tongue.

"I'll never understand how you can smoke these things."

"What's to understand?"

"I keep thinking if I try just one more I'll see the appeal." Another mouthful. Another cough. "No, it's no good."

We took a step back as a crime tech officer in a white jumpsuit appeared in the doorway and made his way down to the van, carrying a box.

It had been one box after another: the collected detritus of Tillman's obsession, taken away to be catalogued, analysed, and finally stored in some airless, lightless vault, all that remained of this strange museum to the past seven days.

There had been three boxes alone of photographs, hundreds of them. Shots of Mary Lynch, Mary Dalton, Nikolaevna mainly, but scores of other women that I didn't recognise, each taken secretly as they were followed, kept watch over, the ground prepared. The bathroom upstairs was his darkroom; countless undeveloped rolls of film lined the shelves.

More photographs had been sellotaped across each wall, together with cards for prostitutes and massage parlours taken from telephone boxes, and photocopies of newspaper stories relating to attacks on women going back five years neatly snipped out and displayed.

There were books too, many of them the same ones that had been in Tillman's rooms in Trinity, and an old portable typewriter whose typeface had been tested and shown to match that on the letters, not to mention plastic bags filled with various items of clothing, mostly underwear, some shoes, items of jewellery; all stolen, I guessed.

And there was one further box, similar to the one from last night, in which the crime tech officers had found the missing feet of the nameless woman in the churchyard, as perfectly preserved as the hands. The box was wrapped in Christmas paper, ready to be sent.

Nick Elliott's name and address were pasted on the front. He'd be furious when he learned what he had missed. A story like that could have been his way back into favour.

There was no sign of the head.

"So is that really it?" I said. "It's over?"

"Isn't that what we were hoping for?" Fitzgerald answered. "That the killer, whoever he was, would just bring this all to an end himself? Tillman even warned us to expect it. He said in his profile that the offender might kill himself if he was cornered."

"But he wasn't cornered," I said. "He backed *himself* into a corner. There's a world of difference. He could have gone on indefinitely and never been caught. Instead he chose death."

You're welcome to come with me if you like, I remembered him joking grimly in that last conversation, *though I'm not sure you'd like the journey.*

"Maybe he just wanted to make sure he never was caught. How did he put it to you?" said Fitzgerald. "He was the undefeated champion, going into retirement where you couldn't follow."

"And that's what he meant by the message? *The last enemy that shall be destroyed is death.* You could be right."

"I hate to spoil the party," interrupted Lynch, and we both looked round as the city pathologist emerged from the gloom and trudged heavily down the steps towards us, "but suicide isn't defeating death. Death still wins, whichever way you look at it."

"Even if you choose the manner and timing of it?"

"Why should death care about details as long as it has you?"

I had no answer to that.

"I don't suppose there's any doubt it was suicide?" I said.

"How many times do I have to remind you that I cannot determine a true cause of death prior to an autopsy, and sometimes not even then?"

"You're not in court now, Ambrose," said Fitzgerald. "We're only after your best guess. It certainly looks like suicide."

"I'll forget you said that. I don't want to have to report a chief superintendent for trying to influence my findings. But," he said, "off the record, I'll admit that it looks like suicide to me as well. At some point in the last three hours, say."

"I spoke to him two hours ago," I said.

"You did? At some point in the last two hours then. I'll know more precisely once I've completed the autopsy."

"Are you going to do it now?"

"What choice do I have? On the seventh day, the Lord rested. But not me," he said. "I still have to work."

"Everyone's working," I said.

"Everyone else gets days off, breaks, sick leave. They don't work every case. I am legally obliged to attend the scene of every violent or suspicious death in the city. It doesn't matter when it happens. Late at night or early morning. Christmas Day, Hallowe'en, my birthday, the Fourth of July. If someone decides they want to play Jack the Ripper with the local population, I have to be there. I'm tired of saying it, or perhaps just plain tired, but it's time I got an assistant."

"Don't look at me," I said. "I'm sick of seeing the dead."

"Aren't we all?"

CHAPTER
FORTY-FOUR

Assistant Commissioner Brian Draker had called a press conference for five o'clock to announce that the investigation was ended. I skipped the celebrations. I wasn't in the mood to see Draker grinning like a halfwit; and besides, it didn't feel ended to me.

"I've been over it a hundred times and the pieces still don't knit together," I said to Fisher when I went round to his hotel and found him drinking in the bar, desperate for news.

He'd been shocked when I told him Tillman was dead.

"I can't believe it," he kept saying.

"In case you've forgotten," I pointed out, "it was you made me suspect Tillman in the first place."

"I know," he said. "That's what makes it worse. I suppose I hoped you might be able to prove to me it couldn't *be* him."

"Well, it's too late for that now," I said. I looked at my watch. "An hour from now, Draker will be announcing to the world that Tillman was a dangerous killer, not to mention taking the credit probably for hunting him down. If only there weren't so many loose ends, it would be easier to accept."

"Loose ends?"

"It's something that's been niggling at me, that's all. When we were in the café this morning and the first call came through, I thought it was Tillman because he reminded me about some story only he and I knew, how when we were driving up to North Vermont on the White Monk case I got lost in a snowstorm."

"And you nearly crossed the Canadian border," Fisher finished for me.

I was astonished.

"You know about that?"

"Tillman told me about it once. In strictest confidence, of course." He noticed the look on my face. "You don't mind, do you?"

"I don't mind — at least, it hardly matters now; but you're missing the point. I didn't *nearly* cross over the border into Canada; I *did* cross the border. It was only when the signs started appearing in French that I realised. But the caller said the same as you. Why would Tillman have remembered it wrongly?"

"Why do I get the impression you're asking me questions when you already know the answers, or suspect that you do?"

"I don't have any answers," I said bitterly. "I'm not even sure I have any questions that deserve answers. I'm just trying to make all those pieces I told you about knit together."

"Who says things always have to make sense?"

His words depressed me. Had I come all this way only to settle, like Draker, for an unsatisfactory ending just because it made things simpler? No. I wouldn't do

490

it. I pushed back my chair roughly and rose to my feet, glad now that I'd refused Fisher's offer of a drink.

"Come on," I said. "We're going."

"Where?"

"You'll find out soon enough."

I pulled to a halt outside Cassidy's Car Rentals with an unintended screech, making the people hidden under umbrellas in the forecourt turn their heads our way with alarm. I'd wanted to make sure we got here before it shut. Already some of the stores had pulled down their shutters and closed up for the night.

"They probably think you're here to hold up the place," said Fisher as we climbed out. "Do you ever think about getting a new wardrobe so that you look more respectable?"

"The way your waistline's expanding these days," I shot back, "a wardrobe will soon be about the only thing that fits you."

"I asked for that."

We ran through the rain to the door and pushed inside.

"Can I help you?"

The standard introduction, delivered by a middle-aged man in a pinstripe suit, hair combed over to hide his bald patch, fingers cupped together in that same priestly way Stephen Clark had. I often wondered if they were taught it at some night-school class.

"Cassidy?" I said, taking a wild guess. "I talked to you earlier today on the phone from Dublin Castle."

"About the car for the American gentleman. I remember."

Another standard salesman's trick: to remember some little detail to make the customer feel they were the most important person in the world. So he remembered about Tillman? Big deal. It would've been remarkable if he'd forgotten. It was only a few hours ago, and taking a call from the murder squad was the most excitement he was likely to get this side of sneaking a quick grope with his secretary at the staff Christmas party.

"I want to look at the registration form Tillman filled out when your car was dropped off to him at the airport," I said.

"Now?"

"No. Next summer should do. Of course now."

A flash of irritation, but he brought it under control admirably.

"Wait here," he said. "I'll get it straight away."

Cassidy fell back to the safety of his filing cabinet and presently returned with a single sheet, which he handed over.

"If you need me, I'll be in my office."

Fisher and I glanced at the sheet.

"That's not Tillman's signature," I said immediately.

"Are you sure?"

"Look," I pointed out, "it's signed Mort Tillman."

He looked confused.

"That was his name."

"No it wasn't," I said. "It was what he called himself, but his full name was Scott Mort Tillman. Scott was his father's name; Mort came from a favourite uncle. When Tillman got older he took the name Mort, to annoy his father mainly, I think, but he always signed himself S.M. Tillman. The boys in the FBI used to joke that it stood for Sado Masochist. Sado Masochist Tillman. Point is, he never signed himself Mort. Never. This is a fake."

I raised my voice to reach Cassidy.

"Who took the car out to Tillman that day?"

"Brendan," he said. "He works for us in the garage."

"Is he here now?"

"No. He called in sick this morning. I can write out his phone number if you need to speak to him."

"His address as well."

Cassidy glanced round for a scrap of paper, but there was nothing to hand, so he lifted down some cheap religious calendar that was hanging on the wall behind his desk. December showed a picture of Christ in the manger, the shepherds and wise men gathered around. He tore off a strip of paper from the bottom where the days were numbered and wrote what I asked.

I checked the address; it was a street not far from the canal where Mary Lynch had died.

I put it in my pocket as I made my way to the door.

"It's all coming back to me," I said as the dark streets unfolded under our wheels back to the city. "I've been so stupid. When we burst into the house and found Tillman hanging there, he had a crucifix in his right hand. It was the crucifix that was taken from the body of Monica Lee. But Tillman couldn't have killed

Monica. That happened two years ago, long before he came to Dublin."

"How can you be sure it was Monica Lee's crucifix?"

"I can't, OK, not yet. But I'd put my life on it all the same. It just fits. And if I'm right, then Tillman couldn't have killed Nikolaevna Tsilevich either, because the knots binding the two women were exactly the same. They must have been killed by the same man. And if he didn't kill Nikolaevna, then what sense does it make to say he killed Mary Lynch and the others?"

"Slow down a moment, I'm getting confused. If what you're saying is right, then that means Tillman must have been —"

"Murdered. Exactly. The killer even hinted at it to me during that call in the café, when I first became convinced he was Tillman. I asked him what he wanted, if he wanted me to say I was sorry, say I was wrong, if that was what this was all about, but all he did was laugh. He said it was too late for apologies. It was too late because Tillman was already dead by then. The message on the wall of the house is the same sort of confession, don't you see?"

"Frankly," said Fisher, "no."

"Mort is Latin for death. Tillman used to make macabre jokes about how appropriate it was that a profiler should be called Death. So when the message said *The last enemy that shall be destroyed is death*, what it meant was *The last enemy that shall be destroyed is — Mort*. And that's another thing about the message," I went on hurriedly before Fisher could raise a counter-argument and knock me out of my stride. The thoughts were crowding my brain so fast now that even my words were too clumsy and slow to keep up with them. "Tillman was left-handed. If he wanted to cut his wrist in order to write a message in the blood, surely he would have held the knife in his left hand and cut his right wrist? Yet it was the left wrist which was slashed."

"But the hands in Tillman's rooms —"

"They were sent to him, it's obvious now, same way that the other parcel was packaged up ready to be sent to Nick Elliott. The box wasn't sitting there that night waiting to be wrapped. It had been *un*wrapped by Tillman and he'd folded up the Christmas paper afterwards and laid it to one side. You remember how crazy he was about being tidy. It was the parcel that made him rush out that night. It confirmed something that he'd started to suspect from his reading. All those books were research; not signs of his obsession, like we thought, but of his tracking down the roots of the killer's obsession. He hadn't given up his interest in the case, he only wanted us to think he had; his interest had actually intensified. Like you said yourself, he was desperate to prove we were all wrong about him, so he went off on a solo run."

"And paid for it with his life," said Fisher. His voice sounded empty as the realisation of how he had misunderstood and failed Tillman — how we *all* had, me for a second time — wormed into his head. "What are we going to do?"

"I'm going to drop you round at Dublin Castle. Find Fitzgerald. Give her the address Cassidy gave us for his driver and have her send someone round to get a description of the man he met at Dublin airport who claimed to be Tillman."

"Where are you going?"

"Back to my apartment. I have a photograph of Monica Lee somewhere in my notes, showing her wearing the crucifix. Draker won't be able to deny it's the same one if he has the proof in front of his eyes. After that I'm going round to Lynch to get a set of Tillman's fingerprints to run against those found in Nikolaevna's apartment. I'll be along as soon as I can."

The lift was broken again. What was wrong with this bloody country? Everything was either broken or, if it was working, useless anyway. The porter wasn't even around for me to complain at. Making himself scarce, if he had any sense.

I didn't think my feet could manage the stairs. The last time I'd slept was in Jackie's house, when I'd dreamt about Tillman trying to make me see what he'd seen. But I made it to my door in the end. One step at a time. The only way.

Soon as I reached the top of the stairs, I saw it.

A box, wrapped in Christmas paper, with my name and address on the top.

I knew what it was at once.

I unlocked my door, stepped over the box and went inside. Left the door open whilst I walked to my phone. I called the porter seven floors below.

He picked up after three rings.

"Hugh, there's a box outside my door —"

"That's right, I brought it up for you," the porter said. "It's been sitting down there for the past two days, but you've not been in to collect your mail. Been busy, have you?"

"Something like that."

"Well, I thought I'd save you a journey, especially with the lift out of order again. Did I do the wrong thing?"

"It's fine, no. I just wanted to know."

Replacing the receiver, I stepped back to the door, bent down and picked up the parcel, then carried it to the table, where I laid it down gently before going to the kitchen for a knife.

I should have left it for the police, but I couldn't.

Like Fitzgerald with the body in the car, I had to know who it was.

I cut off the Christmas paper carefully and laid it to one side. Same way Tillman had. Then I opened the box.

I almost cried out when I saw what was inside. It wasn't what I'd expected. At least, not exactly. But I didn't. The dead could hurt no one. I'd learned that after killing Fagan.

There was no face. Everything which might have identified her had been removed, dissolved, and now there was only bone, the smooth curve of the skull picked as clean as if it had been left out in the desert sun for a decade. But why?

It didn't take a genius to figure out. Because I would have recognised her otherwise. Recognised her face. Recognised — who?

From nowhere, an image came to me of a familiar face. *Go, see now and bury this cursed woman, for she is a king's daughter.*

King's daughter.

I felt suddenly cold.

I put my hand into my pocket and lifted out the scrap of paper which Cassidy had torn from his calendar. I'd forgotten to give it to Fisher when I dropped him off at Dublin Castle.

I'd looked at it briefly before, but the words must have entered my mind at some deep level without me even being aware of it happening, for my hand had reached for it unthinkingly. Now I stared at it, numb with disbelief, and yet calm too, knowing that finally I had the answer.

I picked up the phone again and dialled a number, again hardly knowing how I remembered it. I'd only dialled it once before.

"Hello," said a voice when it was picked up.

"Professor Salvatore?" I said. "Can we talk?"

CHAPTER
FORTY-FIVE

The air was sterile and antiseptic in the autopsy room, but Ambrose Lynch wasn't there. Nor was Tillman; and I wasn't sorry about that. I hadn't wanted to see him lying there. What I'd seen of him already that day was bad memory enough.

A lab assistant was washing down the surfaces and told me he'd been taken back to the morgue, where he would remain, alone, cold, until his family made arrangements to fly his body back to the States. As for the city pathologist, she thought he'd gone back to his office on the first floor to write up the autopsy report. I made my way up the stairs after him.

I found Lynch sitting at his desk, the only light coming from a lamp angled towards the page on which he was writing. He looked up and smiled when I walked in.

"They're on the table over there," he said.

I'd called earlier to tell him I'd be over to pick up Tillman's fingerprints.

"If you hang on a few moments," he added, "you can bring this autopsy report along too. It shouldn't take me much longer."

I sat down in the chair opposite and sighed.

"I suppose I ought to call them," I said.

"Who?"

"Tillman's family. Telling them what happened is the least I can do. Though it might help if I *knew* what had happened. I was hoping you could help me there."

He looked up from the page and frowned.

"What are you saying?"

"You know what I'm saying," I said.

Lynch smiled again over the top of his spectacles, and his smile this time was contorted slightly by the way his face was lit by the desk lamp, like some shadow inside of him was breaking through. And maybe it was. He didn't have to pretend any more.

"It's about time," he said. "I was beginning to think you'd never work it out. This calls for a drink, wouldn't you say?"

He reached down to his side to open the drawer in his desk.

"Stop," I said, and before he could move I'd risen from the chair, pulled the gun from my pocket and levelled it at him. It was the first time I'd seen Lynch genuinely speechless.

I'd picked the gun up on my way to the mortuary from the safe deposit box where it had lain, untouched, since the day after I used it to kill Ed Fagan. Keeping it had been stupid, probably. The sensible thing would have been to fling it into the river at a point where the water was deep and the current would have dragged it out to sea and it could never resurface to incriminate me; but I couldn't. It would have been like throwing a part of myself away.

Besides, I hadn't known when I might need it again. Like now.

"I'm afraid I don't have much practice at this sort of thing," Lynch said after he'd recovered from his initial surprise. "Am I supposed to — how do you say? — stick them up?"

"No," I told him. "You're supposed to stay exactly where you are and shut the fuck up for once. That would do."

I manoeuvred round the edge of the table without taking my eyes off him, then felt down and pulled open the drawer. A quick glance. It was empty save for a bottle of whiskey, three quarters full, and two glasses.

"Satisfied?" said Lynch.

He lifted out the glasses and the bottle, twisted open the cap and poured two generous measures whilst I made my way back to the other chair and sat down again, the gun nestled comfortably in my hand. He slid one of the glasses over to me. He drank deeply. I ignored mine for now.

"I must say, I expected us to be having this conversation sooner," he said. "I had great faith in you, as I told you on the telephone at the café this morning. Even Tillman was on to me quicker. Not that it did him much good. He was so confident of solving this little mystery all by himself that last night, when he found the house, he just walked in. I left the door open and he just walked in. Incredible. But that was our friend Tillman. Good on the academic theory part of the equation, not so hot on the not getting yourself killed part. And now you just walk in too."

"I'm not going to end up like Tillman," I said.

"Tillman didn't think he was going to end up like Tillman either. Right up until the moment when I looped the cord around his neck, and — well, I'll spare you the details. You can't imagine the trouble I had afterwards pulling him up into place in mid-air to make it look like suicide. I should have just slit his other wrist and been done with it, but there was something about the way he looked dangling there, something dramatic, that made it all worthwhile."

"*He* didn't bring a gun," I pointed out.

"True," said Lynch. "He had some rather quaint ideas about obeying the law of the land. Those things *are* still illegal in Dublin, am I right in saying? Not to worry. I won't report you."

He lifted his glass to his lips and drank again.

"Come now, am I drinking alone?" he said when he saw I wasn't doing the same. "This is the last chance I'll get. The least you could be is sociable."

I reached for the glass and took a sip. I was glad I had. I was tired, I'd hardly eaten, everything had moved so fast that I was feeling weak, dizzy. The whiskey sharpened me.

Kept me alert.

I drained the glass and let Lynch refill it.

"Are you going to tell me how you finally figured it out?" he said.

"I'd been drowning in details for days," I said quietly after taking another drink. "Not knowing what was significant and what was nothing. Everything came together when I opened the box. Tillman wasn't sent bones. The box for Elliott wasn't bones. So why was *I* sent a skull? Because I would have recognised a face. Because it was someone I knew. Then it came to me. *Go, see now this cursed woman and bury her, for she is a king's daughter.* King's daughter. You told me right at the start, that night you came to the canal after Mary Lynch died, that your wife's maiden name was King. It was Jean's body that was left in the churchyard."

"My dear wife," said Lynch. "Twenty years I was married to her and I swear she got less observant with each passing year. All of a sudden, she started to notice things. She even followed me out to Ed Fagan's old house. Well, you saw what was there. I had no choice but to kill her."

"You *threw her down.* Like Jezebel."

"*And some of her blood was sprinkled on the wall, and on the horses: and he trod her under foot.*" Lynch laughed lightly. "I wasn't able to supply the horses, alas."

I stared at him and realised for the first time how little I knew him.

How little I knew anyone?

Patiently, because he seemed to want to know, I explained how I'd put together the missing pieces. How a memory had flashed to mind of something half seen at the time but not taken in because I was distracted. It was a scrap of paper torn from a religious calendar, marked with reminders of the saints' feast days. How this scrap had been torn from the page for this week. How it said that today, the seventh of December, was St Ambrose's Day.

When the first letter came, we'd wondered if the fact that the killer had promised that the seven days would start on St Agericus's Day was important. We never thought to look when the seven-day sequence would end and whether *that* was where the real importance lay. It had been the same with the names. We'd thought that Mary Lynch's name might be a pointer because she was called Mary, not because she was called Lynch. And when the next victim was conveniently called Mary Dalton, there seemed no further reason to investigate the first Mary's name as an angle.

From there, the other pieces fell swiftly into place. Salvatore had explained that St Ambrose was one of the ancient Church Fathers and bishop to St Augustine. *Gus Bishop*. That in medieval art he was represented by an ox, a bee and a pen. Like the bee hanging from the keyring in the car that morning. Like the pen that was used to scratch the further riddle on to Liana Cassidy's gravestone: *I know of no bishop worth the name*. Those words had been kept out of the media, but as soon as I told Salvatore about them he immediately completed the quotation for me.

I know of no bishop worth the name . . . save Ambrose.

"Then there were the Hebrew letters," I said. "Aleph and lamedh. They both suggested an ox too, but Tillman had warned all along that the real meaning of them for the killer might be something so simple we'd never even consider it. And what was the most simple explanation of all? Not aleph or lamedh, just A and L. Ambrose Lynch."

504

"Occam's Razor," Lynch agreed. "I told you about it myself. The principle that the fewest possible assumptions should be made when explaining a thing. Your mistake all along was to imagine things were more complicated than they really were. And now you know everything."

"Apart from why," I said.

"Not that one again," said Lynch wearily. "As I explained to you on the telephone today, I hate that mechanistic way of explaining motive. Who really knows why anyone does anything?"

"Surely if you don't ask why, you're just an animal, responding unthinkingly to external stimuli, like a rat scurrying through a maze?"

"Don't start using big words, Saxon, they don't suit you. And you can stop the amateur reverse psychology too. What's the plan? That I will be so affronted at being compared to an animal that I open my heart and reveal the inner Ambrose? Don't insult me."

"Overinflated sense of importance. Easily wounded sense of self-esteem. Classic traits of the serial killer," I said. "You're not even original."

"I didn't become a killer because my self-esteem was wounded," said Lynch. "If anything, it would be nearer the truth to say it was because I was bored. Bored with myself, with this city, my job, with everything. You have no idea how tedious life can be for a forensic pathologist in a city like Dublin. In New York the medical examiner's office carries out seven thousand autopsies a year on suspicious corpses. Seven thousand! Here I get the odd treat, but mostly I'm fortunate if I have one unusual case a year to deal with. Two and I'd be throwing a street party. Night after night I am roused from sleep and called out, only to find that it's yet another drunk stabbed to death outside a nightclub. I've lost count of the number of those."

"So you took to killing because Dublin failed to live up to your refined tastes in homicide?" I said sarcastically.

"Don't be so glib. It wasn't like that at all. Here, have some more."

Another glass filled.

Was he trying to get me drunk so that he could outwit me? If so, he was out of luck. It would take more than a few glasses of whiskey to disorient me. The alcohol may have been working its vague spell on my senses, but I was still in control, he couldn't change that.

"It was Sally Tyrrell's fault really," Lynch said. "I met her when she was a secretary for the police. We had an affair; nothing special. It was me who recommended that she find a new job. It would reflect badly on me, I told her, if I was found to be banging one of the staff."

"Is that how you put it to her?"

"I may have expressed myself more romantically. The truth was, I was growing tired of her, and getting her into a new job on the other side of the city was the simplest way I could think of at the time to get shot of her. When she realised what I'd done, Sally got a bit silly about it. That's women for you, I suppose. She even threatened to tell Jean. I couldn't have that. I picked her up one afternoon on her way home from an office party. She was a little tipsy, which made things easier." He looked almost regretful as he gazed into the dark at the edge of the lamplight. "Afterwards, I was afraid she might have done something selfish, such as telling one of her friends about me, or writing a letter to my wife which she'd left unposted and would be found by the police when they searched her home. But it turned out she'd been touchingly discreet to the end."

"Where did you bury her?"

"That, I think, shall remain my little secret. I have to keep something private now that the rest of my life seems set to be exposed to public scrutiny. And I *was* very fond of her. I wouldn't want her disturbed now."

"You're all heart."

"I like to think so," said Lynch, "though I do still get cross with her sometimes when I look back. I had to make do with prostitutes after Sally. I couldn't run the risk of another woman getting silly about things again. It's not that I would've minded having to dispose of them if they did, but how long would I get away with that if I could be connected to the victims? I couldn't count on luck again after Sally. Prostitutes were safer. Prostitutes knew what they were for."

"Like Monica Lee."

"Like Monica Lee," he agreed brightly. "Monica was very fond of Gus Bishop, but she wasn't stupid enough to think that he would run away with her to a little thatched cottage with roses round the door where they could grow old together."

"So why kill her?"

"You're back to asking why again. Because I wanted to, why else?" said Lynch. "That's the trouble with getting away with one murder. It only gives one an appetite for getting away with more. I blame the police. If they'd caught Sally's killer, none of this would have happened."

"You should write an angry letter to the newspapers."

Lynch chuckled. "I might just do that. It would make a pleasant change from the other sort of letters I've been writing recently."

He paused as the sound of a door opening reached us from outside, followed by footsteps hurrying along the corridor. Don't let it be Fitzgerald, I thought. Not yet. But the footsteps didn't even slow down as they passed Lynch's office. They moved on, faded, another door, gone.

"I *am* right about Sally, though," Lynch immediately continued. He seemed happy to talk now, for all his earlier contempt for explaining himself. "Civilisation is built on boundaries. If there is no punishment for crossing them, boundaries are only pushed further and further back."

"I presume you're talking from personal experience?"

"Of course. For years I'd contented myself with small transgressions. I only nudged at the boundaries, seeing what I could get away with. Lying under oath when giving evidence in court, tampering with autopsy reports . . . Nothing too drastic to begin with. Just little things that could be explained away as the result of an honest mistake or overwork if they were spotted, and then the worst I might face would be early retirement.

As time went on, however, I became more adventurous. Manipulating toxicology levels. Switching blood samples. Tidying up the dead to eliminate signs of foul play. It wasn't hard to do. I work alone most of the time. Dublin hasn't even got to the stage of videoing autopsies. It's positively primitive. But after Sally . . ."

He was growing wistful again.

"After Sally," I continued for him, "tampering with autopsy reports wasn't quite so thrilling?" He nodded absently. "That still doesn't explain," I said, "why you don't care any more about being caught, why you made the riddles all point to you."

"Because it doesn't matter now," Lynch said. "I have nothing to lose."

"Because you killed Jean?"

"Jean? What has Jean got to do with it? No, it doesn't matter because *I* am dying. Cancer. My doctor tells me I should be dead by Christmas. So I thought, why be cautious now, why be careful? I could go out with a bang."

"But why pretend to be Ed Fagan?"

For the first time, Lynch grew annoyed.

"I couldn't believe the attention that man received," he said. "I performed the autopsies on his victims and I don't deny that they were interesting cases, but nothing compared to mine. I left Helen Cranmore in the grounds of Dublin Castle and I even took her there in my own car. Can you imagine the risk I was running? But it was always Fagan this and Fagan that. The final straw was when I saw that Nick Elliott's book was due out and I simply knew it would all be Fagan, Fagan,

Fagan again. I thought, very well, if they want Fagan, they can have Fagan. I would bring him back for them. The Night Hunter, appearing in pantomime for one week only. Book early to avoid disappointment. More whiskey? There's enough for another glass each."

He poured before I could refuse.

"It wasn't hard to make the arrangements," he said. "I leased Fagan's old house and started moving my little photographic collection there. Started picking the victims too."

Mary Lynch because he found the idea of a shared name amusing.

Mary Dalton to provide a passable theory for the shared name

Jackie Callaghan: another cheap joke. Lynch had met him when he came into the mortuary to identify the body of a junkie friend of his. Sealed his own fate in the process.

Nikolaevna Tsilevich just because she was there.

He'd been visiting Nikolaevna for months, which was how he knew Nick Elliott was seeing her too. He'd noticed the reporter sneaking in there one day, though Elliott, observant as ever, hadn't seen *him*. From that encounter, the germ of an idea began to grow. He found out where Elliott liked to drink after work and arranged to turn up there one evening, pretending surprise. Elliott immediately offered to buy the city pathologist a drink, maybe hoping that Lynch might let slip some juicy snippet which would do for the front page; one drink led to another; and one time when Elliott went to the bar for the next round, Lynch

510

wrapped a handkerchief round the bottle from which the reporter had been drinking and slipped it into his briefcase. Elliott's number was bound to come up when Nikolaevna's phone records were checked; and by choosing the journalist as the channel for the faked Fagan letters, Lynch would only heighten the suspicion of him.

Elliott being there on the very night that Lynch had arranged for the Russian woman's death was an added bonus, and one he clearly took great pleasure in.

"What about Tillman? Where did Tillman come into it?" I pressed.

"He was meant to be a simple diversion for the police to allow me time to finish the game. I'd heard about his troubles in America from a colleague over there; and I knew, of course, that you'd had your differences with him. When I heard he was coming to Dublin, it was easy. All I had to do was rent a car in his name, pay for it with dollars, throw some Hebrew mumbo-jumbo into the pot and hey presto, another suspect. What I didn't anticipate was that Mort would try to join in the game, that he would want to beat us all to prove that he could still do it."

"He *did* beat us all."

"Almost all. I still think I came out of the encounter in better shape. But he was on to me unbelievably quickly, I will give him that," said Lynch. "He worked out the A and L business, read all the right books to crack the symbolism. I saw him two days ago, reading St Augustine, and I just knew. So I sent him a parcel for Christmas, and between Jean's hands I put a scrap of newspaper from eight years ago with Sylvia Judge's address on it. He took the bait. He turned up. Alone. He wanted to be sure, he told me, that I really was the killer and that the killer wasn't simply setting me up, as he had with Elliott, before implicating me with the police."

"And you killed him."

"What else could I do? Surrender? Confess?"

Poor Tillman. Doomed by his own sense of fair play. The very sense which had deserted me in my dealings with him.

"There's still one thing I don't understand," I said. "How did you manage to murder Tillman without him resisting? He wasn't the sort to be easily overpowered."

"That part was easy," said Lynch. "I congratulated him on being clever enough to find me, then offered him a drink of whiskey to celebrate. Drugged, naturally. Sound familiar?"

He laughed as my eye sought out the glass on the desk.

As if staring would make things any clearer.

"The only difference," he went on, "is that what I put in Tillman's drink was only to make him sleepy and easily manageable. What we have in here is . . . well, I can't quite remember what. A bit of a cocktail, you could call it, but all the ingredients came from little bottles with a skull and crossbones on the label. And I don't think that meant they once belonged to pirates either."

Poison.

"I don't believe you," I said. "You've been drinking it too."

"Let me assure you that to a man who has been reliably informed that he will be dead by Christmas, the prospect of being poisoned on the seventh of December does not seem so unbearable. Especially if it means he can take some delightful company with him on the journey."

I hardly heard him. I was trying to think.

Trying to count back.

How much had I drunk? How many times had the glass been refilled? Twice, said my memory. Or was it more? Had I even been watching him that closely? And how did I know he was telling the truth at all? No, that was the most idiotic question of all. He was telling the truth. I sensed the poison inside me, a ghost haunting my veins, and even the whiskey was afraid of it.

And all Lynch did the whole time was talk.

Trying to stop me from remembering what to do.

"You *were* supposed to be the fifth victim, after all," he was saying. "*You* were supposed to be at the house; *you* were supposed to track me down. That was the plan from the start. I was saving the best till last. Then Tillman blundered in and I had to let him take your place instead. But I don't see now why I can't add you to the list anyway. Just like you added Fagan to your own little list. Oh yes, Saxon, I know all about that. As soon as the message came through which led the police to Fagan's body, spoiling all my arrangements, I realised. I, after all, had the one luxury the Dublin Metropolitan Police lacked: I *knew* it wasn't me who'd knocked him off. So, as I said in my letter, who had motive, who had opportunity, who had means? It could only have been you. But don't worry, my dear, I'm not going to judge you too harshly for it. We all have our secrets. All have our lists. We killers have to stick together. Besides, where we are going tonight, what does it matter?"

Lynch put back his head and drained what was left of his whiskey.

"Cheers," he said.

I struggled to my feet, and immediately felt afraid. The poison, whatever it was, was inside me now, infecting and occupying my blood. I found myself stumbling almost before I could stand, and the gun was spilling out of numb fingers to the floor.

I tried to swear but my mouth was dry.

Heavily, I dropped down to retrieve the gun.

Where was it? Where was it? There. No.

There.

And then I had to hide it in my pocket again and that took time, and I found that I could barely stand and had to pull myself upright using the chair, which took longer, and then I was striking out on my own for the door, which took years, and Lynch didn't move to stop me.

Made it.

I pulled the door open — and stopped in sudden alarm.

The corridor dropped sharply away.

What had —

Happened? Nothing, I told myself firmly, at least nothing had happened to the corridor. It was me making the corridor drop away, or rather what Lynch had put inside me.

I had to trust my mind instead of my senses.

Somehow, I forced myself to keep going, holding the wall for support.

One step. Another step. A third — steady.

I'd almost reached the door that led out to the stairs when I felt the first pain in my belly, searing, hot, like I'd been stabbed. The pain went deep and twisted, and I had to cling on to the wall to stop myself collapsing.

By the time the pain had passed, my head was spinning, the ground was refusing to stay in one place for even one second, and the sweat felt hard like pepper on my face.

I stood to gather my breath but the next thrust of pain came too quickly and I knew that I couldn't stay there and wait or I'd die. I had to get help. I pushed the door to the stairs and immediately saw a huge window ahead of me, black and speckled with stars.

Or were the stars inside me now?

I couldn't make it.

I couldn't —

Where was my mobile phone? That was it. If I could only remember which pocket I'd left it in, if only I could lift my hand to feel inside, if only —

It was no use. It was too much effort. I couldn't find it. I didn't have *time* to find it.

And the pain was coming again.

I couldn't cry out.

I couldn't even stretch out my hands to save myself as I tried to make a deal with the next flight of stairs, missed my footing . . . fell.

The stairs unravelled beneath me.

The stars turned upside down.

My head exploded into light.

Epilogue

Ambrose Lynch was dead by the time Fitzgerald and the others arrived at the mortuary, still sitting in his chair behind the desk, still smiling; and I wasn't far off being dead myself.

I had Fisher to thank for being found in time. He'd got to thinking about that story Tillman had told him about me crossing the border into Canada in a snowstorm and how he'd misremembered it and how the killer had misremembered it too, and how the only person he could remember telling, or rather mistelling, the story to was Lynch that night when both of them had met at Mort Tillman's rooms in Trinity and the talk had turned to me after they found a copy of my book on Tillman's shelves. It was a funny story, relayed to lift the tension, but Lynch had obviously seized on it to make me believe I was talking to Tillman when he called me the next day.

Fisher still couldn't bring himself to think ill of the city pathologist until he heard the description Cassidy's driver had given of the man who claimed to be Mort Tillman waiting at the airport that morning to pick up his car. And when Healy came back from interviewing the down-and-out who'd been offered money by the killer to send a letter to Fitzgerald, and gave the same description, even Fisher couldn't deny the truth any more. It was then he recalled, not before time, that I'd said I was going to the mortuary to pick up Tillman's fingerprints, and Fitzgerald screamed at him why the hell hadn't he said so before and . . . well, it was over now.

Since then, at various locations round the city, Ambrose Lynch's secret life was being excavated and unearthed. Painstakingly, each item that had been found in Fagan's old house was being traced; each woman in the photographs identified. An enquiry was established to discover the extent of Lynch's abuse of his office as city pathologist. There was talk of ordering new autopsies where doubts remained about his original verdicts, and investigations were reopened into the previously unsolved murders of Monica Lee and Helen Cranmore, the woman whose body was found in the grounds of Dublin Castle a year before Fagan started his killing spree. Responsibility for Fagan's own death was also quickly laid at Lynch's door, and Fisher was soon talking about writing a new book exploring professional competitiveness among serial killers.

Sally Tyrrell's body has never been found, but police did recover the remains of three further women from underneath the floor of the basement in the house that Lynch had shared with his wife for twenty years. Efforts continued to give them names. Traces of Jean's blood were also found on the stairs leading down to the basement, so whether his story about her following him to Fagan's old house was true, or only a construct to justify, in his eyes, a murder which had already happened, would probably never be known. Jack Mullen, meanwhile, was positively identified by two of the prostitutes who had been attacked in London and arrested within days. Denied bail, he now languishes in jail awaiting extradition on charges of rape and false imprisonment.

As for me, it was three days before I opened my eyes and found Fitzgerald at my side.

"The gun," were my first words to her.

"I dealt with it," she said simply. "No one saw."

She said nothing more. She looked at me, that was all, and in that moment I knew she understood everything. About Ed Fagan. About what I'd done. Understood and accepted. Her hand closed over mine and I knew that I was forgiven.

I knew too that I couldn't leave. However frustrated I felt here, however constrained, however much I longed at times to get away, this was where I belonged.

I didn't ask for the gun back, though.

I thought that might be pushing it.

ISIS publish a wide range of books in large print, from fiction to biography. Any suggestions for books you would like to see in large print or audio are always welcome. Please send to the Editorial department at:

ISIS Publishing Ltd.
7 Centremead
Osney Mead
Oxford OX2 0ES
(01865) 250 333

A full list of titles is available free of charge from:
Ulverscroft large print books

(UK)
The Green
Bradgate Road, Anstey
Leicester LE7 7FU
Tel: (0116) 236 4325

(Australia)
P.O Box 953
Crows Nest
NSW 1585
Tel: (02) 9436 2622

(USA)
1881 Ridge Road
P.O Box 1230, West Seneca,
N.Y. 14224-1230
Tel: (716) 674 4270

(Canada)
P.O Box 80038
Burlington
Ontario L7L 6B1
Tel: (905) 637 8734

(New Zealand)
P.O Box 456
Feilding
Tel: (06) 323 6828

Details of **ISIS** complete and unabridged audio books are also available from these offices. Alternatively, contact your local library for details of their collection of **ISIS** large print and unabridged audio books.

1/10/06

Wellfleet Public Library
55 West Main Street
Wellfleet, MA 02667
508-349-0310
www.wellfleetlibrary.org